Waters of Time

Pauline Kirk

Stairwell Books //

Published by Stairwell Books
161 Lowther Street
York, YO31 7LZ

www.stairwellbooks.co.uk
@stairwellbooks

Paperback ISBN: 978-1-913432-16-4
eBook ISBN: 978-1-913432-15-7

Layout design: Alan Gillott

Cover art: Alan Gillott

For Jo

Prologue

Melbourne.

September 1986

My dear Laura,

So that your life should not be distorted by half remembered events as mine has been, I have written this account. You will remember some of the incidents yourself but I would like you to know how they seemed to me. Much of it you will not recall, for the beginning of my story goes back before either of us was born; to the days when Sandhill was a thriving town and cherry orchards and woodlands grew around Arton.

When you are a grown woman read what I have written and snigger if you like, but for your own sake, read. I hope I shall be around to see you do so. Having failed to die young and poetically I intend to go unpoetically, grumbling in my twenty-first century bed. Mind you, I shall feel an idiot when you announce the solicitor has given you a mysterious packet, I shall mumble something about, 'Well, it seemed to matter at the time,' and lock myself in the bathroom. Try not to laugh. Humour after all depends on whether you are the one watching, or the one slipping. Whatever you do, my effort in writing will have been worthwhile. I have taken a journey through the forests of the past, and have come out the other side, a little muddy perhaps and with a few nettle stings, but finding my way.

I will let my great aunt begin the story. During those golden weeks we spent together at Sweetbriar she recorded her memories for me. They give a sharper picture of our past than I could ever offer.

But perhaps I am bewildering you already? Can you recall Great Aunt Mary? By the time you came into her life she was already a very old woman, but even then she avoided confusion like she avoided dirty collars. When I came to transcribe the tapes she had made, very little editing was needed. The part of her life she described then is clear to me, but the rest is a patchwork, sewn from scraps of adult conversation overheard when I was a child.

Great Aunt Mary was over fifty by the year I was born; my adolescence took her towards seventy. All that time her crisp figure came and went through my life, always politely distant but ready in an emergency. When she was a mere seventy-nine and I was already overseas, arthritis forced a compromise with pride and she came to live with us. Even then she remained a visitor, never Family.

If you do recall her, I imagine it is as the old woman who sat on our verandah at Arton shelling peas, or as the slightly severe lady with the old-fashioned lace collar. I suspect that, like me, you will find it difficult to associate passion with such precise gentility. Yet it was a love story she told me, and a requiem for a generation.

I leave you to judge the rest.

ONE: Source

The date is as firm in my mind as if it had been carved on stone: Monday, 3 August 1914. By chance most of us were together that day. We were celebrating the annual Treat, the ritual visit to Arton. It was the last of its kind, a window in my memory to a lost world of summer days. The Edwardian era gathered at Sandhill Wesleyan chapel that day, in all its charm and frivolity; only a day later the same townsfolk had become twentieth century people with twentieth century fears.

I remember the chapel yard was already crowded with children and hampers when I arrived, and the paved space was steaming with horses. Parasols, shawls, muslin blouses and starched pinafores blurred into bright patches of colour. Lakins' Forge had done us proud, lending their biggest wagon for the Junior class. The boards had been swept clean of swarf, and two thick legged horses had been harnessed and decked with ribbons. An equally thick legged man (but no ribbons) stood holding their heads. Jackie Parkes was a reassuring figure as he sat holding the reins. All around and behind him the little ones watched, their eyes almost as wide as their bonnets. 'Morning, Miss Cooper,' Jackie said.

Look what me Mam give me,' Harry Parkes whispered, unwrapping a terrified peppermint pig.

Milly and Richard Lakin were sitting on the Infants' wagon. It would have been fun for us all to have ridden together, but the Infants needed at least four adults to keep them from falling off or choking on humbugs and Milly would be useful there. Mr and Mrs Lakin waited in their motor car. A hat the size of a meat dish was tied on Mrs Lakin's head, and next to her, her husband was sporting a motoring jacket that must have been ordered urgently from Birmingham, for the creases still showed across his shoulders. They had clearly 'gone to town' for the occasion. In the back was Master Henry Lakin, wearing the full rigging of a sailor suit. The Lakins were on holiday, that meat dish hat and sailor suit announced. For at least three hundred days of the year Mr Lakin worked as hard as the meanest sweeper up in his forge, but he knew how to enjoy himself the other sixty-five.

'Read the news, Miss?' Jackie asked.

'I was reading Father's paper before I came out,' I admitted. '*The Leader* was full of the assassination of Archduke Franz Ferdinand.' I was proud of remembering the name, but then I had been practising it as I walked.

'All Europe is on fire,' Jackie agreed. 'Well, not exactly,' he added lest he frighten a young lady. 'That's only a figure of speech editors use.' He fingered the droops of his moustache. 'They will be calling our men to fight soon,' he predicted. 'I shall look spiffing in uniform, don't you think?'

'If I were a boy I would go too,' I announced.

A cheer went up from the senior boys hanging on to Jim Spence's milk float and with a rattle and rumble the procession began to move onto Sandhill Rise.

From my wagon I could see across the whole town, to the Heath beyond. I remember thinking how cramped Low Town looked, compared with the higher parts where the people who mattered lived. Our families had their brass name plates and tradesmen's entrances to prove we mattered; we had lived the same pleasant routine for three generations, since the first forges spread over the

4

hillsides like a skin disease. Nothing less than an unexpected slump in trade or a very long war could disturb our calm. But those in the valley – they had always known smoke and grime and struggle. And they would be the ones fighting our war for us...

Gaining an assortment of butchers' boys and early morning dogs the procession rattled and yapped on to the Birmingham Road and slithered finally into the Station Approach. A special train was waiting and everyone jumped from their wagons, suddenly scornful of transport that till then had seemed the latest fashion. Junior Boys were sorted from Junior Girls while the Reverend Barraclough gave so many conflicting orders it was safer to ignore him altogether, then two coachloads of chatter and delight moved off for Arton Town.

'Now, girls,' the first Miss Turner said, peering in from the other compartment and clapping her hands. 'It's been a very early start for us all. I suggest you settle down for a little sleep.' She was evidently an optimist.

'What a perfectly heavenly day,' Milly Lakin declared, swinging round on her parasol in an abandoned manner which would have shocked her mother. Fortunately Mrs Lakin was sending a telegraph. 'Mama loves sending telegraphs,' Milly confided. 'She forgets things deliberately so she can watch the operator. Were the little ones simply horrid? Ours talked and talked. The Seniors kept flicking bits of chewed up paper at the ceiling. Ever so many stuck. I wonder if they'll fall on the next outing's heads?' Her laughter rippled across the hampers.

Mrs Lakin appeared and immediately Milly stopped pirouetting and smoothed her new muslin dress. 'Oh bother,' she whispered. 'There's a mark on my skirt already. I'll swear spots fly through the air and land on me.'

Bending behind a stack of pigeon baskets we rubbed at the skirt. 'Now don't you tell,' I whispered to half a dozen cooing heads and Milly giggled.

Her dress was beautiful. On any girl but Milly it would have looked entrancing, but Milly was already as tall as her brother, and her frame was as strong as any boy's. Not even expensive kid gloves could make her fingers look slender, and it was fortunate her feet could be hidden under skirts and petticoats. She had been crimped specially for the occasion, with the result that her hair had taken on the texture of a doll's wig, and the curls irritated her so much she shook them back from her face continually.

Scattering small children and railway porters in her wake, Mrs Lakin came towards us. 'There you are girls,' she said, as if we should have been somewhere else. 'I think you two can lead the crocodile.' Clapping her hands she obtained immediate silence. 'Come along everyone. Little ones to the front. Teachers and congregation put yourselves every few yards alongside please. We don't want anyone falling in the river.'

I remember passing a village school, and on the other side of the road, a large corn and seed mill which had *Lakin, Lakin & Hobble* painted across the front. I wondered who Hobble was, or whether he was a Lakin but couldn't afford new shoes. Warehouses crowded the other bank of the river, and a church tower rose above a confusion of red roofs. Arton looked an interesting place.

At the first sweetshop our millipede got its legs tangled, but order was restored and we crossed the road to a fine stone bridge, where a dirt track led off along the river. Puddles lingered there and some of the unattached young ladies found great need of male assistance. Then we were into our first real field. After the smoke of Sandhill the grass was dazzling.

Mr Lakin's mother was already waiting for us in the paddock, having heard us coming along the path, making as much noise as a column of navvies she said. Kissing her son, she greeted the church leaders. Mr and Mrs Carter (the new caretakers the Misses Turner confided) had been busy all morning to have things ready, and two bewildered country girls were carrying dishes from the house. Henry was already making a nuisance of himself chasing

6

one of the girls with the sugar tongs, but Richard and Milly greeted their grandmother with an affection I had rarely seen between them and their parents. A late arrival in the Lakins' marriage, and still barely six years old, Henry had their full attention, while Richard and Milly were left to themselves most of the time. Richard wandered the Heath or helped in the forge and quarry but being a girl Milly was considered unsuitable for such things, with the result that she was intensely lonely, though few would have suspected.

The hampers were laid out on the grass. There were potted meat sandwiches and jam sandwiches, cold beef and chunks of cheese, hardboiled eggs that slithered in your hands and slices of fruitcake impossible to keep in one piece. The adults sat eating with their groups and discussing the Kaiser. The war would be over in a matter of weeks Reverend Barraclough declared, raising his cup to toast the event.

After the eating came the games, with children in sacks, and children holding crock eggs, walking backwards, blindfolded, feeling sick in the corner... At last when everyone was exhausted and the last grazed knee had been kissed, a pause was granted. Guards were posted along the riverbank and for one afternoon in the year Arton Villa and gardens played host to its city guests. Every wide-eyed visitor was warned with threats of never ever, not ever attending another Treat if so much as a leaf was taken or a flower picked, and the games gave way to awed exploring.

For a few moments I tried to stay with my charges, but soon they had split into little groups, timidly testing paths between rhododendrons. Looking for Richard and Milly I went towards the villa and stared about me in pleasure. Though not large – no larger than my own home – with its marble steps and Italian terrace the house was beautiful. There was none of the pompous grandeur of Sandhill Rise, every line of the windows and balconies here expressing quiet good taste. The view from the terrace was superb, over the paddock where the games had been played, towards the river, which could be seen in glints of green and black. On the other side of the water were a few cottages, outskirts of Arton, with orchards behind them and to the right, further upstream there was the beginning of woodland.

'Arton Forest,' Richard explained, as he and his sister joined me. 'Used to be the hunting ground of great nobles.' He pointed to the other bank. 'Those are cherry orchards. You should hear the birdscarers when the fruit's ripe.' He laughed at the sheer pleasure of it all. 'It's a proper commotion. Whole families of gypsies come to do the picking. The fair's here then, too – the town's swarming with people.'

'I love the fair,' Milly confided. 'It's only small of course, but there's a lovely old carousel and its fun just to watch the local people enjoying themselves. Richard can't keep away either.'

'Oh, it's not much really -' Richard began in an attempt at dignity.

'Don't tell fibs. You're always round the shooting booth.'

Sisters could be very trying, Richard's smile suggested, but he could not remain cross long. He had the same enthusiastic manner as Milly, as if life were a wonderful holiday to be shared. We often talked when he called to meet Milly from chapel. In some ways he was more of a brother to me than Harry, who being young and inclined to fill his pockets with dead grasshoppers was poor company as yet.

'I know,' he suggested. 'Let's go for a row and pay Isaac Booth a visit.'

'Who's Isaac Booth?' I asked.

'He's the ferryman up at Arton Ferry – and the best waterman there is. What he doesn't know about rats isn't worth knowing.' Having given the highest praise in his catalogue Richard waited for my appreciation.

'Isaac's a real mystery,' Milly added. 'No one knows where he came from. He has a beautiful voice and when he plays a tune on his fiddle you can't help but jig.'

'He sounds terribly romantic,' I said, laughing.

'Oh, he is. We often go to Arton Ferry to talk to him. He can tell you all the names of the wildflowers that grow along the bank, and he can catch fish with his bare hands. Of course he's terribly poor,' Milly added as if that too were one of his accomplishments.

'Come on,' Richard urged. 'I'm bored with children's games. No one will see us. Henry's with Mama so he needn't tag along. We can take the skiff and be back in time for the train.'

I was less certain. The Misses Turner might look for me and become concerned. There would be trouble soon, surely.

Richard and Milly were persuasive however. They were bored with little children and for them, a visit to Arton had none of the flavour of special treat it had for me. If this war everyone was talking of happened they mightn't see Isaac for weeks. Besides, Richard would be volunteering of course and could be away a month or two. He wanted to say goodbye to Isaac.

And so began one of the most foolhardy – as well as the most far-reaching – incidents in my life.

Taking up the oars and casting off under the safety of overhanging willows, Richard steered us onto the open river. He kept to the bank, rowing hard against the current and round or under over-hanging branches till we were out of sight of the paddock. Though I had never been on water before I was determined not to show fear and sat bolt upright with my hands under my bottom. Small surprised ducks appeared from caverns of willow, and woodland began to replace cottages on the other bank. 'Dragonfly,' Richard said, breaking the silence. 'There's another.' A second green blur darted around us, the most beautiful thing I had ever seen.

We came to a bend in the river. Beyond it was an island. The current was dangerous there, Richard warned, and he pulled into the security of the bank again. Fast-flowing water separated us from the pebbly shore of the island. Very few could row across,

Milly explained: Isaac and a few fishermen, locals like that. There had been a drowning there only that spring, an Arton lad. The ferryman had been paid to drag the river to find his body. She had heard Mrs Carter telling Cook how they found the body quite near their landing stage, all bloated and blue. She herself had seen great branches whirled downstream, where they snagged on Arton Bridge. We were all very quiet as we passed so evil a place, yet it was beautiful to see, a study in wildfowl and ancient trees.

As soon as we had passed the island another bend in the river appeared, and beyond that a railway halt on the nearside bank. Richard rowed steadily towards a small jetty near a riverside tavern. Though he was not quite eighteen, many an older man would have envied his skill and the strength of his strokes.

Looking back over the distance of seventy years I recall a fine young man, one of those blessed by nature, granted good fortune and a healthy body, regular features without over-handsomeness, and a quick mind. In the normal course of events he would take over the Lakins' business and make it still more profitable, for even the workmen at the forge liked him – though they were critical of Mr Lakin's penny-pinching ways and Mrs Lakin's bossiness. Richard was a bright lad they said, who would go far.

We moored at the landing-stage and scrambled up to a path which joined the lane from the station. To my surprise the roadway went straight into the river.

'Haloa Mr, Ferryman!' Milly called, cupping her hand round her mouth. At once a man appeared at the door of an isolated cottage on the other bank, then there was a whirring sound above us as a wheel turned to bring the ferry towards us. All we had to do was walk down the road and climb inside. 'Oh bother,' Milly said, scooping up her skirt to reveal six inches of leg. 'Afternoon, Isaac. We're at the Villa on the usual Sunday School Treat so we thought we'd pay you a visit.'

The ferryman almost lived up to Milly's romantic description. Very dark and with hair that was almost blue-black in the sunlight, he was slighter than I had expected yet, as Milly whispered, had he not been a poor man, how the girls in Sandhill would have fluttered about him! I had often noticed the bargees on Sandhill Canal, and the wiry strength of this man reminded me of them. My main impression of him however was one of intelligence. Dressed in light cotton trousers and a fisherman's shirt, he was barefoot. I had never seen a man's feet before and they fascinated me. Presumably he could grip the boards better without boots but all afternoon those feet distracted me. They were so unashamedly male.

Milly introduced me. 'This is Miss Cooper, my best friend from school. Of course, we've both left now, but we're great friends still aren't we?'

'Pleased to meet you, Miss,' the ferryman replied. His voice surprised me. It was almost educated, with a soft Welsh accent.

'I wanted to say goodbye,' Richard said. 'In case I 'list for a soldier. If war is declared Father will be too busy at the forge making guns to bring us, he says.'

The ferryman shook his head. Silently he wound the boat along its cable. 'Don't you want a war?' I asked. 'Everyone else does. It will teach the Kaiser a lesson, they say.'

'Why must men wish to kill and be killed?' Isaac demanded. 'No, I don't want a war.'

In embarrassment we looked at each other.

The ferry arrived at the bank and Richard paid our three pence. 'Don't you think I should enlist?' he asked.

'No. Your father needs you to help with the business. Besides, men get killed in wars – and so do boys.' There was a call from the other bank. 'You must excuse me while I go about my business. I'll cross back to you and talk when I can.'

The ferry was busy that time of the afternoon with farmers' wives returning with their shopping from the town. In between journeys Isaac sat with us on the bank, chewing a piece of sorrel and talking of the Kaiser.

11

'Do you think there will be a war?' Milly asked.

'Men are stupid enough.

'Reverend Barraclough thinks so,' Richard said. 'He says the Germans have been preparing for a long time; that's why they launched the Dreadnoughts and deepened the Kiel Canal.'

'Father agrees,' I joined in. 'Whenever he goes on reserve training it's the German High Seas Fleet they pretend to fight. He'll sign on again as soon as hostilities begin. They'll take trained men under forty he says, if they are fit and well.'

'I wish I could go,' Milly said. 'Girls miss all the fun.'

In answer Isaac sighed.

Richard laughed at his pessimism. The war would be over by Christmas he said. Our boys would teach the Kaiser a lesson and be home for their plum pudding; everyone said so. Isaac disagreed, however. It would be a long campaign he predicted, and no one would win. Our King and the Kaiser were related; we should be trying to make peace. For a ferryman he seemed remarkably well-informed, though that was because he read the newspapers, he said – one of the gentry saved them for him.

Occasionally children's voices came from the cottage behind us and I noticed two horses cropping the verge. A more peaceful place would have been hard to imagine, nor one more isolated.

'It seems incredible talking of war, when everything's so peaceful round us,' I admitted.

'Sing us a few songs Isaac,' Milly demanded unexpectedly. 'Please. If we can't come again for a while I shall miss hearing you in church.'

Laughing, the ferryman shook his head. 'I should feel a fool sitting here, Miss. I need an audience.' Seeing her disappointment he relented. 'But I'll play you a few tunes if you wish. My fingers are getting stiff and I should be glad of the excuse to practise.' Getting up, he went into the cottage to reappear with a flute, a beautiful silver instrument that was almost absurd in such a place.

For a few moments he warmed it while we sat in fascinated wonder.

'Isaac used to tour the fairs and music halls,' Milly whispered to me. 'He plays better than any of the fancy musicians who come to Sandhill.' Overhearing her, the ferryman smiled. Then he began to play a melody which I recognised as one of the ballads we often sang at the Misses Turners' – *Sweet Barbara Allen.*

My musical knowledge was confined to the church organ and parlour pianos and this instrument was a revelation to me, moving me almost to tears.

The ferryman played other songs, *The Rose of Tralee* and *Annie Laurie, Ye Banks and Braes* and more serious melodies I could recognize but not identify. Haunting in their beauty heard above the lapping of water they melted into stranger tunes which sounded foreign and brought a wistful expression to the ferryman's face. Every note was held in his memory. Two morsels of children appeared at the cottage door and stared at us in amazement. Isaac called them to him but they were shy of the fine young ladies and gentleman and ran back indoors like black-haired rabbits. Others were listening too, for I saw a curtain twitch at an open window in the cottage.

How does one put into words the beauty of music or the skill of a man given its gift? All I can say is that I have heard music so haunting from only one other man, and that was Isaac's grandson.

Finally an old woman appeared at the landing stage, and though she appeared happy to stay a while and listen, Isaac got up and returned to his duties.

After he had gone we were silent. 'I've never heard anything so lovely,' I admitted in the end. 'I'm so glad I came.'

Richard looked at his watch. 'We ought to be rowing back,' he said. Standing up, he waved across the river. At once the wheel began to turn.

We walked down to the jetty, none of us eager to leave. Milly in particular kept turning towards the cottage. Suddenly she was slipping on the muddy path. With a surprised yelp, she sat on her bottom.

'You stupid girl!' Richard said, his good temper for once deserting him.

'Mama will be furious. You'll get us all into trouble.' He softened when he saw Milly's shame. 'Come here,' he ordered and I began trying to brush away the mud with his handkerchief.

'No, that will only rub it worse,' a voice called and we turned in surprise, having forgotten Isaac. He stood uncertainly beside us. 'It looks fine material,' he said.

'It is,' Milly agreed ruefully. 'I shall have no pocket money for weeks and weeks.'

The ferryman tried not to smile and failed. 'Come back to the cottage and let my mother help,' he invited. 'But please – no word to anyone about what you see inside.' We stared at each other in bewilderment. 'If you talk, you may cost me my house and my job, and then where would I be?'

Mystified, we followed him up the river path towards the cottage gate. 'Do you think we ought to go in?' Milly asked. 'Mama says you should never go into the homes of the poor. There may be fever.'

'Do you want your dress cleaned or not?' I asked bluntly. 'Just hold your breath.'

After the sun the scullery was dark. I could distinguish a stone sink with a pail of water standing in it and pans catching the afternoon light. A door was half-open showing jams and stone crocks in a whitewashed store. Another door opened into a main room. Isaac was waiting for us with his hand on the latch and talking to someone inside in a language I did not understand. More reluctant than ever I went in, ahead of Milly and Richard. As I did so a man rose from the table and nodding in a gesture of politeness went out. His hair was long, tied back, but it was not his appearance I noticed most. Beside the range an old woman was

14

standing, resting against the mantelshelf while she stirred a stew on the range. In the gloom there was a flash of gold at her throat.

'This is my mother,' Isaac said. 'You must excuse my brother. He must see to the horses.'

The woman turned from her cooking. 'Come here, Miss,' she said. 'I shall see what I can do. The young gentleman had best step outside.' There was the same Welsh accent but the phrasing was foreign, emphasising the strangeness of the situation. I saw an expression of astonishment enter Richard's eyes, then he and Isaac went out.

Never one to fuss, Milly undid the fastenings on her dress and let it drop to the floor. In her petticoats and camisole she looked more raw-boned than ever. Quickly I went over to a cradle near the fire, so that I should not see her distress. Small eyes watched me with unnerving intelligence. 'What's the baby's name?' I called.

'Benjamin.'

Isaac's mother poured water from a jug and washed Milly's dress in a bowl on the dresser. 'Eh,' she sighed. 'Here's a fine dress to come boating in.' The remark sounded like a judgment on a whole way of life, not one muslin dress. 'What's a lady like you doing talking to my Isaac?'

'I like him,' Milly protested. 'He's the only one who's been friends with us in Arton. It's been much more fun staying here since he came.'

'Oh yes, he's always had a way with him,' Mrs Booth agreed, her voice suggesting her son was allowed a few indiscretions. 'My, you've a way with babbies too,' she added, turning to me. 'And who might you be? You're not of her kin. You're far too dainty.'

'My name's Mary Cooper,' I replied, curtseying in respect for my questioner's age. 'I'm Milly's friend from school.'

In reply the woman turned back to the muddy skirt. Her manner made me nervous and I stared around me. I don't know what I expected to find: vermin perhaps. My mother had told me the houses of the poor were full of lice, and these were no ordinary

15

poor. The scarcity of the furniture amazed me. The dining room in my own home was stuffed with carving chairs, corner cupboards, silver salt cellars, fire irons, fire dogs . . . There were two tables besides, one a small oval inlaid with wooden patterns, the other a monstrous surface on which generals might have fought whole Waterloos. In contrast, though this room served as kitchen, dining room and parlour it contained only a scrubbed table and four chairs to serve a family. Presumably the little ones sat on the tab rugs near the hearth. Poverty was present in every object; in the damp patches on the whitewashed walls, the meagre crockery on the dresser, the curtains that had evidently served at a smaller window in a previous life.

Yet despite the poverty there was pride. A scent of herbs and flowers sweetened the room, and coloured prints had been pasted over the worst of the damp patches. Paper flowers decorated the fringed cloth above the range. Near the window one wall was used for the display of old playbills and public notices, and I read 'Boothman's Fair' on one while another advertised 'The celebrated tenor Isaac Boothman'. A music hall had engaged 'that popular musician Isaac Booth' and in many of the posters the shortened version of the name could be seen. Judging by the dates the ferryman had adopted the name Booth, but Boothman was the original form. He had become quite famous it seemed, for there were postcards of pretty music hall artistes signed 'To Isaac', and one of himself, standing looking surprisingly handsome. Had our Methodist elders not regarded the music hall as a place of sin, we might have heard of him.

Milly had joined me. 'They're show people,' she whispered. 'What do we do? Mama would be furious if she knew we'd been here. They might rob us.' She fingered her gold locket nervously. 'Though they seem decent people.'

'I'll be in trouble, too,' I agreed. 'Get your dress as soon as you can, and let's leave.'

16

We were being incredibly rude whispering, and sensing the old woman's annoyance I turned round. As I did so I noticed a bookcase made out of wooden boxes. In it was arranged an impressive array of books and sheet music. 'Oh yes, Isaac's as learned as any *Gajo**,' Mrs Boothman commented. She sounded scornful, of us and learning too. 'He hankers after your ways, and much good it's done him. If he'd stayed with us he wouldn't be living in such a place. Why, I could buy it now if I wished, all of it.' Taking the dress she examined it in the better light near the window. 'Nothing would make me stay here, 'prisoned in four walls. And your sort hounds him from house to house for his pains.' A whole lifetime of suspicion and insult was conveyed in those few sour words.

*Gajo – non-Romany.

'We wouldn't hound him,' Milly protested. 'He's our friend.'

The old woman grunted. 'There,' she said, in a softer tone. 'All the mud has come away. We'll dry it in the sun and it will look good as new. You will keep your pocket money. Wear Jilly's dress while you wait. She's working today. The harvest must be brought in, holiday or no. Go upstairs – you, the fair one – and bring the Sunday dress hanging over the banister.'

Blinking in the darkness I went upstairs. A dress was laid over the banister as I had been told. Not liking to look round me I took it up quickly, but I could not help but see the mattress lain on the landing and the old coats as blankets.

Coarse and far too short that dress may have been, but on Milly it looked far better than her own. Nothing but fashion had been served by Mrs Lakin's choice and the cost of the material alone would have bought new outfits for the two little ones whose boots waited beside the stairs. Milly had clearly been thinking the same, for she burst out, 'Why can't I wear plain things like this? I wish that hateful muslin had been ruined.'

'There's thanks for all my trouble,' Mrs Boothman snapped.

'Don't be angry,' I pleaded. 'Miss Lakin doesn't mean to be ungrateful. Her Mama made her wear that dress, and it doesn't suit her at all.'

'Miss Cooper's right,' Milly agreed. 'Such dresses are meant for pretty delicate things and look at me.' Though she had meant to make us laugh, her voice snagged.

'You're well enough,' the old woman replied, and there was compassion in her voice. 'In time you'd make a farmer a good strong wife and bear him children by the dozen.'

'But I'm meant to be a lady.'

'And more fool your parents for making you so. You must do their bidding now, but when you are a woman, choose your own way. I know what it is to stand alone. My husband was a fighting man – my father and brothers thought he wasn't fit for me – but I should have spent the rest of my life pining if I had not gone to him. A candle is not made of wax but is all flame. Live for the present. You *Gaje* waste your spirits looking to the future. You make everyone ashamed to live as they are – you have made my Isaac ashamed of his own family...'

I looked at the books and music again and thought of the posters on the wall. 'Why should he settle here, in a place like this?' I asked. 'I don't mean to be impertinent, but he's not from round here.'

Spitting into the fire Mrs Boothman considered my question. 'He wanted that Jilly of his,' she said resentfully. 'And the only way he could keep her was by living her ways. He could do it too, if people would let him. He had a good job, looking after a wealthy man's horses and his farm machines – my Isaac can charm any machine – but they drove him out.'

'Why?'

Mrs Boothman laughed unpleasantly. 'The farmer's wife wanted him for herself, and when he had no eyes for anyone but Jilly, she told the village he was a showman, a gypsy too. A woman's spite can be a vicious thing.'

We were bewildered and embarrassed, two gently nurtured young ladies, hearing of things our mothers would have blushed to admit. I wanted to go home. 'Go outside and talk to your brother a bit,' Mrs Boothman suggested to Milly, and in relief we obeyed.

We found Richard and Isaac sitting on the riverbank. Richard smiled as he saw his sister's borrowed dress, but he was too excited to make any comment. 'Isaac's mother is a true gypsy,' he said. 'Her name's Rupa and she's travelled miles – all over Serbia and Prussia, where everyone is talking about now. His father was a Traveller too, but not pure Romany. He took over a fair when the owner died. That's where the name comes from.'

In acknowledgment Isaac bowed his head. 'I've been trying to explain to Master Richard that to my mother's people I'm a *Diddikai**,' he said. 'Not a gypsy.'

*Diddikai – part-Romany.

'Why didn't you tell us it was your family who run the fair?' Milly asked. 'We wouldn't have minded.'

'You might have done. Once people start calling me a gypsy we shall have the village constable here every time a chicken goes missing. I daren't take risks.'

'Your mother says people keep hounding you from place to place,' I said. 'Why?'

'Nobody wants gypsies or tinkers living in their village, Miss. They're fit to pick cherries or hops, but not to have as neighbours.'

'She says you're ashamed of your birth,' I persisted.

'She's unjust. When my father was killed in the ring I was four years old. My mother took me with her when she returned to her *Kumpania* – her kin. Even after she left them to go back to the fair I stayed with them. I was brought up one of the *Lowara*. It's the way of doing things that matters, not the blood; you must observe the rituals, the ways of eating and drinking, so as not to become *marhime*, unclean. I still keep to such things. I'm more entitled to call myself one of the Rom than my brothers.' His mother's criticism had clearly stung him.

'Why did you settle?' Richard asked.

'I wanted to read and write.'

Milly and I looked at each other in surprise. His answer conflicted with what his mother had said: which was the truth?

'I couldn't read the words of the songs sold in the streets, nor write the music I heard in my head. The Rom don't value learning so I took to touring with the fair again and going to the schools some of the churches ran on a Sunday. I'd missed proper schooling you see. It was a minister who gave me my first flute. It was as if the music was there inside me – I didn't seem to need to learn.' His eyes had taken on a peculiar brightness. 'I found the music halls would pay me to do what I loved.'

'You were quite famous,' Milly prompted. 'Why did you give it up?'

'After I married – my wife's family ran a lodging house where I sometimes stayed – I found it was too difficult to travel all the time. At first Jilly came with me, but when Becky and Sally came along I decided I must give up or lose them. The trouble is, I can't make enough money with work like this, and people have driven us from better things. If you tell people I was a showman – or call me a gypsy – they will drive us from here too.'

'We won't tell,' Milly promised. 'I don't see why people should drive you away in any case, but if you want us to keep quiet we will.'

We had been missed. Though we moored the skiff as quietly as possible and crept up the rhododendron path we were so late it was inevitable there would be trouble. Mr and Mrs Lakin were waiting for us on the terrace, Mrs Lakin's face stiff with anger. 'And where have you been?' she demanded.

'To Arton Ferry, Mother,' Richard replied, remaining admirably calm.

'Might I ask why?' Mr Lakin joined in ominously.

'I wanted to see Isaac Booth -' Richard was struggling for an explanation. 'I wanted to ask his advice about enlisting. I'm sorry we worried you. Milly slipped and muddied her dress. We had to wait while Mr Booth's mother cleaned it.

'Cleaned it?' Mrs Lakin almost screamed. 'You let some filthy old woman clean Milly's dress? Do you know how much that material cost?'

'Mrs Booth is not filthy, Mama,' Milly intervened. 'And she has got all the mud off. Look.' Turning slowly she displayed the skirt. Mrs Lakin snatched at the material and inspected it.

'Well...' she admitted at last. 'She has made a good job of it, though Thompson would have ruined it and blamed the material. But you had no right being at Arton Ferry at all, deserting your duties here and keeping company with such low people. Only the Good Lord knows what fevers you might have contracted there. And you've led Miss Cooper into your foolish ways.'

'They didn't force me to go, Mrs Lakin,' I said softly, 'so it's not all their fault.'

'You are very loyal, young lady,' Mr Lakin said, 'but I'm certain your father will not be pleased to hear you have been visiting such people. That ferryman used to tour the music halls. He's a low sort of man.'

His words brought a flush of anger to my face. 'Old Mrs Booth was very kind, sir,' I said, 'And Mr Booth is a fine musician. He played beautifully for us. They're neither of them low – they're simply poor.' I had no right to speak like that of course and I saw an expression of surprise come to Mr Lakin's face. He was rarely defied.

'Mary's right,' Richard insisted. 'Isaac is a good man. He's taught me a great deal. Only today he's given me a marvellous idea for the Heath. He says it could be reclaimed and turned into a sort of wild park where the people of Sandhill can come and see butterflies and flowers...'

21

'Richard,' Mr Lakin cut in firmly. 'I'm in full agreement with your mother that this undesirable friendship must end. You will be taking over the forge and estate one day, and helping me to manage affairs as soon as possible, I hope. With my health so poor lately I need you. It's not fitting for you to be seen with such people.'

'But Father,' Richard persisted. 'The men who work at the forge aren't respectable, not in the way you and Mother think of; but I shall have to see they do their jobs, and know what to say to them if they injure themselves or their wives die. Isaac teaches me their language.'

'And he can play the flute and the violin like a dream,' Milly cut in. 'It's not right he should be so poor. He works very hard on the ferry'

'You'll find most people are poor because they want to be,' Mrs Lakin said, adjusting her hat. 'Mrs Booth could work I'm sure and help him.'

I wanted to knock that hat off – and all it signified. 'Mrs Booth does work, ma'am,' I said, staring at the ground to hide my red face. 'She was helping with the harvest today and her baby is ever so tiny.' I was very young, and this was my first experience of poverty.

'We ought to help them,' Milly pleaded. 'What we've spent on this afternoon's Treat would feed his whole family for a year.'

A grudging smile softened Mr Lakin's expression. 'You won't solve poverty by not having Sunday School Treats,' he said. 'Perhaps we might do something however.'

'Please,' Milly asked. 'We could at least take them some of what's left over this afternoon.'

'No, Milly,' Mr Lakin replied. 'Even poor men have pride, and I suspect that ferryman has more than most. You must do things subtly.'

'Perhaps you could get people to pay him to play his flute,' I suggested. 'I'm sure I would.'

22

Unintentionally – or maybe intentionally on Richard's part – we had deflected his parents from their anger. Mrs Lakin began to smooth her sleeves. 'I could ask your mother to book him for one of her soirees,' she said to her husband. 'That is, if he really is as good as the young people say. I suppose he can make himself presentable?' she added, turning to us.

'I'll give him my blue jacket,' Richard said, 'I don't need it.'

'Very well, but don't think I've forgotten your foolishness. Still, as Miss Cooper will be spending next weekend with us, the less we say about this silly affair the better.'

'Now be off with you,' Mr Lakin said. 'Go and join the cricket match and do your duty, as you should have done all afternoon.'

'Not Milly,' Mrs Lakin insisted. 'If she can't be trusted not to ruin a perfectly new dress, I shall have to keep her here at the house. Henry is inside already in disgrace. I don't know why the Lord should have sent me two such naughty children.'

'Let her be, Matilda,' Mr Lakin said. 'This may be their last Sunday School Treat for a while. Who knows? Let them remember the day with happiness.'

In chastened silence we walked down the steps of the terrace and through the gardens, but as soon as we were out of sight our mouths were affected by a peculiar wobble. First Milly weakened, then Richard and at last we were all leaning on each other for support. 'I never thought we'd get off so lightly,' Richard admitted. 'Mind you, the Governor's right. It was a stupid thing to do. He can be a decent stick sometimes. It's the business that gets him down.'

The sound of children's voices and the plock of cricket bats came from beyond the rhododendrons. Standing in a gap in the hedge we watched as the Reverend Barraclough scored a single. Jackie Parkes turned to us. 'Heard the news?' he asked. 'Mr Carter took the trap into Styles. He says everyone is talking there. They say war will be declared tomorrow. Isn't it whizzing?'

'Bravo,' a voice called near us as the Reverend Barraclough scored a six. Gentle clapping filled the afternoon sunshine with its restful, utterly English sound.

As Jackie had predicted, war with Germany was declared the next day. In those years before radio and television disaster travelled more slowly than now, but that news reached us remarkably quickly. Little groups of men gathered on corners or at the tennis club discussing how and where to join Kitchener's army, and all sorts of silly rumours circulated. Bert Turner claimed that men with motorcycles were being taken on as dispatch riders – which sent the Homer brothers away to tune treasured toys. Jackie and his mates were for travelling down to Whitehall at once to force the War Office to accept them. There was a great deal of talk of 'poor little Belgium' and 'an Englishman's duty' but I doubt if any of the bright young things chattering so excitedly had much idea what they were saying.

Shameful as it may seem we were not much affected otherwise. The bulk of the regular army was sent at once to France, but only one or two families in Sandhill were involved in their departure, and their men were swallowed up as it were, without message. A few of our group, like Jackie Parkes, travelled to London as they had promised and some joined the local Territorials, but most waited, doing a lot of talking and drinking tea. During that first week the main excitement in our home was my invitation to spend the weekend of Richard's eighteenth birthday at Forge House, though Father was obviously nervous about his own position, being still a member of the naval reserve, though older than most.

My mother scarcely considered the possibility of him leaving. Her thoughts were all on the weekend at Forge House. She fretted, advised one dress and then changed her mind, gave me a hundred warnings, offered me her purse and generally behaved like a schoolgirl. I had advanced in her estimation. Till then I had been the cause of much headshaking. I was too quiet – even worse, I was always thinking. 'Cleverness in a girl,' she warned, 'is like having a sheep that can bark. It may be noteworthy, but it's of no real use to anyone.' Now she found me shrewd and just the right girl for Master Richard, who as everyone knew was clever himself. Mr and Mrs Harper would have their noses quite put out of joint when they found their Gizelle had not been invited, and as for Isabel Hope, I would soon put paid to her chances.

As patiently as I could I listened to my mother's chatter, but I felt uneasy, like a doll being made ready for a Christmas window. I had a nasty feeling that if I returned from Forge House with less than another invitation I would be taken out of the window and returned to a cupboard in my mother's affections. 'Please Mama,' I pleaded. 'Don't hope too much. Richard Lakin and I have been friends a long time. It was natural with Milly and I so close.'

'Stuff and nonsense!' Mother replied. 'Sandhill won't see it like that and Mrs Lakin's too smart a woman not to realise. Isabel Hope is her choice. You are Richard's. It's up to you to see that Richard wins. Isabel will make a nice ornament for some man, but you have as good a fortune as her and five times her intelligence. Fortunately Mr Lakin can rarely refuse Richard anything, and he himself has the sense to realise ornaments soon gather dust.' My mother could make some very penetrating remarks at times. They confirmed my impression that underneath all that practised froth was an intelligence which had never quite lain down.

Father was equally concerned at the invitation, so much so he made an unaccustomed visit to the drawing room. Looking uncomfortable without a pencil behind his ear and a ledger in his hand, he sat beside me and gave advice. 'You're a sensible girl,' he began.

If he had told me I was about to take flight I couldn't have been more surprised. 'Thank you, Sir,' I said.

'I've been impressed by the way you've found work in the shop since you left school ... You may not realise it, but from my window in the cash office I can see over every department, and very useful it has been at times I can tell you. You've been brought up to fear the Lord and I have no need to speak to you concerning your conduct with Master Richard, I'm sure. I have a high regard for Richard himself. He has a clear sense of duty towards his family and his country, and will behave honourably towards any girl.' I flushed in embarrassment and began to protest. 'I know,' Father agreed. 'Your mother is already choosing the wedding gown and you're certain of no more than friendship. I shouldn't have allowed you to go if I had thought otherwise, but when two young people are so well suited to each other there is the likelihood of love, and a better sort of love than most. Your mother and I scarcely knew each other until we were married.' He paused, appearing to lose the thread of his statement, and stared at my needle as if he would find it there. Poor Father. In all other ventures he prospered, but he had evidently entered his marriage in the debit sheets of life long ago.

Just one other time before he left he talked to me alone, trying to explain his decision to re-enlist. 'I shall be sorry to leave you and Harry,' he said (I noticed he did not mention Mother) 'but it's my duty. I'm sure you see that.' He smiled, an unfamiliar pleasure entering his expression. 'I'll admit to you I'm almost looking forward to it. Shop keeping isn't for me. I'm very grateful the good Lord saw fit to leave me so comfortably off; when poor Harold and Malcolm died too soon to enjoy what they expected, but I was sorry to leave the Navy and have been sorrier since.'

A window seemed to open in my mind. My father was unhappy in Sandhill. I had not realised till then adults could share such emotions. Ever since my visit to Arton Ferry I had had a feeling of new understanding. At Miss Beckett's Academy we learned about Africa and India and places with strange sounding names, but our lessons always referred ultimately to England, and to Sandhill in particular. What was Sandhill compared to green fields and a last flowing river, to places like Serbo Croatia, or music which made my eyes go misted at its beauty? And now my father was opening other windows...

Richard called as soon as he could escape from the forge. He wanted to apologise for spoiling my Treat. His mother could be very difficult at times. Fortunately she held no grudges and had spoken well of me on Sunday. He was sorry, he repeated. It was a rotten thing to do, leading someone astray. His eyes were full of amusement.

Pretending to fold an invoice, I smiled. 'I'm quite capable of going astray on my own,' I insisted. 'I thoroughly enjoyed myself I've never seen water so clear and blue, or so many trees. Even our visit to Mr Booth's cottage was quite an adventure.'

'I'll say it was. I'd never realised though I should have guessed. We talked as we'd never talked before, man to man if you see what I mean. He said he understood why I wanted to enlist, even if he was against it.'

'What did your father say?'

'First that the firm cannot spare me, then that Kitchener will want men not boys; that I shall have to be at least nineteen. But I shall feel a coward if I sit around in offices while everyone else is fighting. If they do refuse me I shall walk over to Twynning where I'm not so well known and enlist there. I could pass for nineteen if I put my best suit on.'

'I wish I could go,' I said. 'Why do girls have to wait at home?'

'So there's someone to keep the home fires burning, of course! All the same you'd make a smashing soldier. It'd be a real lark together.'

A slight redness came to his cheeks and he laughed. 'That reminds me why I came,' he said, reaching into his blazer pocket. 'Mama asked me to deliver this letter to your mother. It's about next weekend. I'm afraid she's invited that awful Isabel Hope. I tried to dissuade her but you know what she's like.' He thrust the envelope towards me. 'Here, take it,' he ordered. 'You have got an

27

evening gown haven't you? I've never seen you dressed up. You're always so-' He floundered for an adjective.

'Plain?' I asked drily.

'Lord, no. Serviceable. Personally I can't stand all those frills and curls, and as for beauty, well, it always seems to lead to trouble. Men who marry beautiful wives seem to spend most of their time wondering where they are. I'd sooner have a girl that'd wear well.'

I laughed outright. 'You sound as though you're buying furniture.' My mother had appeared at the far door of the shop and Richard was immediately overcome by embarrassment – as usual. 'I'll have a white thread and two black ones,' he said loudly. 'Will you serve me, or shall I go to one of the assistants?'

'Father likes me to serve occasionally,' I replied, trying not to laugh. Taking the three reels I wrapped them. Afterwards Richard took the packet as if he did not have the faintest idea what to do with it, then wishing me goodbye, turned away.

'Wasn't that young Richard?' Mother asked, sailing like an overladen galleon towards the counter.

'He brought you this letter.'

'Such a nice young man,' Mother commented. 'I told you he was sweet on you my dear. Now don't look so cross. He wouldn't call so often to buy cotton otherwise. His mother must have drawers full of it by now. I'm not sure how much the Lakins are worth but it must be a good deal.' Laughing her tinkly little laugh Mother patted her hair in a gesture I found intensely irritating, as if she were a flighty girl of sixteen instead of a woman of nearly forty. 'Play your cards well with Master Richard. I married wisely and look what it has brought me.' And she sailed away.

Savagely I jabbed an invoice on to a spike. Richard had been too good a friend to think of in terms of 'playing my cards'. Only now as he was talking of going away to fight did I realise how much I valued him. Almost as long as I could remember he had been there, laughing and teasing his sister, offering to carry our school bags, rattling on about some machine his father had installed. I did not know what love was, except that as a solution to problems it seemed over-rated, but if love meant friendship, company, being at ease with one another, I had loved Richard for years. There was every likelihood he felt the same about me. Lately he had begun to say stupid things and go red when he said them. As Mother pointed out, the drawers of Forge House must be full of cotton reels by now. There could be no question of trying to play my cards. Rather be a Miss Turner, yellow bonnet and all, than have him look back and say I trapped him into a marriage he did not want.

Harry burst in, his face red and his tie in its usual sideways position. 'There's a simply spiffing march outside,' he announced. 'The Territorials are parading down to the station. Will Nathan says they're off training somewhere. The fun's beginning...'

My father followed him into the shop. 'You boys don't know what you're saying,' he warned.

Richard and I walked out together several times that week though considering Milly always came too it could hardly be called a courtship. The Thursday before Richard's birthday we strolled across the Heath together, planning the entertainments at Forge House. As we walked I wondered how it felt to own a whole hillside; my mother's hints about marriage had inevitably had some effect.

Lakin's Heath was pitted with shafts, a mess of disused tracks and decaying buildings. Only a stranger would venture there at night, for bits of metal rail and pits even the Lakins had forgotten were protected only by blackberries. But coal and iron had given the Lakins the money with which their quarry was dug and their forge built, raised the family from yeoman farmers owning a scrubby heathland to one of the most prominent names for thirty miles around. Without the Lakins there would have been no Sandhill, and without Lakin's Heath the Lakins would have been nothing. A few cottages would have clustered along the valley of the Dibble, but Town Hall, Infirmary, Sandhill Rise, railway station, shops, forges, brickworks, canal, all the paraphernalia of a bustling town had followed Josiah Lakin's discovery that what lay under his land was more important than the land itself.

'I shall have this lot cleared up,' Richard announced.

'But you'll spoil it,' Milly protested. 'It won't be romantic then.'

'Romance is all very well, but this place is dangerous. I'm sure we'd be held liable if someone fell down one of the shafts. I shall have notices put up till I can fill in the entrances. The spoil heaps could be levelled at the same time to provide in-fill. It would be very economical. We could turn it all into a park then, like Isaac suggested -give it to the town perhaps, or charge entrance fees if we needed.'

He had a way of talking as if he were about to take charge tomorrow which I found puzzling. Like Prince Hal he seemed to be trying on the crown, yet there was no greed in him. It seemed to me his impatience to take over from his father rose from an almost blinding vision. There was so much he wanted to do and so little time. Ever since I had known him he had been full of schemes, some of them quite wild when he was younger. Now his ideas were beginning to sound like sense.

'Doesn't it make you feel guilty?' he asked suddenly.

'What about?'

'All this.' His glance indicated the whole Heath.

'Why?' Milly persisted.

'When you think about it, this must have been beautiful once – covered in grass and heather with little silver birch like you can see in a few of the better places still. And think of the poor miners themselves. I was reading an old ledger last week, all about how young boys used to crawl up and down the tunnels dragging sledges of coal behind them, and the pittance they were paid.'

'That was last century,' I said, trying to be tactful.

'But it was our – what? great-great-grandfather who employed them. I'll bet those shafts could tell some horrible tales. I'm glad I don't believe in ghosts. I don't think I could come here if I did.'

'But great-great-grandfather built the chapel and the school. He can't have been all that bad.'

'That was later,' Richard replied. 'And besides, chapels and schools made them feel better, I'll bet. I'd like to know more about this place, and about the famous Josiah Lakin. If this war fizzles out I shall see what I can find. There's stacks of papers in the Board Room cupboards.'

'You mightn't like what you find,' I warned.

'But it'd be the truth, wouldn't it? It's always best to know the truth. I reckon Mama's family was probably worse than ours. Grandad Piper always seemed a terrible tyrant. He used to rap my knuckles with his pipe.'

Unexpectedly Richard ran on ahead, up a small mound from which he could better survey the land. 'We will turn all this into a park someday,' he prophesied. 'Not laid out in dreary walks like Victoria Park but open for everyone, and full of birds and flowers. I've been thinking about what Isaac said ever since we were at Arton. Did I tell you he camped here as a boy, when he was with his mother's people?' He laughed. 'I'll bet Father didn't know. Isaac said gypsies often stay here – on the Twynning side where we can't see. He says even leaving it for twenty years just as it is, will give Nature a chance to improve things.'

Sliding down the mound he lifted a trail of white flower and prickle. 'See, Nature's beginning to take over already. This bramble's living off the mortar – it'll have this wall down someday.'

As we listened to him we caught his enthusiasm. Milly treated him with the scorn due from a sister, but it was a matter of form. Richard's plans were her plans. They would rule Lakins together. Little Henry was never considered, being regarded by both of them as likely to be 'a poor tool'. Milly's responsibility was to be the offices. For the past year she had been going to Mr Hopkins at the Boys' School to learn bookkeeping, greatly to the amusement of the other girls in Sandhill's society set, who regarded book-keeping as a strange weapon in the matrimonial battle. Mr Lakin however was indulgent towards her wishes. He did not share his wife's conviction that expensive dresses and curled hair would make a married swan out of a single duckling. Milly might be grateful for a life-time interest and a private income.

We sat together, drawing plans in the sand at our feet. 'Isaac says there'll be grass snakes here already, possibly adders. He says we must be careful of them if we explore any of the old mines,' Richard said.

'Oooh, let's!' Milly said.

'Let's what?'

'Explore the old mines.'

'We haven't any rope, silly.'

'You don't need a rope,' I said quietly. 'There's several shafts that open right on to the hillside.'

Richard smiled. 'How do you know?' he asked. 'Which one did you go into?' His tone suggested he too had been doing a bit of illicit exploring.

'That one over there.' I pointed to a dark slit in the hill. 'We need a lantern to go any distance, but there's light enough from the entrance to walk a little way. Today's sunshine should help, too. It was a dull day when I came before and I didn't dare go far.'

'I've never been in that one,' Richard admitted. Then he was silent. The shafts were dangerous; they were forbidden even to Richard and Milly. Sandhill mothers warned their children not to go near them, literally on fear of death; dogs vanished after rabbits and were never seen again. Looking from Milly to myself Richard whispered, 'Just a little way?'

His whisper broke the tension. 'What on earth are you whispering for?' Milly asked.

Together we walked up the overgrown trackway towards the black slit in the hill. Pieces of broken rail jutted from the ground, brambles spilled from the verges, catching my skirt. At one place an upturned bogie lay rusting amongst grass and fern. 'I think this must be the one the ledgers call Shepherd's Lead,' Richard said.

The cave smelt of dampness and stray cat. 'Phaw!' Milly remarked.

'Strays from the town,' I suggested.

'Breed like rabbits up here,' Richard agreed. Unblinking eyes watched us through tunnels of fern.

'I don't think I'll bother,' Milly said, turning away.

We tried to persuade her, but she smiled a funny sort of smile and insisted we would rather be alone, then left us. So together Richard and I went into the tunnel mouth, though the smell was disgusting. A hollowed man-made arch opened up in the far side. 'Don't stand in the light,' Richard called back to his sister. 'Mary and I are going to have a quick look.' He took my hand. 'We'd better hold on to each other, just in case,' he advised. Then in the protection of shadow and a shared nervousness he laughed. 'It's a good excuse anyway.' As we entered the arch the light dimmed with frightening suddenness, though the air now smelt sweet, as if coming from another source.

'Stand still till your eyes adjust,' I suggested.

For a few moments we stood in the cold dusk, waiting as the walls took shape and metal rails glinted. 'I'm glad we're on our own,' Richard admitted. 'Milly's a good sort but she does go on. I wanted to tell you...' Words eluded him and aimlessly he scuffled his shoe. 'I almost hope this war does fizzle out. Not because I'm scared – I'd quite enjoy a good scrap – but I feel as though I'm only just getting to know you. Not even Milly's dared come in here, and certainly not alone. You're special.' He still held my hand in his. 'You don't pour cold water on my ideas either, not like Father. I can talk to you. You seem years older than Milly. Mama keeps pushing that awful Isabel Hope onto me, yet all the time I'm with her I keep wishing I was with you.'

It was almost a declaration of love.

'I shall miss you terribly,' I admitted. 'I can't imagine whole weeks without you.'

For several minutes we were silent. 'It won't be long,' Richard said at last. 'We'll teach the Kaiser a lesson – bullies never do fight long, not once you stand up to them. Then I'll come back and we'll talk for hours and hours about all the places I've seen. And perhaps one day we'll go and see them together.'

The tunnel seemed brighter and we walked further in taking care not to block each other's light. 'I'd like that,' I agreed. Our path came to a halt with nothing but blackness before us.

'We'll come again with a lantern,' Richard promised. 'It'll be the first thing we'll do when I come home.' In the darkness he put his arm round me and turned me so that I could see the circle of light at the entrance.

'It looks an awful long way doesn't it?' I asked. 'It must have seemed a mile if you were dragging a sledge of coal.'

He had not moved his arm and I began to feel confused by his nearness, and conscious that he was equally confused. Milly's voice echoed suddenly. 'Are you alright?'

'Yes,' Richard called back. 'We'd better go,' he said to me. 'It's foolish to stay here.'

Returning towards the light was far easier than the walk out had been yet both of us lingered, pretending difficulty. 'You know what I want to say?' he asked.

For a few moments more we stood in the darkness.

Apart from one boring weekend at Pemberton Lodge with Aunt and Uncle Pemberton, I had never spent a weekend away from home on my own. At first I found the strangeness and noise overpowering, and Richard being constantly occupied with his other guests, I fled to the safety of my room. Milly was not having

34

such cowardice. 'Come on down this minute,' she ordered. 'Put away that wretched book and play tennis with me.'

'But I'm hopeless,' I objected, laughing.

'So am I. We'll chase the ball about together and be thoroughly undignified. No one else is using the court. Richard has taken the others to see the new dyecaster.' Milly's laugh brightened the room. 'You should see Isabel Hope trying to look absolutely fascinated.'

Laughing also, I allowed myself to be propelled downstairs.

The gardens were quiet for the first time that morning. Though not a large house party, made up of two or three families and half a dozen of Richard's friends (Henry having been wisely sent off to stay with his grandparents), the flowerbeds and walks had continually echoed with laughter and voices. Now the heat of midday had sent the older guests to their rooms to change for luncheon. Tennis at that time of the day was madness, but as Milly said, it was at least private. We chased the ball, kicking our skirts away from our feet and bemoaning hot petticoats and high collars. At length Milly glanced up and down the length of the garden and ducking behind a bush, untied her petticoats. They dropped in a puddle of folds onto the earth. Hurriedly she rolled them up as small as possible and hid them under the bushes. 'Don't tell,' she hissed. 'Why don't you do the same?'

'I don't think I'd dare,' I replied, a little shocked.

'Well, why shouldn't we? I can't see why a girl should have to stay hot and horrid while boys can wear nice light suits. I'll bet the Booth girls don't wear petticoats.' Her voice cut the midday air into small fragments.

The party from the Forge returned soon afterwards, Isabel Hope looking hot and discouraged, the others simply hot. They scattered to their rooms to change for luncheon, calling on Milly and me to hurry. There was a frantic scuffling of dresses in curtained rooms then the gong sounded in the hall.

A sense of unreality had afflicted me ever since I arrived and only when I was able to be with Richard and Milly did it leave me. Despite its utilitarian name Forge House, like Arton Villa, enchanted me. It was not splendid. The Lakins had always put most of the profits from their business back into the firm, but compared to my home it was spacious and refined. Most of the decor was great grandmother Lakin's doing Milly whispered in answer to my awed questions: the mother of the grandma who now lived in Arton. Mr Lakin liked the family rooms to be kept as he remembered them as a child, so Mrs Lakin had to content herself with rearranging the gardens and the servants' quarters, which she did at least annually. The tennis court had gone walkabout twice in the last ten years, and the summer house on the lawn was a refugee from the rose gardens. Whatever Mrs Lakin's faults however, she knew how to make her guests comfortable. Her whole life was devoted to seeing the social niceties were observed both at home and at work: that the meals were on time and cooked to perfection, that the latest plumbing was installed and the meanest sweeper-up in the forge touched his cap.

Like my visit to Arton, my stay at Forge House was a glimpse of another world. It was not simply a question of style. Faith it seemed, like furniture, could vary in weight and shade. The Lakins were pillars of the chapel, but they possessed a degree of ornamentation my mother would have thoroughly condemned. The word 'duty' had not been mentioned during our meal yet scarcely an hour passed at home but it was repeated twice. The young people chattered freely about new motor cars and bathing from a special hut at Brighton ('In funny long bloomers my dear – such a laugh'), and the servants had been ignored during the dessert, as if their overhearing their betters were of no consequence. My own mother was forever whispering 'Remember the servants dear,' as if they were handkerchiefs easily mislaid. In comparison to the Lakins I was from a darker, northern land, full of forebodings and duties... I would never quite settle back at Claremount again.

There was to be another outing that afternoon, on horseback to Twynning, where a fair had arrived – or so Jessica had heard. Hacks had been hired from a stables on the other side of the Heath and would be brought to the back gates of the house. I felt shy and awkward but none of the others could ride much, Richard assured me. Milly looked a perfect guy bumping up and down and he himself kept slipping to one side. The only one who cut much of a figure was Isabel he added, and she'd been taught to do everything *properly*. There was a touch of irritation in his laugh.

We bumped across the Heath, taking the old miners track towards Twynning. The horses scuffed up the sand and there was a great deal of laughter and tally hoing, though considering Mr Jobling's hacks were incapable of chasing anything faster than a tortoise it was all for show. Richard dropped back several times, ostensibly to check I had not quite fallen off, but mainly it seemed to laugh and tease me, or to point out some feature of the Lakins' land. Those rocks over there he called Toad's Mouth he said, and that muddy patch was a pool in winter. Once I saw Isabel Hope glance towards me with an expression of surprise and enmity. It was only a brief lapse, then she smiled her practised smile, but to me it was a revelation.

Once the Heath was crossed the track became a metalled road through a few tired fields, remnants of farmland that had flourished before smoke poisoned the soil. Twynning was almost indistinguishable from Sand-hill, another straggling industrial town dribbling along the valley bottom, though since it was on the other side of the escarpment, everything was in a sense in reverse. Lacking a canal, it had never grown as prosperous as Sandhill and with the closing of the pit had begun to decline. Still, there was a good bit of land near the stream, and fairs and revival campaigns visited bringing with them a sense of the outside world which

Sandhill lacked. Already as the horses plodded down Old Mill Lane a sound of voices and bustle rose from the valley field.

'I can't hear any music,' Milly said in concern. 'Are you sure it's a fair and not one of those travelling preachers? I'm not in the mood for being saved.'

'It was there when Polly came through yesterday,' Jessica insisted. Being Richard and Milly's cousin, she regarded herself as entitled to argue. 'Besides, I can see the stalls,' she added, pointing downwards.

Villas and hedges began to close around us and we trotted down without any clearer view. 'Perhaps there isn't an organ,' Richard suggested. Finally we reached the valley bottom and the fair.

'Look,' Milly whispered to me excitedly. 'Look at the name. It's Isaac's family.'

'I shouldn't have thought there'd be two with the same name,' Richard agreed. 'I say, wouldn't it be a lucky chance if Isaac was with them?' Then he remembered the others were possibly listening and stopped.

Leaving the horses in the care of the grooms we began to walk round the fair, causing a murmur of curiosity.

With our smarter clothes and voices our party was marked as 'gentry', and there was a flurry of effort amongst the booth people. Since the fair was only small we quickly exhausted it. A show tent with gaudy frontispiece had been set up near four or five stalls, and a delightful roundabout proclaiming *Boothman's Chariots and Horses Giving Pleasure To Children Throughout the Land'* went round sedately near a helter-skelter. In the middle was a splendid carousel.

'It's the same fair that comes to Arton,' Richard explained. 'We've seen it lots of times.'

'Well, I haven't,' Jessica replied firmly. 'I want a ride.'

'Me too,' Willy agreed. 'Come on, everybody. This ride's on me.' He bayed with laughter. 'Well, not exactly on me. I mean I'll pay the first lot of fares. What d'ye say Rich? You pay for the second?'

It was agreed and at once everyone crowded towards the carousel. The owner could scarcely believe his luck, and those unfortunates already riding were given a short trip. Amidst much laughter we chose our horses and mounted, patting gilt heads. At last we began to rise decorously up and down. 'Faster,' Jessica called.

Round and round the carousel went until the horses floated outwards and the muddy field and watching crowd rose and fell with them. 'Bit better than old Percy's gee gees, heh?' Jamie shouted.

We were given an extra-long ride, in honour of our wealth. At first I sat stiffly, not sure whether I was enjoying myself, and remembering that travelling fairs were disapproved of by my father. But then I began to relax. The motion was exhilarating yet restful and Richard had managed to find a horse near to mine. We rose and fell alternately beside each other. 'Race you to the other side,' he whispered.

At last the ride ended, the man at the centre trying to coax us to stay a little longer. We promised to return, but wanted to visit the other booths first. Then we wandered around the fair trying a ha'penny here and a floating duck there, and leaving at least three delighted stallholders in our wake. 'I wonder why there's no organ, Isabel asked. 'Really, it's rather common without any music.'

'I thought the carousel was splendid,' Milly disagreed at once. 'Still it is rather strange,' she admitted. 'The Boothmans always have an organ. It attracts people for miles.'

'There it is,' Richard called triumphantly, pointing towards the wagons arranged round the outer edge of the field. 'Or rather *was.*'

Lying in the mud were various pipes and parts belonging to a fine old mechanical organ. Now the angels played windless trumpets and a row of putti stood dejected.

'What a pity,' Jessica remarked. 'I love mechanical music.'

The shooting booth had claimed the attention of Willy and Jamie, and Richard joined them. Reluctantly we girls followed. 'You can't keep Richard away,' Milly complained.

'Aren't you the young gentleman who -' the stallholder began, recognising Richard at once but unable to place him.

'Of course I am,' Richard said gallantly. 'My sister and I have been scores of times when you're in Arton.'

'Pleased to meet you again, sir,' the man replied. His manner was both servile and oddly mocking. Again there was that Welsh lilt I recalled from Isaac. His features were like the ferryman's also, but coarser, his whole body heavier. Looking round me I recognised the man who had been in Isaac's cottage. Isaac was evidently one of Nature's cuckoos, the changeling child who preserves a gentler gene throughout the generations.

With exaggerated grace the man took Milly's hand. 'Master Richard can show his skill to his friends,' he suggested. 'There's not a finer shot that's been to my booth.'

Flattered, Richard paid his money and took the rifle offered him. Attracted by the sight of so many well-dressed young people other spectators came from round the field. Flushing at his unexpected prominence Richard waited for the targets – a row of battered ducks. 'Imagine they're wearing Prussian helmets,' the booth tender advised. 'You'll soon have 'em then.'

And so began a contest between Richard and Willy and Jamie, with each of them banging away in turn as the ducks staggered along the canvas booth, wound by some invisible mechanism. The crowd increased but none of the boys were aware of the people watching. Terrence joined them but as he could manage only five and Willy and Jamie scored six, Richard was left undisputed master.

'Let me!' Milly cried out.

'Girls can't shoot,' Willy Hope said scornfully, but Milly was insistent, and taking up the rifle, banged away. Her first attempt seemed to prove Willy correct, but insisting she was nervous, she cajoled her brother into paying a second time. This time she scored seven, equal to Richard's first total. After that, it became a competition between the whole party with even myself making one attempt. No one could equal Richard's nine, which he scored twice, a different duck eluding him each time.

'You can't have one of the enemy getting away,' the rifleman remarked. 'He could be the one as comes around the back and picks you off later.'

I shuddered at the image presented. For me the sky seemed to have clouded over and the joy to have gone from the afternoon. Once more Richard took the rifle, and this time the crowd was silent. Crack, crack, crack. The sound echoed over the whole field. Duck after duck fell. Soldier after soldier. 'Oh bravo!' Will shouted. Milly glared, seeing his interruption as an attempt to break Richard's rhythm. Crack, crack. Crack, crack, crack. All ten targets had been hit and a cheer went up. 'Well done, young fellow,' somebody shouted. 'You'll make a fine soldier for England.'

'Ay,' another voice agreed. 'That's the sort will show the Kaiser a thing or two.' 'I trust you will indeed be going to serve your country?' a woman in a fashionable hat asked. 'England has need of such fine young men.' 'When the call comes, I shall answer,' Richard replied, embarrassed by all the attention. 'We all shall, ma'am,' Jamie said, not to be outdone. Another round of applause greeted his words, then the crowd began to drift away. Somewhat sheepishly Richard replaced the rifle. 'We'd better be riding back,' he reminded us.

'I vote we go back to the house at once,' Isabel agreed. 'Fairs are so common.'

'You've never been to a fair before in your life,' her brother retorted crossly. 'I like it here, so I vote we stay. Rich owes us all a ride on the carousel.'

The atmosphere was becoming tetchy, and ever the good host, Richard compromised. 'We'll have one last ride,' he said pleasantly.

Pacified, the party moved back to the carousel. I saw Richard hurriedly count the money in his pocket. He must have spent a great deal at the shooting booth paying for the ladies to have a turn, and for himself, and there had been other booths before then. Handing over most of the change he had counted, he kept his part of the bargain. At once we scampered on to the horses. As we did so, a horse and trap came rattling on to the field, with one man riding on the passenger seat.

'It's Isaac,' Milly whispered in delight.

We did not know whether we should greet him, though it was obvious he had seen us. The ferryman solved the problem by coming over to us with cool politeness. 'Afternoon Miss Milly, Master Richard,' he said, bowing slightly. 'I have been sent for, to mend the organ.

'Oh, I do hope you can,' Milly said. 'The fair's not the same without music.'

'I shall have to see,' Isaac replied. 'She's an old lady and like a lot of old folk, a bit cantankerous.'

'Richard's just scored ten out of ten at the shooting booth,' Milly boasted.

Isaac lowered his voice. 'Have you been letting Jacob cheat you out of your money?' he asked sharply. 'How much has he talked you into spending?'

The question was impertinent of course and Richard flushed. 'Only a guinea or so,' he said.

'Then he shall give you some of it back. He can talk a man and his money apart in no time.'

'I spent because I wanted to,' Richard replied with dignity. 'You shall do nothing of the sort.'

'Did you really spend so much?' Milly asked. 'Papa will be furious.'

'What's done's done,' Richard replied. 'You're not to say anything, Isaac. It's your brother's business to make people spend, and a fool and his money are soon parted. Besides, I imagine his family needs the money.'

'That's true,' Isaac agreed. 'But not a lot of it will reach them. Jacob's a bad lot, Master Richard. You don't want to be seen spending time with him.' He shook his head. 'Well, I must see what ails the old girl now. I imagine it will take me till nightfall, so I will wish you a good afternoon.' The last sentence had been said more loudly, for the benefit of the others in the party. I was aware that Isabel and Jessica were watching him. Hesitating, he turned back to us. 'Have you still a mind to go as a soldier?' he asked Richard.

'Of course. Won't you be volunteering now it's really on?'

'I have a wife and family. Who would see to them?'

It was rank heresy. Overhearing the reply, Willy Hope interrupted. 'Oh I say,' he protested.

'Have you ever met a Prussian?' Isaac asked.

'No, not exactly, but...'

'But you believe what the papers say. The more fool you.' Offering Richard his hand, Isaac bade us goodbye.

'Where on earth did you meet such a common, disloyal fellow?' Isabel demanded after he had gone. 'Really Richard, I think you might choose your company more carefully.'

'Positively ignorant,' Willy agreed. 'The Government will have to round his sort up and get rid of them. They're a threat to the nation. Probably been working for the Germans for years.'

'The papers say there are spies over here already,' Jessica volunteered.

'Don't talk nonsense,' Richard replied. 'Isaac's no spy and entitled to his views. I don't agree with him, but I can see what he means. The papers are whipping up hatred, and if you've travelled all over Europe as he has, you probably have met decent people even amongst the Germans.'

'Well, really!' Isabel repeated. 'I can't imagine why you should defend such a common fellow, Richard.'

'If you use that word again I shall scream,' Milly said.

'My dear, whatever can you mean?'

'I imagine she means the word "common".' I suggested. Dislike for my rival made me forget my manners. 'There can be few men less common than that one. Could you mend an organ?'

Richard was having trouble suppressing his own anger. 'Yes, do stop being so infernally snobby, Isabel,' he advised.

'Snobby?' Isabel's immaculate voice rose to a squeak. 'Me snobby? Some of us have been taught our place, even if you haven't. That man is clearly no better than a gypsy – probably is one for all I know. I never have enjoyed the company of ill-bred people. They make me feel positively faint.'

She had said too much and knew it. 'How very unfortunate for you,' Richard replied coldly. 'It must distress your friends.'

The ride began, fortunately. 'The business can go hang,' Richard whispered to me. 'Nothing is going to make me tolerate that girl a moment longer.'

'You have to,' I advised gently. 'You can't send her home. Be as polite as you can till she's gone, then make sure your mother knows how you feel, and why.'

And so ended Isabel's chances. So also ended the hopes of an alliance between *J. D. Hope's* and *Lakin Industries*.

'If you ask me, this war will be a good thing,' Richard declared. 'When it's over everyone will have to work together to make England great again. It's all the snobbery and idleness that's dragging us down. The Hopes used to be an honest, hard-working family, but they've made so much money they've taught their children to look down on hard work and those who do it. Willy's always boasting about getting sent down from Oxford and a man like Isaac'd give his right eye to go.'

44

After the ride was ended we made our way back to the horses. To our surprise Jacob Booth was waiting for us, though it was to Milly he spoke. She would not tell us what he had said and became quite distressed when pressed. 'Leave her alone,' Jamie said at last, for despite his occasional arrogance he was not unkind. Only when we had ridden tiredly and sullenly back to Sandhill and gone to our rooms to change did she come to me to confide.

Opening her hand she showed me a gold sovereign. 'The man at the rifle booth gave it me for Richard,' she said. 'I asked if Isaac had told him to do so, but he said not. He said he had a foreshadowing – that was his word. Of most of the men in our party dying somewhere. He didn't see their bodies or anything like that, just their names on a memorial. It was black marble he said, with lettering hammered into it, but he couldn't say where it was. He wouldn't keep Richard's money in case it brought him bad luck.'

'Stuff and nonsense,' I said. 'I don't believe in such talk, and you don't either. It was simply to cover his returning the money after Isaac had ordered him. Rogues like him play on people's superstitions.' I considered the sovereign. 'Put it quietly in Richard's pocket so he doesn't know,' I suggested. 'Then he will have something to spend later, without losing dignity.'

Smiling at the idea of the trick she would play on her brother, Milly went out. Afterwards I sat for a long time beside the window, thinking of the rifleman's prediction.

I saw Richard just twice after that weekend. He came into the shop, pale with excitement at the seriousness of what he was doing. Tomorrow he would be walking over to Twynning to enlist he said, against his father's wishes and lying about his age. Would I meet him that evening at the gate to the Heath? He would see I got home safely in the dark. All he wanted was a few hours' quiet with me.

If I had had greater discretion and had loved him less I would have refused, but instead I nodded, my throat too tight for speech. Then, as soon as I had eaten tea in the old nursery room with Harry, I put on my sensible boots and slipped out of the house. As my mother had Aunt Gwendoline coming to help her play backgammon and demolish reputations, there was no danger of her missing me. In the late afternoon light I walked up Bircham Coppice.

Richard was waiting for me at the gate, and silently we walked through the woods, into the clearer air of the Heath. What we said and how we spent the three hours that followed is too personal to speak of, but by modern standards it was innocent enough. In those days before books and films taught us to expect more, merely to sit close and hold hands was so daring we blushed. For most of the time we sat beneath one of the old hawthorn trees while bees buzzed on the pea flowers and the gorse pods popped around us. We talked of our love and tried to find words to express it, and planned his return. I would help him and Milly run the family business. Of course I would be marrying him, that was decided without discussion. As proof of his love he gave me a silver ring, bought with a sovereign he found he had not after all spent at the fair. That had been a real relief, he admitted. Finally, as the dusk turned to night and there was a risk we would be missed, we returned down the Coppice. At the bottom we parted, and I stood amongst the trees watching as he walked away along Victoria Road.

For nearly two years the postcards came, written first from training camp in England and then headed 'France', or simply identified by a string of numbers. Some showed views of places I had never heard of, seaside towns with fine promenades along which walked ladies in white hats; others were comic pictures which made me smile over breakfast. The ones I liked best were the special cards, of dreamy young ladies sending fondest greetings, or wishing us together again. Though I smiled at their sentimentality I treasured them, knowing they expressed the love he could not put into his own words. Most treasured of all was a photograph sent me the first Christmas and printed on the back like a postcard. On it Richard stood near a make-believe balcony, his face so proud and his figure so fine in his new uniform, my throat tightened each time I took it from my album.

In return I wrote long letters full of plans for the future and news of how Milly and I were learning bookkeeping and shorthand together, or playing with the new typewriter. With her father's health declining, Milly was quietly taking over, young as she was. I told my parents about Richard's proposal and the Lakins were consulted. To my relief Mrs Lakin's liking for Isabel ended as soon as she heard *Hopes* were doing badly with the loss of European trade. At my father's suggestion (who was by then sailing towards the Dardanelles) our engagement was announced on my sixteenth birthday, two months after Richard left. I sent Richard a copy of the *Sandhill Gazette* to prove it, in case Milly's went astray.

Then, almost two years after Richard walked to Twynning to enlist, the call I had dreaded came. Milly stood in the morning room with her face made plainer by crying and her best kid gloves in a screwed mess in her hands. Unable to tell me herself she passed me the cable and I walked to the window to read it. Afterwards Milly and I sat together till twelve, and time for her to return to a luncheon she could not eat. When she had gone I walked to Bircham Coppice, for I too could only stare at the 'little bit of nice fish' Cook had bought to tempt me. Taking the path up to the gate, I wandered the Heath, until too exhausted to walk any further I lay down under the hawthorn tree and cried.

We could not stay in Sandhill that weekend; there were too many people wishing to extend their condolences. Henry was away at boarding school and Mrs Lakin wished to be alone with her grief so Milly and I took the train to Arton, on our first journey anywhere without teachers or family. Not even our maids came with us. We wanted to be together we said, and to their credit our families understood. For a whole rail journey we hardly spoke and when I caught a glimpse of our faces in the mirror on the compartment wall, it was two grown women I saw.

I don't know what made us decide on that trip to Arton; perhaps it was an idea that the quiet of the river would ease our pain. Certainly that was what happened. The Villa had been shut up for almost a year, and we were kept busy by the need to open rooms and discuss repairs with Mr Carter. All that first afternoon we stayed indoors, but too much in demand to sit grieving. As the next two days passed we grew more confident. First we walked in the shrubbery, then we took the path along the river and stood watching the fishermen. On the second evening we dared to explore the woods that had been a king's forest. The pain did not go away but we learnt how to endure it.

Finally, on the third day we untied the skiff and rowed together, each of us pulling an oar. Richard had done the rowing before but we reached Arton Ferry with no more mishaps than a soaked skirt.

To our surprise we found Isaac sitting in the cottage garden. The pillow behind him and the pallor of his face warned us. Till then we had not even known he had gone to the Front. Regretting coming with bad news at such a time we turned to go away, but as soon as Isaac saw our black dresses he understood. Thirteen years in age, and class and fortune had separated him from Richard, yet an expression of utter weariness came to his face.

'Thank you for coming,' he said. 'It must have been hard for you both. Would you excuse me? I should like to remember Richard on my own.' Rising with difficulty he walked down to the ferry and stood on the bank. In concern we looked at each other, for a moment forgetting our own grief.

I heard the cottage door open. 'What is it?' a woman's voice called.

'We came to tell Isaac Richard is dead,' I said. 'Did we do right? We hadn't heard he had been wounded himself. I'm so sorry.'

The woman nodded. Clearly, she had been told who I was. Remembering Isaac's talk of his wife's parents running a lodging house, I had expected a common sort of woman, but instead a slender girl stood before me with an expression of compassion. Though hardship and the demands of children had begun to fade her face, in her plain work dress she was more lovely than any of the overdressed beauties of Sandhill Rise. Her voice suggested she had mixed in many different companies, and once again there was that soft Welsh lilt. A man might well give up a successful career for her sake. Sitting beside us on the bank she watched as her husband stood staring along the river.

'I didn't expect him to show so much grief,' I admitted.

'There've been too many deaths,' Mrs Booth replied. 'He hasn't heard of his mother's people since the war began. And he's seen some terrible things himself these past few months.'

'But I thought he would never fight,' Milly said.

'His views haven't changed, but when it became clear the Government would soon have to conscript everyone, he volunteered to serve as a stretcher bearer. It was a struggle to persuade the authorities, but his case was accepted. He's what they call a non-combatant.'

'I think a man must be very brave to expose himself to fire and not fire back,' I said. 'Braver than those who fight.'

Mrs Booth nodded. 'He's no hero, Miss Cooper,' she said, 'but he's shrewd and will get a wounded man to safety if a way can be found. It was his cunning that saved him a few weeks ago. He and several others were trapped when the enemy made a sudden advance. When the others tried to run they were shot, but Isaac pretended to be dead and lay there till dark. He was wounded by a shell all the same, and I think a less determined man would have died...' She indicated we should sit on the bench beside her. 'I'm sorry. I shouldn't be talking of my own love when you've lost yours. Your brother was a fine young man Miss Lakin – the sort

49

we can ill afford to lose. The old men sit in safety while the young men die.'

Her words surprised me; though it was disloyal I could not help but share her anger. 'Who manages the ferry?' I asked.

'I do. Isaac taught me before he went away. We must keep the house and job till he returns for good.'

We stared at her slight figure incredulously. I wondered which of the two showed greater courage, the husband or the wife. 'You intend to stay on here?' Milly asked. 'Arton's a narrow place and the people are small minded. They'll never accept you.'

Mrs Booth smiled. 'We must settle somewhere, for the children's sake, and we've managed to stay here longer than anywhere since we married. Besides, though I shouldn't say it when the war has brought you such sorrow, it's helped us. Isaac has gained respect among the men who have gone to the Front. I've had several women call to thank me for what he's done to save their husbands. If he can only survive till it's ended I think we'll be able to settle at last.'

That 'if he can only survive' was so telling Milly and I glanced at each other. We had both heard how few of the stretcher bearers had survived even till now. As if understanding us Mrs Booth looked away. 'I've tried to persuade him to seek a transfer to other duties,' she admitted. 'To one of the bands perhaps or to entertain the troops; something that will use his talents and give him a better chance of coming through, but he says it isn't possible.' She sighed. 'I keep praying some officer will hear him play and see how he's being wasted.'

As she spoke there came the sound of the flute, very softly from near the river. Without our noticing, Isaac had returned to the cottage and was now sitting again at the water's edge. I've no idea what tune he played, except that it was hauntingly beautiful, an elegy for the dead. None of the black-edged mourning cards that were being printed, nor the memorial services being arranged at Sandhill Rise, would mourn Richard so exquisitely.

When he had finished Mrs Booth got up and walked to him. Putting her hand on his shoulder she stood beside him, and he turned his head and kissed her arm. I heard the word *'dordi'** used between them, as if it were an endearment. Even in July 1916 gentleness and love could survive.

Dordi – dear.

'Let's go,' Milly said. I offered my hand to her, as her mourning gown was heavy with crepe and ribbons. 'Leave them together.'

We rowed in silence, letting the current carry us. 'I'm glad we went,' Milly said. 'I feel as though I've done the right thing for once. Mama and Papa would never think of telling Isaac, but he has as much right to know as any of Richard's friends.'

'Not one of them could have mourned more sincerely,' I agreed.

The boat carried us slowly. 'I shall see Isaac gets that transfer,' Milly announced suddenly. 'Father was at school with Colonel Hewison and Uncle Kenneth is a Major. Things can be arranged you know, if the right people want them to be.'

'Try Milly,' I said. 'Do try. But Isaac mustn't know it's being arranged or he'll refuse.'

In agreement Milly nodded.

'Are you still intending to take over the business from your father?' I asked. 'Without Richard?'

'If that gentle little woman can manage a ferry we can manage without Richard. We've trained ourselves for it and we know everything Richard intended. We'll even restore the Heath as he wished. You'll see.'

I shook my head. 'I'll help,' I promised. 'But it wouldn't be right for me to run the firm. Your employees would rightly resent me. I've no claim on your family now that Richard's gone, and I wouldn't want to be employed by you however well you meant it.' Milly began to deny me hotly. 'No,' I insisted. 'We've been such close friends I don't want to risk spoiling things. I'll always be around to discuss your plans with you, and I'll check your figures if you like' (Milly's arithmetic had always been a joke between us) 'but I want my own employment. I can't work with Mother in the shop any longer. I shall impale her on one of the spikes, instead of a bill, if I do. So I shall find myself a position somewhere else. I shall become one of those wicked women, independent of everyone and working for my own living.'

Resting on her oar, Milly smiled. 'I can just picture you striding around in one of those mannish suits,' she said. 'Like Miss Roper the librarian. You will become ever so successful and be manageress of a big emporium one day. Then you and I will meet for luncheon in a smart little restaurant, and the waitress will be terrified of us.'

The image she presented made us laugh. Richard was not forgotten but we were both only seventeen and had life and hope before us. As Milly had said, visiting Arton Ferry had been the right thing to do. It had softened grief and brought us closer to one another. Our friendship had matured from schoolgirl giggliness through the bond of a shared love for Richard and finally that day moved to an adult respect. That respect was to last for another six decades and give us strength through the crises and happinesses of life. Unknown to us, our visit had also confirmed another relationship: between three utterly dissimilar families. Ebbing and flowing like the river itself, that relationship has survived time and fortune, and still holds us in an unpredictable love.

TWO: Tributary

It was Milly's 'problem' which eternalised our friendship. For ten years after Richard's death we were a support to each other, good company, but not the necessities in life we became later. The ordeal of Richard's memorial service over we filled the empty place in our souls with work, Milly helping her father at the forge while I obtained a position as under-manageress in a drapery in Twynning. My mother was horrified having expected me to stay at home and be beautiful – we had parted with our own business when Father was wounded. I had no need to work, she protested, there was money enough. That not being the point I worked on, in a world sudddenly run by women. I have never enjoyed myself so much since.

Every Saturday night Milly and I met to discuss our careers, or simply chatter. We went to concerts and plays in Birmingham and sat through incredibly interesting lectures I can't remember a word of now. On Sundays we walked to chapel, soberly dressed as befitted wartime and our new station as emancipated women. Ironically, we both looked far better in our navy suits than when we were in fashion. After the war was over Milly even had a proposal of marriage, which she rejected saying it was made out of love of her fortune not herself, but I think she was wrong. Though she persisted in seeing herself as plain and awkward, there was much that was attractive about her: eyes full of interest and hair that shone however straight she pulled it. It was her character that men noticed most however; the spirit of her, the refusal to do things because they had always been done. Increasingly she rejected the values of Sandhill Rise, thought nothing of putting on a pair of men's trousers and cleaning a dyecaster, or checking a white-hot ingot. Her father encouraged her and shocked the whole town when he died by leaving the Villa and mill in Arton to Mrs Lakin, but the management and inheritance of *Lakin Industries* to Milly.

Mrs Lakin contested the will and it was all very unpleasant, but Milly won, and I think half the work force cheered that day. If it had to be a woman ruling *Lakins,* then they preferred Milly. Mrs Lakin was heartily hated for her snobbery and extravagance, and for persistently denying the meanest pay rise.

And then suddenly I was standing speechless in Milly's office, listening as she announced her problem.

I could think of no answer except, 'You can't be.'

'I think I am.'

'No. Not you, Milly.'

'For two lovely months I was happy, Mary – really happy. For once in my life I did what I wanted, not what others expected of me.' Her face was almost beautiful. 'Do you remember Isaac's mother? Live for the day, she said. Don't waste your spirit living for the future all the time. I lived for the day Mary, and it was beautiful. You don't have to tell me it was stupid. For four years I've built this place up – and undone the harm Mother did. Got the workers talking to me, smoothed things over with the directors – you've no idea how much ill-will she left – and now what do I do? Throw it all away.'

I could not help feeling pity for her and stood chewing some rough skin on my lip. 'Are you sure?' I asked.

'No. 1 don't know enough about such things to be sure, but I got one of the cleaners at the works talking – casually of course – about a supposed girl in the canteen ... What she said makes me

54

think I am.' She wrapped up a packet. 'Nature's very cruel, you know. The man can go away. Oh he's hurt, thinks he'll never get over it, but he does. The woman's stuck. If she gets caught, that is. When we were at school it was always me that got caught. This isn't so very different. Another of my stupid scrapes. Only the punishment's much worse.'

'I can't believe it,' I protested. 'You're not the sort.'

'Who's to say who's the sort? For anything? I discovered depths I didn't know about. Besides, if I'd been more – well, what you mean – I'd have known how to avoid it wouldn't I? I never dreamt...' She paused, almost laughing at herself. 'If you mean I'm too ordinary, perhaps you're right. Except that he didn't find me so.'

'Who is he?' I asked. 'I've never seen you with anyone. I can't imagine...'

'Then let it stay that way, for his sake as well as mine. Let us keep our secret, Mary.'

'But he's to blame as much as you are. He should have to bear the punishment as well. Not that any man ever really does but he shouldn't get away free. Did he -you know? Was it his doing?'

'Of course it was. But it was mine as well.'

In comparison with her calm acceptance my disbelief began to seem petty. 'But won't you be marrying him?' I asked.

'No. He's already married.'

In horror I stared at her. 'Can't he get a divorce? People do. If they have enough money. He'll have to, to save your reputation.'

'My – friend – is happily married with a family. Even if he wanted to divorce his wife I wouldn't let him, particularly as I would have to pay the expenses. What sort of a start would that be to a marriage? He'd hate me within months. I sent him away as soon as I suspected I was with child.'

'Doesn't he know?' I asked, awed into quietness.

'Of course not. How else could I get him to go away? If he'd known he'd have wanted to stay and do the decent thing – though how he could do right by two women at once heaven knows. Still, he'd have tried.'

'Don't you feel afraid?' I asked.

'Terrified. All the same, I got myself into this mess and I must get myself out.' Her manner towards me softened. 'But I do need your help. Please, Mary. You used to cover for me at school – when I forgot my homework or did something stupid. Like the time I climbed out of the window when we were on holiday in Weston. I know this is much worse, but please...'

'You must marry him, Milly,' I advised. 'Sell the business and go abroad till he's free.'

'It's no use telling me to sell the business. I'm having far too good a time. I have my own money, my own house, and a thousand or so men working for me. I'm not marrying either – anyone. If I married, everything would become my husband's. However loving he was he'd want to take over and run things his way. I'd change overnight from Miss Lakin, the owner of all I survey – from this window at least – to a mere Mrs Thingummy, being ruled by one man. I'd be expected to entertain his callers and wipe babies' noses. I'd be hopeless at both.'

'Be practical,' I persisted. 'If you have a child out of wedlock, you'll end up losing the business just the same. It won't only be the old gossips who'll call you names. Customers will, too. So will the men who work for you. And you'll still have to wipe the baby's nose.'

Clipping a pile of correspondence viciously into a file Milly turned on me. 'All right. You come up with some suggestions,' she demanded.

'When will you be -?'

'I presume I shall be confined in September.'

'Let me think about it,' I pleaded. 'I'll try to help if I can, but right now I feel too – shocked, I suppose, to want to say anything.'

The next two weeks are blurred in my memory. In retrospect they still have a quality of nightmare about them. I was agonisingly confused.

I felt let down by Milly and alternately angry and pitying, wanting to help her, out of friendship, but hating what she had drawn me into. There was no ending the nightmare either. Having been brought up 'properly' we were cut off from the knowledge held by our working-class sisters. Our fingers had been taught to tinkle ballads Schubert would have burnt had he heard the catastrophe we would make of them, our voices had been trained to the right pitch of sweetness, our hair groomed by a brush resembling a hedgehog with rigor mortis, and all so we should catch our man. What we were to do with that man once we caught him, no one explained. All we knew was that we were somehow to acquire daughters who would be brought up properly, too. Now, two dignified, terrified young ladies we regarded Milly's pregnancy with a kind of fascinated horror. There was no one we could turn to for advice, scandal being an even greater fear than birth, and Milly must have taken some horrific risks in her efforts to get rid of the child. Nothing worked. She remained as she said, 'Stuck.'

And so, quietly on the Sunday evening we walked the Heath. Concern for the future of *Lakins* was beginning to worry Milly more than her own situation. If she was ostracised by the town orders would stop coming to the Forge and go to *Hopes* instead, or the half-dozen other competitors which had appeared since the war. Though she might herself withstand gossip, the firm would not. Nor would it be fair on the child.

We decided on adoption. I would find a respectable couple and pay them to take an extra child into their family, the utmost secrecy being observed. Till then Milly must stay away from Sandhill, though without arousing suspicion.

But how were we to explain her absence?

For days we talked round and round the gardens at Forge House or walked the Heath in the bleak March winds. Every idea we had became absurd when we followed it through. If we said Milly was in hospital people would want to send cards, worse still, visit. If we pretended she was on an extended holiday or family visit, customers would think she had lost interest in the business. There was no one we could ask to take over *Lakin Industries* without a great deal of comment. Henry was planning to go up to Oxford, and Mrs Lakin had sold the mill and retired to Brighton, using the Villa in Arton as a summer residence only. Milly would not in any case have sought her mother's help. On that she was adamant. Having spent ten years proving she could run the forge on her own, Milly was not going to admit her foolishness now. The thought of hiding herself away in some nursing home or private hotel was equally repugnant. She would go mad reading journals and walking the lawns for six months or so. We must find some occupation for her or she would come back to *Lakins* and never mind what people thought.

'Of course!' Milly said suddenly, clapping her hands. 'I'll join the fair.'

I laughed.

'No, I'm serious. No one would guess where I was and I certainly wouldn't be bored. We'll go and see Isaac straight away. He can keep secrets, and no one round here would be likely to meet him.'

'Don't be stupid,' I replied. 'You? Taking pennies? Besides, it'd be most unwise. Much too heavy. You'd end up losing the child.'

Milly's expression silenced me.

Since there was no dissuading her, the following week end we travelled to Arton, supposedly to inspect the Villa and prepare for it to be opened up in the spring. After seeing Mr and Mrs Carter we set off together upstream, as we had done when Richard died, and so many Sunday afternoons since.

Milly insisted on rowing and trailing my fingers in the water I watched her. I saw her again as the schoolgirl I had adored, the irrepressible one, the girl who was always tearing about doing things I did not have the courage – or skill – to do. She had grieved with me over Richard and then set about running a huge firm in his stead. I could not help but respect her, and in some ways envy her. Just as when she took her petticoats off while we were playing tennis, she had dared more than I would ever dare.

The punishment was terrifying but as usual she would accept it.

'You look horribly disapproving,' Milly said suddenly. 'I can't say I blame you.' Red facedly I began to deny her. 'Of course you disapprove. You've always been better behaved than me. At least wiser. Still, for what it's worth I did love him. I still do.'

A sense of relief made the day seem warmer. If I could believe she had been carried away by some great passion I could forgive her. 'You've never talked to me about him,' I said. 'I don't want to know who he was, just how you felt.'

'I loved him as much as you loved Richard.' The boat drifted as she rested on the oars. 'At first I was in love with love I think. I wanted to experience it before I was too old. It struck me that at twenty-eight we were both pretty firmly on the shell, and I didn't even have the memory of love to look back on. Not like you. Nor did I have much likelihood of anyone turning up – which you probably did. I mean, you're quite presentable. Fashionable hats and skirts look right on you. I look best when I'm at work in men's sorts of things. What chance had I of finding some respectable husband? Besides, I didn't even want one. And then just as I was feeling low, there he was.' For the first time I saw what might have attracted a man to her. 'He would talk to me about his engines instead of treating me like a silly female, or doffing his cap because I was boss. He knew about books and poetry too – things I longed for. He was so gentle, Mary. Like a younger Isaac in some ways, though a city man through and through. You should have seen him playing with his little boys. That was when I first began to love him.'

'Surely he'd want to know about this other child?' I asked.

'Of course he would. Which is why I haven't told him. He would want to look after it, to be a good father. It would put him in an impossible position. Which family should he care for? His legal one or mine? He's a decent honourable man, and I couldn't do that to him.'

'What about his wife?' I persisted.

'She's a better woman than I am – a clean, God-fearing lady. But they married young because their families and friends thought they would, and they got on too well together to object. Getting on together – that's all most people ask for, isn't it? The sort of love he and I found for each other isn't a good thing, though it's what all the songs are about. It makes you do stupid things, and it's not dependent on looks or he wouldn't have wanted me.'

Watching as she began to row again I thought she was being unjust to herself, as well as to him.

Jilly Booth was welcoming as usual, taking us out into the garden where Isaac was hoeing carrot seed. Out of respect for Milly's privacy I left her with them and walked through the far gate, and along the lane. When I returned half an hour later they were sitting on a bench under the apple tree. 'Mary knows,' Milly said, in answer to Jilly's silent question. 'It's all settled,' she added, turning to me. 'The fair will be passing through Hereford the week after next. You and I will apparently set off for Switzerland –'

I interrupted in amazement but she ignored me. 'You must come with me. You need a holiday, and I shall have to have someone over there to post letters and make things look right. After a week or so you'll telegraph that I've had a bad fall while walking along a mountain path. On the doctor's advice I have gone into a private hospital over there and must not be disturbed – flowers and cables to the matron. With Mama and Henry told I've had an unfortunate love affair and do not wish to see them till I've stopped grieving (the man jilted me – Mama'd like that), there's no one likely to pay the cost of a trip to Switzerland to visit me. You'll stay on for several weeks and answer letters and so on, then return to take over the business till I recover. Meanwhile I shall have joined Isaac's relatives in Hereford and travelled with them till they reach Wales. After that I shall board with Jilly's parents in Harlech.'

'It's absurd,' I pleaded to Isaac, though I could not help but admire Milly's resourcefulness. 'Tell her to be sensible.'

'It's a good plan,' Jilly said, though her voice showed her sorrow at it all. 'Miss Lakin can have her baby at my parents' home. They have a decent quiet boarding house. No one would ask questions about a lady waiting her time there. People would assume her gentleman friend is paying the bills. It would be best not to seem too well-to-do though; a nanny or a clerk would be best.'

'And after the baby is born?' I could not look at Milly's face.

She sat iron straight with her hands gripped in her lap. 'You'll arrange the adoption, won't you Mary? I can trust you.' Turning towards Isaac she weakened slightly. 'It will be the best thing, won't it?'

'It's not my place to say. I don't understand your ways. If my Becky or Sal found themselves with child we'd take them in and let them live with us. A child is precious, not to be given away. But then, money and position alter your view.'

'How could Milly keep her child?' I demanded. 'How could she go on running the forge?'

Isaac sighed. 'It would be difficult,' he agreed. 'If you want me to find someone to take the child, I could do so for you. When a mother dies in the fair there's always someone willing to take the kiddy, and there's my mother's kin, too. Rather than have a little one pushed into a corner where no one loved it Jilly and I would take it ourselves. What's one more?'

'I couldn't let you -' Milly began and stopped in discomfort.

'You want your child to have a decent upbringing,' Isaac replied, a sour note in his voice.

'I didn't mean that.'

'Of course you did,' Jilly insisted quietly. 'It's quite understandable. You don't mind playing at living with the fair for

61

a few weeks or visiting us here when the sun is shining and you're on holiday, but it's not a life you want for your child. Well, neither is it what I've wanted for mine. If I could have given them better than this I would have done. But in the long run he or she may not thank you for giving them away, however expensively you do it. Nor will you thank yourself.'

There was a long silence between us. Mrs Booth was right, of course. However much Milly and I might consider ourselves representatives of the New Woman, we shared the values of Sandhill Rise. A decent upbringing was essential, for our children if not for others. And that included a good education and wearing shoes all day. It meant new outfits for Whit and having an inside bathroom with polished taps and a rail on which to hang the towel. We might dispense with servants, and declare our independence of men, but we had our sticking points. Milly's child could never live in Arton, much less at Arton Ferry or with the fair, yet he or she might one day wish we had accepted Isaac's offer.

'Can't you dissuade Milly from travelling with the fair?' I whispered to Jilly as we went indoors. 'She'll do herself harm.'

'She's strong,' Jilly assured me. 'Let her have a bit of colour in her life. Her days are drab enough, always working. If you ask me, that's why this baby's on the way. Besides, it will do her good. She'll learn what it is to be hungry and wet and cold – and to snatch what you can to eat instead of being waited upon. She'll take better care of the men in her business afterwards. Don't you worry, Isaac's sisters will take care of her. They won't particularly welcome her; she's bound to be in the way. But they'll see she gets to Harlech all right.'

'But why can't she go straight to Wales?' I asked.

'Someone might well trace her there. This way she'll vanish as completely as if she had fallen down a crevasse. No, I rather like Miss Lakin's idea. It's a clever plan and few young ladies would consider risking such a life. It shows courage.'

62

Success came so easily as to seem to me immoral. I went to Switzerland and thoroughly enjoyed myself selfish as it sounds. From there I sent postcards to my own family and posted the letters Milly had written in readiness. She had a vivid imagination and almost convinced me with her stories of beautiful walks and spring flowers opening on the hillsides. Then I telegraphed the news of her fall. Concerned telegrams came in urgent reply. For a month I built a maze of lies at the centre of which I was losing myself for ever. I thanked people for their concern, acknowledged gifts and gave interim orders for running the business. The gifts and flowers went to a nearby hospital, the matron of which was paid to accept in silence. The business orders I got from Milly. She wrote from Wales where she had just arrived, enclosing the required legal permissions. Finally I cabled that Milly was recovering but needed complete rest. She had asked me to take over the forge until she was fit to return.

The prospect of running a business terrified me, but I had managed shops in the past, and Milly had often turned to me for advice in the early years. I knew least about running the quarry, but Milly had left me pages of closely written instructions, and letters to each of the various departmental heads seeking their assistance, letters which I posted in Switzerland just before leaving. As it happened, I found it all easier than I had expected. A well-run business can go on running itself for a while it seems. I quite enjoyed myself.

Milly never did tell me much about her time with the fair. It seemed wisest for her to make as little contact with me as possible from England, and afterwards when I was back in Sandhill we were both terrified of someone recognising her handwriting, though we had made careful arrangements for all mail to go via Styles, where Isaac picked it up and forwarded it to me in envelopes written by himself, or Jilly, or one of his daughters. Visits to Harlech were too risky to arrange.

I felt the separation terribly. If Milly could have talked to me more of her love and why she had put us both in such a difficult position I would have been better able to control the feelings of anger and resentment that came to me. For Milly the time in Harlech must have been dreadful, but when she did write it was only bright bland messages, or of business matters.

The adoption was comparatively easy to arrange, though there was some disagreement between Milly and myself at first. I advised a town in another part of England; Manchester perhaps where I had relatives on my mother's side. Milly however could not bear her child going so far from her, for against her will she was coming to care for it. She wanted to be able to watch over the family where it was placed. That seemed dangerous to me. No mother could keep from visiting her child if it were near, I argued; she would raise suspicion straight away. Milly was determined however. She was too sensible to make visits, she insisted.

In the end I gave way, though I knew I was right. One of the churches in our circuit served an outlying part of Twynning and while my Bible group was being entertained to tea there before taking a service, I heard of a couple who had recently lost a baby, their third stillborn child. The wife was desperate for a baby of her own. It was simple to arrange a discreet visit to them. A young servant girl connected with some friends was with child, I explained. Secrecy was needed as it was the son of the house who was to blame. His parents wished to hush the matter up, but being good church people wanted to provide for the child. They would pay well if an adoption were arranged. Mr and Mrs Wallace were wanting a baby. What could be more convenient, or humane?

After all these years I cannot overcome a sense that I behaved dishonestly however good my motives. If only I had met with some difficulty I might have paused to consider what I was doing, but it's not true that evil does not prosper. Fate smiled on everything I did. The Wallaces were delighted; they had the promise of a baby, three thousand pounds down and an allowance for twenty-one years. The payment was so handsome they were unlikely to talk and proverbially cook their own goose. They could even feel they were helping a needy young girl. Milly was equally pleased. She would be able to watch over the child and intervene discreetly should anything happen to the Wallaces. Her reputation would remain unblemished and she could return to *Lakins* with the business in a healthy state.

As Milly's time drew near there were dark moments, of course. She began to dread the thought of parting with her child. I risked one visit to Harlech and we sat in the conservatory overlooking the sea, talking till her resolve returned. Her position in the town was important not only to herself, but to her family and to Richard's memory I insisted. Think too what Mrs Lakin would say – and do – if the scandal got to her! That was the clinching argument, I think. Milly feared her mother's tongue more than she feared live snakes. Finally, of course, there was *Lakins* to consider...

It was one of the few arguments I won against Milly. A few weeks touring with the fair had taught her how much reputation mattered, she admitted. Once when she went with Isaac's sisters into a grocer's, the chit of an assistant had refused to serve them. Another time a farmer set his dogs on them. You had to experience being at the bottom for however short a time to appreciate how important it was to stay at the top. If keeping her baby meant giving up *Lakins* and all that went with it, she would sooner give up her baby.

After that it was simply a question of waiting.

On 31 August 1928 Milly was prematurely delivered of a five and a half pound girl. Such a morsel you never saw. Where Milly was strong and plain – not pretty any rate – her daughter was diminutive and exquisite. Perhaps Milly had neglected herself during her pregnancy, or travelling with the fair had done her harm. Perhaps the child favoured the father's side. I can't say. All

I know is that little scrap touched my heart. Milly lay staring at her child with a horrified, pitying expression.

Isaac and Jilly were coming down to Harlech to visit Jilly's parents and bring the child back to Twynning. Milly was paying them well for their trouble, but Mr and Mrs Booth would have done it in any case, out of compassion. In the meantime Jilly's sister helped with the confinement. I arrived after the baby was born, having made an excuse of a business visit in the area. Taking up the baby, Gwynneth Jones rocked it gently. 'What a dear little one,' she said. 'Our Jilly will love you. I could put you in my pocket.' Round eyes watched us with intelligence, fingers opened and closed like moths.

'She'll not live long that one,' Mrs Jones said optimistically. 'She'll be sickly, you mark my words.'

Gwynneth laughed. 'Always the comforter aren't you, Mother?' she said. 'Never you mind her,' she advised Milly. 'You've a lovely little girl here. She'll grow up to be a beauty.'

Milly stayed in Harlech another two weeks, till the baby was strong enough to travel. I came across at weekends, still pretending business in the area. The season was coming to a close and the boarding house had spare beds. I insisted on paying my keep, not liking to accept Mr and Mrs Jones' hospitality, and feeling I could no longer let Milly pay.

We called the baby Katherine Mary. Till then Milly had refused to consider names – naming someone made them into a person she said – but a legal registration was necessary. The name Katherine had appealed to me ever since I read *What Katie Did,* and Milly insisted the second name be Mary after me, in thanks for what I had done. Sometimes I tried to help Milly care for her baby but I felt unnecessary, an interruption. For moments on end she would sit silently watching the cot, hardly moving except to tuck back the sheets or stroke the child's face. It upset me to see her so absorbed in what she must lose.

Only once did she talk to me of her grief and then it was totally without self-pity. 'It's a mean trick, isn't it?' she asked me.

'What is?'

'Making this little thing so appealing. It's the same with kittens and puppies, baby anythings. They all have great big eyes and tiny faces. It's a defence mechanism I suppose. So you'll want to look after them.'

The situation was painful to me. I did not know what to say. 'You've been a brick Mary,' Milly added, then reconsidered her words. 'That sounds horribly *Schoolgirl's Own* doesn't it? I can't think what else to say, though. Marvellous – a good friend. You've gone trotting off to Switzerland for me – '

'I enjoyed myself,' I said, feeling embarrassed.

'That's beside the point. As I was saying, you've given up your job, gone trotting off to Switzerland, run the business, written letters, arranged adoptions, come tearing down here, and all without question. Well, not quite without question, but without too many.'

'You'd have done the same for me,' I muttered.

'I wouldn't have needed to. You'd never have got yourself into this mess.'

'If I'd loved someone enough I might.'

''Course you wouldn't. You'd have been the soul of virtue or good sense. But you'd have missed a lot Mary. Grim as it's been, I wouldn't not have done it. Even having her, well it's an experience isn't it? I know what other women are talking about. It's a part of life. I'm rather proud of myself too. She is beautiful, isn't she?'

'Very,' I agreed.

'Well, there's one blessing,' Milly added, getting back into bed. 'No one will dream she's mine. She's very like her father though. I hope he doesn't come back into town. People might get ideas.'

'Was he very good looking?' I asked.

'It depends what he was doing. When he was talking about his machines or books his whole face would light up. He was handsome then.' She looked round for something to eat. 'I'm starving. Feeding babies doesn't half give you an appetite.'

Recognising the old Milly I laughed. 'You don't show much remorse,' I pointed out. 'You ought to, you know. It's polite.'

'Why should I be sorry? Oh I'm not going to make a habit of such things. This was my one indiscretion. Totally out of character.' Her eyes were wicked for an instant. I did not believe her and said so. 'Perhaps you're right, Mary. I enjoyed myself that's certain.' Laughing at my disapproval she passed me her plate. 'Someone may come into your life yet and you may feel the same. I hope you do. You're missing something otherwise. But I wish you happiness whatever happens. You've done me many a good turn this past six months and I shan't forget it. Nor shall I forget her,' she added, turning to the sleeping child.

Most of the time I was at Harlech I spent helping Mrs Jones in the kitchen. There I did feel needed, for there were still paying guests other than ourselves, and the comings and goings to do with a baby disrupted the normal routine. I found the old woman kindly underneath her sourness and talked to her a good deal about her own life, and about her grandchildren. Though I had never heard her speak a good word of anyone, she was clearly fond of the 'Artons' as she called Isaac's family. 'Great growing louts' she called his boys and scowled lovingly. It was such a houseful when they came, even with Becky and Sal left to mind the ferry. Fancy two girls managing a ferry. It was a wonder they didn't drown themselves and everyone on it. Still, she admitted, she supposed someone had to keep it running and it had been nice this year for Isaac as well as Jilly to be able to come to Harlech for a break. If you were daft enough to keep a ferry – or a lodging house – for a living you usually had to put up with never going anywhere together.

How did she feel when her daughter married a music hall star, I asked.

'A gypsy, you mean,' Mrs Jones replied, her dour manner even dourer.

'Precious little pleased, I can tell you. We sent him packing first of all. Ungrateful wretch, coming here every few months and eating our meals and smooth-talking our daughter. We warned her he would drag her down and we were right. But what can a mother do? Jilly left town with him next time the company came through. It broke our hearts, indeed to goodness. We wouldn't have any more to do with either of them. And then there on our doorstep the following year was that persistent gypsy fellow with a baby in his arms. Could you have resisted him? Holding our first grandchild, he was, and with a piece of paper in his pocket to prove he and Jilly were legally wed.' The old woman shook her head in remembered amazement. 'She'd got him to chapel and had the baby properly christened. Whether she'd put him up to coming to us I don't know. I think he'd decided all on his own. Said he didn't like quarrels.'

I could not help smiling at her reluctant affection. 'Mr Booth's a good man,' I replied.

'He'll do. He has some funny ways. Can't settle in a proper house or job, and what annoys me most, he's bringing up his children the same. But he's good to Jilly and that's the main thing. I've seen respectable tradespeople too mean to give their wives an extra shilling, or so drunk they knock them about. Our Gwynneth's husband's nothing to boast about, always bullying and shouting. I wouldn't have chosen either of my girls' men, but of the two, Isaac's least worry.'

A higher compliment she could not pay.

Before the third week was up Jilly took the baby quietly from its cot as Milly was sleeping. At least I hope Milly was asleep and not just pretending. Then wrapping it in one of her own shawls she left for the station, where Isaac was already waiting with their own children. It was neatly and cleanly done and I cried the whole morning.

Milly did not let me see her feelings. Dressing herself quickly she went for her first long walk, along the dunes.

The adoption went smoothly. Jilly looked after the baby for a week or so at Arton Ferry, then as arranged took her to Twynning and Mr and Mrs Wallace. I paid her train fares, and the cost of a decent lodging afterwards. Later I called on the new family and found them delighted with each other.

There Katherine's story should have ended, for Milly and me at least. The adoption was made legal and binding; her natural mother had no claim upon her. The forge was her child now, Milly declared, spending every waking moment on her business. Cheerfully she thanked everyone for their concern during her illness. Yes, it had been touch and go she agreed, but the Lord and good mountain air had pulled her through. She had her story immaculately prepared, even to the silly details that convince hearers of truth, like the bar of chocolate she was holding when she fell and the bells in the valley which used to wake her each morning at the hospital. With the aid of the list I gave her she called on each of the families who had sent her good wishes, and at each the story was retold. I have never come across anyone with such a capacity for lying with conviction. What it did to her soul is another matter. She was no longer the careless irrepressible Milly I had known.

As quickly as possible we put the whole 'unfortunate affair' behind us. I obtained another position as manageress of a chain of draper's shops in the city, and began to travel back and forth each day by train. There was little time for us to spend together, and apart from calling to thank Isaac and Jilly for their help, we did not go near Arton Ferry for months, a reaction which must have hurt the Booths even while they understood it. Milly had reason to beware of the Booth family. As well as finding them a painful reminder of what she had lost, while they were at Harlech it was possible their younger children had seen Milly with the baby, though every effort had been made to ensure they did not. She paid few visits to the villa in case one of the children should see her in town, and ultimately her mother rented it to a French family spending a few years in England. Since they lived mainly in London the house was empty much of the year.

It was as if all the nice things in our friendship had ended; no more visits to Arton no more rowing on the river, little time or will for visits to concerts or plays. With the Depression deepening Milly's energies were increasingly taken up at the forge and quarry. Besides, she had been deeply hurt and began to retreat into herself. She had committed her one indiscretion. There would be no more.

I was busy with my own affairs in any case. Though I had thought love had died with Richard, there it was again, and in the most unlikely place and at an age when everyone had parcelled me up and placed me on the shelf. I need not trouble you with the tattle that resulted – that belongs to my story not Katherine's – but it kept me occupied for a year or more. By the time I was coming through my own problems I had marriage to sort out. That took another year. I should have noticed that all was not well with Katherine but I was quite simply too busy living my own life.

I should have been more observant. We had had cause for unease for several years. Foolish as it sounds, we had never foreseen that Mrs Wallace would one day have her own healthy children. When we heard she had produced a baby boy we were surprised but not disturbed. It would be nice for Katherine to be brought up in a proper family we thought. The Wallaces were sensible, well-meaning people and their adopted child had first claim on their affections. It was Milly who first realised all was not well. Ever since the adoption she had been watching the family from a distance, occasionally attending the chapel in Twynning (she was a lay preacher by then) or listening to the gossip at work. Mr Wallace had obtained a job as a clerk at the quarry in Bircham Coppice, either through chance or Milly's engineering, I'm not sure which. Milly made it her concern to call there regularly 'to meet the staff and show willing' though in the past the forge had occupied most of her attention. The little girl Katherine was clever everyone said, too clever for the Wallaces altogether. She went to a good school, paid for by her natural father rumour had it, and was learning fancy ways. Her adoptive brother resented her and there were a lot of squabbles, Mr Wallace particularly taking the side of blood rather than law. He didn't see why Katherine should have chances his Douglas didn't.

Finally Mrs Wallace came to me. Would I contact the family who had arranged the adoption? They must make an allowance for Dougie as well. It would make things happier all round. Otherwise she would have to take Katherine from her fancy school and return their money.

Mrs Wallace's arguments had some force. Clearly it was unwise to have one child enjoying privileges another did not. Going up to Forge House I put the problem to Milly.

'It's blackmail, isn't it?' she asked, then reached for her pen. 'Moral blackmail. I can't afford to have Katherine victimised.'

'She's not your child now,' I pointed out. 'By rights you should turn your back and make no further enquiries.'

'Could you do that?'

'No. Not with her so near. You'll remember I advised another town.'

'Don't say "I told you so" Mary – it's most annoying, especially when you were right. I shall have to do something, and I've seen this coming for a while. The wretched woman shall have her allowance for Douglas and Katherine shall have no more – and no less – than him. But make it clear there's not unlimited money to be had.'

'I shall stipulate that I'm allowed to visit occasionally.' I said. 'To see the child's all right, and to report to her father's family. It might make them more cautious.'

'Excellent,' Milly said. Then looking up from her desk she smiled suddenly. 'We've not seen much of each other lately, have we? There's a concert next week I'd like to go to. I think your John and my *Lakins* can spare us for an evening.'

And so one good thing came out of Mrs Wallace's visit. Some of the old intimacy between Milly and I was restored, and both of us were happier for it. We remembered how to laugh together, and strode about the Heath or swung about on the top of trams. A woman's friendship is an easier sort of pleasure than a man's, and it sustained us both through the worries of work and oncoming war. There were even walks along the river at Arton again, and times when we were silent and at peace watching the water flow. Katherine's birth had strained our friendship almost to breaking point; concern for her well-being brought us back together.

Every two months or so I visited the Wallaces, making a pretext I was a friend of Mrs Wallace. By then the girl was seven years old, a bright vibrant little thing promising beauty but unpredictable as an English summer. The Wallaces were good to her, but she was out of place in their home. Her cleverness made them feel uncomfortable and irritated their son, who though only five was powerfully built and able to hit hard. Even in appearance she was set apart from him, colourful and striking while he was pallid, as if he had been bleached by his mother's constant washing. With the aid of Milly's allowance Douglas was sent to Mrs Scott's crammer also but two short planks had more intelligence. Still, a fancy uniform and a posh accent will buy a good deal.

Then a second child arrived. The situation worsened dramatically. Katherine was squeezed to one side of the family. Mrs Wallace had the daughter she longed for, her kith and kin who thought and acted as she did. The toddler was everything Katherine was not, robust, easy going, chubbily pretty. Besides, war was threatening and few adults had time for a difficult, introspective child. Katherine was left, to read and draw by herself if she wished, or snivel in a corner. There was no cruelty, just a slow turning away.

Milly made an additional allowance for the new child but beyond that she could not go – would not. All three children were sent to schools far above the family's status in the town; only Katherine profited and then fitfully, never really settling to work. Since she was chided at home for 'always having her nose in a book' and mocked by her adoptive brother that was hardly surprising.

As he grew older Douglas made her life a misery. A lusty lout of a boy who was his father's joy, he had the sort of bullying streak that makes some little boys pull the legs off spiders. His resentment at his elder sister's different nature turned to malice and he never missed a chance to interfere with Katherine's books or tell on her. To be fair, I think Katherine could give as good as she got, but verbally. I heard her wither him several times with a well-timed insult. It was not a happy situation for anyone involved.

Having arranged the adoption I felt miserably responsible. Though I had no way of foreseeing the birth of the other children I felt I should have recognised how different Mr and Mrs Wallace would be from the baby they were taking into their home. In self-defence I argued I had not known what sort of child I was being given. Had Katherine been more like her mother, outgoing and cheerful, she would have coped better. Not knowing her father how could I guess the whole personality? And perhaps it was the circumstances of her birth and adoption which made her so moody and inclined to be obstinate? Who can say what makes one child thrive and another wretched?

Finally I became so anxious I offered to take the girl on a brief holiday in Arton. Perhaps I should explain how this came about.

Just before war broke out Henry inherited Arton Villa from his mother, but as he was serving in the RAF the gift was more of a worry than a blessing. He decided to sell off the paddock in small plots, and sought Milly's help. Without Mrs Lakin's favouritism poisoning their relationship, brother and sister discovered a belated friendship. We profited from this for Milly persuaded Henry to give us one of the plots, though both insisted their generosity remain unknown. On it we built a chalet – a hideaway from the war we were sure would come. Katherine could be our first visitor. She would have peace there from her brother's bullying, while Mrs Wallace would find life easier with only two children to attend to, and perhaps be a little sweeter when her adopted daughter returned. My proposal was accepted, enthusiastically.

Milly was hungry to see her daughter, but too sensible to ask for close contact. She would come down to the Villa and stay a few days while we were at Arton. The terrace overlooked the riverbank; perhaps she would see her daughter from a distance.

I was very careful, so careful I had not even told my husband of the girl's origins. For a time I think he suspected she might be my own child, but in loyalty to Milly I said nothing, and the suspicion passed. By the time Katherine came to stay with us I think he had worked things out, but he was too kind a man to ask questions.

Katherine was eleven when she paid that first visit: tall, rather ungainly and so shy she reminded me of a young deer forever starting at the least noise or anxiety. Those first few days were difficult. War had been declared and though Sandhill and Twynning were as yet little affected, the atmosphere there was tense, and all the forges were working flat out making munitions. The girl was suspicious of adults, having found them unsympathetic and impatient; other children were assumed to be hostile. But gradually with people who shared her tastes she lost her aggressiveness. There was no need to assert herself when her ideas were listened to, and the birds sang all round us.

From disgust at everything creepy and crawly she moved quickly to a fascinated interest. The country was full of surprising things. She loved it, she decided, and from that moment she blossomed. As soon as it was light she would be up, running along the riverbanks or sitting on the stile overlooking the fields. Arton

Woods were a paradise to her. Sandhill had its bluebell woods but these were so much wilder, so much deeper. Having been brought up in the town she had very little country sense and would have got lost but for our watching, but she would not have cared, she said. She wanted to stay in the woods for ever and ever.

As the second week drew to a close I took her to the villa, to see the gardens. With perfect composure Milly got up from her deckchair and greeted us.

'Pleased to meet you ma'am,' Katherine said, having been taught manners.

'You're staying with Mr and Mrs Chapman I gather?'

'Yes Ma'am. Mrs Chapman invited me for a holiday.'

'Are you enjoying yourself?'

'Oh yes, it's beautiful here. Much nicer than Twynning.'

And that was that. A brief tour of the gardens followed by an inspection of the terrace and we were gone. Glancing back, I saw Milly watch till we were at the end of the drive. I'm still not sure whether she was crying.

As soon as I could I took Katherine to Arton Ferry. I felt Isaac and Jilly should see the child they had cared for eleven years ago. Lest surprise should make them say something indiscreet I called young Saul Booth to me as he was passing in town. 'Tell your father and mother I shall be calling this afternoon,' I asked. 'I've got a young girl from Twynning with me and I thought she'd like a trip on the river. Her name's Katherine.' Hoping he would remember the name and mention it I turned away.

Isaac and Jilly were impressive in their tact. It was a long time since I had been to the cottage and I was disturbed to see how much both had aged, though with a child to entertain they were soon as young as ever. Isaac took us back and forth on the ferry and let Katherine help him wind the cable. He even showed her how to bake and skin a hedgehog to her squeals of disgust and delight. (It gave her a weapon against Dougie for weeks, on the lines of 'Bet you couldn't skin a hedgehog'.) It was a magical afternoon which has stayed in my memory. Finally, as John and Katherine were going down the path to the skiff I called that I had forgotten my bag and must go back inside for it.

Standing briefly in the cottage amongst the smell of flowers I held out my hand to Jilly. 'She's growing up a beauty like Gwynneth predicted,' I said.

'Yes indeed,' Jilly agreed. 'You've not done badly by her.'

'But she's not happy where she is,' I admitted.

'No – she'd rather be free,' Isaac said. 'You can see it in her face. Still, she's being schooled well and she speaks proper. Miss Lakin's daughter couldn't have had less.'

'Has Miss Lakin seen her?' Jilly asked, dropping her voice as one of her sons passed the window.

'Yes. Briefly. I think it hurt as much as pleased.'

Katherine stayed with us two weeks. Almost the whole of the last Friday she spent at the fair, watching the booths and rides being set up and talking to the show people. It was the last visit *Boothman's Entertainments* paid to Arton before war broke out, and I think many of us realised years would pass before we would ride again on its gilded horses. A nostalgic sweetness seemed to flavour the candy floss and toffee apples; I have never known the organ play so plaintively. Katherine was entranced. Apart from buying a few gifts, she had spent very little of her pocket money till then. Within hours on the Saturday afternoon she had not a penny left. She loved the carousel, chose a different horse each ride, had names for every steed she touched. Isaac's brother, Ben, was managing the till and took quite a shine to her. I doubt if she paid for many of the rides she took. Looking across the field I saw Milly standing as if idly, watching her child.

Later that night John and I could hardly refuse the girl's silent appeal as the music floated across river, and took her again, to 'see the lights'. It ended with John and I seated on the carousel beside her and loving every minute. Her happiness was wonderful to see.

And then when we came to leave on the Sunday, she must go back to the field, now quiet with sleep, and say goodbye to 'her horses'.

She was not my child, I kept reminding myself. Nor was she Milly's in anything but blood, but when I took her back to Twynning I felt as guilty as if I were returning a paroled prisoner to jail.

For a few months in 1940 I was able to do more than watch over the girl. After the false war ended I came down to Arton for a few months to live, taking refuge in the chalet. Sandhill would be terribly hit once the bombing began, with so many forges working on munitions and a river to guide the planes. For those of us who had already lived through one war and grieved at the losses it brought, the waiting was awful. For the first few months I stayed, doing my bit fire watching and working long hours at the shops, but remembered grief and years of overwork made me ill. John suggested I go down to the chalet, while he travelled back and forth to Sandhill each Monday and Friday. We were reluctant to be parted, but my doctor insisted on rest, so I obeyed. I could not be idle, however. The children were being evacuated from Sandhill and Twynning and I offered to take the Wallaces' three.

Mrs Wallace was overjoyed. By then she was irritable and sickly, one of those women who wear headaches like others wear hats. I can't say I enjoyed those two months, having taken a thorough disliking to young Dougie. Maureen was easier to handle, and generally content if given enough slices of bread and dripping, but I was unused to children and they were unused to the country. With relief I agreed to them returning to Twynning when Mr Wallace announced he wanted his children back, Jerry or no Jerry.

Katherine stayed on however, at her own request. She was happy with us she said. She went to school in the village and played with children her adoptive parents – and her natural mother come to that – would have been horrified to know. And in the evenings I rowed her on the river or paddled about with her, looking for ducks. John grew almost as fond of her as I. So too did Isaac and Jilly. Whenever Isaac rowed downstream to shop in the town or one of his sons was coming to work, they would pause at the jetty at the foot of our garden and call out, 'Is the little 'un coming for a row then?' and she would look at me for permission and go running down the path to join them.

In return she adored Isaac. Jilly was her favourite old lady she said, next to me (I was all of forty then) but Isaac was special. For hours on end she would sit on the riverbank at Arton Ferry and listen while he played the flute, or wait till he had returned from the other bank with his ferry. Like Milly she had a keen ear for music and I think she would have made a passable pianist if she had received any encouragement at home. Certainly she was quick to pick up the few tunes I could teach her on the secondhand piano we bought.

Her talent lay more in developing other people's gifts however. Isaac composed little pieces specially for her – it was a kind of game between them. She would suggest a word or idea and ask him to 'dream up' some music for her. It grieves me that those pieces were never written down. One in particular haunts me still. Isaac called it *Aquarelle*. Even the word was beautiful. Yet when we asked him what it meant he admitted he didn't know. He heard it when he was travelling and loved the sound the letters made. Katherine hunted for it in dictionaries in the library at Styles – she had the sort of intellect that will not allow ignorance. Aquarelle meant delicate watercolour painting, she found. Ever after she called Isaac's pieces Aquarelles. I saw what she meant. While his grandson's music was bolder, painting in oils, Isaac's had the delicacy of water.

Our chalet overlooked the riverbank and the constant lapping of water began to blend with all our dreams. For Katherine it took on a special meaning. It was as if her imagination had been starved in the town. Now it peopled the riverbank with the strangest of creatures. Her smart private school had been strong on the classics, thought to be an antidote to revolution, bad breath and other working-class habits. She knew the names of all the gods and heroes, was on speaking terms with the lesser deities. Talking to Isaac gave her a fourth layer in the hierarchy, spirits and warriors he created for her in his stories. Some of these were from old Welsh legends, tales of the giant Idris, of Arthur, and the Witch of Llyfi, the Tylwyth (fairies) and Non the mother of David ... Some were English legends, heard from farming people round about, many of whom still put out saucers for the fairies even in those days. A few were from his mother's people, the doings of distant relatives long dead, the cunning of one, the strength of another...

In the way of the lonely, Katherine created from such tales and her own dreams imaginary people to accompany her, or long involved games which could be picked up at the end of school as if held in suspension from the night before. Sometimes she was a spy, at others a famous war ace, single-handedly fighting Battles of Britain. It was war time and many children played such games. Fewer pretended to be Prince Madoc voyaging the sea, or Elen of the Hosts challenging mighty Rome. We used to smile at her fantasies and ask her to explain them, but they were private, and not to be discussed with prying adults. So we learned to leave her alone. One game did puzzle us however. A peculiar blend of school learning and Isaac's tales, Katherine called it her river game. In this, the willows and inlets were inhabited by fantastic creatures, all temporarily frozen into trees and birds liberated only in her presence. The woods were peopled with run-of-the-mill dryads, nymphs of woods and trees, but along the river were the more important fairies of waterfalls and streams. They had names adapted from a book she had brought with her from school – the adaptations were more by accident than art, a glorious misspelling and mis-pronouncing of ancient Greek. Prymno (whom she called Primmo) was trapped in the outflow from Arton Brook, Galaxaure (Glaxure) lay in the river, her hair floating to form the trailing reeds. Rhodia's army of elephants waited in the dark bank of burdock, only their ears showing. She herself was Halimeda, a sea nymph trapped in the river and always looking out to sea, and who must hide from mortal beings. I lost count how many times we called for her, only to see a tantalising flick of summer dress.

Katherine's wanderings worried us, for we were responsible for her safety. When she took to sitting astride an overhanging tree ('It's my horse, Auntie Mary – I'm riding to the King of the River') our concern turned to alarm. John took her in hand. If she was going to play along the river she must prove to him she could swim.

And so that weekend he took the child to the inlet above Arton Villa and swam with her, till we felt she stood a chance of saving herself if one of her imaginary horses tossed her into the river. Strangely enough she never did fall in the water. For all her wild imaginings she had a strong sense of self-preservation.

Milly shared our anxiety, but there was little she could do, except call out as a friendly neighbour, advising care. How she managed to stay so near without making herself known to her daughter I cannot imagine. Fortunately Milly was not often at the Villa during those months. Like the other forges in Sandhill *Lakin's* was caught in a frenzy of activity and with the bombing beginning she was afraid to leave the site. I think the war was a relief to her, a way of deadening her soul.

Our chalet was too cold for winter living, and reluctantly I began to make arrangements to return to Sandhill. It was not fair to make John travel so much, and I could not stretch my sick leave further. I advised the Wallaces I could find another family to take Katherine, but to do them justice they said her place was with them.

After that her visits to Arton were shorter, a matter of weekends and summer holidays, sometimes with Dougie and Maureen, more often alone. Twynning was less savagely hit than Sandhill, being shielded by the Heath and having fewer important works along its valley, and since the Wallaces lived on an estate well away from the industrial areas, the girl was as safe as anyone could be in those times. Still, she loved to escape the noise and the black-out and join us, as did half of Sandhill Wesleyan chapel.

As she grew older the passionate imaginings faded. They never again had the vividness of those months of evacuation. But she loved Isaac's company still and used to row upriver alone sometimes. It was risky of course even on a calm day, and perhaps we were being foolish letting her do so, but though she lacked her mother's physical strength she had the same fierce determination. It caused talk in the town. No girl should be allowed to do such things alone, and the Booths were not fit people for her to associate with. If the town had minded its business I might have agreed, but having heard the tongues wagging I was at once on Katherine's side.

We took other risks too. Sometimes we would go for tea at the Villa and sit at a white table on the lawn while Mrs Carter waited on us, bringing bread and home-made jam. When Katherine was at ease she would chatter away and her mother would listen, her face turned away so that we could not see her expression. Katherine loved those afternoons. They made her feel like a fine lady, she said. The remark touched me. Born in wedlock she would indeed have been a fine lady, and the Villa might have been hers one day.

I advised against such visits at first, but Milly's will was strong and her self-control awesome. Never once did she give any indication of her relationship to the girl. In the end she became so secure she visited Katherine in Twynning. An introduction having been effected in Arton, she could claim she had called while on her way to preach at the chapel. By then Milly was respected and feared in the area; she was Miss Lakin, the only woman in a man's world of business and money. Mrs Wallace talked of the honour for months afterwards. She was convinced it was her Dougie who had won the single woman's heart, and had high hopes for him ever since.

And what else should I tell you?

The years blur in my mind. When I see Katherine it is one minute as a girl riding her imaginary horses along the riverbank, and the next with her own children, still visiting us, and still finding in Arton the peace she rarely found elsewhere. We watched her grow to be a woman, beautiful and erratic, like a butterfly flitting from experience to experience, while Milly and I wondered at her loveliness and feared for her future.

She should have been gracing a ballroom or studying in some fine library we agreed, not hidden in a semidetached off Twynning Road. Whenever I visited her, I thought of Wordsworth's Lucy, flowering alone and unseen. But Milly and I were prejudiced. Thousands of girls have bloomed briefly in semi-detacheds and have faded unknown and unseen. At least we were able to pay for Katherine to have books and paints and to taste the few goodies an expensive cheat of a school could offer.

And though her life sounds wasted to you perhaps, in ways the world does not usually measure it was a rare achievement. She was that little bit special, always. It's hard to define. Her gifts were never fully developed, her intellect remained unchannelled. Yet after she left them people talked as if they had been privileged to receive her visit. Her presence always seemed to lighten a room, to bring laughter into shops. By then she had learned to govern her own tendency to dark moods. I doubt if those who met her in adulthood suspected how much of herself, she kept secret, for she had a way of diverting attention from her own feelings and back to the questioner. Her greatest gift remained as it had been in childhood, an ability to bring out the best in others.

Nowhere was that clearer than in her dealings with the Booths. One incident has stayed vividly in my mind. I think it was the time

Milly stopped regretting her daughter's birth, and felt pride in what she had become.

Some money was stolen from one of the shops in town. There was a lot of talk. Arton had very little crime, like most country places those days. Constable Lammie was certain it was a local affair, since the thief knew Mr Houghton kept his takings locked in a drawer under the counter. People took it into their heads that the Booths were involved. All gypsies are thieves the reasoning went – the Booths were not much more than gypsies and Isaac and his sons often came into the shop for fishing tackle. It had to be them.

There was no proof and people were reluctant to suspect Isaac himself. By then he had gained considerable respect, as had Jilly. His daughters were married and settled locally, so was Benjamin; they were respectable country people now. His two eldest sons had joined the family fair and were away. Had the fair been anywhere in the area there would have been no hesitation in blaming them. Zac and Cal were wild lads, made rougher by a life of travelling, and the pubs often had trouble when the fair came through, though not I must add from Cal and Zac themselves.

That left Saul.

Saul Booth was never trusted in the town. Isaac and Jilly's youngest, he was the best-looking and strongest of their sons, and impossible not to notice, for good or ill. He seemed to take pleasure in shocking the staider folk of Arton, cultivating a hard-living, hard-working image that made him popular amongst the farmhands and woodcutters he worked alongside, and dangerously attractive to local girls. I think quite a bit of the gossip had jealousy at bottom. Katherine saw good in him however, and they were friendly – insofar as the gap in upbringing and class would permit. With her he was always respectful.

Constable Lammie decided Saul had taken the money. He was arrested, but there was no evidence and he was acquitted, in law that is. In the minds of Arton folk it was a different matter. People used to cross the road to avoid him, and most of the local farmers refused him work. The war had just ended and Saul had returned from the army with no trade. The situation became increasingly serious for him, forcing him back into the family fair with which he had often toured as a lad. His departure was viewed as a sign of guilt.

One night a dead crow was nailed to the door of his parents' cottage, with a note saying 'We don't want your sort here. Clear off.' Poor Jilly was bitterly hurt and angry but she shared her husband's pride and would not be driven out. Katherine was with us that weekend. She was eighteen, the age when injustice matters. She deliberately visited the Booths, and sat talking to them where drinkers at the Fisherman's Rest on the bank opposite could see her. Afterwards she went on to Arton Villa, and called on Miss Lakin. Could her brother find Saul some odd jobs around the estate? There must be lots of work needing doing with Mr and Mrs Carter getting older, and it would save the young man from perhaps really turning to crime, and enable him to come back from the fair. Milly spoke to me in amusement later, seeing the irony of the situation. Her daughter had been so appealing and so charming she could not have refused she said, even if she had been no more than a neighbour.

And so Saul found temporary employment and with the support of Milly and Katherine, and ourselves of course, the Booths stuck it out, but the resentment remained, the sort of poison in-breeding and prejudice create in a close community. It began to affect Isaac, with fewer bookings at fetes and weddings coming his way, and fewer people calling at the ferry for a chat. Those who had to use it to cross the river continued to do so, but less politely, and with the increasing number of cars coming on the roads, the eight-mile round trip to Arton bridge became less of a labour for some.

Then a dead rat was hung on Isaac's door. Again there was a note. Isaac had destroyed both before Jilly saw them, but she learnt what had happened from a passerby and came to us for help. There was little we could do except comfort.

A few weeks later Katherine was with us again. Once more she rowed to Arton Ferry. This time she found Isaac sitting by the river, almost crying, strong man that he was. His dog had been strung up in the orchard. It was the only time I knew Isaac's spirit give way. The whole business was horrible, the work of a sick mind. Everyone knew Isaac's dog, a thin sandy haired sort of wolf hound, the best ratter for miles. While Isaac was never sentimental over it, he respected that dog's character. 'Prowler thinks,' he used to say. 'Some dogs work by instinct, but old Prowler thinks.' And then to find the poor thing garrotted and hanging from an apple tree... It beat Isaac how anyone could do such a thing, however much they might hate him. Nor could he understand how anyone could have got near enough to do it, never mind silently. I'm afraid that pointed to a neighbour or regular visitor, someone the dog knew, which made it all the more horrible.

Wrapping the dead animal in her jacket Katherine rowed back down to Arton. Going into the police station she laid it on the counter. Nor would she leave until Constable Lammie had promised to investigate who was persecuting the Booths.

No culprit was ever found, though many of us had our suspicions, and the worst of the affair passed. There was sympathy in the town for Jilly, who fell ill out of worry and humiliation, and Isaac was regarded as an honest man illtreated, but Saul remained a sort of outcast. He did little to help himself, refusing to deny the rumours, out of pride I think. There was never regular work for him and he used to travel with the fair in hard times, even after his marriage.

I'm sorry. My story is beginning to ramble. It's hard to sort out events when my mind is so tired. Still, what happened to the Booths is part of Katherine's story, for she remained close to Isaac and Jilly until their deaths, while in turn Saul and Isaac helped the Lakins many times, cleaning up after floods nearly ruined the villa and working on the estate. Whenever the fair was in town Katherine loved to ride the carousel and wander round the booths – even after her marriage she would do so, taking her own children 'to see the horses go round'.

Of all her links with the family one slight action has had longest effect. It was she who spotted the talent in Saul Booth's third son, before Isaac himself. Saul and his wife had moved into the old caretakers' cottage next to the Villa – that's another story I will tell you some time – and whenever Katherine visited us she brought sweets for their children, who would have had precious few otherwise. One afternoon after hearing little Paul playing a school recorder she sat chatting to him about his grandfather, and well, one thing led to another as it usually did when Katherine was around, and the boy was invited into the chalet to try the piano. No one in the Booth family had a piano. If Saul could have afforded one he would have regarded it as a 'nancy' instrument, while Isaac thought pianos were only for the gentry, though he played the organ at chapel.

The boy was no prodigy, if by that you mean an ability to play Rachmaninov's concertos at the age of seven, but he was clearly gifted. Any instrument would make simple tunes for him within hours, be it mouth organ or old violin. I think our piano appealed to him precisely because it was associated with 'the gentry' in his mind. Even so young he was looking beyond Arton, and out of his family. Amongst them he was so out of place as to be like a cuckoo, except that cuckoos place lusty offspring in stranger's nests, and until he was thirteen or fourteen Paul was anything but. Yet there was an inner strength in him which we all learnt to respect. He used to remind me of the reeds along the riverbank, apparently weak, but fixed so firmly at the root not even a flood could dislodge them.

Every time she came Katherine taught him the tunes she knew and gave him Teach Yourself books, or slipped him a ten-shilling note towards the cost of music. Every bit as proud as his father he would refuse anything savouring of charity, but 'Auntie Kath' was different.

As indeed she was. She saw in a pale-faced boy the talent of his grandfather, born anew, and when others mocked his ambition, she encouraged him. I wish I could draw for you what he was then – so shy he used to hide in the woods when there were garden parties next door, unable to keep up with his stronger brothers, and one winter so near to death Dr Miller joked afterwards he had the certificate already written out. What the river had been to Katherine, the woods were to Paul. He knew every path through them, would vanish for hours, occasionally whole nights when there was trouble at home. I think Katherine saw herself again in him, and that was why she loved him.

Now I must rest a while. When my brain is clearer I will tell you the end of my story. If I went on now I would only become confused and a little emotional perhaps. I have always had a tendency to get emotional when I'm tired, and I should hate you to think me old and foolish.

Before I sleep there is one thing more I must say. I wouldn't want you to think I still blame Milly. Hers was the hardest part, to love and to stay at a distance, to watch over and support without return. It was I who had the joy of her daughter. I have been blessed indeed.

THREE: Homeground

Like most children I found my relatives' tales boring or bewildering, told as they usually were above the clatter of cups, and with knowing pauses and nods. Some of the events in Great Aunt Mary's story I had heard, but never thought of as having meaning for me. Some I had actually experienced but saw from a different height if you like, the people seeming terribly big and important when I was a child. Saul Booth used to terrify me with his strength and loudness, and the Lakins were the grandest folk in Arton and Sandhill. I never considered they could have feelings, much less personal tragedies. I think I imagined Miss Lakin went to bed with her clipboard in her hand, and that Isaac Booth was always eighty.

How my great aunt came to tell her story and why it was never finished – I will tell you in due course. I only heard it in full after I had begun to sort out my own place in its events, and to accept my part in the sequel. That sorting out took place over a period of months, and was not without pain. The pain was merited no doubt, for I had my own foolishness to hide. Like Milly I had learnt to keep silent, so silent I had almost forgotten how to speak of myself that is; I could babble on for hours about the Frankfurt theorists and the concept of negation, and was positively eloquent on Marcuse. Looking back, I see myself as one of those terribly clever people riding for a fall. I am being harsh on myself no doubt; even without Aunt Mary's nudging I would probably have come to terms with myself and my past actions, honesty being one of my few virtues so I'm told, but the process would have taken longer. As it was, within a matter of months my values, and my life, had been turned inside out.

Let us start with the day that process began: the day of Great Aunt Mary's eighty-eighth birthday, and my return home.

Home? Well I suppose the word will do. While I was away I thought of Sandhill as home and grew quite sentimental over it, painting in cosy firesides and hopscotch under the streetlamps. Yet the day I returned it was a foreign land to me. My eyes had grown accustomed to brighter light. The blackness of the canal and factories appalled me, and the patch of grass beside the War Memorial was lurid green. I had not predicted the modern estate built where Lakin's Forge used to be, nor the subway that dived into lavatory smells and emerged where the Palace Cinema once stood. Evidently Sandhill had been overtaken by Troglodytes I remarked, and promptly went up the wrong exit, into a car park. Fortunately I sorted myself out, though my efforts to enter the Gents brought a stare from a woman in sari and fur boots. Even the things I remembered were smaller, or tattier. Miss Haley's drapers still sold pink knickers by the yard, but her brassieres were unlikely to arouse fantasies in any modern man – except a pumpkin salesman perhaps.

As I climbed the hill towards Sandhill Rise, I felt an absurd seeping away of confidence, the sense that I was a little girl about to be corrected by my relatives. Every return home has that effect I suppose. One's own old people are never old; they remain suspended in the images of childhood, like those poor creatures set in plastic to make paperweights. This time however my nervousness was worse than usual. I felt as if I were coming home to face some ordeal. Eating Aunt Lizzie's scones, while risky, was hardly sufficient to explain the feeling.

Aunt Lizzie herself was watching from behind the geraniums, letting the curtain fall as I pushed the gate. Our house seemed bigger. I had forgotten how grand it was: No 28 Nightingale Road, the house with the gothic windows and imperious door ... 'Did you have a good flight Martha?' 'Have you had anything to eat?' The greetings were banal but sincere, a cover for emotion.

'Come and say hello to Aunt Mary,' Dad said. An insignificant little man who only moved from behind his newspaper in times of national emergency, or dinner, he had a gift for leaving unsaid the things you did not want saying. His silence was more welcoming than all Aunt Lizzie's chatter. Quietly he led me through to the back room with its mantelpiece blooming with cards. Great Aunt Mary was sitting beside the window. It was good to see me, she said. I was doing well she heard, getting my picture in the paper and writing books. Their Lizzie had told everyone as came.

'I can imagine,' I said, and could. When I last came back Aunt Mary had been a sprightly, determined old woman; now the sprightliness had gone but the second adjective still applied. Though her skin was like polythene across her cheeks, the line of her mouth was as strong as ever. Thirty years ago she had been the perfect manageress and her manner had never quite lost its organising edge. Her mind was as active as ever, plotting, judging, remembering. We all had occasion to laugh when we found ourselves committed by some quiet word from Aunt Mary. Vicars assured us we had volunteered to help with bazaars; neighbours thanked us for the loan of mowers or stout pairs of legs.

'I suppose you'll want to go and freshen up,' Aunt Lizzie suggested, careful as ever about dirt behind ears.

Staring round the bathroom with an increasing sense of bewilderment I noticed the margarine pots waiting for their nightly teeth, the ancient tins of talc. The same piece of pumice stone as had pumiced for twenty years lay on the soap dish and when I lifted the toilet mat silver fish slid for shelter. The atmosphere of dampness and 'using up' bothered me, the cut-up squares of vest for flannel, the evidence of poverty, made only more touching by pride. My throat ached with love. 'Things' had clearly been going badly since my mother's death, but Dad had never told me. He had talked generally of 'Things getting a bit tight' with teachers' salaries not keeping up with inflation, and 'Things being a bit difficult without Katie' but I had never visualised 'Things' in terms of a faded bathmat and a cracked mirror.

Like many families ours had its legends of lost fortunes, but in our case they were true. In my childhood we were genteel-poor, the sort local wags described as wearing fancy hatbands and no knickers. Nightingale Road was far too posh for us; the house far too big for a schoolmaster's income, but we all fell in love with it and would not hear of Dad selling when he inherited it. Besides, Dad's good fortune was an excuse for Mum to leave the suffocating world of the English private school, which she had hated ever since she and Dad took up residence at St. Bart's. The life of a house master's wife was not for her she said. Genteel poverty in Nightingale Road was preferable to High Table and the Headmaster's speeches. Now her death left an emptiness in the house which was like toothache, continually felt but rarely mentioned. Without her gift for making a pair of jumble sale curtains look like a Victorian heirloom, tat was tipping the balance against gentility. Yet the table in the parlour would be groaning with the weight of trifle and ham and scones, and peaches out of a tin, and orange squash for the children – for Harry's three would be there – and cake too, Murdock's best hideous in blue icing. My stomach revolted at the prospect. And it was all for my sake, and for the birthday of an old woman. But we were family and entitled to indigestion.

Below me I heard the doorbell ring and Aunt Lizzie's voice passing along the hall. Dabbing a blob of scent behind my ear I prepared a face to meet my brother, then went into my bedroom. Putting my bags beside the wardrobe I stared round the room. It had changed little since Lydia and I shared it. For hours we had lain talking and laughing till Mum shouted dire threats from below. Several of our possessions remained. An old teddy bear, four schoolgirl albums and a Sunday School prize or two littered the shelves, while a china dog of appalling wickedness watched from the mantelpiece Paul's first present to me, won from his uncle's stall on a summer night. Other reminders of Paul lay on the bookcase; an encyclopedia of music and a collection of folk songs. At once I saw him playing the piano for us on a wet evening, while we stood round and sang.

In anger I turned away. I did not wish to be reminded. A sense of acute shame and distress made my hands go sweaty. Condensation was forming on the windows, an unfamiliar dampness entering the house now that the sun was dropping, and I shivered.

Furious at my own foolishness I went downstairs.

For the rest of the afternoon we adults talked of Old Times. I did try to explain a little of my life during the past four years, but apart from a few questions about the cost of things and the weather, that topic never got going. There was a brief canter about the mysteries of airplane toilets then the conversation was wooden again. My experience was too remote for the others to share. Fortunately Harry's laugh brayed good naturedly, filling the space between us. It wasn't his fault he couldn't take me seriously. After all, he remembered me in spots and gym knickers. It must be hard to imagine his sister as a dignified sociologist, writing books and appearing on those late-night telly shows no one stays up long enough to see. He'd warned me no good would come of studying something ending in 'ology'.

Sue was a fit match for him. When we were girls together in the Sunday School she was the happy sort, roly-poly and easy going. She would end up like most Sandhill women, a flock mattress with the stuffing shaken to one end. Harry wouldn't mind. He was going to fat himself. In their company I felt like a Victorian spinster. Then gradually the old family magic returned and we were laughing again, recalling the silly stories every family treasures and an outsider can never find in the least bit funny.

Finally, after hearing the story of Aunt Lizzie's shepherd's pie for the five hundredth time, I escaped to the garden. Following Dad around in the evening light, I admired the winter cabbage and the greenhouse full of seedlings. Cement fairies and rabbits still crouched in the little garden he had made to amuse us when we were children, and the pool still boasted two fishermen and a flamingo. Since I was last there one gnome had taken to drink and the flamingo had mislaid a foot.

Walking down the garden I stood at the back gate looking over the park. A girl was running towards the swings, long hair slashing in the wind, dress tucked into blue knickers. Suddenly it was Lydia I was seeing. The laughter left me. Just as before, there was cold sweat on my hands.

We ate tea dutifully, all of us taking more than we wanted rather than offend Aunt Lizzie, who measured love according to the number of scones one ate. Harry was at his best. He had an endless supply of 'Doctor, Doctor' jokes, which proved to be international, since to everyone's hilarity I completed many of them before he could. (There's a thesis to be written on the world distribution of 'Doctor, Doctor' jokes.) Sue was in good form too, smiling benignly over her spectacles as she handed round a second piece of blue concrete. Aunt Mary would not join us at table, preferring to sit in her chair at the fire, sipping tea and keeping an eye on the proceedings. Her age gave her confidence. A very old woman can get away with rudenesses not permitted the young, with comments on people's hairstyles for example. Harry's mop needed cutting and mine made me look older she volunteered. At one point she announced Dad shouldn't eat with his elbows on the table, and to everyone's amusement he did as he was told, though he was all of fifty-five himself.

After the washing up, we adults wandered into the garden again. Standing beside the french windows we admired the sunset over the park while Aunt Lizzie described her cystitis. A few children were still playing on the swings but the fair-haired girl had gone. I wondered who she was and why she should have reminded me of Lydia. It was going cold, and we all returned reluctantly to the back room.

It was then that the key to my future was given me, though for months I did not recognise it as such.

'There's some old biscuit tins on Aunt Mary's table, Martie,' Dad said. 'Bring them down when you've unpacked. She put them out to show you.'

I was surprised and pleased. Aunt Mary rarely trusted anyone with her confidences. Having spent so much of her life alone, though with others, she had retreated into herself and her books. Just occasionally I had been privileged to be shown some treasured memento, as if I were the only one who could understand, as perhaps I was.

As soon as I entered Aunt Mary's room a smell of lavender greeted me and I was surprised to see how bright and delicate everything was. A photograph and a gilt carriage clock stood on the sideboard, reminders of thirty years' happy marriage and forty as a manageress of a chain of drapers. Beside them lay a Bible, its binding torn. Though I handled it carefully the back cover fell to the floor, and in bending to pick it up, I let the whole book slip in my hand. Several pages floated downwards like golden edged feathers, and an image of falling leaves in autumn came to me, startled from some recess in my brain, though at first I could not fix it in any time or place; would not, perhaps. The biscuit tins lay on the table, three in all. I picked up the first. The lid was marked with rust and bore the picture of a Spanish dancer performing to a guitar-playing lover. When I turned it over I found a plan of the original contents, specialty biscuits no longer available at any price.

Not liking to look inside without permission I put the tins to one side while I finished unpacking.

All the time, that image of falling leaves troubled me.

'You wanted to show me these', I said later. Aunt Mary motioned me to join her in the corner. Her deafness made conversation difficult but I enjoyed trying to talk to her. I judged that a woman who could remember fields between Sandhill and Twynning must have something of interest to say. So, pulling my chair as close as possible I put the first tin onto her lap.

Aunt Mary lifted the lid. 'I want you to have these, Martha,' she said. 'There's no one left now – not of my generation.' She glanced towards Aunt Lizzie. 'I'm not saying anything against our Lizzie. If it weren't for her I wouldn't have been able to cope after your mother died, but I don't owe her any favours. She's always had my money regularly and I've had to fit in with her likes and dislikes. I want you to have my few treasures before I go. If I hang on to them much longer, they'll like as not end in the rubbish bin.' Again she glanced towards her niece, with dry humour pretending a Black Country whine. 'Her's always clearing out.' Then she was serious again. 'Postcards are worth a good deal now, I've heard. I started this bit of a collection when I was a girl and I've kept it up ever since. Just what folk sent mind, and what I could beg from others. I never felt justified in buying them – that would have been self-indulgent.'

Dipping her hand into the box she brought out six or seven cards and let them fall back – a collector's dream.

'Are you sure you want to part with all these?' I asked, though I would have howled if she had changed her mind.

'I'd sooner you had them safe. There are a few bits besides I'd like you to have. You'll appreciate them.'

Eagerly I began to thank her, but Aunt Mary put her hand on mine. 'You're the only one who has ever shown any interest in me since I got old,' she said. 'I was touched when you made a special effort to be here for my birthday.'

'What's that she's giving you?' Aunt Lizzie called across the room.

'Only some old postcards,' I replied.

Aunt Lizzie was pacified. Her expression was easy to read. 'I don't know what she's giving you,' it said, 'but it doesn't sound valuable.'

Aunt Mary had read her response too, for she smiled grimly. 'I'm glad you've come back,' she said. 'I don't feel so alone in the house now.'

That night I looked through the boxes. It was better than Christmas. Between them the three biscuit tins contained about five hundred cards, all neatly arranged in two rows from front to back, and separated into subjects by bits of paper labelled in my great aunt's copper-plate writing.

She must have begged every card thrown out in our house as well as saving her own throughout a lifetime. Messages were addressed to Dad and Mum, even myself. Some of the pictures I recognised as ones sent by me from Australia. I had never imagined they would be so carefully preserved. Others were familiar too: faded views of Ilfracombe and Weston, places we visited as children. One particularly recalled my childhood; a novelty view card that depicted a little Scots boy dressed in a kilt. When the kilt was lifted a string of Devon beaches fell down. Goodness knows what a Scots boy in a kilt was doing in Devon, but we thought he was ever so daring at the time. There were other specialty cards too, birthday greetings with a sprig of lily of the valley, famous beauties from the Edwardian age ... It was like opening a door on a simpler world.

Picking up a view of Arton church I was startled to recognise my own childish handwriting, messy and impractical like myself. *Having a good time with Mummy at the chalet. Pip chased Mr Booth's hens and got spanked. Aunt Mary baked a cake for Lydia's birthday and Harry ate the sweets on top.*

For years I had tried to forget our visits to Arton, and now all those weekends were before me.

Sitting in a damp bedroom I allowed myself the dangerous pleasure of memory. I picked up another card. It was dated 3 August. *'Dear Mum, We're fine, so you mustn't worry about us. We rowed to the island yesterday with Mike Booth. It was heavenly except that Paul had to tag along. He looks like a beanpole.'*

Tucked into the box next to Lydia's card was my version of the same few days, our first holiday at the chalet without a grown-up.

'We're having a nice time though I wish you could come. We've been on the river in Mike Booth's boat, as far as the island. Harry and Lydia went off leaving me stuck with Paul, but we got on famously. He knows all the birds of the river and plays the piano better than ever. He intends to be famous, like me.'

As I read those forgotten words I was thirteen again, tall and awkward, permanently dreaming of higher things and missing half of what was going on round me. I remembered that stay at Sweetbriar vividly; Lydia loving the freedom and at fifteen feeling quite the woman, lounging about in her shorts where the passing fishermen would see her, and flirting with the boys at the fair until one of them gave her a coconut, so old we had to smash it open on the back step with a hammer afterwards. Without Sandhill's chapel presence she grew like a fern after rain, leaving me behind, still a child.

Even now as I stared at the cards I felt that first pain of disappointment. I had looked forward to our stay so much, made elaborate plans for the imaginary characters we three always assumed when alone – Lydia was Group Captain O'Hara, heavily based on Worrells from the W. E. Johns books, while Harry was Biggles himself and I was assorted Resistance heroines or emigre' aristocrats. But that time Lydia did not want to play. Instead she wanted me to experiment with the lipstick she had bought in town, or expected me to wait while she wandered around the fair. I could see no fun in painting different shaped lips on myself or in

98

propping up stalls while Lydia laughed at the witticisms of spotty-faced youths, even if they did wear rings in their ears. Mike Booth hanging around didn't help. He was the same age as Lydia and helped to run the boats for the tourists. Ordinarily I liked him. He could row better than any grown man on that stretch of the river and knew as much about nature as did Paul, but for those four days there was something new in his manner, some knowingness – I could not name it even to myself. Harry did not understand when I tried to explain to him. He worshipped Mike with all the passion of a younger boy dazzled by greater strength and skill. Lydia laughed when I tried to talk to her of it, but I was certain she did understand.

I should never have allowed myself to read Aunt Mary's cards. A sense of nausea began to overcome me; real physical sickness however intangible the cause might be. Through the scuffling echoes of time I became aware of Dad and Aunt Lizzie coming to bed, and was grateful for the distraction. Picking up some more cards I examined the stamps on them – they were safer than the messages. Many bore the head of Edward; most depicted George VI and the young Elizabeth. There were foreign stamps too, not just mine from Australia but from France and Spain as Harry and Sue took to having themselves packaged in Sandhill tourist bureau. I could not understand why Aunt Mary should have given me such a valuable collection. Yet her gift was an ambiguous pleasure. It laid my childhood before me in disturbing fragments.

I slept badly that night. My body was still on the plane, throbbing with the engines. Having spent the previous night in a hotel airconditioned to a 'cool' 70 degrees, my bedroom seemed both airless and cold and I could not stop listening to Aunt Lizzie snoring in the next room. But it was the sounds I could not hear which kept me awake most. Just as when I was in London it was the swoosh, swish and thump of the forges I missed, now I was listening for cicadas outside my bedroom window and for bullfrogs in the distance.

Finally I fell asleep, but it was an unpleasant troubled sleep. Sometimes I was trying to find my way through a bewildering city that opened a new subway each time I turned to cross the pavement, at others I was shouting above the drone of engines. Later I was walking around the back of a fairground, peeping inside the tents. In one a bearded man was tattooing himself across the arms and chest. Snakes writhed as he flexed his muscles. Suddenly one became real and slithered down from his chest, straggling across the floor towards me. In alarm I moved on. In the next tent a woman offered to read my fortune. 'Fear death by water,' she predicted. 'I see a man with three saves and a broken branch. Fear death by water.' Thanking her, I got up, knocking over a stuffed parrot in a cage as I did so. Outside, the swing boats were waiting for me, and letting the attendant help me in, I grasped the rope. A young man sat opposite me. He was laughing and handsome. *Fear death by water...*'

With a jerk I awoke, my dream only half-completed. Trying to drive the images from me I forced my eyes open, but I was worn out and the room was dark. Slowly I drifted back into that semi-conscious state where sleep and waking are confused, and memory blends with dream. The swing boat had become a rowing boat, and the young man's face was distorted with fear and effort. He was trying to row us away from the island but all the boat would do was turn, sluggishly, downstream. I heard Paul's voice yelling about the current, and I tried to shout too, but my mouth was stuck together. Then the branch was on us, big as a small tree, twigs smothering us even before the boat tipped. 'Jump!' I shouted, suddenly able to move my mouth. Gulping air, I threw myself forward. I tried to dive away from the tangle and swim back upwards to see if Mike was near me, but the river was dark with flood and the current too fast for me to see anything. 'Mike – here...' I screamed. But I was gulping water, not air. I was drowning, threshing out at twigs and roots and water. My ears and chest were bursting. My mouth tasted of blood.

I woke sweating and sick. For a long time I stared at the streetlamp outside. *Fear death by water.* In dreams it was still there in my mind though my consciousness pushed it as far as possible from me. Amnesia is after all a rare complaint, despite being suffered by T.V. soap characters with the regularity of the common cold. Since I was neither beautiful nor rich and did not wear outsize shoulder pads, I could not take refuge in oblivion. The mind remembers, however much it tries to forget.

Reaching across, I put on the bedside lamp. The china dog stared at me from the mantelpiece, as ugly as when it sat on the shelf at Cal Boothman's stall. Paul's voice said. 'Every time you look at him you'll think of me'.

'Looks like you,' my voice agreed, and we chased each other round his uncle's stall.

Impatiently I got up, and fetching one of the biscuit tins began to examine the cards inside. It was two o'clock. I would not sleep any more that night.

***

The next day I was shown off. That is to say, I was taken round Aunt Lizzie's friends and displayed like a new hat. 'This is our Martha.'

'You remember our Martha? The clever one that went to Awstraylia?' 'Come back on a year's holiday you know. Sabbatyical they call it out there. Nice for some...' 'Her writes books you know...'

Smiling wanly each time, I took the hand offered me, and asked after faulty knees or sons in Manchester. I did protest feebly when put down for the Ladies' Bright Hour – my slides were all in my trunks at sea I protested, but that was over-ruled. I could use the few I had sent my father, and talk generally about the country afterwards. The ladies would love that. When my trunks arrived I could be put down for a proper slide show on another evening. Too amused to resist effectively I was also dragooned into visiting the Sunday School, complete with boomerang and didgeridoo. The fact that I did not possess either was only a temporary problem. I would just have to send back to my friends for some. Mrs Timpkins wasn't going to look a gift Sunday School in the mouth.

I must admit I was rather naughty. The huntsman spider I found in the shower was only four inches across, and I never did see any tiger snakes in the wild. Still, it's nice to give one's audiences what they expect, and the funnel web under Dr. Aston's loo seat in Sydney was true. I drew the line at agreeing that everyone in the suburbs wore knee-high anti-snake boots, but all in all it was not an unpleasant way of spending a morning, though one morning was enough.

At lunch we had a family meeting, in Cooper tradition. The subject was me and what was to be done with me. Having been granted Sabbatical leave early to suit the department, I had to find somewhere to live where I could research another book, hopefully as successful as my last *Working-Class Tories in the West Midlands Conurbation*. Obviously I was welcome to stay there Aunt Lizzie invited, but her voice implied what we all knew that that would be a disaster. Before I left I fitted into the Nightingale Road household as well as an onion in a potato patch, and now I had been away so long the tensions would inevitably be greater. No, it wouldn't work we agreed amicably. The only thing we had in common was love, and not even love is sufficient when too many people are sharing the same bathroom.

And so, if I was not going to stay at Nightingale Road, where would I go? It was Harry who came up with the solution, having called en route to a client in Stourbridge. Why didn't I take over the chalet? It was still Aunt Mary's and not properly used. Dad and Aunt Lizzie only went down occasionally and it was too much for Aunt Mary. Though he and Sue had meant to do the place up, Sue had never forgotten their first weekend there when she found ants in the sugar and earwigs in the Weetabix. Sweetbriar would be all the better for having someone live there again.

The suggestion was a sensible one, at least for the summer months. Even so I felt uneasy. I was afraid of going there, particularly if as Harry said Paul Booth was back home, but such a reaction was childish I told myself. When there was a perfectly good building available to me rent free, I would be foolish not to use it. What was more I would take Aunt Mary with me I announced on impulse. Give Dad and Aunt Lizzie a break and let Aunt Mary see her old summer home. She could help me a bit with the housework.

My intention was greeted with enthusiasm, particularly by Aunt Mary. 'A holiday?' she asked. She hadn't had a holiday in four years, not since she went with the Ladies' Bright Hour to Weston, and that wasn't much of a holiday, helping the old dears on and off the coach and hunting for their spectacles. Harry would run us down in his car he offered (and the way he drove, he might) – take the day off work perhaps. And so it was agreed, and a more hairbrained scheme was rarely concocted amongst consenting adults.

Within half an hour I was developing doubts. Harry had an attack of conscience, too. 'What 'you want to invite Aunt Mary for?' he asked. 'You'll never cope with her. She's getting to be quite a trial, coming out with things that make your hair curl.'

'I'll manage,' I assured him without conviction. 'I thought Dad looked as though he could do with a bit of quiet, and Aunt Mary and I always get on. I meant what I said about her being useful to me. I don't think I'd like to be at the chalet on my own.'

We were both silent after that. 'Do you still dream of it?' Harry asked. 'I do. I wake cold and sweating and spend the next day wondering what more I could have done.' He wiped a large hand across his face. The bottom button of his shirt had come undone, showing a triangle of vest and stomach. 'I dreamt of it last night,' he added. 'Seeing you started me off again I suppose.' Awkwardly he put his hand on my arm in a gesture I found unexpectedly touching. 'Things have never been the same since, have they? Do you know, Lydia didn't even send a Christmas card? Did you get one?' I shook my head. 'Dad was awfully hurt when she never visited him. He's getting to look a lot older. You must have noticed with being away so long...'

His voice trailed away in apology – apology that for once he could find no protecting joke, that he was not what we had hoped, that his stomach was too heavy and his wife was a careless, self-centred woman . . . For a rare moment we were in unison, understanding each other's failure.

Aunt Lizzie came in, fretting as usual about pots not washed. 'Well, must be getting back to it,' Harry said, rubbing his hands like a probationary Shylock. 'Got to make my million.' Still with his button undone, he went through the gate to his car, his feet echoing as he left.

I retreated to my room early that night, justifying my rudeness by saying I was tired after the flight. Sitting on my bed I opened the second tin.

Most of that collection was given over to *First World War*. I turned each faded picture reverently. Men in uniform posed before their kit, unwieldy guns ready for action waited beside smiling teams; a field full of bell tents was marked with an illegible squadron number. On others dreamy young ladies sent greetings from France. The best card of all was an embroidered one, almost certainly valuable. Too sweet for modern taste, the design was stitched under a handsewn verse, and included the words *'Remember Me'*. Pulling the lamp nearer I tried to decipher the pencil on the other side. *'To my own Mary'* it said. The signature was blurred but I interpreted it as *'Richard'*. There was no address, just the word *'France'*. A date was given; *'29 June, 1916'*.

At first I thought I had misread the signature. The card must be from Uncle John. Great Aunt Mary wasn't the sort to have had more than one lover. There was no way I could make seven letters into four however, and when I came to think of it, Uncle John would have been too young to serve in France. Aunt Mary had startled the whole of Sandhill by marrying a man nearly ten years her junior, long after she had been pigeon-holed as a spinster. In 1916 Uncle John would have been nine years old, too young even for a war in which volunteers prided themselves on lying about their age. Whoever Richard was, he had come before Uncle John.

It was as if the Past had reached out and touched me with gentle icy fingers. June 1916. The year of the Somme. Dates and figures returned to me from a lecture I had given. 'The first of July 1916: in a single day's battle which opened the Allied Offensive on the Somme, the British Army in France suffered sixty thousand casualties, of which one third were killed.' Aunt Mary's card gave unexpected life to those figures and I sat helplessly, marooned in a bedroom. A scent of furniture polish and lavender filled my mind and from next door I heard the gilt carriage clock rasping, as if the balance were scraping inside. 'Remember Me.'

I had never known my great aunt. Not one of those weekends we had spent at Sweetbriar had revealed her to me. Despite the rather strange phenomenon of Uncle John I had never associated Aunt Mary with romance, or considered how she had been shaped by the events I had studied. Now her postcard collection was revealing her secrets to me, as it had begun to reveal my own.

Turning back to the cards, I examined others. One young man in an Edwardian suit held my attention. He looked no more than fourteen yet on the back my great aunt had written laconically, 'Killed in action'. The same brief description had been written on several others: a lad called Willy Hope, and another, Jamie Thompson, both of whom looked scarcely any older. Feeling a deep sadness I began to look for more cards from Richard.

There were fifty-one of these I discovered, though some were scattered under other categories in the collection. Many had no more than the word 'France' upon them, yet through them I could trace the progress of Sandhill Battalion from training in southern England, to the Front, and then to the trenches and death. The card I had found first was in fact his last – *'Remember Me'*.

Sighing, I began to sift the last tin. To my surprise I found other messages signed Lakin, but they were from Richard's sister, Milly. When I came to consider the issue more carefully however, I saw I should have expected as much. We used to visit Arton Villa with Aunt Mary quite frequently, and the elderly lady in the deckchair used to receive us cordially. There would be sweet biscuits on a Japanese plate for us children and wafers of sandwich for Aunt Mary and Mum. We should have realised the two older women were friends rather than mere neighbours, but then, what child ever does consider an adult as having friends? Friends are a characteristic only the young possess, like love and hope...

Curiously I read some of the cards from Miss Lakin. She had been a remarkable woman. As late as 1974, four years before her death, she was visiting London, negotiating an order for the forge it seemed. I wondered whether at the age of seventy-five I would be capable of making such journeys. To the end she had fought the compulsory purchase of her land, her last illness rather than the council defeating her, or so people said.

Eerily I suddenly found myself looking at Miss Lakin's brother He was standing beside a studio balcony and even in a faded image he was handsome, without being conceitedly so, what people of Aunt Mary's generation called 'A real gentleman', and meant as a compliment. On the back of his portrait was written *'Christmas 1914. With all my love, Richard. Be with you soon.'* Those simple words touched me more than any passionate declaration, and putting the photo back in its polythene holder, I sat thinking about a whole generation of 'real gentlemen' who sent their portraits and never returned.

'Well – fancy Aunt Mary being engaged to Richard Lakin!' I thought in the end and put the tin away. Poor Aunt Mary. Had he lived she would have been mistress of one of the biggest businesses in the town. And we dared to think her worth no more than an armchair and an unwilling cup of tea.

There was one last category of card I had not explored. Knowing very little about the entertainers of Edwardian times I had left *Music Hall'* untouched. Now I glanced idly through the beauties in their fancy hats, the dapper men posing beside stage curtains. *Who has the prettiest smile?'* one caption asked and five different ladies smiled in heart shaped appeal. Some had been signed by the star concerned, and probably had collector's value but they rather bored me, I'm afraid. Then abruptly I was jerked into attention with a sharpness that left me shaking. It was as if Past and Present had blurred in one of those chilling sci-fi movies where double selves exist and haunt each other's time. The face before me was familiar though the dress was Edwardian. Eyes and mouth, even the line of the hair was known to me. Pulling the bedside lamp nearer so that I could read the torn inscription, I distinguished the words *Isaac Boothman, Gypsy Violinist'*.

I had never seen Paul as a grown man, yet I knew he must look like the image before me.

Once again the sense of physical discomfort, almost nausea returned to me. I wished to God I had never returned home. For years I had refused to remember, and now everything, even a tin of old postcards was forcing me to do so. I could not grieve, even so – not now, not ever.

Taking a handful of cards I went downstairs.

Aunt Mary was making her evening drink. Her fingers would not close round the cocoa tin nor around the saucepan handle and I watched nervously as milk slopped into the cup. 'Let me do that,' I suggested, knowing I would be refused.

'I can manage,' Aunt Mary said, and then immaculate as ever added, 'Thank you. I like to do for myself as long as I can.' She held the mug to her as she stirred the cocoa into the milk. With every week the effort was evidently becoming greater. 'I've managed to look after my own needs till now, and please God I shall continue to do so.'

'I didn't realise you knew Richard Lakin,' I said.

'We were going to be married. We had many plans.'

'Is that why you married Uncle John so late?'

'There weren't enough men to go round after the war, my dear. Besides, I didn't seem to want anyone else.' She paused. 'There wasn't any point in pining. I'd learnt how to do a man's job while the soldiers were away, so I carried on doing it. I was lucky. No one came back to take my place. Then John joined the firm. A nicer, decenter man you couldn't imagine – and well, time passes and new feelings grow. People only grieve forever in books.' She smiled, a rare softness entering her expression. 'The amount of headshaking that went on over our wedding would have suited a dervish's tea party. Yet John and I had over thirty very good years together. My being older gave a different slant to things of course, but my only real regret is that he died before me. I seem to be like the spider who outlives her mates.' She sighed. 'Still, there it is. I was born the lasting sort and he wasn't.' A malevolent note came to her voice. 'I may outlive our Lizzie yet.'

I laughed. 'You don't like Aunt Lizzie do you?' I asked.

'I'm not saying anything against her,' Aunt Mary began, which remark I've usually found means the opposite. 'Lizzie is a good woman. She did her duty looking after you children when your parents were abroad, and nursing your mother in her last illness, but well, she's the sort that's marvellous in a crisis and bores everyone silly the rest of the time.'

Dad entered, seeking the evening paper. For years he had never seemed any different, the sort of timeless respectable little man who could be thirty or fifty, never following any fashion. When cufflinks were the rage he wore buttons. Now no young man would be seen dead in cufflinks he stapled his shirts together with the abalone pair Mum gave him. His own standards were upheld in all things: neatness, rectitude. I wanted to tell him I was glad to see him again. Instead I asked him how Sandhill Grammar was faring.

'Not too badly,' he replied. 'There's cut-backs of course and morale's low amongst the staff, but we're coping better than some schools. Miss McClean runs a tight ship.' He smiled grimly. 'She throws anyone overboard who doesn't swab the decks.'

'Any hope of a deputy headship?' I asked.

'Not without moving. We're all waiting for the one above us to die or take early retirement. I've found several bars of soap at the top of the stairs and Jenkins' roller skates appear in the corridor regularly.'

'We haven't seen much of each other have we?' I said, smiling. 'I've been swallowed by other people.'

'I was thinking the same myself. You will be all right at Sweetbriar, won't you?' He coughed hesitantly. 'I admire your courage – going there.'

'Oh – I'll be fine. I won't stay long. In any case, as soon as I've got my book started I'll come back for the weekend. Aunty'll be all right, won't you?' Aunt Mary nodded emphatically. My words tumbled out, just as they used to when I was a child.

'That'd be nice,' Dad agreed, and put the cat out to hide his embarrassment. We paused, not knowing what to say. I realised I still had my great aunt's cards in my hand. Not certain whether she would like me to talk even to Dad about her private affairs, I paused. 'Would you like a drink?' I asked.

'A cup of coffee'd be welcome.'

'I'll make it,' Aunt Mary offered.

'Then I'll run upstairs and put some things away,' I said.

In my bedroom I hurriedly replaced the handful of cards, trying to remember the order in which I had found them. I had not meant to delay but a picture held me. Turning it over, I read the message.

The concert went well, at least I think it did. People clapped and said nice things. I can't say thank you enough for lending me that quid. If I hadn't had

109

some music to practise with this week I'd have had to give up. Dad's sorry now of course. He came to the concert, but it's going to take me an awful long time to forgive him this time. You hit someone in anger and then it's over, but burning my music is different. Still, that's my problem. Love you, Paul.

P.S. I haven't said that before have I? Well I do, so there.'

Stupidly I reread the words. That pound had never been repaid; I would keep it as hostage I said, but in his pride Paul was determined I should have it. We grew quite bad tempered over it. How old were we? Fifteen? I had kept the card for years, then thrown it out before I went to College.

Putting the tins back on the floor, I went downstairs.

Dad and Aunt Mary were already sitting at the table. 'There's some biscuits in the barrel,' Dad confided. 'Lizzie keeps them on top of the cupboard. Can you reach them? Lizzie uses the steps.'

The idea of Aunt Lizzie hiding the biscuits reduced me to such hysterical laughter I could scarcely reach the barrel. Then with a fine sense of mischief we sat together eating bourbon creams.

The next day I walked round Sandhill.

For a desultory hour I examined the shops and town centre, having first bought myself a leaflet from the library. The writers managed to make two main streets, a pelican crossing and a drycleaners sound like the gateway to Europe. Afterwards I sat on the pocket handkerchief of a lawn the guidebook called *'Sandhill Green and War Memorial.* Recalling old pastimes I counted the steps to the black marble slab, and read the names, checking how many must have belonged to the same families: Hope and Parkes, Barraclough, Homer and Turner, Thompson and Langdon. They were arranged in alphabetical order and there between Walter King and Jonathan Langdon was Richard Lakin. The letters had new meaning for me. For the first time too I considered the implications of that long list. Not one of the prominent families had remained unscathed. It was as if an angel of death had passed over the town, taking not just its eldest sons, but its brightest and best.

And the town had declined. One only had to talk to Aunt Mary to realise that. It was still declining – had done so since my last visit.

In my youth Sandhill was a bustling place, coarse and ugly, doing nicely out of the Midlands car boom. We used to boast a mechanic could put a car together just by walking round the local factories with a barrow. There was a constant shout and throb and coming and going in grubby overalls, a whistling and cheerful obscenity. The place stank to high heaven. One day I cycled through a white mist and my nylons promptly dissolved on my legs. We were all probably dying of Somebody Or Other's Lung but we intended to go to our graves well-fed. There were bacon and eggs and slabs of fried bread for breakfast, and fish and chips in greasy newspaper for lunch, with a bottle of cider to wash them down. Good large Black Country bellies hung over Belmont's best trousers; no nonsense about designer jeans here.

And we girls, we staggered along in our high heels with our skirts so tight we had to bend from the knees so as not to tell the world our secrets, and every Saturday night the beauties used to stand outside the Palais with their legs mottled with cold, and size up the local talent. And the local talent would come swaggering round the corner, knowing he had money in his pocket and a barrel chest to match any rival. Now the young men had lost their swagger. They were sitting on the wall waiting for the Green Dragon to open, or standing while their wives chattered outside the shops. Some were pushing toddlers in buggies, though any man seen doing so in the past would have been satirised as 'soft'. Unemployment was altering all the old values, for good as well as ill.

I was shocked by what had happened to my town. In seven years it had died. 'To Let' had appeared all over the trading estate, and many of the new Wimpey houses were for sale. The Tower bingo had turned into a supermarket; the coffee bar had eloped to the east and married a tandoori chicken.

More than any of these changes what distressed me most was what had happened to Bircham's Coppice, the Wild Wood of our childhood. Bircham's Coppice had gone.

It had only ever been a narrow area, about half a mile across and a mile and a half long, leading up to the Heath, but it was an oasis in an industrial desert. Armfuls of bluebells grew in sheltered hollows where bikes could not reach, and birds sang in the branches, flying in from 'the country' as we all reverently called the imagined lands beyond the Heath. We made dens amongst the trees and carried bits of tin roof and tyres begged from neighbours a mile or so through the streets to do so. The more daring looped ropes around the oak tree and became Tarzan for a morning, or scrambled up the sides of Lakin's quarry, an illicit dumping ground for lawn cuttings and old mattresses. Nature was fighting a rear guard action even then, but at that time she was holding her own, putting forth new growth each spring and barring our way to her innermost recesses with bramble and nettle. And what splendour was hidden there! Further up the hillside and too far away for most Sandhill residents there was quiet, such as we never heard elsewhere, the sound of insects, the scent of leaf-mould and damp earth. Primroses grew in season under the trees, and down the slope a blue waterfall of sweetness cascaded each May. The Bluebell Woods were our Paradise, our one sweetness in a harsh little town.

And now they were gone. Men had come with machines. They had built a new road straight through the woods and put a Little Chef restaurant in the quarry. I could just trace the outline of our hermit's cave rising above the smart plush and pine building, but the birds had flown and the primroses with them. Clay banks rose either side of the road, treeless. There had surely been no need to take it all.

One tree remained, the oak we used to swing on and make our dens in; dying back at the top it stood like a gibbet on the furthest bank. I could not reach it. To cross what had been mine by right of childhood I would have to slither down one clay bank, climb a crash barrier, risk my life amongst the speeding cars and climb another bank. Furiously I turned away.

Returning along the Birmingham Road I came to the back gates of the park. Rusting in Victorian splendour they opened onto the rhododendron walk, and taking that path I crossed to the playing area. At least that had not changed. The roundabout looked as if it had never been painted since Lydia and Harry and I played our wild games around it. Sitting on one of the swings I paused before returning indoors.

A thickset man was pushing a toddler back and forth in the baby swing at the end of the line. Absorbed in my anger I did not see him come across to me leaving his son swinging his fat little legs, safely tucked behind the bar. 'Hello, Martie,' he said, offering his hand. 'Mam said you was back.'

I was delighted to see him, though embarrassed, as I always was in his company. Meeting an old flame tends to leave you feeling you've got smuts on your nose. Looking at Lol Jackson I wondered how I could have found so much flesh alluring, and no doubt he was wondering what could have induced him to get that prim-looking creature against the corner of the cricket pavilion. 'That your little one?' I asked.

'Yeah. Brought him out for a bit of a play, out of his Mam's way. Josie reckons her cor' get any work done, not with us both under her feet.'

In his prime Lol had been irresistible, to a rebellious genteelly nurtured schoolgirl at least. Leader of the local bikies, he was wonderfully undesirable in black leather and slicked-back hair, feared by every wimp who had to cross the road past his gang.

Now he sat on a playground swing, watching his son. 'How long you back for?' he asked.

'A year.'

'Staying here then?'

'Only a few weeks. I'm going down to the chalet – at least till I find something better. I'm over here to work, and I wouldn't get much peace in Sandhill.'

'You always did like it down there,' Lol agreed. 'Me – I cor' stick the country. All that muck and farmyard smells. Mind you, I'm thinking of getting out of this dump meself. There in't nothing left for me now, not with Langdon's closed. We've had to move in with my people – sell the house. It's driving me round the bend. You'll have to tell me about Australia someday. I fancy going there meself, but Josie don't. She don't want to leave here – it's her home she says.' In resigned disgust Lol looked about him. Then unexpectedly he nudged me. 'You'd have been more adventurous, wouldn't you? I've always reckoned there's more to you than you let on. And I'd have found out too, if that bloody aunt of yours hadn't come out!' Nudging me again he laughed, being crude because he knew it annoyed me. 'Fancy running off with me now? We could go to Australia together.'

He was joking of course and I would have hit him hard if he hadn't been, but it was good to know I was still worth the odd proposition. 'What would Josie say?' I asked.

'She'd call me an effing fool – like her does already.'

'I'm sorry things have gone badly with you,' I said. 'The whole town's gone down hasn't it?'

'Yeah.' Smiling at me wryly he retrieved his son from the swing. 'Be seeing you,' he said, then paused. He was still a fine-looking man, standing watching me with his son tucked in the crook of his arm. 'You look tired,' he said. 'Your Dad's worried about you, you know. He says you in't sleeping like you should.'

'I'm OK.' I assured him. 'This term's been particularly heavy, arranging to come home and trying to finish lecture courses first.'

'You always did work too hard' Lol agreed, sitting again on the swing beside me. 'It in't good for you, you know. Oh, you're ambitious and all that, but there's more to life than work. Would you take a bit of advice from an old friend?'

'I'll listen to it,' I replied, smiling. 'But I can't promise to take it.'

'Find yourself a steady bloke. You in't the sort to spend your life alone. You'll get hard and clever.'

'Oh, give over,' I protested. 'What makes you think the blokes are queuing up for me?'

'You underestimate yourself- always have done. I'll let you into a secret. I'd have given my right arm to marry you meself once, but I could see it was saft. You fancied me a bit because I was number one round here, but you weren't my sort. Besides, you loved that boy of yours in Arton. Every time you spoke of him there'd be a different note in your voice to when you spoke of me. Find yourself a bloke like him again. Then you won't want to work so hard.'

'Don't open old wounds,' I replied gently.

'Naw, it in't fair of me.' In apology he pushed his great hand through my hair, scuffling it into a hopeless mess just as he used to. 'I've missed you,' he admitted. 'I could've done with you to talk to, this last year, with *Langdon's* shutting and the town going down so much. We were good friends, weren't we? You was the only girl this way as'd talk to me, for all you were so different, and I used to get a lot of pleasure when you lent me books and things. Your people have been good to me too. Your Dad's given me bits of decorating and plumbing to do on the side ever since I was made redundant.'

Acknowledging his friendship I smiled. 'You must introduce me to your wife,' I said.

'Yeah – come for a drink with us one night. There's a few of the old crowd left you'll remember.' He paused, evidently considering his words. 'We were talking about you last night wondering if you could help now you're back.'

'In what way?'

'I dunno really. Just that we can't let this place get any worse, and it will if Lakins' Heath is built on like they're threatening. They've dug up the Coppice – have you seen? I used to love walking there with me dog. We got a petition up, but there in't much you can do once the big boys move in. Besides, most people didn't seem to care not till it was done. They didn't want to shift their arses off their bloody chairs. You might know how to find out what they're planning for the Heath, before it's too late to save that, too.'

'They couldn't build on the Heath,' I protested. 'There'd be subsidence all the time.'

'You know that and I know that, but the planners don't – or pretend they don't. They want to put up warehouses. So long as they hold up a few years that's all the Council cares about. The only thing that's stopping them at the moment is they can't find the owner. Milly Lakin gave the deeds to someone before she died, and no one knows who. If they're still alive, they're keeping quiet about it. Don't want it built on any more than us perhaps. But we ought to find out – before the Council does – then perhaps we can get a preservation order on it or summat.' As always Lol was the leader. 'Your family used to be well, almost gentry. You might know how to find out. Besides, you've got the education. I haven't.'

I could not resist such an appeal, and nodded.

'Don't go over doing things though,' Lol added, evidently feeling guilty. 'You don't look all that well.'

'I'm all right,' I repeated. 'Coming back's thrown me a bit, that's all.'

In understanding Lol touched my shoulder, gently. 'Memories can hang around, can't they?' he said. 'I always reckoned it'd catch up with you sometime. You didn't grieve proper at the time.

116

Grieving's Nature's way of coming to terms with things. You have to grieve. All the psychologists say that – least ways from what I've heard.'

'Leave it alone,' I replied quietly. 'Didn't Miss Lakin leave a will?' I went on, abruptly changing the subject.

'I imagine so, but it was all done secret. It was a queer business.'

'Charlie Warwick may have a few ideas,' I suggested. 'I'll ask him.'

I kept my promise to Lol.

Mr Warwick's house, like Mr Warwick himself, was one of the last remaining bits of Sandhill's glory, an ugly red-brick monstrosity that had once been a manufacturer's home, built high on the Sandhill Rise so that the owner could watch his workmen come and go to the factory beneath. Gothic windows gave it the same oddly religious air as our house in Nightingale Road, and the balcony round the top of the bay was surrounded by wrought iron of such intricacy that people waiting at the bus stop were kept amused for ages, counting its tendrils. A heavy privet hedge engulfed the garden, as old no doubt as the house itself, and just as dusty.

Mr Warwick was alone, sitting at his desk in a confusion of books and stale cups. Venus and Aphrodite, his cats, blinked at me unwelcomingly but old Charlie was delighted, shaking me vigorously by the hand. 'Sit down, sit down,' he urged. 'It is kind of you to call.' Removing the remains of an eclair on a saucer ('Naughty but nice,' he joked), he cleared a pile of files on to the floor, where they promptly fell over. 'And how's the research? You are still writing, aren't you?'

I assured him that when I could find the time I was.

'Ah yes, time. Always my problem. There's never enough of it. When you reach my age you're even more short of it. Do you know I was seventy-two last week? It's indecent. I don't feel the least bit different to when I was twenty-two, not inside me. Of

117

course, the machinery's packing up – waterworks don't function as they should and the oil's dried out from the joints.' He held a misshapen hand to the light and examined it in amazement. 'But me, the bit that's me, that doesn't alter. I'm working on another book you know, a history of Sandhill. It'll take me at least another five years to complete. Masses of material.' The papers around him confirmed his statement, spilling on to the window-ledge and the hearth, and even, seen through the open door, into his kitchen where they decorated the fridge. 'I've moved over into local history now. Well, it's what every body wants, isn't it? The nostalgia craze. We can't stand the mess we've made of the present, so we hanker after the past. Not that that was any better. Do you know, the average life expectancy of a man employed in the wireworks below us was thirty-two? That was as late as 1840. And those are the Victorian values everyone wants to go back to! Well, I can't complain. They're buying my books, and coming in droves to my lectures. Never did better ...'

'Do you still lecture, then?' I managed to ask.

'Wouldn't dream of stopping. Not while the audiences keep coming, and I can get through the door. I'll offer you the life of the Brontë's, readings from Charles Dickens, Sandhill history, whatever takes your fancy.'

It was impossible not to smile at his enthusiasm. Learning was still his single love affair. No woman had ever been able to equal its charms. Trivialities like dirty cups and unmade beds were sheer waste of time when there was all Scott to reread and the latest Booker prize winner to discover, and now local history to absorb him too.

'You might be able to answer a question for me,' I said. 'Who owns Lakin's Heath?'

Mr Warwick laughed. 'Don't know, my dear – I'd be all the rage if I did. Who's got you involved in that one? They didn't waste much time.'

'Lol Jackson was talking to me. I gather there's quite a few people concerned to preserve the Heath.'

'Oh yes, big Lol. A rough diamond as they say.' Shuffling the papers in a file, Charlie Warwick examined the past. He was himself an anachronism, a splendidly enthusiastic, *Boy's Own* teacher from the days when the triumph of the first eleven and the summer production of *A Midsummer Night's Dream* were the main events of the calendar. Unlike Dad, he had not survived the change at Sandhill Grammar. Of course he would have had to retire in any case, but that was his good fortune, not his hardship. His values and manners would have caused laughter amongst the rougher boys suddenly tipped into the school when it went comprehensive – boys like Lol Jackson with plenty of intelligence, bright and hard as a whole box of buttons, but under the old system too lacking in formal learning to be admitted along the leaky corridors of Sandhill prestige. Charlie Warwick found it difficult to imagine that anyone in the world had not read *'Season of mists and mellow Fruitfulness ...'*. That they should not appreciate the line once it was explained to them was unthinkable.

'What happened to the Lakin estate then?' I asked, recalling him to my presence.

'When Charles Lakin died it was split up – always a mistake. The Villa and the corn mill in Arton went first to his wife, and then through her to their youngest son, Henry. The forge and quarry here went to their daughter Milly. Richard, the eldest had been killed at the Somme. It must have caused a lot of talk – a woman taking over the business, but from what I've heard she was stronger than her brother. I remember her well. She cropped the Coppice and strode about the forge like a man. A few years ago Christopher – that was Henry's son – sold the Villa and the mill. Most of the land had already gone in bits. Your chalet's on part of the old paddock, so I believe.' Mr Warwick shook his head. 'Christopher was the dilettante sort, still is for all I know. He must be quite a youngster even now; no more than forty or so. Fancied himself as a writer but never got anywhere.'

One cat watched him from beneath the table; the second jumped on the chair beside him and Charlie absentmindedly wiped his hand on it. 'Miss Lakin hung on to her share better, but part of it was compulsorily purchased to build the new road, just before her death, though she fought for years to prevent it. Someone's made a nice profit letting it stay idle so long. I mean out of the land alongside the road, where all those horrid brick boxes have gone up. Miss Lakin was determined the Council shouldn't have the Heath as well, so she gave the deeds away before her death. The Council have tried to follow it up, but you know Sandhill. They've never really put their minds to it till now. Daft really – with *Langdon's* going bust, building warehouses up there's even sillier.'

'We were forbidden to go up there,' I volunteered. 'That's not to say we didn't.'

Mr Warwick's eyes expressed understanding. 'Fascinating place,' he agreed. 'But thoroughly spoilt, with all those shafts and disused workings.' Putting some of his notes away he looked at me properly for the first time. 'Come now, I've been doing all the talking, as usual. What have you been doing this past four years?'

I think I got a few remarks in about my work, but I'm not sure. It wasn't important. My visit was not only for Lol's sake, but a pilgrimage, a confused mixture of thanks and 'See, haven't I done well?' Absurd though he might be to some, Charlie Warwick with his school plays and Dickens lunches had awoken some hunger in me that sent me leaping every establishment hurdle towards some imagined goal of learning. Which is a horrible mixed metaphor, but so were my feelings for Charlie.

It was only as I came to leave that I managed to ask one more question. 'What was Richard Lakin like?'

'A fine young man from what I've read, full of idealism, yet sensible too. His letters from the Front are preserved in the library.

120

They make fascinating reading.' I stopped with my hand on the doorknob. Mr Warwick laughed. 'Martha Cooper,' he said. 'There's a gleam in your eye. Yes, I'll share Richard Lakin with you. I have more than enough to be going on with, and you'll approach him from a different standpoint.' Reflectively he stroked Aphrodite. 'I think Sandhill might have been very different if he had lived – he and those who enlisted like him. They had courage and vision. We lost a whole generation of leaders. Now we are run by small-minded men who don't value education because they never had it them selves. If your generation had stayed things might have been better. You, Tich Matthews, Peter Sampson, you would have been the teachers, the doctors, the lawyers, the professional class Sandhill lacks, but you all left. Not one of the good ones in your year stayed, and yours was the best year we had.'

Charlie was right. We had sought our fortunes like a whole generation of Dick Whittingtons. Peter Sampson ran everything he touched at school, whether it was speech night or painting: Just Married' on Miss Hewison's car (and her every bit of fifty and like a bus with it). And I too, once I had learnt confidence, was always up at the front. I even organised a concert in the lower sixth. We raised two hundred pounds for the school organ fund, a good deal of money then. It was Paul's first big engagement...

'I'll tell you who might know something about Miss Lakin's intentions,' Mr Warwick said. 'That dark lad who played at your concert. Lived near Arton Villa. His grandfather sometimes worked for Miss Lakin, he told me – was a sort of friend even, and his father did a lot of heavy work on the estate.' Rubbing his hands together Charlie smiled with pleasure at being able to add further information. 'Now then, where are you going to spend this Sabbatical of yours?'

I explained about Sweetbriar, and my need for quietness.

Mr Warwick approved entirely. 'Can't work with people coming and going all day,' he agreed. 'Wanting to clean your windows and collect for children's homes. The Greeks never had such problems and I don't suppose Shakespeare did, either. Anne Hathaway would have sent them packing.' His eyes narrowed in an expression he always imagined conveyed extreme cunning. 'If you're going to Arton you can ask Paul Booth about Miss Lakin yourself. Come to think of it, what did happen to him? Did very well for himself, didn't he? Remarkably well for a lad from such a background. Won some international competition, I heard.'

Twice in one week was too much. 'He's working in America,' I replied. 'When he's not travelling the world. He's probably in Kathmandu at the moment.'

'Don't have any concert halls in Kathmandu,' Charlie replied cheerfully. 'All right my dear, I can take a hint. You don't want to match off with any old flames, and quite right too. Go and get your book written and I'll carry on with mine. If you want to cry on my shoulder round about page 132, you know you're welcome here.'

Even as I shook hands an idea began to tantalise me. I ran long stretches down Sandhill Rise, such was my excitement. Then hot and undignified, I ran upstairs to look at Aunt Mary's cards.

We took torches and anoraks in case the clouds that threatened decided to break. 'What did Josie say?' I asked.

'I told her I was going for a walk with my fancy piece, and she laughed and chucked me a quid. "You mean you'm going down the Green Dragon"' she said.

'You're lucky to have such an understanding wife,' I remarked. 'You're not bad at understanding things yourself, coming with me, and asking no questions.'

'Aw.' In confusion Lol offered me a mint. 'I'm not saying I'm not curious, but I reckon you'll tell me when you're ready.'

As we walked the last part of Sandhill Rise we kept glancing at each other, both struck by the absurdity of the situation. Like kids on a scrumping expedition we had met half-way up the hill, on the other side of the park to our own. In such a confined town every movement was observed and any deviation from convention noted. Lol and I could argue all we liked that we were old friends, that we had helped each other through the usual crises of birth and death and burst water pipes, but no self-respecting guardian of Sandhill morality would accept our plea. Friendship between people of the same sex was regarded with suspicion; between a man and woman it was considered unprintable. I had no wish to cause Lol or his wife any trouble.

Even so, for a few moments I paused beside the old gateway to Forge House, Lol waiting while I stood silently, paying homage. Nothing but the gateway was left; a close of houses having been built on the site of the Lakins' home and gardens. The stonework was 'a bit fancy' no doubt, and had caught the architect's eye as a feature worth preserving. Then, turning away, I walked on towards the edge of the Heath.

Children were playing around the old mess huts, kicking a ball or chasing each other down the shelters. I smelt the same stink of dog piddle and tramp that used to fascinate and repel me as a child. Goodness knew who still used those mouldering shelters but there were cigarette stubs near the entrances, and in their dark insides the flash of a can or broken glass caught the failing sun. Near us, an obsolete sign announced *War Department. Keep Out.* Broken barbed wire coiled from posts and concrete foundations. Crossing the camp, we took the path up the Heath proper, the wind off the hill blowing fresh and clean as we did so. We were already above the fumes and noise of the town, and that ancient track took us into the past with every step.

It was a steep climb and after ten minutes we were glad to pause and look back. The route was not the one we were used to, but Bircham's Coppice had gone, and we had no choice. Below us, the great gash of road crossed our view, the red clay at its edges giving it the appearance of an inflamed sore. The scene was a little less smoky than in my childhood, but much more confined. Even the handkerchiefs of green had gone: the bomb sites where an odd field mouse could still be caught by a patient cat. Without Bircham's Coppice it was stifling, worse in spring than in winter since one instinctively hoped for leaves and flowers.

'It do'arf look a dump,' Lol remarked. 'It wasn't this bad when we were kids. Or do you just remember thegood things?'

'A bit of both I imagine,' I replied, smiling.

Beyond the last of the concrete posts the ferns began. Here there were the beginnings of scrubby trees, mostly birch and beech with the occasional hawthorn or holly marking the line of an ancient boundary. Ruins of building were almost lost under growth. All around us was a wild beauty. Chimneys sprouted trees, trees sprouted chimneys. The first ragwort of the season was growing amongst the ruins, and above us the clouds passed in dark bands, creating a changing pattern of green and gold on the open space awaiting us. In delight I saw a butterfly alight on a young nettle, where it lingered, wings open to warm in the sun. There was nowhere else for miles a butterfly could have been seen except perhaps the odd tortoiseshell on a garden buddleia, and a sense of the preciousness of Miss Lakin's estate came to me. She had been right to preserve it by any means she could. Nature was returning there, healing the scars of a hundred years.

Turning off the main track we took a path that led upwards towards the Shepherd's Lead. A sign proclaimed *Danger. Keep Out* but by unspoken consent we both ignored it.

Lol switched on his torch. 'Fancy a bit of exploring?' he asked. 'It's still safe. I went down only two weeks ago after me dog. Silly mutt ran after a rabbit, and to make two silly mutts I went in as well. The roof's fallen in at the bottom, but the air's still sweet.'

What form of madness overtook us I couldn't diagnose, but climbing over the planks that barred the entrance, we went in. The coldness of the air touched my face. Our torches lit only the sides and roof immediately around us; in front was blackness. 'Imagine working here all your life.' I said. 'And having to drag every bit of coal back to the surface on a sledge.'

124

'Or in a basket on your back,' Lol agreed. 'You'd be so tired after twelve or fourteen hours of it you'd do nothing but eat and go to bed. No wonder the poor sods had such large families. It'd be your only pleasure between dinner and sleep.'

We reached the place where the branch of the shaft entered, and there was space to sit against the wall.

'Switch your torch off a second,' Lol suggested.

We turned off our lights simultaneously. The darkness was a tangible thing, filling my mouth and eyes. 'It's terrifying,' I admitted.

'You never see darkness like it in town. There's always some light, even at three or four in the morning. And to think all they had was a bit of candle.' For a few moments we lingered, using only one torch so as not to flatten both batteries. 'I wanted to be quiet with you a bit,' I said awkwardly. 'Just to talk. Nothing funny.'

'We used to talk for hours didn't we? Putting the world to rights.'

He sat down against the wall of the shaft, indicating I should do the same. 'Tell me why you asked me to come up here with you.'

'I wanted to look round – but I thought I'd be safer with company. I've been making a few enquiries, like you asked. Can you keep a secret?'

'Cross me heart and hope to die.'

'I think Miss Lakin gave the deeds to my Great Aunt Mary.'

'But they asked her earlier this year! Mr Homer reckoned she was too senile to know what he was talking about.'

I laughed out loud. 'Aunt Mary's as senile as you or me, probably less so. Of course, I've no proof, but Aunt Mary and Miss Lakin were clearly close friends – that's obvious from a collection of old postcards she gave me last week. There's a little writing box she guards very carefully ... she's already said she wants to take it with her to Arton. I think the deeds are in there.'

Lol stared at me in amazement. 'But why didn't she let on? Miss Lakin died years ago. I mean, the land must be worth thousands. Even the Council would have to pay Compensation.'

'I imagine she promised Miss Lakin she wouldn't sell, unless the Heath was to be preserved.'

There was a pause between us and silence around us. 'Do you reckon she'll leave it to your family?' Lol asked.

'If she does, I'll have to make sure we don't sell, shan't I? We should be able to do something better with it than build warehouses on it, though without money I don't know what. The shafts must be fenced, or I'm sure we'll be held responsible if there's an accident.' Water spotted along the floor ahead. 'Miss Lakin trusted my great aunt – judging by her cards she even handed over the running of the business to her for a while, though don't ask me why. I don't intend to do anything that would break that trust.'

Leaning against the wall Lol rubbed his chin reflectively. 'Is it legal just to give land?' he asked.

'I don't know. If there was a proper will it'd be all right. When Aunt Mary and I are alone at Arton I'll try and discuss it with her. I thought I'd tip you off, but please, not a word to anyone or we'll have developers sniffing round the next morning.'

'You're a bright girl,' Lol said quietly. 'Always have been.' He considered my information for some minutes. 'Do you think your great aunt intended you to work it out?'

I was impressed that he too had seen the possibility. 'She may have done,' I agreed. 'She's always been intensely private – words don't come easily to her. Perhaps it was her way of telling me.'

'When do you go to Arton?'

'Next week – straight after Easter.'

'Are you wise going? I'd hate the place after what happened. I dunno. I can't make you out. You saw a friend drowned and nearly got drowned yourself – that'd be enough to send most people round the twist, without finding the body into the bargain, yet it never seemed to affect you.'

Sitting against the cold shaft wall I tried to think of something to say. 'You don't understand,' I said lamely. 'It's not that it didn't affect me. It changed me forever. It dried me up somehow. I've never felt anything, not deeply, since it happened. I couldn't feel at the time. Everyone else was crying or shouting and I was completely calm, as if it was all happening to someone else. It was me that told Mr Booth and called the police. Lydia just stood there screaming and Paul was too shocked to do anything. It was like something inside me died in that water – emotion, whatever you like to call it. It's never come alive again. It's better that way perhaps.'

'It was shock I suppose,' Lol agreed. 'It affects everyone in different ways. When I came off me bike I laughed, made a big joke of it, yet me leg was gone. I wasn't being brave, it was some sort of reaction.' He smiled. 'The way I remember, you weren't all calm and collected as a kid, that's for sure. Your Aunt Lizzie used to be terrified you'd run off with the first handsome stranger. I'd only got to appear and she was out. She was convinced I was going to have a crack at you.'

'You make me sound like the north face of the Eiger,' I complained.

'You might as well have been, for all the chance I stood.'

'I was a very moral young girl,' I insisted, laughing. 'I'd have never thought of handsome strangers, if Aunt Lizzie hadn't been always talking about them.'

Suddenly the torch went out, leaving us in that terrifying darkness. 'We'd better go,' Lol said, switching on the other light. 'I don't fancy having to feel my way back to the surface.' He helped me up and we brushed the dust off our clothes. 'Take care of yourself. I don't like to think of you getting hurt again.'

'I'll be all right,' I assured him.

We began to walk back to the surface. 'Is Josie what you hoped for?' I asked.

'She's a good sort. She's seen a lot of trouble in her life, been married before – I suppose you've heard that? It didn't work out. Well, she was only seventeen and her boy wasn't much older. I mean, you're still growing up then aren't you? At that age I was tearing around on me bike thinking I was a right villain, but I settled down. There's blokes I know who were the apple of teacher's eye and are sods now.' He had lost his place in his argument and paused, trying to recollect it. Introspection was. not familiar to him. 'Josie's husband walked out on her after a couple of years, leaving her with a little 'un to support. She got whatever work she could. I'd like to see some of them that turn their noses up at her, coping on a few quid a week. Then, well, the kiddy got knocked down and she seemed to turn to me somehow. Dunno why.' I knew, but it was not appropriate to say so. 'I've no complaints. She's a good wife to me, and having a second family like, she's happy herself. I won't have nothing said against her.'

'I gather a great deal has been,' I replied gently.

'Aw – you know this place. Sticking our nose into other people's business is the main occupation. Still I'm not grumbling. Not much, anyway. I'd have no real grievance if *Langdon's* hadn't shut.'

An arch of daylight had appeared, growing larger as we walked. 'I'll keep in touch about the Heath,' I promised. 'If I learn anything more from Aunt Mary I'll tip you off – in confidence of course.'

'Of course.'

Sleep and I were in dispute that night.

Lol's concern had forced me to think of Arton again, and now I could not stop. For hours I lay in a state of wakefulness that made my headache. When I did sleep I woke wishing I had not done so. The nightmares I could cope with; they were only fantasy. It was the half waking pictures that distressed me most. Every night after Mike's death I had seen the same image. I thought it would never

128

leave me, but time makes even such terrors tolerable. Gradually it became a matter of bad dreams on occasional nights, until ultimately it hardly returned. Now it was back with me, every detail as vivid, even to the scent of water and reed.

'We've been looking too far upstream,' I shouted to Paul. 'Remember how that plank washed up beyond the bridge, and then shifted down to Pelham Rocks? I'm going down the rocks. You can do what you please.'

We waded amongst the reeds below Arton Bridge, neither of us wanting to speak, hating each other but held by a shared fear. I went on ahead, wanting to be free of him. The silence of the rockface above me was welcome, though the air in that bend of the river was cold and damp, like the smell of death. The water scarcely moved beneath the shadow of the rocks, so deep was the channel. There were stories of a great pike which lived there, and of bathers who disappeared without trace. I began to feel afraid, there on my own, but I waded on, keeping to the edge of the water, lest I too slip and fall.

And then I saw the hand. It lay open, fingers a little curled. In horror I parted the tangle and found him lying as the storm had cast him, on his side. I knew it must be him, but could not at first recognise the features, so bloated and discoloured was the face, and half-hidden in mud. Bending down, I turned the head so that I could see the whole. If I had been less appalled I would have screamed, but no sound came from my throat. The whole of the one side of his face was smashed, crushed by some heavy object which had driven against him – the keel of the upturned boat perhaps, or the tree itself. Even the eye was pushed downward out of place. There was little blood; the river had washed the flesh clean, though mud caked across it now. Mechanically I took out my handkerchief, and dipping it in the water, tried to wash the mud away. The skin came away with it, making everything worse. In frustration I started to cry. Paul must not see him as he was.

Finally I had cleaned off the worst of the mud, and turned the face back gently on to some broken reeds which I laid beneath it. In the distance I could hear the sound of Paul's voice. 'Martie! Martie – what do you think you're playing at? Where are you, Martie?'

He must not come yet. Wringing out my handkerchief, I flattened it across my hand until it was clean and smooth again, then laid it across Mike's shattered face. I had not closed the eyes, I remembered. People always closed the eyes of the dead; I had read it in books.

There was no time for me to do so. Paul came running across the field above the bank, and along the path into the shadow of Pelham Rocks. 'Where are you, Martie?' he called again. There was a note of fear in his voice, as if he dreaded something had happened to me too, but when he saw me standing there his face was cold again.

'Don't come down here,' I said.

'You've found him!'

'Don't come,' I repeated. 'It'll do no good. Run back and fetch someone. We'll need someone to carry him back to town.'

But he would not listen to me, and crying out, ran down the bank towards me. 'Poor Mike,' I heard him say, and then he turned the body towards him.

In fury I got up and walked around the bedroom. 1 dared not switch on the light, in case the clack woke Aunt Lizzie next door. And so in the darkness I sat at the window, staring out on the street. It must be after midnight; the lamps had been switched off. Feeling cold, I got back into bed. A dog barked, the sound suspended on dampness and cold. A dog had barked at the farm, when we walked down the track. Paul was carrying his brother's body, though in life Mike had been by far the stronger. How so slight a boy found strength I could not think even now, but grief will make us all do irrational things, I suppose. He would not let me help, threw the handkerchief away; would not speak to me,

130

beyond that first awful statement. 'This is your doing,' he said. That was all. The whole ghastly way to the farmhouse he walked apart from me, silent, hateful, as if I were not there, not grieving too. In the end I could stand it no longer and when I heard the sound of feet coming towards the door turned away. If he wished to be alone with his grief, then I would not force myself upon him.

Getting up again I put on my bath robe so that I could sit at the window longer. Impatiently I tried to recite to myself some silly poem I had learnt at school about a Highwayman, but I could get no further than *'Over the cobbles he clattered and clanged.'* 'An example of alliteration children,' I heard Miss Brown say. *'Over the cobbles he clattered and clanged.'* It did not drive away the sound of Paul's weeping, heard softly beyond the hedge. I turned my head. I too had been crying, but inside me somehow tears would not come. I envied Paul his grief; it was something open and healthy, whereas mine was all inward and unexpressed. People thought I was cold, that I didn't feel as a normal girl would do in such circumstances. Aunt Lizzie called me unnatural. But I could not cry, not as Paul cried. When I turned Mike's face and saw the skin brush away under my fingers crying stopped – for always.

Something phutted against the windowpane and I realised with surprise that it was snowing, the wet splatting snow of late March. Shivering, I tried to distinguish the flakes as they came down. My hands were stiff with cold. There would be no more sleep that night. I must risk the sound of the light switch, or drive myself half demented. I would read a while. It was about time I settled to a bit of work.

I'm not sure how I ended up addressing my old school, whether Dad set me up or Great Aunt Mary volunteered me, but it later proved to have been an important visit. At the time I found it distinctly embarrassing.

Miss McClean ushered me down the corridor, talking all the time about the achievements of her 'owd girrls'. The same smell of chalk and hot plimsoles as used to greet the owd girrls fifteen years ago greeted me, and the corridor still leaked in the same places. I felt nervous, as if I were about to receive one of Miss McClean's dressing downs. Why it was never dressing up I never worked out – the association of any downward motion with Miss McClean being difficult. Even her chin was stiffened to keep her upper lip company.

In my day 'Muckie McClean' (Muckie Drawers as we knew her) was the terror of the Latin room, rolling her r's around 'A, ab, absque, corum, de.' I hated her with the venom only an unclassical schoolgirl can nourish. And now she was Head of the School and leading me down the corridor to speak to her 'boys and girls' on the virtues of hard work, achievement and overseas travel.

In a flurry of eau de cologne and permanent pleated skirt she led me on to the stage. One finger held aloft silenced a babbling throng. 'I would like to introduce Dr Cooper,' she proclaimed, 'who has come to talk to us about Australia. Dr Cooper is one of our most successful owd girrls. While she was here she distinguished herself as a scholar, and took an active part in school societies, representing the school in the second eleven hockey team, and being particularly noticed in the end of year plays. After winning a scholarship, she went on to University to study Sociology'- (a slight hint of disapproval entered Miss McClean's voice but she overcame it). 'She is now a lecturer in Australia and has written several books, one of which is already a standard work. Boys and girls, I hand you over to Dr Cooper.'

Having aroused a fine dislike for me in the mind of every self-respecting listener, Miss McClean stepped back. At first I thought it was Lydia she was remembering. I was a hopeless mess at school – aggressive, awkward, not even good academically until about the fourth form when I suddenly began to understand the language my teachers were using. Joining the school in the second year after we moved to Sandhill from St Bart's didn't help. The second eleven team was host to me for a very short time, a matter of a few rides on the bus as reserve, and no one being more maimed than usual those weeks, I never got a full game. If I was noticed in the school plays, it was because of my gift for playing slave girls, who entered left, spoke one line, and exited right. One year I was left out of the programme altogether, and was credited on a slip of cyclostyled paper stapled inside. For months afterwards I was known as 'Addendum'. Which all goes to show the retrospective effects of fame, but left me with a horrible start to my speech.

Somehow I managed it. Faces beneath me actually smiled and the lengthened assembly was clearly not too bad a way of missing first lesson. As I talked, I looked down at the girls in their grey skirts and blouses. They seemed happier and more relaxed than we had been. No doubt they hated their uniform as much as we did, but at least they were permitted a waist. When I sat in those rows the standard schoolgirl shape was up-ended plum, gymslips being designed to mask all traces of femininity. I imagine that was what gave the quick grope behind the bicycle sheds half its thrill. Exploring beneath those serge tubes must have been like trying a lucky dip.

Later Miss McClean walked with me back towards the main lobby. It was kind of me to spare the time, she said. I had spoken very well, though she had thought at first I sounded unusually nervous. It must be difficult having my father on the staff nowadays.

Her introduction had confused me, I replied. I didn't recognise myself. Most of it simply wasn't true I added, smiling to soften my criticism. I lived in Lydia's shadow all through the Junior forms. I was nowhere near as gifted as her.

'I know that,' Miss McClean added brightly. 'Pack of lies, but we have a sprinkling of high-fliers who might be encouraged. Besides, Miss Harpur will be sending a report to the local press. They might print some of it.'

Her cynicism was so outrageous I laughed. 'I hope they do,' I remarked. 'For your sake and the school's, though all this returned heroine stuff makes me feel an idiot.'

We were moving towards an uneasy understanding after years of mistrust. We would never like each other, but liking is not the only foundation for respect. I asked after the school's progress. It was a trying time Miss McClean admitted, with so few opportunities for school leavers, but otherwise the comprehensive system was working quite well. One had to adapt and Sandhill was becoming isolated in its refusal to follow other towns. After all, it had always been her school and she had managed to keep standards up, whoever was in power. (She spoke as if she envisaged standards fixed to a pole, as in a sense I think she did.) This year was the school's Jubilee – presumably my father had reminded me. She and her staff were looking for some means of celebrating, not with a party but something that would last. There had been various suggestions: a new science block, even a statue, though what Sandhill would do with a statue she couldn't imagine.

'I'm afraid I can,' I admitted.

Miss McClean smiled. Yes, so could she, now I mentioned it. No, what she wanted was a project that would benefit the whole community. In a sense it would be her own memorial, for she had spent her whole teaching career till then at Sandhill Grammar, and as I knew, she had been a pupil there herself. At the entrance lobby we paused. 'See if you can come up with an idea for our project,' she said. 'You often used to have bright ideas. You could let me know through your father.'

I took the hand offered me. 'I'll try,' I promised. 'I owe this place a good deal. For all its faults it was a window, for those of us who wanted to look out.'

Awkwardly I turned to leave and pushed the door when I should have pulled.

I had one final appointment to keep before leaving for Sweetbriar. To please Aunt Lizzie I went to chapel, to hear the Easter performance of Stainer's *Crucifixion*. She was a member of the choir, having still a shaky but powerful contralto voice. The seasons of her life were marked by a progression from *The Messiah* to *Crucifixion* to *Elijah* and back to *Messiah*. It was traditional for all visitors and long-lost relatives to be taken to hear her sing, so feeling conspicuous I walked with Dad and the others up Sandhill Rise, and entered the chapel that had been almost home in my youth. It was huge, solemnly Victorian, the sort of building that takes itself so seriously it becomes unintentionally comic. Around the vast balcony were painted the reminders *Labour Overcomes All* and *Honour the Lord in Your Daily Work*, values which had built the chapel itself and the villas and factories crowding the valley beneath it. The pulpit was a monstrous affair with a canopy designed to brain any speaker forgetting the virtue of humility, and around the communion table ran a rail only surpassed in brasso consumption by the plaques that were screwed to chairs and walls – any flat surface in fact.

In its prime Sandhill Rise Wesleyan was magnificent but even when I was a child it was declining, though we still had our Sunday School teas on trestle tables and Whitsuntide Walks. With the advent of the family car it became difficult to fill even one of Meddicks' charas for an outing, and the charms of TV did for many of the meetings. Now the building was a liability, too costly to heat, with the regular congregation scattered around the pews like currants in an overbaked cake.

That night the rows were better filled however, and the doors to the balcony had been opened. Remembering the joys of stained glass and views over Sandhill, I begged to 'go upstairs', and humouring me, Harry and Sue and Dad trudged behind. We arrived as the chorus of behatted women and bald men filed into the choir rows either side of the organ – as splendid as any fairground instrument.

135

Aunt Lizzie was resplendent too, in new hat and bifocals both of which gave her an unfortunate tendency to peer down her nose. I watched her settling into her seat and could predict every one of her fifty separate movement: opening and shutting her handbag and taking out her glasses case; opening the case and putting away her bifocals, shutting the case and putting it back in her handbag; taking out her second case and opening it to reveal her favourite pair of reading specs ... By the time she had chatted to Mrs Homer and nodded to Mrs Hope, I was ready to scream. Other people's aunts have similar habits but it is the mannerisms of one's own relatives that become unendurable.

I was annoyed by my reaction. One of the difficulties of adulthood is that you begin to see everyone's point of view. Aunt Lizzie was a good woman. She had done her best for us. The trouble is, good women are often insufferable. Their virtue gives them an interest in everyone else's sin, to know what to avoid I suppose.

When we were young we provided Aunt Lizzie with plenty of material for research. Mum had no idea of discipline. If we wanted extra biscuits we got extra biscuits. If homework was too difficult we were told to put it away and it would all come right in the morning. We worshipped her and Dad encouraged us. She was his dear, brilliant Katie. When he was home from St Bart's he spoilt her irrevocably, pampering her gaiety and beauty, because he could not believe such a bright butterfly creature could have chosen to rest in his home. Dad was so very mundane, his idea of romance limited to a cup of tea in bed on Sunday and two weeks in Weston. Mum's mind was full of dreams of knights in shining armour. She read inordinately, though her mental portfolio was made up of bits and pieces gathered enthusiastically but without order. In her youth she had been to a smart but cynical private school, and given the opportunity, I think she would have gone to University and become a scholar, the sort of long-skirted researcher one sees in places like the British Museum, ferreting at some by-way of chivalry, and leaving worldly matters to those more gifted – or paid – to handle them. As it was, she had to cope with three small children and an eccentric house on her own each term-time, or admit defeat to the other wives at St Bart's. We respected her determination to lead her own life, but suffered a perpetual chaos of half-done washing up, and library books with pastry prints on their pages.

Into this disorganised household Aunt Lizzie found herself consigned by chance and her own sense of duty. When her brother accepted a post in Italy and her sister in-law was taken seriously ill, no one expected Aunt Lizzie to step into the breach. She was not usually associated with breach stepping, but Grandmother died, leaving her feeling unneeded. She had always maintained her brother's wife was 'not strong', as if marriage required an ability to lift ten kilo weights and her predictions were confirmed. Katie should go to Florence too, and get properly better. She, Aunt Lizzie, would look after us.

It was a kind gesture and gave Mum a year's freedom but it wasn't a practical one. Aunt Lizzie had no experience of teenagers and she rightly said we had been ruined by our mother. She grew increasingly horrified by our carelessness with morals and dirty knickers. We must be taught proper ways before it was too late, manners and the Bible – all sadly lacking from our repertoire.

Poor Aunt Lizzie. She had no grounding in new-fangled psychology. All she had was her sense of duty, her Bible and the key to the attic door. I spent a lot of time in that attic reading her Bible. Had she known the passages I was reading she might not have been so keen to shut me there.

Looking at my aunt across the distance of a Victorian chapel and twenty years, I almost forgave her. I hoped she could forgive me.

The choir began to sing. It was four years since I had been into the chapel, and that was for my mother's funeral. I felt like an outsider on show, conscious that I had been recognised by some of the congregation beside me. Trying to appear unconcerned, I looked out of the window to my right. Through it I could see over the chapel yard and the road, then in a gap between two villas, the sweep of the valley. Victoria Park was already yellow in the haze of a cold spring evening. To the east was the running sore of the new road, to the west an area of empty sheds where *Langdon's* and *Lakin's* forges used to be.

Slowly the music began to demand my attention. I had come expecting to need patience and make allowances; instead I was increasingly aware of beauty. The acoustics were good, the choir only a little less fine than in its heyday, and the piece known and loved. Though the outside was raw and cold, inside there was warmth and security. Some good remained in Sandhill.

The realisation set me evaluating my own attitude to the chapel and Sandhill generally. As a student I poured scorn on my childhood; killed my accent overnight. Yet my values were those of Sandhill, and not just Sandhill generally, but Sandhill Rise Wesleyan. The Reverend Grace and a whole series of sermons had taught me to suspect the temptations of the flesh, and value the mind – the spirit perhaps – above all else.

Reverend Grace – his name used to strike me as one of the great misnomers of history – believed in keeping his congregation to heel with graphic portrayals of the terrors of Hell and the joys of Heaven. If you were 'In' you got the works, harps, angels, cloud cushions; if you were 'out' you were for it, the long fall, nasty little devils, boiling oil. There is a violent streak in the Black Country character I think, which appreciates a good bullying. The Reverend Grace packed the balcony as well as the hall, long after such theology was out of fashion elsewhere. His congregations used to pour out of the chapel yard, congratulating themselves on being the 'In' lot, and contemplating a good dinner. No matter how much my reason, and to do them justice my parents, tried to balance his influence, his sermons used to make me wake in the night with fear. Though I was barely fourteen when he retired, he coloured my view of the physical world for years, with Aunt Lizzie acting as a kind of treasurer for his ideas after his departure. I knew before I did anything that it was likely to prove a sin, and that I would be found out. I usually was.

Poor Paul did not stand much chance against such an influence. He had no such hang-ups. There was a spontaneity in everything he did whether it was in love or anger. With the greater wisdom or caution of adulthood I would now be much better able to cope with such a situation, just as Sandhill Wesleyan had mellowed, but it was what I was *then* that mattered.

The music rose higher and higher, carrying me to other services and other *Crucifixions*. It took me to Arton chapel and an Easter when I was about eight, and it was my mother who was singing. She had a sweet, pure soprano. Her music shaking in her hand she stood before that much smaller congregation and we thought she was the most beautiful woman on earth. Even Isaac Booth came over to praise her, and old man that he was, we loved him for it. Of course he was too infirm by then to play much himself, but he had music in his soul and we valued his judgment. Thoughts of Isaac led me on to Great Aunt Mary, sitting at the front of the hall below me. She had been collected by car before we left, as befitted her status as honoured member of the church. Like Isaac, she had wasted in body but not in spirit, and I respected her for it. The next weeks at Sweetbriar would no doubt be difficult, but I began to look forward to them as a time of quietness, and friendship even. It would be good to get Aunt Mary talking. And perhaps she did own the Heath – that was an intriguing possibility. I felt almost childishly excited.

My mind had travelled a long way, the choir receding from my thoughts. Images of Arton returned to me: Isaac playing the fiddle or flute at a Vicarage garden party while fat little girl guides danced on the lawn; a church organ and the old man teaching his grandson; the school at Larch Lane with its pocket handkerchief of playground and coloured windows ... dredging for sticklebacks while Paul held the jar.

For thirteen years I had suppressed such images, crowding them out with constant business because they always led to other, awful pictures, to that blue-black face and bloated body. Now I felt I dared consider them a little.

Beyond the empty forges the sun was dropping in a fat balloon, its light catching the glass roofs and windows as if the furnaces had been relit. It was an eerie sight, something I had not seen since the days when Sandhill was thriving, and Lakins' and Langdons' throbbed in a frenzy of competition. Turning round so that I could see out of the rear window I watched the Heath begin to blacken. With a last flare the sunlight caught the lower edges of the wasteland, and ruined chimneys and roofs took on an appearance of solidity, as the gold filled in missing bricks or shaded out broken doors. Why couldn't the Heath come alive again? What the sun could do, people might do also.

My skin had developed that strange tingling sensation I have occasionally felt before, when an idea for a book or article has come to me. I must talk to Charlie Warwick – and Miss McClean. There was potential in my idea for the memorial she wanted. We might get the children to clear the rubbish though we would have to keep them well away from the open shafts. Miss McClean would know her way round the latest bureaucracy. I was out of touch, and acronyms like MSC or WOW bewildered me. (I thought the last was an outsize fashion shop, till I discovered it was a course for women). Charlie could advise on the history of the place. Lol Jackson would be interested too. Securing the old shafts and clearing broken rails would be a huge job but that sort of work would be no problem to big Lol, and might give him a sense of being needed. As I thought about my vision I became increasingly excited.

Then I pulled myself up sharply. I did not know for certain the Heath was Aunt Mary's. Even if it was, she would will it to Dad or Aunt Lizzie. No one would blame them if they decided to take the money offered by the first developer who came along. Miss

McClean might think a Heath a peculiar memorial. I must find out who owned the land, and work out my scheme in detail so that I could persuade them, and Charlie, Lol Jackson – half a town if need be. I would also need to find out more about the Lakins, for a good story is always a help in catching people's imaginations...

The music had reached a crescendo and ashamed of my lack of attention I turned back, to find Mrs Homer glaring at me, and Harry blowing his nose.

FOUR: White Water

We arrived in a confusion of blankets and borrowed saucepans, dumping everything on the track at the top of our land. 'I kept meaning to do summat about that,' Harry admitted, kicking the broken gate to one side. He carried our cases to the verandah. I followed, discovering that a well-placed heel could shoot one of the wooden steps to an angle of forty-five degrees. A coot watched me, worried by the prospect of new neighbours.

Gingerly I went down the path to the bottom of the garden. The lawn was meadow grass, blooming with early buttercups and daisies, and tendrils of vetch were taking hold near the trees. Self-sewn broccoli had over taken the patch where Uncle John used to grow his vegetables though raspberry canes survived along the edge. In a wild way the place was more beautiful than ever, the wooden bungalow improved by the air of mystery that neglect often brings. I thought the jetty might still stand my weight, but was not willing to test it, and instead peered over the bank to see if the rowing boat was still there. I found it half submerged under the willows, with a rope tying it to our mooring post.

It was a lovely spring afternoon, and seen in the slanting sun, few places could have been more enchanting.

'I've got the door open,' Harry called to me. 'And there's a chair waiting for Aunt Mary. We'll help her down now if you like.'

Stiff after so long cramped in the back of a car, Aunt Mary needed pulling and pushing to get her out, and then her left leg would not behave itself until she had leant against the bonnet and muttered imprecations against old age in general, and her own in particular. Finally we shifted her down the path. Seeing how lame she was, I wondered if I had been wise in bringing her, but her legs would ease up soon she assured me, and her obvious pleasure at being back at Sweet briar was reward enough. Afterwards Harry and I went back to unload the car. For a few moments we paused on the verandah, recalling the times we had come to the chalet as children. 'We've had some fun here, haven't we?' I remarked.

Harry grinned. 'Remember the time I went through the roof?' he asked. 'I'll never forget Dad's face when I landed in his dinner. Ruined his sausages he said. He didn't half belt me. I would never have thought him capable.'

'Oh, Dad'll defend his sausages,' I replied, laughing. 'Besides, you were climbing a daft branch. You were lucky not to break your neck.'

Trying to tuck his shirt back into his belt Harry grinned again. Harry and shirts parted company. As a child he always had a dirty band round his vests where they'd hung over his trousers. 'I'm glad you're getting some use out of the place,' he said. 'It's been a refuge whenever we've needed it.' Giving up the unequal struggle with his shirt he set off to the car.

'By the way,' he called as he emerged from the boot with Aunt Mary's hat on his head and the crockery box in his arms. 'The cooker's not working. I forgot to tell you.'

In amusement and anger I turned on him. 'How the hell am I to feed us?'

'There's always the chippie downtown. I'll have another look at the gas bottle before I go. There's probably a dead mouse in it somewhere.'

'Is the kettle working?' I wailed.

'Oh, that's all right! I couldn't survive down here otherwise.'

With the practice of a whole childhood I aimed a pair of shoes at him.

The hat slipped in surprise. 'You nearly made me drop the crockery,' he protested. 'It's not my fault things go wrong. There's a conspiracy against me.' Plodding back with the hat perched on his head he stood on the loose board and nearly removed his kneecap. 'Seriously though,' he added. He had a way of saying that phrase which sounded like the interval turn at a working man's club. 'I'm glad you're going to stay here a bit with Aunt Mary. It's broken my heart seeing it going to wrack and ruin, but Aunt Mary hasn't been able to do anything lately and Sue resents every hour I spend here, and as for paying any money on it ...' His voice was genuinely serious now. 'There's a sort of selfishness in our Sue which can't abide people having different tastes to her own.' It was the first time I had heard him speak ill of his wife, but the judgment confirmed my own.

Knowing Harry too well to reply, I followed him indoors.

Aunt Mary had not exaggerated when she said the bungalow had been a bit neglected. A smell of mould greeted us as we entered the kitchen and there were mouse-droppings near the cupboard. Something long legged and malevolent had made its home beside the wastebin and a spider with peculiar habits watched from beneath the window ledge. Fortunately water still ran from the tap when I turned it on, though the gushings and groanings that preceded it would have done justice to a Hammer Horror movie. Harry had kept the building together structurally; new boards hammered into the floor and fresh putty were witness to his efforts, but with Sue actively disliking the place I suppose he was right to be careful about doing more. He used it as a fishing retreat he said, and valued it as somewhere quiet he could make to, from the demands of unwilling clients and a persistent wife. He usually 'dossed down' on the camp bed, he said – a crumpled sleeping bag and a pair of stale socks proved his claim.

Together we cleared the worst of the mess while Aunt Mary sat in her chair and smiled like a cat in the sun. Grunting in response to Harry's jokes, I removed a foul-smelling dishcloth complete with earwigs' nest from the bottom cupboard. Harry was amused at my lack of concern for all things creepy and crawly, but as I said, when you've found spiders the size of your fist in your bedroom, earwigs are merely practice. The cooker was all right once the calor was properly turned on, and after an hour's work I felt the kitchen was in a state in which making a meal would not actually poison us. Then we sat in the main-room and ate baked beans on toast. Afterwards Harry repaired the bottom fence, using an old bedstead he knew would come in handy someday. We tied the slats of the gate together with twine and the hinges needed no more than half a can of oil. None of our efforts would stop a determined old lady but Aunt Mary was too sensible to take midnight strolls along the river path. Then Harry left us, kissing me wetly on one check.

As soon as Aunt Mary was safely in bed with a book I stood on the verandah in the dusk. In the silence of evening I heard a water vole plop from the bank, and the alarm call of a blackbird. The scent of damp grass and water was sweet. Two figures walked along the river path towards me, emerged as a courting couple, then walked on. In the garden next door a cat was crouching, tail swishing. I wondered if the Marsh boys still lived there. The garden looked well-tended and the chalet was in good order. Older than us, they had been good friends nonetheless. They were GI babies, born to two sisters within months of each other, after their fathers had returned to America. In the city their mothers would have been ostracised but in Arton they were cared for, though not invited to tea. Poor silly girls people used to say. And so the two girls moved into one of the empty chalets when their mother said there wasn't room for them in her cottage, and Jackie and Sammy swam in the river or went scrumping and brought us stolen fruit. They made a tremendous fuss of us when we were little. Standing there in the dusk I thought of what Harry had said about Sweetbriar being a refuge. All the houses along that stretch of river were refuges of one sort or another. The chalets owed their existence to the war and fleeing Black Country families who scraped together a few pounds to buy a plot from Mr Lakin, then built a wooden bungalow with their own hands and a fine disregard for planning. When I was a girl even Aunt Mary and Uncle John had an earth closet at the top of the garden, and we used to pad out with a torch in one hand and cut-up squares of *Radio Times* in the other. I used to look forward to a good read. Several of the chalets still had no sanitation, having been left by their original owners to local folk too poor to afford a proper house. And River Cottage too – well, that was never very special, though Henry Lakin was a good landlord and saw to it that that there was water there. It was after Christopher took over that the place went down so badly.

Walking along the river path I forced myself to look over the hedge surrounding River Cottage. Despite the failing light, what I saw shocked me. The garden and orchard had the appearance of over-use which comes from attempting to live on insufficient land. Hens scratched around on ground already bare, and bits of corrugated iron provided shelter for a few geese and ducks, though these obviously spent most of their time escaping through gaps in the hedge and wandering along the track. A goat was tethered to the fence and browsed on whatever it could reach, sheltering at night in a stable made from a tarpaulin weighted with tyres. There was an appearance of neglect I did not recall. Brambles were beginning to gain hold and weeds grew amongst the vegetables. Beside the house was a car on blocks.

My eyes stung with pity. However much the Arton boys might have jeered, River Cottage had been a model of country thrift, with hens cackling in contentment and apple trees banded and staked. Now the chorus of 'Tinker! Tinker!' seemed justified.

Yet when I looked more closely I was aware that a return to self-respect had begun. Broken panes were being replaced and the fencing repaired. An area of bramble near our land was being cleared, the refuse piled neatly ready for burning. It was clear Saul had been ill, or perhaps had left with the fair as he used to in bad times, and now he had returned was taking the place in hand. Yet even as I considered the idea I saw Saul sitting in the half-light, a chair pushed into the kitchen doorway, and I knew from the sticks beside him that he must have met with some accident. I knew too who had begun that return to self-respect.

I felt confused and ill at ease. I had returned expecting to hate Paul – wanted, to do so. Now I found myself respecting him.

Startling me, Janie Booth appeared from the wash house, carrying a bowl of meal for the fowls. In the dusk she appeared scarcely any older, her figure slight as ever and wrapped in a blue pinny, just as I remembered. Calling to the hens she scattered meal in a practised arc to encourage them to return for the night. Then she filled the feeding trays inside the huts. There was a timelessness about her movements which I found touching, my emotion increased by the song she sang as she worked. Janie was always singing, thin Irish sounding tunes no one else could make sense of, but that seemed to linger in her head since childhood. It was too much for me and I went indoors.

As soon as breakfast was finished, I explored Arton. I had thought so often about Beechmast Lane and the Silent Wood I was longing to visit them. Most emigres share the same unreasonableness: the assumption that the place they have left will remain the same, awaiting their return, as if a ghost should resurrect and expect dinner to have been kept warm in the oven. I wanted to go the same walks, climb the same trees, eat the same pink ice cream. And of course half of those things had gone.

In fact most of the changes had been for good. True, the toy shop had been attacked by space invaders, but the trendy little craft shops behind the church were acceptable, and the general appearance of the town was improved. When we were children the lovely eighteenth century houses were in a terrible state, with slumping roofs and evil-smelling backyards. Many of the people were products of in-breeding in a small community, a bit simple and inclined to prejudice. In earlier times they would have tied the whole Booth family to stakes and watched them burn; in our day they merely tripped Paul in the playground and refused his mother entry to the Women's Fellowship. Now the old houses were being taken over by bright young things who owned Austin Sevens and commuted to Styles each day. There were few passers-by I recognised and fewer knew me. In ironic contrast to Sandhill, Arton had gone up in the world.

A conservation order had been passed on the whole central area, or so I discovered from what used to be Mary Miles' bakery and was now the Civic Society. Grants were available. As a result the tiniest cottage on Back Lane was advertised as 'having potential'. 'Scope for modernisation' seemed to mean 'the roof needs replacing', while 'quaint' meant 'six foot by six, and five feet between floor and ceiling'.

Grudgingly I recognised the town had gained more than it had lost, though I could not reconcile myself to the sense of being newly enclosed. Open space and freedom had been the birth right of every Arton child; now there was a constant throb of through traffic and where there had been cherry orchards the valley sides were covered with suburban homes.

Finally I found my way through what used to be Miles' farmyard to the Tourney Field. The stretch of stream beyond it had been diverted by a local farmer, leaving the water course as an empty hollow. Slow-worms and adders used to live in that channel but they would have found too little cover now. Crossing the field I went through the kissing-gate and paused on the bridge, looking along a dry valley.

Gradually I began to feel I was being watched. There was a rustling beneath me and I caught a glimpse of a dark-eyed child. A dog ran up to her, the long-tailed mongrel sort that has forgotten its father before birth and learnt to avoid boots. A piercing whistle came from behind and the girl and dog both turned and trotted back in that direction. Long after they had gone I felt ill at ease, starting violently when a thrush flapped out of a laurel bush in one of the old gardens. Beyond some iron gates I saw the child again, solemnly watching me, her hair almost blue-black in the leaf light. Later, as I walked up Beechmast Lane I was certain I saw that same dog and child running across an open space. There was another path I remembered, overgrown years ago, which cut up from the stream and re-joined Beechmast Lane. Yet when I reached the fork neither dog nor child were to be seen. I heard the same whistle however, to the right of me. It reverberated through my brain. By now I was thoroughly cross. I did not know who the child was, but I was certain who owned the dog. 'I know you're there,' I yelled furiously. 'Come out and talk to me or go away.' But there was no answer. The dog and child, and the man who had whistled them, had gone.

They were sitting waiting for me by the stile overlooking the wood. Or perhaps it was simply coincidence. They had chosen a parallel route and had reached the style ahead of me. Either way I must meet them or turn back.

All right, so it was an act of cowardice, but I turned back. As I did so I saw Paul look up in surprise and flush deeply. He had only just recognised me. Still, I was committed. If he wished to speak to me he could cut down whatever path he had used to outdistance me so far.

All the way back to the Tourney Field I cursed myself for my stupidity, putting myself in a false position when I had meant to be rational and grown-up. It was the child who had disturbed me most, watching me with those familiar eyes. In the sunlight they were not quite as dark as her father's and her hair lacked the intensity of colour his possessed, but it was obvious whose child she was. I had not known of her existence.

As I had expected, when I reached the bridge both were already in the Tourney Field beneath me. The child was running around and the dog was chasing her, young and foolish. Paul was calling it to him, but the child was shouting conflicting orders, patting when scolding would have been more appropriate.

'Laura!' I heard Paul call. 'How am I to get Tiger to behave himself if you're always petting him? He's got to learn to do as he's told.' The combination of the dog's stupid name and Paul failing to keep his child in order, amused me. After so much foreboding and hurt, it was a wonderful anti-climax.

'Why? I think he's beautiful.' Her voice carried to me clearly, with a distinct American accent.

'Of course he's beautiful, but if he steals any more chickens he'll be very dead too.'

'Oh *Daddy.'*

'It's true, Laura. Mr Lewisham will shoot him. He only let Grandad keep him because I promised to train him myself. You're in the country now.' I noticed he had gained a faint accent himself.

For a moment the child stood crossly in the middle of the field then she ran off towards the barn in the furthest corner. Not liking to watch unobserved, I walked to the kissing-gate where I could be seen. For years I had imagined the meeting between us, but I had never envisaged it like this, with a curious child watching and a stupid yellow dog lolloping around.

It was clear he would not speak to me, so I spoke, out of sheer cussedness. 'You startled me earlier' I said.

'I'm sorry. I didn't recognise you. Laura and I were playing Indians. We must scare quite a few people that way.' His voice was studiously polite.

'That's quite all right,' I said sweetly. 'Harry told me you were back in England. How are your parents?'

'Dad had a fall a month ago. That's why I'm over here – to help out. My wife has stayed in the States. She has contracts to fulfil.' The reference was awkward and clearly for my benefit.

'I see,' I replied. 'But you brought your little girl with you.'

'I thought it would be nice for her to stay with her grandparents.'

Laura had returned and stood near her father, watching me uncertainly. She seemed to sense her father's hostility to me for she looked up in bewilderment. 'Your father and I used to be friends,' I explained. There was a difficult silence.

'How did your father fall?' I asked.

'Pruning trees for Ben Parker. He's a poor patient.'

The likeness to Isaac Booth's image on the postcard was disturbing. So too was the change in Paul. He had grown at least two inches since I knew him, and his whole body had strengthened. The beanpole had turned into a good-looking man. I appreciated the irony. The kids had mocked him as 'gyppo' but those dark eyes and hair were probably part of the reason for his rapid success. The blue-rinsed ladies would take him to their hearts, and he would be oblivious of their admiration, or laugh at it.

Taking a collar from his pocket he slipped it expertly round the dog's neck, then in the brief pause the animal's silly bounding allowed, he tied a rope round the collar, securing it. 'I know you don't like it' he said softly. 'But needs must.'

I was only half-concentrating on what Paul was saying. My attention was taken by his hands as he stroked the dog. They were badly scratched, as if from cutting brambles. If he intended to continue playing the piano professionally he should never have undertaken such work.

The child looked from her father to me uneasily. She seemed used to playing hostess and embarrassed by the coldness of her father's manner. She began to tell me about the Tourney Field and how Daddy said knights and ladies used to watch from the banks while the brave men jousted. Remembering how that field used to fascinate me as a child, I listened and showed interest. Aged seven or eight, she had the solemn manner which suggests too much time spent in adult company, and my heart went out to her. In return she seemed to take a liking to me, perhaps because she was not used to strangers listening to her ideas. Impulsively grabbing my hand she led me over to see the barn Daddy said was really an old chapel, and then across to the dried-out channel where adders used to live. 'Daddy knows ever so many things' she confided. 'All about the woods and the river.'

'Your father's a very clever man,' I agreed. Overhearing our conversation, Paul shrugged his shoulders. 'I've forgotten most of what I've learnt,' he admitted. Though his manner was guarded there was a flatness in his voice which concerned me. As he sat on the bank stroking the dog every line of his body conveyed Exhaustion, mental as well as physical tiredness. I wanted to reach out to him and say I was sorry, to suggest we forget the past thirteen years and were friends again, but his coldness repelled me. If I could have hated him in return it would have been easier but seeing him so obviously in trouble left me confused, torn between compassion and anger. 'Give your Aunt Mary my regards,' he said.

I saw him several times during the days that followed. The Booths' land being next to ours, from the top of our garden their comings and goings were clearly visible to me. Though I settled to work as quickly as I could, sifting through the notes I had brought with me, I made myself take regular rest periods in the open air. Aunt Mary saw to the meals at her own insistence, pleased to be needed again. Slowly she worked her way from cooker to sink, or sat at the table preparing 'nourishing stews' or cakes rich as royalty. I had not been so well fed in years. Taming the vegetable garden seemed a useful way of gaining room for the next meal, and I attacked the top end of our land.

I could not help but be aware of Paul. He worked constantly, continuing the struggle against neglect and despair which he must have begun as soon as he returned. If it rained he wore an old fishing cape and carried on. Within days of my arrival he had put the car back on its wheels and arranged for a mate to tow it away. By the Thursday the brambles were burnt. Occasionally his mother helped him, wearing her blue wrap-over pinny. Most of the time she worked closer to the house however, feeding the animals or milking the goat. She seemed to be employed at the Villa also, for in the mornings she set off up the track and returned at one. When I investigated I found Arton Villa had become an old people's home, catering for the privileged elderly whose families could afford two hundred pounds a week for the benefits of river views and country air. Presumably Janie was employed to help out.

Paul's two sisters visited and took away washing, but of all Saul's sons Paul seemed to be the only one who had returned. One other person visited during the first three days – the doctor, who came twice. The silence of the house troubled me. When he was younger Paul used to practise little while his father was around, fearing his irritation, but the rest of the time there was distant music, played over and over again, till we all got fed up with it and Uncle John complained tactfully. Now there was rarely the sound of a radio and Paul worked outside for hours in total silence. Once or twice he saw me over the hedge, but he did not acknowledge me.

Since he clearly intended to go about his business as if I did not exist, I adopted the same unforgiving manner. It was absurd really, with both of us so near each other. During the days I cared little what he thought, but in the evenings the strain of his nearness, and of the ever present sound of the river, made me restless. I worked far too hard; work having always been my aspirin. When I was too tired to continue I encouraged Great Aunt Mary to talk, trying to gain her confidence so that I could ask her about Lakins' Heath. She told me many stories of the Lakins and of Arton when it was a quiet country village. We talked too of the times I used to come there as a child with Harry and Lydia, but all mention of Mike's drowning was carefully avoided, though the topic never left the conversations completely, hanging around somewhere in mid-air, like the last war does in the company of middle-aged Germans. She talked of the Booths however, and that I found distressing enough.

One poignant story touched me: After various 'No, it can't have been then becauses'. she placed it in 1950. Having been unable to find work locally Saul Booth had joined his uncles' fair. In the early afternoons while the older men were resting, he and his cousins were in the habit of going wenching, as Aunt Mary put it. He found himself a girl from one of the back streets nearby. Janie however was not content to be a one-week romance. She followed the fair to the next booking, and no amount of persuasion could send her home.

What possessed Saul Aunt Mary did not know. Perhaps it was love at first sight, though she doubted such frivolities. Perhaps it was pity. Whatever the reason, he brought Janie to Arton and placed her in his parents' protection.

Isaac and Jilly were used to waifs and strays and Janie's elfish figure became familiar around Arton. She was city bred and Aunt Mary doubted if she had seen a cow close to, but she had courage and determination. Within a week she had found work in the fields. Then as soon as she was old enough, Saul announced they wished to be married. He was twenty-three, Janie just sixteen. Isaac called his son a fool, but bowed to his wishes, and set about finding them a home. The old caretaker's cottage at Arton Villa was empty. Could Miss Lakin persuade her brother to rent it to Saul and his young wife?

I had never heard the story of Saul and Janie's wedding before. We only knew she had left her home and family to follow a showman and thought her terribly romantic. She became an object of fascinated wonder when we were children. Neighbours said she was 'a Roman', and coming as we did from Sandhill Wesleyan that made her doubly interesting, particularly as Saul had a fine reputation as a heathen. We used to see her walking in the early morning with a book in her hand, and all three of us would peep through the hedge to see if she were crossing herself. Later we discovered a little wooden Madonna in her kitchen. When I found courage to ask her about it she replied that the kitchen was her kingdom; if her husband wanted his dinner he had to let her do as she wanted there. At the time her answer puzzled me but watching her stubbornly helping her son fight months of despair, I found it revealing.

Glancing over the hedge and seeing Saul sitting in his chair it was possible to imagine him as a vigorous youth taking his pleasure amongst the local girls, but there had been a change in him, worse than that of age. Before his accident he had been splendid in his strength, his body perfectly balanced, browned like an oiled knife. He knew how to enjoy himself too, whether it was siring a large family or drinking in the Black Bull, though he was never a drunkard, nor brutal, except once or twice, to Paul. Now he sat in a chair, staring at the orchard. As Paul had said, his father was a poor patient, clearly bitterly resenting the loss of his strength, and his dependence on the son he had despised. Whatever Paul did was wrong, whether it was the way he tied back the raspberry canes or grafted the trees in the orchard. The situation was one of those sad, apparently insoluble impasses where two wills are in permanent conflict, Saul grumbling and sniping, Paul silently continuing as he thought fit.

I could not help but admire Paul's patience. His father was evidently improving despite himself, and he took to stomping about the garden with the aid of a metal frame. His son had even less peace now, for Saul could check his efforts and prod about with his foot. I only heard Paul raise his voice once.

Then on the Friday, evidently unable to stand the atmosphere any longer, he went out with the dog.

Mr Booth saw me working in our vegetable patch and came over to the hedge. 'So you're back?' he began. 'Heard you'd returned.' He eyed me up and down, like a piece of bloodstock. 'Grown into a good-looking bint, haven't you? Bit thin for my taste- I like more flesh on my women.' He was teasing me of course, but over fifty and crippled as he was he was still a handsome figure. When he was not grumbling his features were good, his heavy black hair turning to silver rather than grey. 'How'd you like Australia?' he asked.

'Very much, thank you' I replied. It was too complicated to explain the things which infuriated me and the things I loved.

'You and Paul certainly put the world between you,' he remarked. 'Never could understand you meself. If I tired of a woman I left her alone. No need to go to t'other ends of the world to avoid each other.'

Disliking the turn the conversation was taking, I began to be busy sorting cabbage plants. 'You want to hoe the rows a bit deeper first,' Saul advised. 'Catch the rain a bit. This soil's too dry. You did right planting crossways, though. Smart for a woman. I've seen newcomers lose half their soil into the river in one storm. Your aunt's let the place go a bit, hasn't she?'

Resisting the temptation to remark on the wildness of his own orchard I continued planting. 'I suppose you've seen the state of our place?' Saul asked, speaking for me. 'Bad do. It's got a bit much for me, with having to find work. There ain't much for my sort round here anymore. I've been having to walk an hour or so first or catch a bus up to the Oak Leaf, and most of the forest's gone round there, too. This bloody accident's put paid to everything. I don't like being laid up I can tell you. I've always been independent.' There was a note of anger in his voice. I thought of Great Aunt Mary struggling from sink to cooker and admired them both.

'I was sorry to hear of it,' I said. 'Paul told me you fell from a ladder'.

'Ay- fair broke me back. Fell awkward somehow. I've fallen afore but never this bad. Paul told you, did he? He would. It suits him fine to have me laid up.'

The remark was so unjust I looked up in embarrassment. 'I'm sure that never entered his head,' I said. 'He came back to help.'

'Him? He don't know the first thing about the land. A namby-pamby city gent, that's him. Been living in an apartment in New York, without so much as a blade of grass to his name, and he comes back here, telling me what to do. I never asked him to come back.'

And he wouldn't have done, I admitted to myself sadly. It seemed wise to let the conversation drop.

Saul did not want to do so. He had someone to complain to at last. 'He came back because that silly woman his mother asked him to, that's why. Well, all right, perhaps it was his duty to come and see his father when he was in hospital, but now I'm home we can do without him.'

'I doubt it' I replied coolly. 'Not if the orchard's to be got into order and the cottage roof repaired.' I should have kept silence but the man's ingratitude annoyed me.

'It's Christopher Lakin's job to do the roof,' Saul replied, 'and I'll do the rest meself when this stupid back of mine's better. What do you take me for? An invalid? I've whopped two fellows Paul's size only a few months ago – just for calling me a Tinker. Let him go back where he belongs. He's left his wife. Did you know that? Deserted her. I may have been a bit free in my time, but I've stuck by the woman I married, and so should he.'

Saul's statement pulled me up short. 'He told me she had contracts to fulfil,' I insisted.

'Load of shit. He's left her that's what he's done, and grabbed the kiddy. He ain't staying here out of caring for me, but because it suits him. Perhaps we do need a bit of help, but I ain't taking it from him. And you want to keep clear of him too. He's quite a charmer nowadays. But he's a married man, and don't you forget it.'

The man's spite infuriated me. 'If Paul's marriage is breaking up, he needs help,' I said. 'Not turning away. But you would never help him would, you? You do him an injustice, Saul Booth. There's nothing 'namby-pamby' about Paul as you call it. It takes courage to do what he's done all his life – what he's doing now, putting things to right while you complain and find fault.' I saw Janie Booth come out of the cottage, and unwilling to be overheard by her, spoke more quickly. 'You've never understood the talent he has. Nor have you ever stopped seeing him as he used to be. He's not weak now if he ever was. A weak man couldn't have cleared the land like he has. Look at him as he is *now*, Mr Booth, at what he's become.' I could not express myself properly and grew impatient. 'Whatever you may think of him, he came back. Where are your other sons? The ones you boasted about? Where's Artie? He was your darling, wasn't he?'

I had hit him unfairly and knew it. 'Artie's married and working away,' Saul replied sullenly. 'There weren't nothing for him here.'

'I can understand Artie leaving,' I agreed. 'But I don't see him coming back to visit you. I do see Paul, working here all weathers, ruining his hands. They're as much his tools as saws and axes are yours. If he starts practising again tomorrow, he'll take weeks to get back to concert level, and every day he stays here, the less chance he'll have of performing in public again.' Janie was coming towards us. 'Mr Booth,' I pleaded. 'If you can't do it because he's your son, do it out of common humanity. Show Paul a bit of gratitude.'

I could not speak any more and gathering my tray of cabbage plants went indoors.

The quarrel pained me. I should not have spoken so harshly. At the time I hated Saul for his cruelty to his son, but with the hindsight of adulthood I was aware how much pain he himself must have felt, knowing he was being judged by his son and found wanting. As a boy Paul had the same solemn watchfulness his daughter now possessed, and which had made me so uncomfortable near the Tourney Field. Everything about the lad was darker, more intense than the rest of the family, dominated by a talent which burnt him from the inside. And much of it was Paul's fault, too. If he had bent himself a little towards his father's idea of what a son should be like, things would have been easier for them both. But Paul could not bend, any more then than now.

And there was love between them, of a sort. Paul would never allow others to speak ill of his father and Saul gradually learnt to be proud of his son's achievements. That stubborn love had obviously continued, too. No one in Arton would have judged Paul if he had broken all connection with River Cottage, yet there he was, working away in the orchard, and for all Saul's sourness, it was he who poured Paul a glass of beer, or brought him the fishing cape when it rained. Some time I must apologise.

The knowledge of my own unfairness made me edgy and discontented with myself. For a while I talked to Aunt Mary, briefly mentioning the argument but too uneasy about it to give many details. As usual she saw through me.

'You 'll never make those two understand each other,' she said decisively. 'All you can do is recognise they've both got right on their side. They used to remind me of D. H. Lawrence's Sons and Lovers you know, Paul Morel and his father. Even the name used to seem right. You didn't see them as much as I did. You only saw the outside.'

'But with Mr Booth it wasn't just a matter of wiping his hand across his mouth and eating without washing,' I protested. 'He used to mock Paul – make fun of his ill health, even. I've seen Paul hide along the riverbank like a sick animal rather than admit he was ailing again.'

'And how much was that his own pride?' Aunt Mary asked. 'Leave them be. They're nothing to you now – nor can they be with Paul married.'

'That has nothing to do with it,' I said coldly. 'It wasn't love that made me stand up for Paul – it was a sense of justice.' I sounded pompous, and knew it, but for once what I said was true.

Aunt Mary's advice was wise. Let them be. The trouble was, having them so near each day was like having an ulcer in your mouth. Your tongue will for forever keep rubbing at it, making it worse. If I was to adopt a proper attitude towards living beside River Cottage I must heal that ulcer. Though I had walked into Arton several times since my arrival, I had never gone further. I didn't have time for long walks, I told myself. Aunt Mary shouldn't be left alone. Excuses of course, or cowardice. While I could accept the judgement that I was a bit of an idiot, I did not like to think of myself as a coward.

Settling Aunt Mary in her chair for an afternoon nap, I gave myself a good talking to, on the lines of one of Miss McClean's dressing-downs. By the time I had finished I felt as if I had been set two detentions and a thousand lines. Then, closing the door quietly, I walked downriver.

I cannot explain to you the sense of dread that accompanied me on that walk. You would have to be inside my mind to understand the dryness of my mouth and the sickness in my stomach. I would have turned back a dozen times, but for that head teacher inside me saying I was a silly little girl, and a coward besides. It would have been so easy to pretend I had shopping to do in the town, and turn up the path to the bridge, but I kept on walking, under the old arch, and along the cobbles towards the gardens beyond. Children were playing around one of the seats, and a woman was sucking the first ice cream of the season. So the tourists still came – by car now rather than bus.

A rowing boat negotiated the bridge and then passed below me, gliding down-river. Then as it approached the shallows, it turned

160

in mid-stream, and pulled back against the flow, as I had seen a thousand boats do before. The scene was so tranquil a sense of unreality began to afflict me, as if the events imprinted in my brain had been an illusion. I would rub my eyes and they would go away.

It was half an hour's walk to Pelham Rocks, and with every moment the sense of dread grew stronger. And what for? The day was calm, promising the end of winter. The birds sang. Clouds scudded across the sky as clouds do at that time of the year. The only discordant thing was me. When I reached the rocks I sat down. In their shadow the air was cold, and the same smell of damp sand and rotting reed filled my mind as it had done in memory for years. There, winter still clung, the river still flowing high on the bank, the reeds half-covered and bending in the current. I saw the usual signs of storm, the bits of paper and polythene trailing from overhanging willows, the driftwood washed up on the narrow beach opposite, and under the shadow of the overhang the river was black, pockmarked by eddies and small whirlpools where the current tried to negotiate the sudden bend. Getting up, I took off my shoes and walked down to the river. It was ice cold to my feet. Wading through the shallows I forced my way into the reeds until I was level with the beach opposite. Somewhere there – I could not tell exactly where.

And then I saw it and cried out in fear. Pushed into the reeds was a shape, rising and falling with the current. In panic I waded forward, to find merely driftwood.

It had been carried down by the same current as Mike's body and forced by the water into the same projecting spit of reed. Already green and slimed on its upper surface, the bough strained at its net and sought to continue its progress downstream, but the reeds were too tangled, and too strong. It would lie there till it rotted, or another storm raised the river's level and freed it.

My skirt was soaked, and my feet cut by the sharpness of reed and root. Anyone seeing me there would have thought I was mad or determined on a watery death. Not being quite either, I waded

161

back to the bank, and sat on a patch of bare earth overhanging the water, wondering what I had achieved. I had visited the place again and given myself an unpleasant few moments. And having done so, what was there to say? I had found a friend's body there and looked at death for the first time. What was so special about that? In olden times girls of seventeen must have been thoroughly familiar with the face of death, having helped lay out fathers and brothers, killed in routine disasters. The face I saw was badly marked, true, but the boys who went away to Richard Lakin's war were scarcely any older and saw much worse. Paul's anger hurt me deeply of course, but I ought to be able to find forgiveness. Besides, the man who worked in the orchard next to me was not the boy I had known then and holding grudges for past actions was a bit pointless.

By the time I got up I was almost calm.

Aunt Mary asked me where I had been. When I told her, she simply nodded. 'You have courage,' she said. 'Now apologise to Mr Booth.'

To my surprise it was not I who had to make the first move, but Janie Booth. Later that evening she came to the river gate, calling up to the chalet for me. Puzzled, I left my papers.

The creation of seven children from her body had left her painfully thin, a little wisp of a woman but still surprisingly pretty. Wearing her inevitable pinny, and with her Irish hair and pale face, she reminded me of one of those blue primulas splashed with black about their centres. Her fragility was deceptive. Like Paul she had an inner strength. Saul might lord it over his children, but it was to her they turned in times of trouble. 'I wanted to say I was sorry,' she said. Even after thirty years in Arton a faint Dublin accent lifted her voice. 'It's a fine welcome for you, but you must excuse Saul. Being tied to this place – to a chair until a few days ago – makes him rage like a caged bull.' She shook her head. 'He was becoming bitter and low before this. There's not much room in the world for a man like my Saul. He can't cope with the new-fangled machines they have on the farms, or with the smart folk moving into the town.'

I nodded in acknowledgment. 'I shouldn't have answered him,' I admitted. 'But I was angry on Paul's behalf.'

'I have had words with him myself since,' Janie agreed. I smiled at the image of Saul being the object of 'words'.

'Mr Booth said Paul had deserted his wife,' I remarked. 'I find that hard to believe.'

'I don't know what's happened, Martie. Paul has always gone his own way and told me little of his mind. I can see he's grieving and I've asked him why, but he smiles and tells me not to worry. I think it is his wife's wish he should stay away a while, what smart folks call a trial separation. They go in for such things in America; perhaps it's with all those film stars carrying on.' Her simplicity was touching. 'His wife's a singer, you know. Travels all over America giving concerts like Paul. The kiddy can't hardly see them. Do you know, I have six grandchildren – can you believe it? – and that little girl touches my heart more than any of them.'

On the following Monday I deliberately walked up the river path, towards Enchanter's Island.

It was Paul who first gave the island its name, after the Enchanter's Nightshade that grew in shady places in the woods nearby. Most of the names we used came from him, for he had a rich imagination. We were quite willing to believe the island was enchanted, just as we were willing to believe the strangely marked stone he called an adderstone and kept it in his pocket was a talisman against the evil eye. Looking back, I'm certain a lot of it was deliberate hokum, to confuse city children, but some of his stories were ancient and came from his grandfather. Approaching the oddly shaped island I was once again held by its magic, and once again afraid.

It was a necessary journey, a laying of the past finally to rest, so that I could get on with the present. Enchanter's Island had haunted my imagination more beguilingly than Pelham Rocks, for there was beauty in my memory of it as well as horror.

Cut off from the main bank in some terrible flood, the island was a secret world, where kingcup and police man's helmet splashed yellow and pink in season. Even on dull days the sun seemed to catch those magnificent elms and waterfowl dabbled along its banks. Only the Marsh boys and Paul and Mike Booth could steer their way across the current to it, and in their company we were privileged beings, given access to a magic land. It was hard to imagine anywhere more peaceful than the island on a summer's day, yet Death had hovered round it as long as I could remember. A swimmer had drowned there the year before Mike died, and there had been two other drownings since, so Miss Timpkins at the drapers told me. And each time Saul Booth had been called out to search the reeds with his grappling irons, for he knew the current better than anyone. What he must have felt as he searched for his son I dared not think, nor what Paul must have thought as he rowed beside him. My own memory was enough.

Sitting on the bank I tried to look at the past directly, without flinching. There were few other walkers to disturb me; school had not yet been dismissed and the fishermen were sitting patiently on their stools nearer the town. It was one of those pale April days when the world is fresh and new, but terribly vulnerable, rain menacing on the edge of the sky. I was aware of the beauty round me, but a creeping deadness seemed to be taking over me; a sense of dissociation, of remoteness – it's hard to find the word. It was the same deadness which had afflicted me at the time of Mike's death. I could not feel. I wanted to feel, to cry like people expected me to, but nothing came.

Beneath me the river sucked at the bank and near the island two wild ducks flew past in a beating of wings. I tried to visualise where we had been rowing when the branch struck but found it unexpectedly difficult. The shape of the beach had altered, and the current ran less erratically, water parting smoothly about the spit of land and rolling under the alders.

I had brought some biscuits and an apple with me, and mechanically got them out. In surprise I stared at them, wondering what kind of woman could sit eating, whilst looking at a scene of past tragedy. It was then I recalled a passage from Richard Lakin's letters – the letters to his sister that Charlie Warwick had found in Sandhill library.

'I am sitting writing this to you on an upturned bucket, my feet deep in mud. It is amazing what one can accept after a while. You begin even to joke. We laugh at some appalling things, you know. I suppose it is a form of protection. No one can feel deeply forever. You must cut off your feelings or go mad.'

Beginning to eat my apple I considered his words. Even the fact that *I* had nearly died at Enchanter's Island brought no emotion, only a vague interest, as if I were recalling events I had read of in a newspaper. 'Well then, let me recall them,' I thought. 'As if they did belong to someone else.'

We should not have gone there of course, but the island had held a fascination for us ever since we were children. It was so beautiful and so temptingly near. On such a day, with a storm breaking and rain falling in the hills upstream we were mad to stay so long before attempting the crossing back to the bank. So why had we done so? Both the Booth boys knew the river's moods intimately; they had worked the tourist boats since they were twelve or thirteen and were as sure-footed crossing a line of moored craft as any cat. Lydia and I were sensible enough on water too, having lived so many weekends and holidays with the river flowing through our sleep. So why did we stay so long?

The apple began to go sour in my mouth. For the first time I felt the nearness of the water. It was as if I had begun to awake, to take part in life again. A memory returned to me, vividly complete.

Lydia and I were lying in bed in Sweetbriar, both of us too lazy to get breakfast, hoping Harry would be driven by hunger to find the cereal packet.

'He's fifteen, for heaven's sake!' Lydia said. 'He can take a turn.' Lying back against the pillow with her hair tumbled about her head she looked – I could not find the right word, but her manner and appearance shocked me.

'I'm bored with rowing to Arton Ferry,' she said. 'I vote we go to Enchanter's Island and have our picnic there first. I'm in the mood for a lazy afternoon. Harry can mess about pretending to fish and Mike and I'll spend a little time together.'

'Aunt Lizzie's going to hear, one of these days,' I warned.

'So what? I'm nineteen, old enough to be married and have a couple of babbies. I shall get a nice little flat this autumn, then I can do as I like. Mike can come and stay with me if he wants.' She laughed. 'He can be my itsy bitsy country mouse. I shall feed him on bread and cake.'

'I think it's mean of you to mock him,' I said. 'I don't understand how you can lie around with him on the island when you don't intend to marry him.'

'Marry Mike Booth? Don't be ridiculous! He's not much more than a Tinker.'

'Then how can you …?'

'Martie, you're so pi sometimes you make me laugh. I let Mike Booth make love to me because I like it. I don't have to marry him.'

'Don't you love him at all?' I was becoming upset.

'He's rather a dish and we have a laugh together, but you don't imagine he's faithful to me, do you? He's got several girls in town; he's told me so himself.'

'I'm glad Paul's different.'

'Of course he isn't. Don't be such a fool. All this eternal love stuff makes me laugh. If you're not careful you're going to get

caught. It's always the innocent ones that do. Are you and Paul –
you know? You're not chancing it, are you?'

My face went hot with shame. 'No. He asked Mike.'

'Well, that's a mercy,' Lydia said briskly. She looked for her
hairbrush. 'I could just see you ending up in a grotty little house
with a couple of babbies. You'd have hated every minute, and he'd
have let you clown in the end- that's supposing he would have
married you in the first place. Those Booths arc drifters, the lot of
them.'

'If you must know,' I replied 'I'm breaking it off this weekend.
I've made up my mind. I shall fail my A-levels if I keep on seeing
him. I couldn't think during my Mocks for seeing his face – that's
why I did so badly. He won't do well either if he keeps on
hankering after me, and he'll never forgive himself, or me, if he
doesn't get into that college. I never meant it to get the way it
did....'

'Oh give over. He didn't *make* you do anything.'

Throwing the apple into the water, I sat staring as it bobbed
about. Suddenly it was caught in the current and sucked forward.
I felt myself being drawn forward with it. My hold on life seemed
suddenly to weaken. Once again I recalled Richard Lakin's letter.
For years I had coped with my guilt by cutting off my emotions.
Now they forced themselves upon me. Lying against the bank I
pressed my face into the grass. A spasm of sickness passed over
me, making me retch. I had come to the heart of the matter, the
black hole at the bottom of my mind. Getting up quickly, I began
to run from the place, back towards the chalet.

If I could have talked to Aunt Mary I would have felt better, but
what could I say? That I had been responsible for another person's
death? For a while I hung aimlessly about the kitchen, then I went
outside and wandered the garden. My head had begun to ache. It
would be sensible to go indoors and lie down, but as soon as I did
so the restlessness returned. The walls of the chalet were closing
in on me, so I went back outside. Work would make me feel better.

Contemplating trying to repair the old rowing boat I pulled on the rope, but the weight of water defeated me. Aimlessly I returned indoors and equally aimlessly came out again. Grabbing the spade I set about clearing the upper patch. In a blind fury I hacked the dock leaves and sorrel. They had no right to be there; they must go this minute.

But I could not keep it up. For a while I rested, until my mind began churning again. Furiously I dug the docks, yanking their long white roots. The sun had come out and a fly kept crawling across my face. Each time I swatted it, it flew up, only to return. Suddenly it was another fly I was swatting. I was lying under the elms of Enchanter's Island and a persistent fly kept crawling along my arm. Paul flicked at it with his fingers and then instead of moving his hand began to trace the shape of my throat ...

I could not stay there hacking away. The woods had given me peace before. The weather was deteriorating but I was not afraid of a little rain, and my anorak was sufficient even for an English April day.

Laura was watching with her solemn eyes as I turned up-river. I sensed Paul was nearby, but I wanted no one to speak to me. Speech would be tiring, and I wanted quiet. I discovered my hands were shaking as if I were shocked after an accident, and the digging had brought up blisters on my palms. Scarcely noticing the walk I reached the ride that led into the wood. I had warned Aunt Mary I would be out until dusk, and there was an ancient track that would bring me back through the forest to the main road and so home to the chalets. I would take that route rather than the shorter one back to the river.

Already I was tired from walking and gardening so absurdly. If my judgment had been clear I would never have undertaken another six miles, but clarity had left me. Subconsciously I think I wanted to lose myself in those silent woods.

For the first mile or so I was scarcely aware of my route, but gradually my vision cleared. My mind had begun to settle, and I

168

could appreciate the beauty of a Brimstone fluttering purposefully along the ride ahead of me.

As always, the woods were beginning to offer healing. It was then I made my second and genuine mistake. Aunt Mary would worry if l was not home soon. Rather than continue along the ride I decided to take a shorter path which cut off a large triangle of woodland, bringing me out lower down the main road. It had obviously not been used much lately but there were signs of a few walkers passing that way.

As I remembered, the path dropped steeply into the bed of a stream, then climbed through denser woodland. The light was fading among the closer-growing beech, so I went up the last part of the ascent quickly. Overhead a plane droned, and I felt reassured, reminding myself I could be barely two miles from the road.

Suddenly I came to the barbed wire. I was over two thirds of my way home and stretched across my path were five strands of taut barbed wire. Presumably they ran from Deepdene Farm to some new hunting lodge, for a sign hammered to one of the trees said *Deepdene Hotel. Private shooting.* My path was not marked as a right of way, but we had always walked it as we pleased. Anger made me reckless. I would not be kept from my path, trespassing or no. Besides, if I was to reach the road before dark I had to follow the old route.

Putting my anorak across the barbs I tried to find a way over or through. The strands were too close and too high however, and though I attempted to glide underneath the bottom, I could not cross the fence. All I achieved was several deep scratches and a wasted ten minutes.

There was no alternative but to make my way alongside the fence to its outer limit and hopefully turn back towards the right, finding a route along the road or near the farm. The walking would have been difficult even if I had been less tired, for a tangle of last year's fern and bramble grew on earth disturbed when the fence was erected. I needed Wellington boots to protect my calves; by now fern and briar clung to my trousers. Several times I stumbled. Ultimately my foot caught in a root and I fell heavily. Scratches appeared on my hands and a nettle-sting rose in white lumps. Instead of a peaceful shelter in which I could hide myself, the wood had become a malevolent place. I could find nowhere to rest, except a fallen bough that crawled with tiny red mites and broke into damp powder at my touch. I was getting too exhausted to go on however and was forced to sit down on the firmest part of the log. Taking out some mints I had brought with me I began to open the packet, only to drop it in my tiredness. Without looking where I was reaching I put my hand down to pick up the packet, to recoil in horror as it touched something moist and fleshy.

A dead rabbit lay beside my seat, its bowels torn out by some predator. Carrion beetles swarmed from the corpse. At once I noticed the stench and wondered how on earth I had not smelt it before.

It was a trivial incident, but it played on my mind. No doubt I was overwrought and a little unstable. I wanted to shout out to keep myself company but when I did so I felt foolish, for my voice merely echoed back from the valley. Startled birds clattered from the undergrowth. It would be dark soon amongst the trees, though in the open fields dusk would linger another hour or so. I was alone, out of my proper route and exhausted. Even the weather was turning against me. Large spots of rain fell on the twigs and I hurriedly pulled my anorak about me. Unexpectedly a woodcock flew up from the gully near me, making my heart race. An irrational terror was beginning to disturb me. In the distance a cuckoo was calling, like a human voice calling me on. Rustlings and watchings announced the coming night, while above me a nightjar churred. 'Bracken-clocks' Paul used to call them. I saw the bird drop off a dead branch twenty feet up an oak tree and flick downwards against the darkening sky. 'Goatsucker' was the other name Paul used. In olden days people used to believe nightjars fed on goats. Involuntarily I shuddered, closing my eyes. As I did so I saw the dead rabbit again, its entrails spilling across the fern.

Urgently I began to walk but my shoes would not hold firm on the rain-soaked leaves and I slipped several times. At one point the path cut alongside a steep gully and I wished I had proper climbing boots on instead of shoes. The rain was incessant now, making everything greasy and insecure. Suddenly my foot touched a loose stone and I was slipping downwards. Though I tried to save myself my hands would not grip on the wet shale and I fell twenty feet or so, down into a half-full stream. My head caught on a stone at the bottom and dusk turned to blackness.

When consciousness returned I found I was lying on my side while water seeped around me. More than anything in the world I wanted to sleep. I would lie there and rest, just as I was.

Mercifully self-preservation returned. I was shivering uncontrollably, feeling violently sick. I must move at once. Like a drunken bagwoman I climbed out of that wretched gully, though I still do not know how my hands gripped or my feet held on that wet shale. When I reached the top the trees were laughing at my slurred state; faces began to form on the bark. In lines they walked alongside me, grinning and pointing. I heard their laughter, and it became the sound of water. A river flowed down the hillside towards me. I shouted, and my voice echoed around the woods. Now the trees marched through the water. In terror I tried to breathe and could not. I was drowning again near Enchanter's Island.

Then suddenly I was in the old clearing; not even darkness and semi-consciousness could take my sense of direction from me.

It was a long time before I opened my eyes. The rain was pouring down. That was the water I had felt. My clothes were stained with wet and mud and my hands were stiff with cold. Somewhere nearby was an old saw pit. I must seek shelter there; trying to struggle on in darkness would be insane. Reduced to

171

crawling in the last grey light, I searched for the hollow, finding it at last, obscured by dead leaves. A flash of humour came to me. 'Some babe in the wood,' I thought.

All humour left me that night however. As darkness deepened around me an inner blackness seemed to settle on my soul. I had been responsible for another person's death. My fall that night was Nemesis at work. Anxiety concerning Aunt Mary increased my fretting. Perhaps she would come to harm struggling around in that rickety chalet. Stories the Booths had told me returned to my mind: an adder nearly eight feet long curled on a piece of shale, a wild man living in one of the sawpits. I turned over amongst the leaves, catching my head, and cried out. Movements amongst the leaf-litter set me staring into the night while fear strutted around inside my brain. I saw a pair of eyes burning and screamed.

Whatever it was ran away at the sound. Later I heard a swish and a terrified squeak. Beyond me in the blackness something small had died. I had reached the darkest point of the night, and of my soul. I cannot describe what thoughts came to me then. My civilised self-fell away from me, leaving me a terrified animal like the night creatures I heard scurrying for food and shelter around me. Even my name seemed to be taken from me. This was my real self, lonely and afraid, at the mercy of a Nature which found me no more significant than the dead rabbit beside a fallen branch.

As the hours passed I dozed a little. The rain continued.

Gradually I became used to the darkness and the movements around me. It was an experience, I decided. Not many modern people had spent a night alone in a sawpit. It would be something to talk about.

'You can't die in an English woodland,' I told myself. 'Not two miles from a road.' It was this thought that kept me going, that if I died I would never forgive myself.

Slowly I climbed back from the depths into which I had descended. A second pair of eyes watched me but this time I lay still, listening. Another pair joined it. There were shufflings and gruntings and a strong alien smell until whatever it was caught scent of me and blundered out of the pit. Badgers, I decided and felt a thrill of wonder. Later, as the rain stopped briefly, and the moon shone through the twigs above me, I could just distinguish another shape as well as sense it. Suddenly a hot stink of fox passed me. Everything was as it should be; the animals were returning from their hunting.

Perhaps it was simply sleeplessness and pain, but I saw visions after that. A sense of my oneness with Nature brought me comfort. Nothing would be the same. My values would be changed. I had heard badgers in the darkness, smelt the stink of fox.

Was I responsible for Mike's death?

At the time I thought so. I accepted Paul's anger as justified. But had I been right in taking all the blame?

There is always a combination of events involved in a death, and the atmosphere of that day was as much to blame for Mike's drowning as I was. All five of us created that: the continual emotion, the competitiveness which made it impossible to admit fear, the anger at parting. We should never have crossed to Enchanter's Island with the weather so treacherous. Even setting out to Arton Ferry was foolhardy.

There was some blame attached to my actions, of course. I should not have chosen that afternoon to tell Paul I was parting with him. Delaying our return from the island by trying to make him understand my reasons was foolish. It cost us valuable minutes during which the river rose with frightening speed.

But it was not malice, and if I had delayed us another five minutes that branch might have gone by safely. Who can measure chance, God, whatever one likes to call it?

We were none of us to blame, we were all of us to blame – Lydia for her wilfulness and panic, Mike for his bravado, Harry for his weakness. Even Paul must bear some of the guilt. He should have followed his judgment and refused to cross to Enchanter's Island.

If he had insisted Lydia would have given in, for where the ways of Nature were concerned we all respected his judgment. Perhaps that was why Paul could not forgive me because he could not forgive himself.

Turning back into the leaves, I slept.

When I awoke a cold morning was flickering through the trees above me. It had stopped raining; the earth smelt sweet. King Charles' Oak spread all around my vision, a vast comforting shelter. Goodness knows why we called it that. King Charles must have undertaken a Cook's tour to visit so many oaks and all of them fifty miles off his route. Then I heard it again, the same shrill whistle. I put my fingers to my lips and tried to remember how to whistle in return. My mouth was stiff with cold and at first I only managed a rather rude noise, then one clear reply sounded. Immediately the response came, seeking direction as we used to do as children. Again I whistled. There was a long pause. My legs and arms were stubborn but I pulled myself out of the sawpit, into the clearing, where I sat trying to rub the mud off my clothes with screwed-up leaves. The whistle came again, near enough for me to call in return, 'Near the old sawpit.'

Within minutes that stupid yellow dog was bounding through the trees, knocking me on to the bracken. The silly animal must have been ordered to fetch, for its chief ambition seemed to be to lift me by the neck and carry me back. Rolling in a painful heap I petted him till he must have wondered if Christmas had come early. I was kissing the silly mutt's ears when Paul appeared through the trees. 'Tell Tiger to put me down,' I shouted.

'That's the first time the stupid idiot's obeyed an order,' Paul said. 'You can't expect him to obey two.' He crouched beside me and in relief I leant against him. 'Hell, Martie, what have you been doing?' He was confused, not knowing what to do for me first. 'You're in an awful state. How did you do this?'

'Falling in the gully. Is Aunt Mary all right?'

'She knocked us up about midnight. My mother took her back and spent the night with her. How she managed to walk round to us in the dark and on that slippery path I don't know.' I thought of Aunt Mary struggling through the rain. That hundred yards must have been as long for her as my last mile. 'What were you doing so far from the path? It's not like you to get lost.'

'I wasn't lost,' I insisted. 'I knew perfectly well where I was. There was a bloody great fence in the way.'

An embarrassing dizziness was making it difficult for me to focus on him, so I closed my eyes. My mind was marching around giving orders which my body refused to obey. 'Mum put us up some coffee,' Paul said. If he had offered me hemlock I would have drunk it so long as it was warm, but my fingers would not close over the cup. In utter humiliation I had to let him hold it for me.

I would have chosen anyone else in the world, rather than have Paul see me in such indignity. 'Why did you come?' I asked. 'You of all people could have refused.'

'I'm not heartless, even if you think I am. Your aunt was worried sick. Besides, if she'd called the police they would have knocked me up. With Dad lame I know these woods better than anyone – or did till I left.' The statement was made as a matter of fact, not pride. 'There was nothing I could do till first light or I'd have set off earlier. Laura had seen you go up-river, but she hadn't seen you come back. I reasoned you were either in the water or had taken the path into these woods.' As he talked he examined the cut on my head. I did not like him touching me and flinched away from him.

By now the dog had bounded off to chase phantom rabbits. Paul let me lie back against him. His mother had laced the coffee with whisky and its warmth crept through me. Then he found me a sweater and a dry jacket my great aunt must have given him. 'Put those on before you die of pneumonia,' he advised. Obediently I began to change from my wet anorak, but my fingers would not

175

close over the zip. 'Come here,' he said. Once again I was forced into letting him help me. His manner was awkward rather than unkind, my weakness forcing a truce between us.

'How did you know where I'd be?' I asked.

'I remembered us playing here. Thinking of the mess I got into myself with that fence last week, I reasoned you might have done the same and sheltered here when night carne on.' He attended to the wound on my head.

'Have you slept at all?'

'I saw a pair of badgers, or rather heard them, and a fox.'

'That wasn't the question I asked.' Hesitantly he examined the scratches on my hands. 'You'd better let me put something on these too.' In annoyance I turned my face away. 'Some of these are deep. They'll fester if you don't let me see to them.'

'Then let me do it myself,' I insisted, taking the cream and cotton wool.

I attended to myself. Twice I dropped the cap and had to let Paul find it. There was a long silence between us, hostility returning now that the first compassion and gratitude were spent. 'We'll walk to the farm, if you can make it,' Paul suggested. 'Perhaps one of the Catford boys will drive us to Casualty.'

'I don't want to go to hospital,' I objected.

'You're going all the same. That cut needs stitches and you're probably suffering from exposure. I'll see your Aunt knows where you are.'

I was in no state to argue with him but bitterly resented his control over me. 'I should have warned you about that fence,' he added unexpectedly. 'Apparently there's new owners at the hotel – one of those syndicates. They're putting up fences all round their land. Dad's clashed with them several times. You could have walked alongside and got around to Deepdene Farm if you'd known.'

'I did walk along it,' I protested, 'but I started to feel too tired to go on.'

'I'm not surprised. You were going at that garden like a maniac. We could do with employing you round our place. It'd save hiring a JCB.'

Despite my annoyance, I smiled. The wind was cold and I shivered. Taking off his jacket, Paul gave it to me. He was being too gentle to me. I could not maintain the distance I had intended.

'I've been nearly frantic Martie,' he said suddenly. 'Mum was convinced you'd gone in the river and set about me because of it. She said I'd been cold to you ever since you returned – that it was my fault if anything had happened to you.' Looking away from me, he watched the dog amongst the trees. There was nothing I could say in reply, though my silence inevitably expressed agreement. 'For a quiet little woman my mother has a savage tongue. She said I was hard and unforgiving, that it was hardly surprising my marriage was failing. I think that hit me hardest.'

In silence I considered the movement of the trees around me. 'She said I still blamed you for Mike's death, and that I was unjust.'

Anger returned to me, making my voice unsteady. 'You were unjust to me,' I agreed. 'Bitterly unjust. Mike's death was no more my fault than it was yours, or Lydia's, or even Harry's. You turned on me so savagely because you felt I had cast you off out of snobbery. If it's worth anything now, I didn't. I thought neither of us would get to college if we went on seeing each other. Sex and exams don't mix.'

His mouth set into the hard line I recognised. 'You delayed us. If we'd left earlier, we would have been safely across before that branch came down.'

'If I'd delayed us more it might have passed already. You should have refused to go on the river in the first place – but you didn't want to appear chicken in Mike's eyes.' We were going back over old ground, but this time I could defend myself. 'You were as much to blame as I was, and you know it. If you'd stopped to listen to what I was saying we'd have left that island quicker in any case ... Your mother thought you were partly to blame. She has a habit of being right.'

For several moments we were silent. In such a helpless state I was crazy fighting with him and I saw him smile slightly at my stubbornness. 'Please, Martie,' he said quietly. 'I'm too tired to fight with you – or with anyone. We've both been unjust to each other. You didn't mean Mike to drown any more than I meant you to end up in this state.' Tentatively he pushed the hair from my face.

We had come to a still point after years of anger.

'There's some soup,' he offered.

Sitting against a tree I drank the soup he gave me. Then I tried to make myself look more presentable, tucked my blouse back into my trousers, felt in my pocket to see if I had a comb. Finding one in his jacket, Paul passed it to me. 'You've no right to see me like this,' I said.

'I know how thin a coat human dignity is,' Paul replied. 'You've seen me in a low state several times. Still, you'd better look a bit more civilised or Mum won't half fly at me.'

It had been a carefully chosen response, opening the possibility of conversation between us. 'You sound afraid of her,' I said.

'I am. So's Dad, though don't tell anyone. The trouble is as you said, she has a habit of being right.' The faint American accent was vanishing. He had the ability to adopt any speech near him, and for my sake he was slipping back into the language of his youth.

'Your mother shouldn't have worried,' I assured him. 'I'm a tough old boot. Nothing's going to make me throw myself into any river.' Explanation slithered from me.

'I'm glad I spent the night out here, probably wanted to do so all along. I've looked my demons in the face. I'm sorry I frightened everyone and got you up so early, but that's all.'

'Have your demons troubled you a lot then?'

'Yes.'

'We've made a right pig's ear of things, haven't we?' Paul asked quietly. 'We seem to have sent each other chasing halfway round the world, trying to find some illusion that's nearly broken both of us, and taken about the same time to do it. You've worked yourself nearly to death – Harry's clear about that – and I've just about wrecked my career and my marriage.'

'It's not that bad,' I insisted, smiling at the extreme way he saw everything. 'I've seen a pair of badgers and I haven't died of cold or beriberi. We've both of us got where we wanted in life, even if we've lost a lot of other things along the way.' Taking the flask of water I began to clean my face and hair. From the amusement in his eyes I gathered I had merely streaked the mud and had another go. 'What else have you got in that rucksack?' I asked. 'It's like Aladdin's cave in there. You don't happen to have anything more to eat? Steak and chips? Bacon and eggs?'

'Mum put us up five loaves and two fishes.'

'Don't tell me she's sent one of her lardy cakes?'

'Naw. I said I couldn't carry heavy weights.'

Against my will I laughed. We were slipping back into the old silly banter and I was conscious that I was happy. The feeling did not go away as soon as I thought it, but remained, warming me like Janie's whisky. Opening the rucksack further, Paul took out a package. 'You'll have to make do with bread and cheese,' he said. 'I should warn you the cheese has a government health warning on it. Mum's started making that too, when we can catch the goat.'

'Judging by what I've seen of that goat's diet,' I remarked, 'yours must be the first privet-flavoured cheese on the market.'

I ate the lot and looked round for more. 'You're on the mend,' Paul said drily. 'There's one last cup of coffee each, then that's your lot.' Feeling cold, I put his jacket back on. It was too long at the sleeves and I saw Paul smile.

'Are you going to carry me?' I asked.

'Not on your life. I'd probably drop you.'

179

The dog had caught three phantom rabbits, dispatching each in a fury of growling. Paul whistled to fetch him back. Repacking the things he had brought, he sat considering me. 'I knew you must be hurt or ill,' he said reflectively. 'You wouldn't leave your aunt alone. Nor did I believe you were in the river. You've always had too much fight in you.' Turning away from me he shook his head. 'You see, I have remembered you, and not always with bitterness.'

Bounding towards us, the dog knocked the rucksack flying. 'Gerroff you daft thing,' Paul complained. Then he laughed. 'I'm entering this one for the Silly Mutt of the Year award.'

'I reckon he'll win,' I agreed. Feeling ridiculous in his jacket, I stood up. For a full moment Paul tried to be polite, then he burst out laughing again. Even after he had returned home, low and tired, to his father's bad temper and the town's curiosity, his sense of humour had not deserted him. 'Come on, Penguin,' he said. 'Can you walk? We'll cut across to Deepdene Farm and hope the Catford boys haven't left yet.'

'Of course I can walk.' I fixed my attention on the furthest tree. If I aimed for that tree I could reach it, and then I could aim for another.

The next three days were among the happiest in my life. After I was released from the hospital (mercifully they let me go by teatime) I lay floating between sleep and contented wakefulness at Sweetbriar while Aunt Mary and Janie Booth rattled cups in the kitchen. Later in the quiet of evening I listened to the sounds around me. I had forgotten the sense of closeness to Nature living in so flimsy a structure could give. Beyond the wooden walls the river lapped at the bank and I knew from the muffled water and sense of damp that a mist had fallen. My awareness of sound and smell seemed sharper. Never before had I been so conscious of the life flowing in me, or of its pleasantness. Unable to sleep any longer I got up, and careful not to make the floorboards creak, crept to the kitchen.

Aunt Mary heard me, of course. I had reckoned without an old lady's instinct for disobedience. Within minutes she was pulling herself along the corridor from the sitting room, demanding to know what I was doing.

'Making a drink, Auntie,' I admitted sheepishly. 'Then make me one while you're at it,' she ordered. I had expected a scolding and smiled at the saucepan.

We sat together in my room drinking Ovaltine while the alarm clock ticked beside my bed. It was eleven o'clock. Leaning back against my pillows, I began to talk of the day Mike died.

'I thought there was some trouble behind your disappearing,' Aunt Mary said. 'You'd never got lost before. Well, you wouldn't be the first that has hidden away. I've often thought that's one of the problems nowadays; there's nowhere quiet, or green, to hide.' The remark struck me as perceptive. 'You're very like your mother you know. You bottle things inside you. If you'd told us you thought the lad's death was your fault we'd soon have squashed the idea. It was a stupid thing for the lot of you to be doing – rowing over to that wretched island with a storm breaking. Lydia should have had more sense – she was the eldest – and so should Paul. Next to his father, he knew better than anyone. As for Mike Booth himself, well, I've no wish to speak ill of the dead, but he was always a daredevil, foolish sort of lad, all mouth and charm. He brought his death on himself.'

'But I was partly to blame,' I insisted. 'I delayed us ....'

'None of us is ever completely free of blame. When you reach my age you look back and see scores of things you shouldn't have done, or that went wrong when you meant them for good. There's things I could tell you that affect yourself and lie heavily on my conscience, but they seemed right at the time.'

'What sort of things?'

Aunt Mary shook her head. 'I've kept silence all these years, Martie. For the sake of the dead I'll keep silence a little longer.'

Her remark intrigued me, but she would say nothing more. As she looked at me there was a blankness in her expression which troubled me. The skin across her face was stretched tighter than ever and her whole body appeared frailer. Even more worrying, a red spot had appeared in one eye. With an obvious effort she drew herself up in her chair and smoothed her dressing gown. Once again, the intelligence returned to her manner.

'Are you sure last night hasn't done you any harm?' I asked.

'Of course it hasn't. The Booths were kindness itself, even Saul. I was frightened, but knew you'd be all right. You're too capable to come to harm in such a silly way. To be honest, I thought it was meeting Paul again that had upset you. That was partly why I went to the cottage instead of asking the Marshes to phone the police. I reckoned Paul would know where you were, and if he didn't it was his place to go looking.' My great aunt's mouth set into a firm line. 'Much as I admire that fellow, I can't help feeling he's treated you badly. I may be old fashioned, but I still believe if a man has his way with a girl, he should marry her.'

In bright red confusion I exploded with laughter. 'Aunt Mary, you have a peculiar way of putting things,' I protested. 'And we thought you were fooled. As it happens Paul would have married me – I think. It was me who broke it off.'

Aunt Mary grunted. 'Too independent for your own good,' she remarked. 'It runs in the family. And why haven't you married since? You can't tell me no one's asked you.'

'I've never felt like it,' I admitted. 'Besides, it's not usually marriage the gentleman has in mind. Oh it's all right, I had a good Methodist upbringing ... I drove one poor fellow crackers finding some excuse each time he suggested bed – I was too hungry, the milk bottles needed putting out. In the end he announced I was thoroughly repressed and gave me up as a bad job.' Glancing towards my great aunt I wondered if she was shocked, and saw she was smiling slightly. 'Well,' I added, 'he had to say something clever. He was a psychologist.' Then I was serious again. 'I would

182

have thought you of all people would have understood. You didn't marry for the sake of it, and that was in days when the pressure must have been much greater. Nor did Milly Lakin from what you've said.'

'No,' my aunt agreed, and I thought I detected a sadness in her voice. 'It's time you went back to sleep, my girl.' Lying back on my pillows I wished my great aunt goodnight. It occurred to me she did not like talking about Milly Lakin, even though they had been such close friends, and grief did not seem to be the only reason. That fact, and the passing references she had made intrigued me for a good half hour.

Indeed, so intrigued was I that getting up softly, I went to the old tins stacked on the floor beside my wardrobe. Taking out bundles of cards I began putting the ones sent by Milly from Wales into order. When I had finished my head was aching, but I had found thirty dated 1928, covering a period of ten months. They were all so vaguely worded I could not determine what she had been doing there so long, except that she seemed distressed, but trying to be cheerful. There were references to going to amateur concerts or walking near the castle at Harlech.

It was as if she had deliberately avoided any remark that might arouse the curiosity of a gossipy postmistress, and yet could not help but by her very reticence suggest all was not well. There were odd phrases like the fact that the hill was 'getting too steep now,' or 'of course I go out less now than I did', which began to give me ideas. Finally I found one card which must have been sent inside an envelope, for the address space was written across in pencil. It was dated July 1928.

'I thought you'd like this very old view of the town to add to your collection. I imagine it will become quite valuable in time. I am fine still, but tired and sick of myself. I must talk to you. Can you come down? I begin to love when I should not and the thought of parting becomes painful to me.'

The tone of that brief message touched my heart.

Perhaps a man would not have understood, but to a woman the meaning was clear. Milly Lakin was pregnant and hiding herself away till her baby was born. After that the child would be quietly adopted. Even now her situation would be difficult enough, unmarried and with a business to run. Supposing I found myself in that situation, what would the reaction of my colleagues be? In those days when her condition would have lost her the respect of everyone in her employ, it must have been almost unbearable. Except of course that she had money, could pay to stay somewhere for nearly ten months, pay to find the child a home . . .

Acting on instinct rather than reason, I crossed to the spare room I grandly called my study, and began looking through files, seeking a sheet of addresses I recalled bringing from Australia with me. This time my aunt did not appear. Finally I found what I was wanting and sat down to write a letter. *Dear Sir,'* I wrote, *'I am engaged in research into the history of a family connected with the industrial development of Sandhill, in the West Midlands. I have reason to believe a child was born to one Millicent (Milly) Lakin in August or September of 1928, within the Harlech area. I would be most grateful if you could send me a copy of the relevant birth certificate, and will of course send the appropriate fee. Unfortunately, I do not have any details of the father's name, but the child was probably illegitimate.'*

I should have used the proper form of course and my letter was badly constructed, but there was a chance the entry might be traced.

The stitches in my head had begun to sting. Enclosing a stamped addressed envelope, I sealed my letter and went back to bed.

For the next two days Janie Booth Took Over. There is no other way of describing her encampment at Sweetbriar. On the first morning she arrived at eight with a basket clanking with jars of calves' foot jelly, and bottles of elderberry wine which cured headaches by the simple principle of replacing them with a hangover fit for an office party. Since I was 'a mere slip of a thing,' though five inches taller and probably able to put her over my shoulder, I must be cossetted, fed, watered, and generally rubbed down. Feebly I protested, but was put in my place, though in the nicest way possible, with an 'indeed you don't, my dear' and a 'sure, but the Good Lord knows best'. She even altered her hours at the Villa so that she could see to me first before going to see to her old dears. If either she or Aunt Mary offered me another slice of cake with the words 'It'll build you up my dear,' I promised myself I would scream. I was not a cathedral requiring another stone, or a motorway. After my fifth cup of sweet tea (I don't take sugar), I pleaded to be allowed to sleep. Afterwards, however, I must be entertained to prevent me dozing again, or I would not sleep that night. Janie had heard of my nocturnal habits from Aunt Mary and did not approve of them. Which is why I was shown the family photos.

As a recipe for wakefulness Janie's album was none too successful. It consisted mainly of photographs of children, taken at those four-for-the-price-of-three stands in supermarkets, or caught in the act of suffocating themselves in candyfloss. She had six grandchildren in all and five of them were represented in every stage of dress, undress, and the knickers in between. Only Laura was poorly recorded. Three studio portraits showed her as a baby and a carefully groomed little girl, while a handful of holiday snaps portrayed her with her parents. With a peculiar sense of unease I examined the latter and found them unexpectedly poignant. The couple with the baby looked so young, so careless and handsome; the father holding his daughter on his shoulders or playing ball with her on a beach, the mother disconcertingly pretty, far too pretty for me to represent competition. The man and woman sitting beside the pool a few years later were still handsome, but the carelessness and happiness had gone.

Seeing my interest, Janie turned to her ultimate weapon, what she called her 'Mother's Pride Book'. It was a scrapbook, made up of cuttings and reviews, stage photographs or publicity handouts, and all of them concerning Paul or his wife. It began in the years when I knew him, with several small clippings regarding school speech days and distinctions in Piano grades six, seven and eight – two in one year – and included a report of the concert at Sandhill Grammar in which I had been involved. Even in those reports there were references to 'outstanding promise' and 'gifted young pianist.' Then, six months before my parting with him there was the first full-length feature, recording an award under something called 'The Dr Halliday Trust', given since the nineteenth century to a local youth of outstanding promise and poor family background. So much was made of the last point I cringed on the Booths' behalf.

After that first feature others steadily appeared in the *Examiner* announcing, *'Local musician wins Scholarship'* or *'Young pianist comes third in National Competition.'* The column space grew from an initial one inch to a full-page profile with the announcement of a scholarship to the United States, then dropped back to a few lines as he began again to establish himself in another country. I found a brief notice of a charity concert soon after his arrival there and scanning the list Janie pointed out to me the name Aileen Russell. That was how Paul met his wife, she confided. On the next page was their wedding invitation, glossily printed in gold italic, and dated only six months later.

'Mr and Mrs Stuart Russell request the pleasure of your company at the wedding of their only daughter Aileen Janine to Mr Paul Booth of Arton, England. Ceremony and reception to take place at The Cedars, 2210, Bellavista Avenue.'

He was not yet twenty-three, his wife twenty-four.

Less than a year later there was an announcement of Laura's birth, fifteen words in a New York free paper. I could not help smiling. Paul certainly didn't hang around. At thirty-one I regarded myself as still young, with no need to rush into marriage. He already had a child eight years old. Then, recalling my great aunt's description of Saul's impulsive marriage I was serious again. There was so much likeness between father and son, yet neither could see it.

Turning the pages with Janie's expert commentary, I read the programmes and reports that followed. About the time of Laura's birth Booth suddenly changed to Boothman. Presumably Paul had to take a stage name to avoid some already existing Booth and had used his family's original form. After that the two names Russell and Boothman appeared frequently in small-town concerts and charity shows, until three years after Laura's birth there was the review which must have altered everything. *Brilliant young newcomer wows audience.'* The picture beside it was smudged, but recognisable, a darkly brooding Paul in his Chopin mood. It made me laugh outright. Within months there were other more balanced reviews, but always the same points were made: technical brilliance, intensity of feeling, the youth and sensitivity of the performer. Within eight pages Paul had moved from playing one-night concerts in small towns, to the status of soloist. As one programme writer gushed, his rise was meteoric. But then, as long as I recalled him he had crammed more living into the space of a year than anyone else I knew. He was still driving himself too; that was evident. His debut recording had won some prize or other, and a foreign tour was planned. I could not think what he could be doing coming back to Arton, risking three or four months away from his career. 'Aileen's done very well for herself,' Janie prompted me, finding my turning of the pages too slow. She had too, rising from the Christmas concerts and social functions of a struggling singer to a permanent place with one of the leading opera companies, though American names and conductors meant little to me. It was all very impressive, and horribly poignant.

I was surprised Paul should have sent such proofs of success to his mother, for it savoured of conceit which I knew he did not possess, but seeing her pleasure, I forgave him. Perhaps after all it was a kind of anger, a reply to all those louts who called him Gyppo and all those women who refused Janie entry to their coffee mornings, to his father too for the times he burnt his music and ridiculed him... Janie had every reason to keep her Mother's Pride Book. Even allowing for the usual critical flannel, her son had established himself within American musical circles with remarkable speed. The progress from Dr Halliday's Bursary for poor boys to the last, acclaimed tour had taken fourteen years, fourteen years of constant achieving, constant work and dedication, with almost no private life in between, judging by the meagre photographs of himself with his family. It was hardly surprising he looked tired.

'He's done so very well,' Janie said, shutting the book with satisfaction, 'It can't have been easy, coming from such a different class and all ... particularly when his wife's family are so well-to-do. He must feel it returning here.' Her glance took in the direction of River Cottage.

'It's not what he's used to now. Do you know, they have a man at the apartments where he lives, who does nothing but let people out and in? They can put their washing out at night and someone will collect it and bring it back all cleaned and ironed. It's a wonderful place, New York.'

'It must be,' I replied gently. 'Do you like his wife?'

'I hardly know her, my dear. She's only been here the twice. I felt rather sorry for her.'

The answer surprised me. 'Why?'

'She seemed so out of place. Saul was his usual self, and the fair came through the second time she was here, so there were his brothers around, too. There were times I thought she was near to tears, poor thing. In the end Paul took her away touring with him for a bit and left the kiddy with us. It was a kind gesture – the sort of thing I'd have expected of him. I don't think the visits were a success all the same. I wasn't surprised he left her behind this time.'

Early that afternoon Paul himself came to visit me, bringing a bowl of late hyacinths so sweet they scented the whole chalet. He stood at the foot of my bed making conversation about Laura and the changes in Arton. I assured him I was the greatest layabout ever and thanked him for coming to look for me. Friendship was at least possible. As he stood there I was struck by the change in him, which seemed to mirror what had happened to his town. He would be perfectly acceptable in polite society, able to hold his own in a highly competitive profession, but to someone who had known him as he was, the cost was painfully clear. Already faint lines had begun to form around his eyes. Then, for just one moment he relaxed, and the old humour flashed through. 'I'll bet you didn't know you could still whistle,' he said.

I laughed. 'Once learnt, never forgotten,' I replied. Still he lingered beside me. 'Is there anything you need? Mum will see to the shopping, but perhaps there's something ..."

'Would you post this letter for me?' I asked. Taking the envelope from under my pillow, I passed it to him.

'I'd also like to write to Dad. There's some writing paper in my study.'

In a few moments Paul came back with a sheet of file paper and a pen. 'I'm sorry, I couldn't find the writing pad. I didn't like to rummage. '

I stared at the blank paper. No opening chapter had ever been so hard to begin. 'What do I say?' I asked.

'If you want me to tell him you've been hurt, I'll drop him a line.'

'Would you? Just say I'd like to see him. Don't worry him.' Still the paper stared at me. 'I feel I want to say something myself all the same.' Taking the pen I wrote just one line. 'Could you come down? I'm missing you.' The words looked sentimental on the page, but unable to think of anything else, I folded the paper and passed it to Paul. 'There's some envelopes somewhere' I began. 'I was using them last night.'

Smiling, Paul shook his head. 'Stop trying to be efficient,' he said. 'You were in hospital yesterday. You're entitled to lose envelopes.'

'Thank you for coming with me,' I said inadequately. 'I loathe hospitals.'

Again he smiled. 'I'll send Laura round with some books after school,' he offered.

Paul kept his promise. That afternoon Laura arrived, together with two library books and a huge jigsaw. A thousand pieces, she confided and all looking the same. After that, as soon as she came home the next day, she sidled into the chalet like a hesitant crab, 'to see if Miss Martie needed any help with the jigsaw.' Then, since I was clearly incapable of doing such a splendid puzzle on my own, I invited her to sit on my bed, while we struggled with bodyless legs and at least two miles of sea. At first, we worked in silence, but gradually the talking began, about America, her home, the peculiar grown-ups who called round. 'Musicians,' she added, as if that were sufficient explanation. If Paul had known how much of his private affairs was being shared with me he would have been acutely embarrassed. School, swimming pools, concert halls, everything she could think of was described to me with the speed of the lonely. I even heard about Grandad and Grandma Russell, though the impression I formed of them through her eyes was scarcely favourable.

When the jigsaw beat us into exasperated rest, we played snap and strip Jack naked. Aunt Mary told me I should call it 'beggar my neighbour,' lest I deprave the child, but Laura much preferred to be depraved. Aunt Mary invited her to stay to tea, and after Laura had run round to check that her father approved, she sat beside me eating sausage and chips and blowing an empty crisp packet out and in. It was nice with us, she announced. Grandad Booth was a grump.

'Don't you like it at the cottage?' I asked.

'Oh sure, I like it *really*. It's much nicer than that smelly school.'

'Larch Lane?' I asked.

Politely but firmly she explained she meant her school in the States. Daddy had taken her away because she hated it so much, but Mummy wanted her to go back. They had paid too many dollars to waste she had shouted at Daddy, and Daddy had replied money was nothing compared to a child's happiness. Then Mummy had said Daddy should have consulted her, and there was a terrible row right there in the hotel foyer, where everyone could hear. The child's eyes were uncomfortably bright. It was worse than any of the other rows.

The immediate reason for her parents' separation was being given me, the final quarrel that is no more the actual cause of breakdown than the bottle broken against a ship actually launches it. Gradually I gathered the hints and fragments. It seemed the other girls had taken a disliking to Laura. Perhaps her sharp cleverness had made them feel inferior; perhaps there was the same sense of difference about her that had turned the Arton boys against her father. Whatever the reason she had been subtly bullied until she was sick with misery. Then her father visited her, and they spent the day together. Clearly, he did not visit often, and he had driven across two states to be with her that time. When he started to say goodbye Laura cried so much her father became almost equally distraught. He took her back to the Principal and receiving no satisfaction – 'Miss Harrington said I invent things. I don't! I don't!' – he gathered her clothes from her locker and took her away. For the rest of his tour she shared his hotel room.

I could understand the mother being furious. Of course Paul should have consulted her; he ought to have found Laura another school; the money would be wasted, and he was no doubt in breach of some school attendance act. Yet if the woman had

191

known her husband's childhood as I had done she might have understood. And perhaps there was genuinely no time for him to make proper arrangements. After all, he was on tour and having to rehearse every minute he was not on stage. 'Mummy's mean saying I should go back,' Laura said with ominous quietness. 'When she marries again I shall stay with Daddy.'

'Do you think she will marry again?' I asked sadly.

'Course. Nearly all the girls at school had two Daddies or two Mummies. They said it was quite fun really. You get two lots of Christmas presents. Except that you have to buy two lots back and visit lots of boring aunties and uncles. Samantha had an extra Grandad and Grandma, too. That's all right I suppose if they buy you presents or take you to the movies, but I wouldn't like it if they were old; not falling-apart old like Gramp. One Gramp's enough.'

Though what she said was tragic in its implications, I could scarcely help laughing. 'Don't you miss your mother?' I asked.

The child looked at me with hurt, determined eyes.

'Yes,' she said. 'She smells nice and she's ever so pretty – prettier than you are – but she's always off singing and having to rush away when she's promised we can eat burgers together. Daddy used to go on trips too, but he's stopped now we've come to England. He's teaching me how to swim and to catch fish. He never taught me to catch fish before. He's much nicer here, even if he is always sad inside. He misses Mummy, so you'd expect him to be sad, wouldn't you? When he marries again he won't be sad. I'm going to look for someone for him to marry.'

I was being given a child's view of adult behaviour. For an eight-year-old she had an amazing vocabulary. She spoke like a small adult though without the prevarications and deceptions of adulthood. As we talked, a window opened into Paul's life and mistakes, and my sympathy went out to him, and to his wife also. Strangely, I felt less concern for Laura herself. That bright determined manner promised strength. Finally she got up, thanked us for having her, and announced she must be getting back. Daddy had lots to do; he needed her help.

Soon through my open window I heard her voice again. Helping Daddy seemed to involve playing football with him and I listened to their laughter as the ball thumped and bounced. It touched me on a raw place, reminding me of my own childlessness.

I had had enough of lying in bed; it was making me morbid. I had read Paul's books, two rubbishy thrillers I adored even while I laughed at them. The books I had brought with me bored me; the latest critical successes I should have read months ago but promised myself I would read when I was ill, and then said I was too ill to read. When Aunt Mary came to see if I needed anything I took her hand. 'Let me tape your memories,' I suggested.

'But I don't know anything worth recording ....'

'Of course you do,' I replied firmly, having heard the same excuse from a hundred old ladies, each of whom turned out to be a sociological textbook. 'I brought the postcards with me. Harry thought I was mad carting biscuit tins along. Let's make the carriage worthwhile. You can go through them and tell me who everyone is.'

'Well, if you really want me to ....'

And so began the telling of the story I thought was Aunt Mary's and found was my own.

On the Friday I got up. It was tempting to stay being coddled. – or is that something cooks do with eggs? – but Aunt Mary needed my help. I had seen that drawn look around her mouth again, yet she would not leave the housework undone. 'We've enough crockery for three days,' I protested. 'When I'm fit I'll hose the lot down in the garden.' My suggestion was met with the expected dignified rejection. So, since she would not rest while I did, I took over again.

For some hours I sat with my great aunt on the verandah, then when she fell asleep in her chair, I went outside. The sense of freedom was intoxicating. After walking slowly up the top track I stood beside the gateway to Arton Villa.

A smart sign announced 'Arton House. Residential Home for the Elderly.' The proprietors had got the name wrong. The Lakins had built and named their country residence on the Italian model with marble floors and a rococo porch. It must have changed a good deal since we visited Miss Lakin there, judging by the adverts I had seen in the local paper. The gates were open and brazenly I walked in. A large area of formal walks had been sold since my youth, to make space for a modern bungalow. Stuck-up people Saul said, who drove up and down the track in their Porsche without a word to anyone – he hoped the potholes broke their springs. Chairs and tables were set out on the lawn and three elderly ladies wrapped in blankets sat looking blankly at the remaining bushes, but clearly it was too cold for most of the inhabitants. I passed the old ladies, who looked blankly at me too. The front door was propped open with a wooden block, so I entered.

A woman in a blue dress and white cap sat in an office, once the butler's pantry. Feeling an idiot, I explained my errand. I had an elderly relative living with me. I wondered if they took short-term residents to enable me to go on holiday sometime. At once all was efficiency. I was shown round the public rooms, peeping in on a lounge already laid out with television and a circle of chairs, and then taken to a sample bedroom, a bright cubicle overlooking the river. Partitions had evidently been erected across a larger room, for the moulding round the edge of the ceiling continued along three sides and suddenly vanished. Everything was neat and bright and compact, and with every fibre of my being, I hated what had been clone to a once proud house.

Thanking my guide, I followed her down the marble staircase. A floral carpet had been laid over the steps and the hallway beneath to deaden sound and increase warmth, but the beauty of rose-pink Carrara stone shone at the edges. Pausing at the French windows

194

I admired the view over terrace and river, amused to see the back of our chalets and River Cottage discreetly hidden by a line of new leylandii. For an absurd minute I wanted to confide in that cool little woman, to see if there was any feeling beneath her efficiency, but I resisted such silliness. Taking the literature she offered me, I shook hands and left.

Outside I paused, pretending to savour the atmosphere of tranquility. A private ambulance approached along the path and I had to step to one side, against the bushes. The suddenness of the movement made my head hurt. For a second I saw the faces of the halest of Arton House clients, returning from a shopping expedition perhaps. I watched while the driver parked in front of the house and lifted out sticks and walking frames.

For a few moments I looked at the house, trying to picture its former grace. Suddenly the man stared at me, and feeling embarrassed, I turned to go. Picking up a cone from one of the decorative firs I tossed it thoughtfully in my hand.

I was absurdly impatient for a reply to my letters. So ill at case was I – though I could not imagine why – I woke at dawn on the Sunday and went out on to the verandah to watch the river while Aunt Mary slept. Once again there was a mist hanging white and dripping on the trees along the bank. Through its deadening silence I heard a gate close and saw Janie Booth walking along the path from River Cottage. She was dressed for a long walk but appeared to have a smarter pair of shoes in a polythene bag. As she drew level with the chalet I stepped back, unwilling to be seen in my dressing gown. The gate clicked again, and Paul ran along the path, calling softly to her, and still pulling on his jacket. They paused together outside our land and talked quickly and quietly before walking past the chalet together. Puzzled, I went back to bed.

It was only after I had dozed for half an hour that I realised where they were going. Janie had set out to walk to first Mass in

Styles, and Paul had unexpectedly joined her. In all the years I had been friends with him I had never known him go inside a church. None of the Booth boys did. They either shared their father's conviction that religion was a lying cheat designed to oppress the poor or feared him too much to appear to be sharing their mother's faith. Religion was a living issue in that household, fought over every Christmas and with the birth of every new child. Saul would have none of Janie's 'papery' and refused to have his sons baptised, though strangely he compromised over his daughters. As soon as she was well enough, and Saul was at work, Janie nonetheless walked with each new baby boy in her arms and the toddlers straggling behind, across four miles of fields to Styles and the nearest priest. I've often thought Saul must have known and grudgingly respected her stubborn faith. Without such undeclared truces I doubt if any couple can live together long. The constant warfare affected the children however, and I'm sure it contributed to the strange intensity each of them possessed. Even now Paul's decision to join his mother suggested either deliberate mischief or faith; I could not make up my mind which.

Aunt Mary and I breakfasted late that morning. We were still sitting over our coffee when the sound of an old van laboured up the track. Presuming it to be heading for River Cottage or the Villa we paid little attention until it stopped.

'Company?' Aunt Mary asked, just as she used to in the old days when half of Sandhill Wesleyan arrived unannounced. To my joy the van door opened, and Lol Jackson squeezed himself out, followed by Dad and from the back a woman with a toddler in her arms.

'Your father said he'd like to see you,' Lol said, shaking me up and down by the hand. 'He was worried like, being as you'd had an accident.' His voice dropped to a whisper even Aunt Mary could have heard. 'He gives me summat for the petrol, so I thought it'd be a chance to take Josie and the little 'un for a run. You don't mind me bringing them?'

196

In delight I kissed him, calling to Josie in apology afterwards. Josie herself stood awkwardly on the top path, obviously viewing the nearness of the river with concern. She was a heavy woman, what Harry would have called big and bosomy, and with her bottle-blond hair looked as though she might work behind a bar. Aunt Mary folded her hands in her lap after she had greeted her – a sure sign of polite disapproval – but I took to Josie at once. I was prejudiced of course, for Lol had told me she was a good sort.

During all these greetings Dad hesitated beside the van but I would not have it and brought him down to the verandah. 'Paul wrote to tell me you'd hurt yourself,' he began. 'Are you better?'

'Better than I've been for years.' Putting my arm awkwardly round him I pressed my cheek against his.

'Come and have a cup of tea with me. I'll tell you about it then.'

The little 'un was beginning to show a determination to roll headfirst down the path, and scooping him up, Lol announced he wanted to see what I had been doing in the garden. Then he and Josie would take a stroll along the river. His effort at tact was amusing.

I know now why we British always make a cup of tea at times of great emotion. It gives us something to do with our hands, and somewhere to look. As Dad and I sat together on the verandah there were many pauses, each filled by a sip of tea or a shuffling of a saucer. For the first time I could bring myself to talk of my own feelings, fumblingly explaining what I had felt when I lay in the woods. Neither of us used the word breakdown, or even implied there was any pain other than the physical, but we understood each other. Finally I could ask about Lydia. She seemed to be fine Dad said, though with her marrying again and moving around so much they'd tended to lose touch a bit. The last time she visited was, when? – over a year ago. Her new husband seemed nice enough though he wasn't really our sort. It wasn't that there was any coolness between them, I mustn't misunderstand him, just that going around the pubs of a Sunday lunchtime and driving smart cars, well, it wasn't what Dad had been brought up to share. Still, Lydia seemed happy enough.

The teacup saved him from further explanation. 'She's moved out of our world Martie, into another I don't trust or like, but she's a grown woman. I sometimes wonder if I could have done more to guide her.'

'She would take guidance from no one,' I said. 'Even when we were girls. Mike dying as he did made her worse.'

'I wouldn't have thought Mike Booth's death affected her much,' Dad remarked, looking up. 'It must have been upsetting, being there, but he never meant much to her. She told me so herself.'

'Perhaps – I don't know. I think he meant more than she was willing to admit. Nothing's ever gone right for her since. I've lost count how many men she's got through one way and another.'

Dad shook his head. 'From anyone but you that'd be spiteful,' he replied. 'But it's no more than the truth. I wish you weren't right. Lydia threw away her chances and it made me angry to see her do it. Your mother would have given her right arm for the education she got, but Lydia herself didn't seem to care, though she had Katie's cleverness, and more. You would work at life though, and you always knew what you wanted. I've been very proud of you Martie. You've given me something to boast about. The family sees me as a failure, you know.'

Getting up clumsily I put my arm round him.

We pottered about the garden after that, Dad admiring the planting I had been doing. As he examined the seedlings he glanced towards River Cottage in concern.

'Saul Booth's had a bad fall,' I explained. 'Though he must have let the place go before then. From what they say downtown he seems to have lost his self-respect. I don't think he can cope with the changes round here.'

'Who's started clearing the place then?' my father asked.

'Paul.'

He had clearly expected my answer.

Josie and Lol were returning, swinging the little 'un (who I never heard called any other name) between them. It was good to see them so relaxed and happy and to hear Sweetbriar once more alive with the sound of voices. To increase the confusion Janie and Paul chose that moment to return, appearing at the stile along the river path, Paul with his jacket slung loosely over his shoulder and Janie flushed with the warmth of her walk. In the seconds before they became aware of our presence Paul lifted his mother over the stile and then swung her round as if they were dancing. It was a gentle gesture which set her laughing and made me remember the boy I had loved. Then seeing our figures around the chalet, they were serious, embarrassed to be amongst unexpected company.

Janie excused herself. She must see to the dinner. That old range was getting so cantankerous the roast could be as black as coal by now, for all she'd put it in the side oven. Paul lingered, greeting Dad. The respect between them was obvious, even after years of separation. Standing beside our gate, Paul still with his jacket over his arm, they talked of America until Lol greeted Paul too, saying he remembered him from the weekends he had spent in Sandhill. Since Paul had stayed there as my recognised boyfriend the reference could have been embarrassing, but both men were too thoughtful to make any comment on the matter. As they stood talking I could not help but compare them: Lol all bulk and sandy hair, Paul so much darker and slighter, yet both possessing sensitivity as well as strength. It occurred to me that the three men I cared for most were together and 'getting on fine' as Lol put it later. If I could have brought happiness to any of them by magic I would have started whittling my wand that minute; a job for Lol, reconciliation with his wife for Paul, promotion for Dad. Fortunately I could not, or I should have been guilty of managing other people's lives.

Laura came running up the path. 'You didn't tell me you were going out with Gran,' she complained, her voice taking on an edge of insecurity.

At once Paul was bending to her. 'Didn't you find my note? You were sound asleep, so I wrote you a letter and put it beside you.'

'Not for ages and ages. I thought you wouldn't come back.'

'Whatever gave you that idea? This is the new regime — remember? If I go away, I come back. Was Grandad angry?'

'He was ever so cross with you, but I took him a bowl of cereal like you wrote, and he said I was a clever girl and told me funny stories about when he was little.' Possessively she put her arm round her father's neck, half strangling him. Then she spotted the little 'un. 'Can I play with the baby?'

I smiled. 'I imagine his mother would love you to,' I said. 'Go and ask. You must keep him well away from the river mind, and he'll wear you out. He's gone through three adults already. Can't you see the corpses?' I indicated two deck chairs filled by Aunt Mary and Josie, and the third in which Lol was struggling to persuade a wriggling little 'un to 'stay still for five minutes, can't you?'

'Are you sure?' Paul asked uncertainly. Looking at me he smiled. 'I would be grateful,' he admitted, lowering his voice. 'There's liable to be trouble when I get in and I'd rather she was out of it.'

For an hour Laura played with the baby, trotting up and down the paths and round and round the verandah. Twice Paul came out to see if she was all right, the third time joining us and sitting with my father beside the river. They talked quietly for half an hour. Tired of running around with a tireless toddler Laura flopped on the lawn beside me. She wanted to join her father, but I distracted her, taking her down to the water's edge to see the minnows. As we scrambled back my father rose, placing his hand on Paul's shoulder. For a few moments more Paul sat alone on the bank, staring into the water, then he got up and went back into the cottage.

Aunt Mary had begun worrying about lunch, but after various surreptitious trips back and forth between River Cottage and the chalet platefuls of buns and biscuits appeared, together with one of Janie's lardy cakes. For weeks afterwards I remembered that lunch.

Finally Lol decided he ought to leave. The little 'un was getting fractious. First Dad came to wish me goodbye. 'Don't overdo things,' he advised. Taking my hand he lingered. 'I've been thinking about what you said earlier.

Perhaps you were right. Perhaps Lydia did care for Mike Booth more than she said. I'd like to think so. It'd make her life since easier to understand. For all her hardness I think she feels more than she makes out. You've always seemed more like your mother, being so studious, but I reckon Lydia has a lot of Katie in her, too. Katie was always hard to pin down.'

Dad seldom talked of his Katie. Grief still lingered in his mind. 'In what way?' I asked. 'I remember Mum as full of life – and talk.'

'But it was often talk about nothing. She very rarely talked about what she was feeling. In all our married life she never told me who her natural parents were, yet I was convinced she knew who her mother was at least. I never liked to push it. I reasoned the woman might be local and the fewer people who knew the better.'

My heart suddenly raced. 'How did you meet her?' I asked.

In surprise Dad looked up. 'Aunt Mary introduced us. She knew Katie's family – the Wallaces.'

Lol and Josie were coming over to say goodbye and my father moved away. In gratitude I held out my hand to Lol. 'Thank you for bringing Dad', I said. 'You'll be able to tell Saint Peter when you're waiting at those pearly gates ... Today will discount a lot.'

'Aw,' Lol replied grinning. 'It must be strange you having Paul Booth so near,' he added, dropping his voice. 'Take care. I wouldn't want to see you hurt, and there's still a lot of love around between you two. I'm not saying it's conscious-like, but it's there all the same. You could slip into something without meaning.'

Foolishly I stood, still holding his hand. 'You give sound advice,' I agreed. 'As always.' Josie was calling. 'Sounds like I'll be in bother next,' Lol said and laughed. 'It's the first time I've known our Josie jealous.'

***

Laura appeared on the verandah the following day, after school. She insisted I come for a picnic along the river. was simply heavenly weather and I should take lots of holidays if *1* was going to get better. Grandma said I was just as bad as Daddy, working all the time. Besides, she wanted to show me how well she could swim. Within minutes an embarrassed Paul arrived to claim her. She had escaped him he said. Laura clapped her hands in excitement. Grandma would give us some cake and we would all go swimming together.

'No, my pet,' Paul said, flushing slightly. 'Miss Cooper's probably busy and I certainly am. You mustn't plan things without asking first.'

'You're not busy,' she declared. 'You're only clearing the vegetable patch and Gramp said he didn't want you to do it.' Victoriously she turned on me. 'What are you doing?'

Working on my book,' I replied, taking my cue from Paul.

'Have you got lots of ideas?' Laura persisted.

'Well, actually ...' I could not lie to her. 'No, but they'll come.'

'You'll think much better if you have a holiday. Grandma says so to Daddy all the time.'

She was unanswerable and in amusement I glanced towards Paul. 'Laura, you don't understand,' he began.

'I do. You're making excuses and you promised me we could go for a swim the first nice day. I like Martie and I want her to come with us. Mummy isn't here and Martie can help me get dry. You're hopeless.'

I could see Paul intended to refuse her demands on principle, but something checked him, some gesture of the mother perhaps which left him weakened. 'Let me come, for her sake,' I whispered. 'If we persist in refusing she's going to wonder why. I'm not going to start any funny business. I've no desire to get involved with a married man.'

He pushed his hand through his hair in confusion – and then nodded. 'Are you well enough?' he asked.

'Of course. I can't go in the water, but I'll help Laura.'

And so we adults found ourselves manoeuvred into an arrangement we would never have made ourselves. At first we did not know how to speak to each other and sat politely side by side. Still, as Laura had said it was a heavenly afternoon, taking us from spring into summer. Settling down with a book I lay back under the willows while Paul watched his daughter.

Delighted with her new skill, she splashed about in the inlet. Even when Paul was apparently dozing, his eyes were half-open, checking she was not straying into deeper water. Once he was up and calling her before I had registered she was venturing too far. Yet despite his apparent absorption in his daughter's enjoyment I remembered him well enough to know he was grieving inwardly.

Evidently Laura was anxious for him also, for she kept coming to him with pretty pebbles or to ask him the name of birds that flew along the riverbank. Her concern was touching even while it must have been irritating. I could not help wondering whether our picnic had been engineered by her in the hope that company would help him. After all, they had shared hotel rooms for nearly two months while Paul was on tour; now he was the one person she knew in a foreign land. It would not be surprising if she were sensitive to his moods. Finally I took her hand. 'Let him alone a while,' I whispered. 'He needs to be quiet.'

We played together at the edge of the water until Laura was hungry. As we returned to find something to eat, our voices startled Paul. He had been transposing a piece of music but as he looked up his expression suggested he had seen little of the manuscript pad before him. With what must have been a considerable effort he smiled and joined in our conversation.

That picnic, eaten with the usual seasoning of river sand and flies was surprisingly successful. For Laura's sake we confined ourselves to the present, told each other traveller's tales or bemoaned the state of England. A sensible hour after eating, Paul took Laura back into the river, teaching her how to improve her stroke and to jump into the water to him. I could not resist looking at him. There was not an ounce of spare flesh on his body, but the painful thinness of adolescence had gone; he had the physique of an athlete, hard and spare. Running down the bank to the overhanging branch we used as children, he dived into the river, reappearing beyond Laura and making her laugh in surprise. Again and again he dived, as if he found release in the repeated physical effort. As I watched I wondered what it had all been about: all that anger and hurt between us, all those years of bitterness.

Sitting there in the quietness I tried to evaluate my emotions. It was the taste of ashes which had made the day of Mike's death so hard to bear, as much as death itself. I had loved Lydia with the passion of a less exotic being, dazzled by greater strength and skill. She could throw a ball further than me, jump better, run faster, laugh more gaily. I knew that even if she and I were the same age I could never achieve as she did, so effortlessly. That Mike Booth should love her seemed natural. He was Adonis to her Venus, worshipped by lesser mortals like Paul and Harry. When he and Lydia vanished into the woods I quelled my uneasiness and allowed myself to be goaded into a similar relationship for which I was not yet ready, as if love were a race and once more I was competing with her and losing and worshipping her for winning. Paul's feelings for Mike must have been the same. Everything a younger brother could envy was combined in Mike: strength, handsomeness, confidence. He knew about things. If he wanted he could have had half the girls in Arton. To a hesitant boy permanently fighting ill-health he must have seemed godlike.

Then that day with its quarrels and parting and death, we saw with adult eyes. I recognised Lydia for what she was, a bit of a tart, however attractive; Paul saw Mike's womanizing and fecklessness. His grief was as much for what Mike had already lost as for his death -for the boy who had been the only one in the family to appreciate Paul's talent. In our pain and horror we turned on each other afterwards. Paul thought me a snob and a coward, responsible for his brother's death. I saw his hardness, his unforgiving nature. Suddenly he was no longer a genius but just a talented, rather cruel boy. There was truth in what we saw but not the whole truth.

Playing the genteel lady sitting on the bank dissatisfied me and I walked along the branch overhanging the water and sat trailing my feet in the river. It was ice-cold. Only a man who had grown up playing along its banks would have gone swimming so early. The child's mother would probably be horrified, yet she would have denied Laura a day she would remember all her life. Paul played the clown pretending to be Jaws and chasing her while I shouted encouragement, then swimming underwater, he made me shriek in surprise by grabbing my feet. A fine silly game ensued.

Finally we sat beside each other shivering on the bank. I helped Laura to dress, while Paul lay on a towel in the late sun. 'Aren't you freezing?' I asked in amusement. 'Or are you waiting for me to help you too?'

'That's an idea.' His eyes laughed at me. 'It is bloody freezing now you mention it.' Putting on his shirt he considered me. 'You're equally mad, scrambling up and down banks with stitches in your head. I'm glad you came, though.'

Feeling foolish I hunted for a sweater. 'You seemed pretty low,' I said.

'I was. You've done me a deal of good, indeed you have.' He had caught his mother's lilt and I laughed.

Laura was by now sitting playing on the beach, making a mixture of river water, sand and leaf which she stirred in some yoghurt cartons Paul had brought. 'You realise you're going to be asked to eat that lot,' Paul warned.

'It can't be worse than airline food.'

For a while we watched the child in silence. 'You get on well together,' I said.

'I've got to know her this last couple of months.'

I felt I dared to question him a little. 'She says she wants to stay with you.'

It was some time before Paul replied. Sitting up, he traced a pattern in the sand. 'That may be difficult. The courts usually give custody to the mother.'

'Then you are splitting up?'

'I don't know, Martie. I keep expecting a letter from Aileen. We agreed to part for three or four months and she would let me know how she felt during that time.' The pattern grew more and more intricate. 'I did receive something from her this morning, but it was only some business mail she had forwarded. When I opened it I was sick with nervousness but there was nothing, no message. If she'd just added a note, asked how Laura was or sent her regards to Mum and Dad – she didn't have to ask after me.' Disappointment still flattened his voice.

'What's your wife like?' I asked.

'Very talented and very temperamental. We make a bright pair. I think it was her voice I first loved. It haunts me even now.'

There was a long, awkward pause. Paul's manner puzzled me. It was too calm. Only the ever-increasing pattern in the sand betrayed emotion. Otherwise, he might have been speaking of someone else. I admired his self-control, but recalling the boy I had known, I felt anxious for him. It was as if he had screwed a lid down on his emotions and dared not – or could not – loosen it in any way.

'How did you meet?' I persisted.

'It was just after I went to the States. I won a scholarship to study there straight from college. Perhaps you heard? We were appearing in the same charity concert. I was playing the Rachmaninov of course.' Absurdly he conducted the air, his self-mockery typical, but sounding forced afterwards. 'Funny, isn't it? While we were students struggling to make a name everything was good between us, even after Laura was born. We bought ourselves a stack of baby books, took it in turns to look after her and thought we were the cleverest parents ever. In a year or so we managed to scrape enough money together to buy a little house on the hill and mowed the lawn and had barbecues with the neighbours. Then our careers took off.' As if that were sufficient explanation, he shrugged his shoulders.

'And that's what broke it up?'

'I suppose so.' We watched the river in silence. 'It got more and more difficult to be together. We had to put Laura in school. Agents were getting the bookings wrong or the venue had to be changed and the weeks we'd meant to have together as a family vanished. While we were together there was too much emotion to squeeze into too short a time. I was forever fighting her parents' influence too.'

'Are they very wealthy?' I asked.

'Not by American standards, though Mum and Dad'd think them so. It's not really a question of money, more of – I dunno – if I'd tried I couldn't have married into a family more different to my own. Now Aileen and I seem to be returning to our origins, somehow. She values possessions more and more; I hanker after being here. The last straw was when we sold the house and bought a smart apartment with everything laid on. I felt like I was shut in a cage.'

'I felt the same when I was in London,' I agreed.

In relief he turned to me, the unnatural calm at last beginning to give way. 'I longed to smell the woods and the river,' he said. 'There was nowhere I could walk, yet I had to get out. The strain of performing was beginning to get to me. All the right breaks were coming, and it was meaningless.' Lying down he watched the willows.

'When Dad had his accident it seemed fortuitous. It gave Aileen a chance to be free of me. There was a dispute over the tour I'd planned, and I decided to do the prima donna bit and refuse to continue with it. Laura had scarcely met my parents so it seemed sensible to bring her with me while Aileen was working. We tried to do what was best.'

'Who's the other fellow?'

The question made Paul turn away in humiliation. 'Did your father tell you?' he asked.

'No. He wouldn't breach your confidence. I guessed.'

'He's in the same Company as Aileen. She sees more of him than of me.'

'Do you have grounds for divorce?'

Putting his hand over his eyes he caught his breath. For several moments he lay apart from me in silence, and I wished I had not spoken. I wanted to reach out and comfort him but could not. Instead, I sat playing with a stick.

'I could sue for adultery if I wanted,' he replied at length. 'But I don't. I love her. It's not the same sort of love I felt for you, but it's deep. Besides, divorce isn't part of my way of seeing things.'

There was so little I could say. Revenge would have been easy; I could have made some smart comment, rubbed it in as Harry would have said, but I had no desire to do so. Lying back beside him I let the sun warm my face. 'I'm sorry,' I said. 'So very sorry.'

'It all seems so far away now,' Paul said quietly. 'This is real, lying here with the sun and the river... We go chasing our tails and what does it matter? I've been happier today than I've been for months.'

Laura was standing beside us. She passed us two cartons of mud.

'I've made you a cup of tea,' she said.

We went back to River Cottage. Janie had evidently expected me, for she smiled as she opened the door and led me through the house. Everything was clean and neat as I remembered it, though

208

emptier without children running from room to room. Outside in the yard Saul was sitting in a chair where the last sun could warm him. 'Your Ma wants some logs,' he said to Paul without any other greeting. 'The fire's low so you'd best get a move on.' Unexpectedly he pulled himself out of his chair and stomped into the scullery, to reappear later with a tray of glasses balanced precariously. 'Have a drop of me own brew,' he invited.

'This'll put hairs on your chest,' Paul said, passing me a glass. 'A couple of these and you'll look just like me Dad.'

FIVE: Fairground

The fair was due in Arton that Friday. Days before I saw the posters I guessed as much from the tightening of the atmosphere at River Cottage. Janie was uneasy, as if fearing trouble Saul made an extra effort to walk with only one stick. Even Paul seemed affected by the sense of waiting. All week he was restless, walking along the river on his own when Laura was in bed. Several times we met and sat beside each other talking. Since he would understand my dream, I shared with him my suspicions concerning Aunt Mary. Without my great aunt seeing, I fetched the cards from Miss Lakin and let him read them. His interpretation was the same as mine. He was quick to see what I intended for Lakin's Heath and to make me think my ideas through, having a fine logical mind when he wished.

On the Friday morning the first vans made their way along Arton bridge. By afternoon the long lorries and trailers had appeared, like blackened dragons, each with parts of gaily painted rides strapped in place. All day there was a shouting and unloading, a hammering and tapping of bolts that echoed across the river from the field to the south of the chalets. I had some shopping to do for Aunt Mary, and making that my excuse wandered to the end of Larch Lane, together with half a dozen unemployed youths and assorted dogs. There would be the usual roundabouts and dodgems and a new ride optimistically called the

'Hell Rocket', which I decided to avoid. To my delight I saw the old carousel being assembled. Splendid in horses and gilding, it had been repainted, as had several stalls. It seemed *Boothman Entertainments* had struck lucky with the nostalgia boom, and Zac Booth had had the vision to save the old attractions till such a time. A delightful children's roundabout had already been set-up; that too, recently refurbished in red and gold. The lettering around the frieze proclaimed *Boothman's' Chariots and Horses, giving pleasure to children throughout the land.'* A helter-skelter looked splendidly inviting.

Wondering if they had brought out the old organ, I crossed to the carousel and was delighted to hear it burble a few tentative phrases. To my surprise Paul's brother Artie was assembling one of the rides. Saul had told me Artie was married and working away, not that he had joined the fair. Since he recognised me I went and introduced myself. The eldest of the Booth boys, Artie had been most like Saul's image of a proper son. He broke half a dozen hearts in the time I knew him, having the strength of his father as well as the striking good looks of all the Booth children. I nearly laughed out loud when he introduced me to his wife. A bright little brunette, she was quite clearly another Janie, and just as capable of ruling her husband, however stubborn.

I complimented Artie on his family's wisdom, in bringing out the traditional amusements. His reply puzzled me. 'That was our Paul's doing. We can't compete with these modern corkscrews and things. That new ride nearly broke us.' He nodded in the direction of the Hell Rocket. 'Paul said old things were all the rage in America and he reckoned they would be here too. We'd still got the Victorian stuff dumped at the back of the trailers, and he said we should do it up. Judging by the way trade's going it looks as though he was right.' There was grudging respect in his tone; the kid brother had brains.

'I didn't realise Paul had anything to do with the business,' I admitted.

'Yeh – he does the paperwork regular. Zac sends it over to him once a month. He's got the best head for figures of the lot of us. Zac'd like him to take over the business side of things when he retires, but Paul prefers to ponce around playing the piano.'

School had just turned out and two dozen excited children joined us, vying with each other to claim the longest 'go' last time or the sickest night afterwards. Several adults drifted onto the edges too, mothers who had been to meet their children or old men who felt they might as well stand and spit with a bit of entertainment as stand and spit at home. Amongst the newcomers were Paul and Laura. At once the child saw me and ran across the field, grabbing my hand. 'Come and see,' she instructed. 'It's a fair. Daddy knows them, he says.'

I allowed myself to be dragged towards her father.

He was talking to an elderly but mountainous man. Uncertainly Laura examined this apparition. 'Allow me to introduce Laura,' Paul said, lifting her so she could see into the man's face. 'I brought her over with me this time, so she could see Mum and Dad.' Putting her down again he turned to another man, older but with a keen expression, whom I remembered as Zac. 'These are my Uncles, Laura,' Paul said quietly. 'Your great uncles, Cal and Zac.'

Artie had come to join us. 'How 'you doing?' he asked Paul. Holding out his hand he noticed the oil on it and withdrew it in apology. Laura stepped back and mutely demanded explanation.

'Didn't your father tell you his family ran a fair?' I asked. Dubiously she nodded. Clearly, he had told her, but she had not understood. 'Do they live in those funny lorries?' she whispered.

'They have to. They're travelling round all the time.'

'Like hippies?' There was a world of disapproval in her voice, the tone of middle America, of her smart private school. I suddenly realised how far Paul had left his family behind.

'Your father's family travel with the fair,' I repeated at last.

212

'Then Daddy should tell them to go away. Nice people live in proper homes.' My own snobbery sounded in her voice. At once I turned against it. 'Not always,' I pointed out firmly. 'I don't live in a house. I live in a flat.'

'That's an apartment, silly. We live in an apartment. Only hippies and gypsies live in lorries, and they're all thieves, Grandad says so.'

'Perhaps Daddy will take you inside one of the vans,' I said, trying to be patient. 'They're very pretty inside. And I haven't always lived in an apartment. Some of the homes I've had have been no more than a room in someone else's house. You mustn't judge people by where they live.' A small child ran by. Goodness knew what relationship she was to Paul; niece perhaps for the family likeness was clear. 'I'll bet that little girl wouldn't swap with you,' I added briskly. 'She doesn't go to school. Not often anyway.'

I had judged Laura accurately. She turned with a mixture of admiration and fascination in the girl's direction. 'I still think Daddy should send them away,' she insisted. 'They're dirty.'

For the first and only time I lost my temper with her.

'Don't you ever let your father hear you say that,' I warned. The tone of my voice startled her and I tried to soften it. 'He'd be very hurt,' I added. 'You'd be dirty if you'd been assembling one of those rides.'

Fortunately Paul had not heard. He had been talking to his uncles. Picking his daughter up, he swung her onto his shoulders. 'Auntie Hilda's got some cake for you,' he said.

'I don't want any cake.'

'Well, I do. I'm hungry. Auntie Hilda makes the best cake in the world. Even better than Nan Booth's.'

'How can she make cake in there? Cakes need ovens.'

Paul laughed. 'Of course she's got an oven, silly, and a refrigerator, and a television. Don't be a snob.'

'She doesn't approve,' I whispered.

For an instant I saw Paul's eyes take on a weary expression, then he swung her down again, making her shriek with pleasure. 'Come and see a house on wheels,' he said. Her lips still pouted but she could not resist the idea of a van with an oven and a television and a refrigerator.

Gathering my shopping I went back into town.

For a supposedly clever woman I could be remarkably stupid. Till that afternoon I had never visualised what it must be like to live on the edge of society; the polite sneer in the grocer's, the whispers behind closed doors. Laura spoke with the tactlessness of a child, but so did all those other children when we played together in the Tourney field or messed about along the water's edge. The fair was welcome in Arton for a few gaudy days but having one of its people living permanently in the town was another matter. I should have visualised how much the gibes would have hurt, the nicknames, the refusal to sit beside a particular boy in class. One wretched harridan insisted the Booth boys sat apart 'in case they had nits.' My face burned at the memory. My rejection of Paul years ago must inevitably have been misunderstood.

Father and daughter returned later that afternoon when I was out in the garden. Laura was sitting on Paul's lap in the back of a wagon, her face bright with excitement. She laughed as he lifted her down, then ran through the top gate to tell Gran and Gramp she had ridden all the way home. Paul had won her back to him.

An hour or so later Saul came stomping up the garden path, together with his sons and older brothers. 'Now you hurry up and mend,' I heard Cal saying. Indeed it was impossible not to hear. 'I'll send the Chevrolet -you'll ride more comfortable in that.' The old pick-up started in a cloud of smoke. Saul went back into the cottage, but Paul came towards me. 'Put your spade away and come and have a chat,' he said. 'Please. I'll see you at the inlet in half an hour.' He laughed at my expression. 'I'm not going to make a proposition, me dear. I simply want to ask a favour.'

In bewilderment I went into the chalet to wash. The fairground had started on the opposite bank, its music blaring across the water. There would be little sleep till twelve for the next few nights. One of my earliest memories is of lying in bed in the chalet trying to sleep above that music, and wishing I was on the other side of the river.

Paul was waiting for me. 'I wanted to talk privately with you,' he explained. 'Would you do me a good turn? Meet Laura from school for the next few days? Perhaps a week or so?'

I burst out laughing. 'That's a new one,' I admitted. 'Why?'

'Uncle Zac wants me to help out on the dodgems. They're short of a man. One of my cousins has got himself into a bit of bother.'

I raised an eyebrow, not sure whether I could pursue the issue further. 'Nothing unusual,' Paul said resignedly. 'No more than the standard brawl with a gang of local lads looking for aggro, but this time one of them got hurt and Phil's likely to be doing time. It's not his first offence. Our Phil has a temper. It doesn't pay.' He shrugged his shoulders. 'The family reckon he wasn't to blame. Perhaps he wasn't. There's usually a fair amount of provocation. Either way they've had to leave him behind. I've suggested they send for our kid. He's on the dole up north and could do with the work, but till he comes down I'll fill his place – if you'll help with Laura. I don't like to ask my mother to keep coming and going. There'll be enough trouble about me joining the fair as it is.'

If he had asked me to run off to Kathmandu I would have been less astonished. 'Join the fair?' I repeated.

'You must be joking.' Evidently, he was not. 'Why?' I demanded. 'You've always avoided helping in the past, taken any job rather than do so. Will you even cope? It's not work for a musician.'

Paul laughed, 'I'm not the sickly kid you remember,' he said. 'While I was at college I used to help Zac every summer. I made good money.'

'When you're a student you'll take anything,' I agreed. 'I worked on a conveyor belt one year, but not now. Surely your uncle can find someone else?'

'Not with an HGV licence.' Once again, I stared at him in astonishment. 'Zac doesn't want a kid to help out with the fares. He needs someone to take charge of the dodgems altogether, see to setting them up and running them.'

'When did you get an HGV licence?' I asked, amused at the idea.

'In the States. I have hidden depths. I worked as a trucker when I couldn't get bookings. I used to do the Eastern seaboard route. I've got lost in the best of places.' He shrugged his shoulders. 'It was either that or accepting money from Aileen's father.'

In understanding I nodded. 'I doubt if she'd approve of you working on the fair now.'

'There's a lot of things Aileen doesn't approve of. Hell, what's it matter? Or are you going to come the respectable middle-class lady on me?'

'No' I replied, 'I hope not. I just want to know why you've made up your mind to go. Even if the fair does belong to your family you turned your back on it years ago. From the day you went to Grammar school you set yourself apart.'

My opposition had clearly been expected. 'The longer I stay here, the more my father will rely on me,' he said carefully.

'True,' I agreed. 'But you can leave without joining the fair. Hire a car and take a bit of a break with Laura.'

'I need the money, Martie. Turning this last tour down has cost me a great deal. I can't live off Mum and Dad and I'm certainly not writing to Aileen to ask for money.'

'That's a better reason,' I agreed. 'But you could give lessons. I gather people have been asking already. Your name's worth a good deal.'

Evidently, he had expected two arguments to be enough. Picking up a pebble he skimmed it expertly across the water before replying. 'Martie,' he said quietly. 'Please, because we used to love each other, if for no other reason. You buried yourself in the woods when you wanted to sort yourself out ...' His voice tailed off, the explanation incomplete but sufficient. 'For six years I've done nothing but rehearse and perform. Even before then it was practise, practise, practise. How else do you think I've made a name for myself, won competitions?'

Reaching out to him, I stayed his hand as he picked up another stone. 'Of course I'll look after Laura,' I said.

The spell of the fairground was upon us all those five days. All weekend the music throbbed through the town. Great gangs of young people collected at the entrance to the field. There was little enough to do in the town otherwise. Bikies came from Styles, revving their machines till the echo clattered off the buildings and it was easier to go through the eye of a needle than find a place in the car park. Respectable Arton disliked the intrusion but was quite willing to sell it scones for tea.

Each day Laura and I went down 'to see Daddy'. As soon as we arrived she was unutterably spoilt by relatives she could not even name. Mercifully she had a nausea- proof stomach or I should have run out of paper bags by the end of the afternoon. Every quarter of an hour she went clown the helter-skelter (or slip as Paul called it) wearing a hole in her knickers, and afterwards ate candyfloss till her face was a pink blob. Sometimes she rode on the old children's roundabout, but she preferred the carousel and used to stand watching the horses float up and down or listening to the organ burbling its sweet Victorian melodies. It was clear she had inherited some of Paul's talent for she could sing the tunes to herself within minutes. Most of all however she liked to wait beside the dodgems and watch her father working his way from car to car while the girls screamed, and the electricity spat above him. Her father was not the serious man she had thought, always practising and bowing formally at the end of a concert. She much preferred this other man, but she did not know him. He was as sure-footed on those rapidly moving dodgems as he had been on the boats in his youth, and I too watched in bewildered admiration.

217

Respectable Arton was mystified. Paul was its local boy made good, the lad with the talent who had lifted himself out of a splendidly awful background (as befitted genius) and returned with an American wife and a sheepskin coat. The town could not begin to understand why he should go back to the fair as if he were no different from his brothers and came in droves to discuss the matter. Girls giggled in queues just to have him push their car and I'll swear the Boothmans' takings were doubled, simply because Paul was managing the dodgems.

The whole world of River Cottage and the fairground mystified Laura. It was outside her experience, beautiful, but cruder, coarser. In the mid-mornings before the fair opened the Chevrolet bounced up the track to take Saul to join his brothers in the pubs in town. Ridiculous in its silver trim and custom-sprayed panels, it bounced back soon after two o'clock, bringing her grandfather, by then several pounds lighter in the pocket and several pints heavier in his belly. The second day Paul joined them. When I told Aunt Mary she shook her head. Those Boothmans were heavy drinkers and would ruin him. Yet when the car returned Paul was still self-possessed, helping his father and patiently listening, for Saul was argumentative in his cups.

On the Tuesday when Laura was at school Paul asked me to join them and feeling like a prim spinster I sat in the Black Bull while Saul and his brothers told increasingly noisy anecdotes about towns they had known and good times they had shared. Paul sat quietly beside me listening, with that intent expression I had seen before when he was absorbing information for subsequent use. Like myself he was an observer, though he was with his own family. Aunt Mary need not have worried. He drank very little. When his brother began goading him on the matter he shrugged his shoulders and replied that he preferred to keep a steady hand. The subject was dropped. I had the distinct impression Paul would have got up and walked out had it not been. Apart from that one discordant note the afternoon was very pleasant, though I was aware that people around me were watching.

On the Tuesday the fair made ready to move on. The generator was stopped, and an uneasy silence fell over the whole town. An urgent hammering out of pins and tapping out of bolts began, though there was surprisingly little shouting or movement, each man knowing his job. It was as if the colour and noise of arrival were purposely created to bring in the crowds. Laura was at school, so I went alone to wish Paul goodbye. Jumping down from one of the rides he came across to me. 'Thank you,' he said awkwardly. Then he pushed something into my hand. It was a ten-pound note.

'What the hell's that for?' I demanded, genuinely annoyed. 'I didn't expect paying.'

'One pound, for sixteen years at eight and a half per cent – compound of course. I came to a different answer each time 1 worked it out, so 1 rounded it up.' Which was an errant lie of course; at school he came top in maths with boring regularity. 'Oh give over,' I complained. 'We were kids then.'

'But I never paid you back. We've settled our debts in other ways Martie. Let me settle this one. It'd make me feel better.'

Shaking my head in vexation I accepted the money. 'I'll spend it on Laura,' I promised. 'Take care.'

'Of course I will. I shall only stay till Ian joins us.'

We did not know how to part. 'Laura wants to come with you,' I remarked. 'She can't understand why you'll take Tiger and not her.'

'If I leave that dog behind I might as well shoot it myself. Try to make Laura understand. Tiger's education is with me- hers is at school. If I keep her off any more I shall have you social workers after me.'

'I am not a social worker,' I replied frostily.

'Professional pride has been wounded I see,' Paul replied, laughing at my reaction. 'Good luck with the book.'

'I need it. I've hardly touched it this last week or so. You're a thoroughly bad influence.'

'So I've been told. I must go and help. We have to be near Shrewsbury tonight.' Yet still he did not go. Half a dozen youths were watching us. 'Be seeing you.'

I lingered as he walked towards the ride, then pulled himself up on to one of the girders.

River Cottage empty after he had gone. Foolishly we had assumed that within a couple of days Paul would return, walking up the path with his coat slung over his shoulder and the dog trying to knock him into the river. Instead, on the Thursday we received a lettercard from Shrewsbury. He was very sorry. It looked like being a week. Ian was travelling himself, having gone looking for work, and they had been unable to get in touch with him. The fair would be moving on Friday and Paul would go with it. He hoped Laura was being good and would send her a present in a separate package. A brief note had been added for me. Would I write to him, care of the Red Lion? He would like to know how Laura was and his parents weren't much of a hand at letters. Sitting down straightaway I wrote an answer, persuading Laura to add a sentence and sign her name.

Janie stood looking through the window, the line of her shoulders expressing more than any words could say.

'He'll come back,' I assured her.

Silently she turned and considered my promise. 'I used to dread the fair coming through,' she said. 'I never knew whether Saul would be with me afterwards. If they needed a man, or the mood took him, he'd go off with them, just like Paul has. Sometimes it'd be months till I saw him again. Oh, he'd send me money regular, and I'll not pretend it wasn't useful. It bought the kiddies new shoes, paid for a bit of curtaining perhaps, but I was left bringing up three or four little ones on my own. It's claimed my sons too, one after the other. Artie could have been anything he wanted, but no one would give him a decent job and he was too proud to go cap in hand looking for work, or to take the dirty things they gave him. He would just join his uncles for a summer he said – he's never lived at home since. If he hadn't died when he did, Mike would have joined them too, and Ben's always coming and going with them.'

'What draws them to it?' I asked gently.

'It's like that old carousel, Martie. The life's colourful and bright, beautiful in its way, but the horses go up and down and round and round and get nowhere. They waste themselves on it, all of them. Zac's one of the cleverest men I know, indeed he is and even Cal's shrewd, a bit of a philosopher; as for my Artie, he was so fine, and now look at him. I hoped Paul would stay away from it. I was even glad when he went to the States. I thought he'd break with all the old ways and I was happy for him, though I shouldn't see him myself. If I'd known he would go off with Zac I would never have asked him to come home.'

'It's only for a week or so,' I insisted, but Janie shook her head.

'You shouldn't have agreed to help with the kiddy,' she said. 'He wouldn't have asked me. If he'd had to see to her he couldn't have gone.' Angrily she turned on me. 'We'll be left with that little one, mark my words.'

'No,' I persisted, feeling irritated myself. 'Paul wouldn't desert Laura.'

Aunt Mary was equally cheerful when I returned to the chalet. Paul was throwing away his career. There would be no going back to routine afterwards, much less to the hours of practice he would need if he were to perform in public again. It was strange how there was that restlessness, that persistent gene. She had hoped Paul with his determination and talent could resist it. Again she shook her head.

Despite such prophecies of doom, for me those days were extraordinarily happy. I felt like a schoolgirl who has just finished her exams. Poor Aunt Mary must have found me horribly noisy.

Laura treated me as if I were an ungainly classmate and instructed me in the niceties of feeding chickens or stroking the goat – not easy skills to acquire with the chickens vanishing upriver and the goat with as fine a set of teeth as you saw on a dental technician's shelf. Each day I rose early to feel the beauty of the morning. When I stood on the verandah soon after dawn fishermen waded like herons in the water; others squelched past me in wellington boots and I waved in a shared joy. After I had taken Aunt Mary her breakfast we sat in contented silence, our awareness of every detail sharpened by the knowledge she might not see it another year: the whiteness of the hawthorn along the bank, the pink of the cherry tree Harry had planted as a stone. As soon as I had taken Laura to school I returned to the chalet to work for three or four hours. In the afternoon I talked to Aunt Mary, taping her memories of Sandhill and Arton, the Hopes and the Langdons, ready to transcribe in the evening.

During those first days I walked a good deal, too. Aunt Mary advocated a daily constitutional. I used to think these daily constitutionals were something to do with America, a sort of twenty-four hourly Declaration of Independence. I even managed to persuade Aunt Mary to accompany me a few hundred yards along the river path. It made her feel young again, she said. It was then I persuaded her to admit she had been entrusted with the deeds to Lakin's Heath. For some moments she played with me, assuring herself of my secrecy, but at last she nodded. 'It's time I told someone,' she admitted. 'If I had been younger I would have set about restoring the land as Milly wanted, but she left me no money – that all went to charity -and I couldn't do the work myself. Besides, while the land lay idle everyone forgot it.'

'What did Miss Lakin intend?' I asked.

'It was Richard's idea first – and Isaac Booth's. They dreamt of a sort of wild park where animals and birds would return and the people of Sandhill could walk. Milly always hoped to carry out their plans herself, but she was too busy keeping the business together. For a while after she died I went up to see things were safe, but the hinges have gone on my legs now. I haven't dared ask anyone else. I've kept faith with Richard and Milly, but not as I would have wished.'

On the Friday a second postcard arrived, while on Saturday there were separate ones for his parents and me. I added my own to Aunt Mary's collection, just as Aunt Mary had added those he sent me when we were at school. No doubt a postcard was easier for him to send than a letter, but he had always been able to sense what would give me pleasure.

There was a brown envelope for me too that Saturday, postmarked Gwynedd. Inside was a birth certificate. For a long time I stared at it. The date was 31 August 1928; the child's name Katherine Mary Lakin. In the space for father's name was written 'not given'. My hands shook as I refolded the paper. Feeling I needed fresh air I walked through the woods to finish aimlessly standing at the gates to Arton Villa. How Milly Lakin's child could have come to marry her best friend's nephew, I could not imagine, unless my great aunt engineered the match as a kind of belated justice. But the birthdate was right and so were the Christian names.

All morning I could not make up my mind whether I should tackle Aunt Mary. It was none of my business. My mother had been legally adopted; her name before then was irrelevant. Yet the idea tantalised me, giving me a sense of responsibility I did not have before. If my mother had been born in wedlock the Heath would have gone to her, and through her to her children. As it was, it would probably come to our father via Aunt Mary. There was a peculiar appropriateness about the patterns forming in my life.

Shutting myself in my study I wrote a letter to Miss McClean. I had a proposal to make for the school project, I said. Without going into details, I suggested it might be possible to trace the owner of Lakin's Heath. I believed I could persuade him/her to co-operate in its reclamation for the good of the community, as an open space or an industrial museum, possibly both. If she approved of my suggestion, perhaps she could begin making enquiries concerning finance and so on, without of course committing me in any way? The Community Programme would presumably be the right body to approach, but she would have more knowledge of such matters than myself. As soon as I returned, I would discuss the scheme in more detail.

Then I wrote a similar letter to Charlie Warwick. Both would understand, of course. They would know I would not write unless I was certain who was the owner of Lakin's Heath, and was confident of obtaining co operation. If they shared my vision, Lakin's Heath might be saved. Richard Lakin and Isaac Booth would have their memorial.

Suddenly the theme of my book was before me: the relationship between the First World War and decline in a typical industrial town, the loss of potential leaders like Richard Lakin and a whole generation of the brightest and best. Putting the biscuit tins on the table I went through the cards again – the nice-looking men with 'Killed' written across their pictures, the Sandhill Battalion parading with its cumbersome gun carriages, preparing to face an enemy with twice the efficiency and twice the speed. There were even horses, horses to pull wheels stuck inches in mud. All the names in Aunt Mary's anecdotes were there – Lakin and Langdon, Hope and Norman: a whole generation of leaders and businessmen. Sandhill's decline mirrored that of the whole country. Those who had survived were unwilling to go back into the family firms; they had seen too much. Weaker relatives took their place, sisters like Milly Lakin who lacked experience and male respect however courageous; brothers who being less adventurous had been slower to answer the call, or were refused because of ill-health. Whole estates had been broken up with the loss of a male heir. Like soundwaves from one of those charges we used to hear fired in the quarry, the repercussions had spread beyond Sandhill, as far as Arton even. With the loss of Arton Villa and its grounds there was no 'Big House' employing local girls, no work for such as the Booths, and nowhere to hold the church fetes. All that was left of my own family's estate was a rubbishy, half-derelict heath, and River Cottage.

I was moving into social history rather than pure sociology and was out of my depth. I needed someone to talk to, some sympathetic wall against which I could bounce my ideas and sec if they fell limply to the ground. If Paul had not gone chasing his own dream I should have used him, as I had done when we were at school. Then I remembered his first letter. In it he had given me the telephone number of *The Rising Sun* in some small town in Shropshire. We had no telephone in Sweetbriar and there was none at River Cottage either, so I decided Laura and I would go to Styles. The post office there had one of those fancy pay phones with buttons, which would take money in advance. That would be easier than shoving ten-penny pieces in every few seconds.

Hurriedly Laura and I caught the bus on the main road. It was the first time I had left Arton since my return. My life had become bounded by the river and the woods beyond it, and I had been content to have it so, as if I had buried myself deep down, as I did amongst the leaves in the sawpit. Now I wandered the market town, finding the traffic exciting, the market exhilarating. There were stompings of hooves in cattle sheds, shoutings of men, bustle and clatter and colour and I loved every minute. Then we reached the post office and for some reason I was immediately nervous. Had I got the number right? Would the telephone be in working order? Laura was oddly quiet too, her eyes taking on the uncomfortable brightness I had seen when she spoke of her mother. I was aware of her love for her father, and the pain it brought. At last we were through to a stranger's voice and the sound of laughter and glasses.

I heard the voice turn away and call, 'Tell Paul it's for him. Cal, where's that nephew of yours?'

We were awkward, unused to speaking to each other at a distance. In embarrassment I passed the phone to Laura. Her speed made up for my slowness; she talked of everything and nothing, rattling so her father could scarcely have followed her. Yes, school was all right. Grandad was getting better. Gran had made her a new dress with a bow on the collar. It looked like a butterfly but she was sick of the dresses she had brought with her. Would he buy her a pair of shorts for school? She had to have green ones. Gramp said to tell him the strawberries were flowering well. Thinning the plants had done them good. The last remark pleased me. It was the nearest to a thank you Saul was likely to express. Finally she passed the phone to me.

A burst of laughter in the background almost drowned Paul's voice, never particularly loud. 'I'm sorry Martie. I didn't mean to leave you holding the baby, even if she is a big baby nowadays. She sounds OK. I owe you.' There was a pause. 'How's the book going?'

'Fine. It's suddenly gelled in my mind. Don't laugh at me, please, but I've unearthed something rather odd. My mother was Milly Lakin's daughter. Illegitimate, of course. She was born in Harlech for some reason.'

'Well, now,' Paul said quietly and as I had feared, he was amused.

'I think it's sad not funny,' I answered stiffly.

'I imagine it was sad, for Miss Lakin and your mother, but can't you see the funny side? Your family has always been so above mine, so respectable – so chapel. And as for the Lakins!' I could visualise the amusement in his eyes. 'My Dad did odd jobs for them and touched his forelock. I'm not laughing at you Martie, or what happened, but at the whole business – class, respectability, whatever you call it. Putting it crudely, if the chemistry's right, the mighty breed like the rest of us.'

It was ironical, I had to admit that. 'When are you coming home?' I asked. 'I want to talk to you about it all.'

'We've managed to get in touch with our kid, so it shouldn't be long. He has to finish a job he's doing and get down to us. He's found himself a girl. She's joining us too.'

'Aunt Mary thinks you'll stay with the fair for good. So does your mother.'

'I couldn't stand the noise. I can put up with a lot of things, but not that bloody music. Stop worrying. I'm not going to the bad – not yet. I just can't leave Uncle Zac a man short.'

A woman's voice called in the background, 'Paul, your beer's going flat. Who are you talking to?'

My money had almost run out. 'Are you all right?' I asked.

'I've got bruises where I didn't know I'd got places, but I'm enjoying myself.'

The money ticked remorselessly. 'Martie ....'

'Yes?'

'I'm sorry if I sounded heartless a minute ago. A thought occurs to me. My grandmother's people lived in Harlech. They ran a lodging house there. It wouldn't surprise me if Miss Lakin stayed with them until her baby was born. She'd have hidden somewhere. Dad would know the address. Take care of yourself.'

'And you.'

The money clicked into nothing.

Both of us quiet and drawn in on ourselves, Laura and I walked round the town afterwards. I felt ill at ease, as if the conversation had been left uncompleted. The woman's voice had been young and demanding. It reminded me of my great aunt's description of Saul's marriage, the wenching, the girls who hung round the fair. Paul's quietness and agility would attract attention as much as his looks; he too would have the girls hanging around.

We could not be depressed long. Styles was too interesting. Laura took the statutory hour to spend her pocket money, becoming the proud owner of a rubber dinosaur and a spider that stuck to walls, then we sat on a park bench eating real English fish and chips out of a paper bag. I had forgotten how good that could

227

taste. Half the fun of entertaining a child is the excuse it gives you to do things adults aren't meant to do. Afterwards we talked of school, America and the solar system. 'Do you like Daddy?' she asked suddenly.

'Yes. I've known him a long time – since I was your age.'

'Mummy says he's no good to us. She says she wouldn't have married him if she'd known what he was like. I heard her telling Grandma Russell.'

I sighed, wondering what to say. 'His values are different,' I began, but my reply was of course incomprehensible to her. 'Those big men you saw with the fair, his uncles, they're not poor you know. The fair's doing quite well nowadays, but they spend their money on different things to us: gold, nice crockery, things they can take with them when they travel. Their vans cost thousands, almost as much as a house – at least the new ones do, with the shiny metal all over the outside. Your father doesn't belong with the fair, but he shares a lot of his family's attitudes.'

'Mummy likes Uncle Mark better.'

'How do you know?'

'She used to bring him to the school sometimes. I stayed with them in a big hotel once.'

'Do you like Uncle Mark?'

'No, he wears silk pyjamas. I saw them on Mummy's bed. I hate silk pyjamas, so does Daddy. When I told him Uncle Mark wore silk pyjamas he sat with his eyes closed for ages and ages. I didn't know whether he was laughing or crying. He must have been laughing, mustn't he?'

'Of course.' My eyes stung. 'Come on, pet,' I said, 'I've got ten pounds to spend on you. Let's start today. What do you want?'

'A recorder.'

'Haven't you got one?'

'It's at home in the States. Daddy wouldn't let me bring hardly anything?' Already she was beginning to pick up the Arton speech, in self-protection I imagine. 'He woke me up and said we were going to England. Miss Felpham says I must have a recorder. Daddy might play it, too. He never plays the piano now.'

I stared at her in delight. 'Of course he might.'

We finally found a music shop and the recorder was paid for. Laura left the shop looking like a grin on legs, then played *Frere Jacques* all the way home.

On the Sunday I took Paul's advice and asked his father if he could remember the Harlech address. A few weeks ago I would never have dared approach him on such a matter, recalling the loud man of my youth; now I found him quietly sitting beside the open door and glad to have someone with whom he could reminisce. Yes, he remembered the lodging house. When he was little his grandparents lived there, and it passed into an aunt's hands after that. His grandparents were respectable folk who kept a decent house – none of your bawdy places, though they took women as well as men. No, he had never heard stories of Miss Lakin staying there and thought it highly unlikely. Still, come to think of it, she was always close with his father, so close there'd been gossip in the town. Miss Lakin was a most unusual woman, didn't care for rank or position, though she knew how to make a forgeful of men respect her. Funnily enough, I often reminded him of her. Perhaps it was with my being so ambitious and clever for a woman.

The conversation came to a stalling point, yet having for the first time got him to talk I did not want to leave. Would he be offended if I asked him a little about his family?' The fair had always fascinated me and with Paul travelling with it I needed to be able to answer Laura's questions.

Saul was delighted. Outsiders like myself must be envious of such colour and vigour. If he were free, and quite clearly he did not regard himself as such, though his children were all grown, he would consider joining Zac and Cal himself. Arton stifled him, it was getting so built-up, though he would miss the river and the woods. He could earn better money with the fair too...

I found it difficult to piece together Saul's anecdotes, the references to Cal and Zac and the sisters who had married 'outside' as he had done. In effect Isaac Booth had had two families with the war between. Benjamin and one of his sisters being so much older had been remote from Saul, but the second, Sal, had taken over the ferry from her father after she was widowed and plied the trade now. Zac and Cal were closest to him, even though they had gone back to the fair- been driven back Saul added, spitting to show his disgust at the cruelty of Arton folk. Zac had taken over from his uncle when he died, Isaac's other brothers having set up on their own.

It all got very confusing. I gathered there was another fair with which the Boothmans joined for big occasions like Wakes weeks, and two static ones at the seaside, all of which were run by relations. In addition a small travelling circus had toured for years under the name of *Boothman* & *Jolly*' though that had been bought out recently. Clearly, in the world of popular entertainment the Boothmans were successful, and talent ran through the family, both for giving pleasure and parting the public from their money. In marriage the family seemed to have done its utmost to perm every combination. Benjamin Senior had chosen an Art on girl; most of the others had married girls from the fairground world. Goodness knew what nationality half of them were. Paul's Aunt Hilda was German according to her place of birth, while his Aunt Tilly was Polish, but one spoke with a cockney accent, the other sounded Welsh. Even Artie's wife was a mystery, coming from a family called Oblonski and speaking broad Brummie. When Saul added to this a tendency for cousins to marry each other it got horribly complicated. At one point it seemed somebody's uncle was also their grandfather, but that couldn't be right.

Listening to Saul's vigorous stories I felt myself being drawn into a world so different to my own it might have been another planet.

230

He never romanticized it, never spared the mud and the babies that used to die – and still occasionally did – nor did he undervalue 'learning' as he called it. There was a need for people like Zac and Paul. They knew how to deal with councils and keep up with the trade. I began almost to like the man, sinner that he was. He was not unintelligent himself and his coarseness was largely a response to other people's expectations.

I felt I might ask him about matters nearer to myself.

He began talking about his own marriage. 'Now that's one thing I've always been grateful to Miss Lakin for,' he said. 'Persuading her brother to let us have this place. Dunno what we'd have done without. None of the farmers would rent us a cottage – we weren't polite enough for them.'

I saw my chance. 'What's Christopher Lakin like? 'I asked. 'No one seems to think much of him.'

'He's not as bad as they make out. He let us stay on anyway, when the Villa was sold. Mind you, I think that was partly because of our Paul. They get on alright -talk the same language.'

It was a revelation to me. For the first time I wished to meet my second cousin.

'Talking of Paul, what are you two up to? I've tackled him and he says he's faithful to his wife and he usually tells the truth. If you ask me you're going to get hurt, being so close. What are you intending?'

'Nothing,' I replied foolishly. 'Nothing at all. Just friendship. We're both too busy to want fresh complications. Besides, we're nice people.'

Saul voiced his disbelief with a noise like a mating rhinoceros. 'You must be a bloodless young lady,' he remarked, 'or a very forgiving one. You have every right to expect summat from that son of mine. I'm not talking about a bit of hanky panky behind the car park – how else is a lad going to gain experience? But a one-night stand with a girl who's been around is one thing. Making a childhood friend love you and then taking her maidenhead is another.'

'Mr Booth!' I protested, and in anger got up, nearly knocking over my garden chair. Fortunately I had the grace to laugh at myself. First it was Aunt Mary and now it was Saul. If Paul and I had put placards round our necks advertising we were lovers we could hardly have been more public. And we thought we were so discreet ... All the same I promised myself I would hit Saul someday. It was a matter of honour.

'It wasn't like that,' I insisted. 'In any case it was me who broke it off.'

'Did he ever mention marriage to you?'

I tried to remember. 'No,' I admitted. 'He was too set on getting to college.'

'Of course he was. Hasn't he always been? His sort make great musicians and lousy human beings. Why else do you think his marriage has failed? If he'd looked after his wife proper she wouldn't have needed another man, and he knows it. That's why he's giving himself such hell. He's taking from you now, ain't he? Trading on your love and offering you nothing in return.'

'Please, Mr Booth,' I pleaded. 'I know Paul's faults, but you're being unfair to him. The wrong can't all be on his side. Going after another man's something I hope I wouldn't do, but I understand it. Doing it so even your little girl knows is beyond me.'

For a few seconds Saul was silent. Evidently he too had heard Laura talk.

Presumably that was how he'd learned of the situation, for Paul would not have told him. 'That'd get to me,' he admitted. 'Well, I must admit I didn't think much of a woman who's always off somewhere, leaving her husband and babby. In my day a woman stayed at home and knew her place. If she didn't, her husband give her summat to remind her.'

My hand had begun to itch. For an absurd moment I found myself defending Paul's wife. 'You don't believe that yourself,' I retorted. 'In the fair women run half the stalls. I've seen them.'

Infuriatingly Saul grinned. 'You rise to the bait every time,' he remarked. 'Naw – I don't believe it meself. My Janie's never known her place. I wouldn't think so much of her if she did. All the same, I don't like a woman who can't take a bit of time to sort things out with her husband. It wouldn't have hurt her to have a holiday here and see if they couldn't stitch summat up. She must have seen how exhausted he was getting. She ought to have made allowances.'

The trouble with Saul was that he could come out with such sense, mixed with deliberate vulgarity. Talking to him was like trying to walk on ribbed sand. 'You said earlier Saul was giving himself hell,' I remarked. 'Why?'

'He don't say much,' Saul conceded. 'But he's my son and I know him. Why else do you think he's joined up with Zac? He's helping the family out I'll admit, but he'd have found some reason they needed him. He's deadening his mind. If you'd worked the rides, you'd know what I mean. There's no room for thought. There's too much coming and going; the days begin to blur one into another, and all you care about is whether it's raining or what the crowd's doing. You've done him a very big favour taking the kiddy so he could go. If you're trying to tie him to you, you're going the right way about it. Gratitude's the strongest noose.'

'That wasn't my intention,' I replied coldly. 'I have my own life and ambitions and Paul doesn't feature in them. He can't feature if I'm to have any self-respect.' I got up to leave. 'I genuinely hope Paul and his wife can make it up.'

'They won't unless he fights a bit harder,' Saul prophesied. 'I dunno, he's always fought for things before, but where his marriage's concerned he seems helpless.'

'What can he do?' I asked. 'Tell me what you'd do.'

'Give her another baby. That'd tie her down a bit and stop her thinking of other men.'

'Things aren't so simple nowadays,' I replied, flushing slightly.

'And you reckon that's progress? A nice little kiddy as hardly knows her parents and has no brothers and sisters to play with? I call it loss when a man like our Paul goes wandering with a fair. He's about as suited to the life as I am to dancing with the chorus line.'

There was pity in his voice. Taking his hand I nodded and wished him good afternoon.

Since Paul clearly intended to write each day, I felt I should reply equally often. A peculiar correspondence was developing, my letters being sent to a succession of different addresses, garages, shops, even vicarages, wherever the fair had 'friends.' That month Zac had a series of short bookings, some of them for only a day, and already since Paul had joined them he had moved four times. I visualised the small towns and the journeys overnight, the muddy fields in the morning. Sometimes I found myself thinking of a woman I had never met. If she had known, she would never have let her child come to England without her. Every day Laura spent at River Cottage was drawing her closer to her father and taking her from her mother. The spell of the fairground was upon her. She had ridden in a battered pick-up, seen the rides assembled. Now she traced her father's journeys on a map each night and longed for his letters.

On the Tuesday of the second week Laura brought a form from school concerning a coming medical examination. Neither Janie nor I could complete it. We suddenly realised how little we knew of the child. Had she had measles? Laura herself was not sure. Writing urgently to Paul and running down the river path to catch the post, I asked him to ring me on Thursday lunchtime. And so, while the old men played dominoes in the Black Bull, we filled in the form, though there were answers Paul himself was unsure of, as if his daughter had almost vanished from his experience during the last year or so.

For a few moments afterwards we talked of ourselves.

He was ringing from the home of a priest he had known since his student days and was enjoying an afternoon's quiet. At night he was sharing with his uncle Zac and Aunt Hilda he said. It was good to see them again and he would be sorry to leave them, but he would come back to Arton next week whether Ian arrived or not. It wasn't right for him to stay longer.

'Miss Lakin did stay at your great grandparents' lodging house,' I said. 'The address matched one on a card in Aunt Mary's collection. Why should she have gone there? I'm not trying to be snobbish but -'

'I think my grandfather protected her. Despite the difference in class, they were friends. Why don't you ask your great aunt? She was obviously involved in it all.'

'I'm afraid it will distress her. I think she feels bad about it.'

'I've an idea she wants to talk. Why should she have given you those postcards otherwise? You're a bright girl; you were bound to work out what had happened through them.'

There was silence between us, but it was the quietness of understanding not emptiness. 'Where are you now?' I asked.

'Near Dolgellau. Some of us drove to the coast this morning for a swim. It was worse than the river. I haven't made friends again with my legs yet.'

There was a long pause. 'Martie?'

'Yes?'

'Good luck with everything ...'

For a long time that evening my aunt sat silently in her chair. 'I did it all for the best,' she said at last. 'But that's what everyone says. At the time it seemed right. If Milly had kept her child her family would never have spoken to her again, and none of her workers would have respected her. Just supposing you were expecting a married man's child. How would you carry on with your job, unless you had it adopted- or worse? Nature is very hard on the woman. It repays her love with punishment. By keeping her child Milly would have lost everything she valued; by giving it up she lost what she valued most.'

'Who was the father?' I asked softly.

'Milly never told me, though I have my own ideas. He was a good, decent man who had the misfortune to marry and discover love afterwards.'

'I thought you said Milly was very plain.'

'She was, but beauty has never mattered as much as we women are led to believe. Her courage and good sense attracted several men, but the only one she wanted was married. On that one matter her good sense deserted her.'

'Who do you think it was?' I asked.

'It doesn't matter. There's no great fortunes to be claimed my dear, or dark secrets to be told. Let him rest in peace. All you need to know is that he was a craftsman at the forge. To some extent I think Milly chose him rather than him choosing her. She wanted to experience love, and had her mind set against marriage.'

'Why?'

'Because that would have meant giving up control of her affairs, and her money. I think her manfriend would have left his wife for her if she would have married him, but Milly wouldn't have it. So when he could no longer live with his conscience he moved away from Sandhill and that was the end of it. Milly never told him she was pregnant.'

The room was silent again. 'Poor grandmother,' I said. 'And poor him, whoever he was.' Unaccountably I wanted to cry. 'Why did the Booths protect her? They did, didn't they?'

'They were very good to her. The Booths didn't set much store by convention. They protected many people in their time.' She smoothed her dress, found a tiny mark on her sleeve and rubbed it clean. 'Isaac and Jilly knew a great many people's secrets.'

There was no point in pressing the question of identity. Aunt Mary had told me enough for me to trace my grandfather if I really wanted to do so. It didn't seem particularly important, except that I would always have a peculiar entry in my family tree. Still, that is nothing unusual. Most families have the odd misshapen bough.

In Paul's absence Laura and I grew closer, inevitably. I found her lively and generally good-tempered, though with a disconcertingly strong will. She had that sort of wisdom which comes from too early a knowledge of adult troubles, and while she was no prodigy, she was clearly gifted. As yet it was hard to say exactly where her talents lay; her life till then had been too formless for her to settle to anything, but she picked out tunes on the recorder with a speed which startled me. She also liked to sit drawing for hours, her tongue poked slightly between her lips to aid concentration. Constantly she played with words turning them around and around in a way I remembered from my own childhood. One of the trendy new dress shops in town was called 'Serendipity' and all one afternoon we had 'Splendipity' and 'Send a pittity' till Saul and Janie were worn out by the noise of her. Yet in quite basic matters she was way behind. Paul had given her lessons while she was touring with him- when he should have been resting between performances – with the result that she could read a sheet of music at sight or discuss the trajectory of Halley's comet, but was totally deficient in the mysteries of tables or the spelling of 'their' and 'there.'

Sometimes she asked me to help her with her school-work, for she felt any failure as keenly as her father did. School was a habit she had lost, and though she much preferred Larch Lane to the smart academy in America, she was always glad to leave. Each afternoon I would be loaded with the latest cereal packet monster, cardigan, and a couple of out-of-date cyclostyled notes. Gradually I became aware that some of the mothers were talking about me, and I caught one phrase which angered me so much I am afraid I was very rude. After that the whispering got worse, but at least they left me alone. As soon as we were away from the school gates none of it mattered. Laura and I played hare and hounds in the woods and bit the heads off jelly babies, and generally behaved like truants out of school. I was growing to love the child almost as much as I had loved the father.

There were occasions when the clarity of her vision pulled me up short. Grandad didn't really want to get better, she told me; he was angry with everyone and stomping around on walking sticks was a way of making people sorry. Daddy was angry too; that was why he didn't play the piano anymore. Saying there wasn't one to practise on was just excuses. He could go up to her school if he wanted. Once that vision was turned on me. I could make myself look a lot prettier if I tried she announced, but being pretty scared me, though she couldn't think why. I was also much nicer than I pretended. In fact she had decided I would be OK.

'OK for what?' I asked, laughing.

'For marrying Daddy.'

'But Daddy's married to your mother,' I replied, no longer finding the conversation funny. 'There are laws against such things.'

'Mummy and Daddy will get divorced first, silly.'

'Daddy doesn't want to get divorced,' I said, very firmly.

She ignored my warning altogether. 'That's why he's gone with the fair,' she said illogically, 'so I shouldn't love him anymore. He thinks I shall go with Mummy, but I shan't you'll see. I shall run away.'

There was a note of conviction in her voice which promised trouble. 'Daddy went with the fair to help his uncles,' I insisted.

Despite my reply I sat on the riverbank afterwards wondering if she were right. Perhaps one of Paul's motives was a wish to prepare Laura for future separation. That presupposed a sacrifice on Paul's part few men could have been capable of, but knowing him it was credible. Ironically, if that had been his intention he

238

had failed completely. By writing so faithfully and sending her presents, he had bound her more closely to him, just as through time men have bound those they leave behind.

On the second Saturday we went to Styles again, to telephone Paul. He sounded easier than I had heard him since my return to England. 'I paid a trip to Harlech yesterday,' he said, surprising me. 'It dawned on me it wasn't far, so I put on my clean undies and hitched a lift.'

I laughed. 'What for?'

'My mother always told me to have clean undies, in case I got knocked down.'

'I don't wish to know about your undies,' I persisted. 'Why did you go to Harlech?

'To see if I could trace my grandmother's family. They're still there. It's a hotel now, quite posh. I introduced myself as a long-lost cousin and got myself invited to lunch. They were tickled pink when I announced I was travelling with a fair. They'd always been taken by their Jilly running off with a showman. Mind you, they kept their eyes on the silver. They didn't remember anything about Miss Lakin, but they promised to look through the old registers.'

'How did you explain about my grandmother?' I asked in delight.

'I said I had a friend who was writing a book about her. It's partly true, isn't it? There's some nice bits of china I'd say were too expensive for my family to have bought – looked nineteen twenties to me – but I didn't dare pay too much attention in case they thought I was casing the joint.'

He was deliberately fooling, but his absurdity could not hide the kindness of his gesture.

Laura wanted to speak to him, so I passed the phone back to her. Abruptly she squealed with delight. Daddy was coming back. I took the phone from her. 'When?' I asked.

'Next Monday. I don't know what time. Zac has a long haul to Llandudno, so I'll drive the dodgems up for him, then hitch my way back to Arton.'

'Laura will be glad to see you,' I replied inadequately.

It was eight o'clock when he returned, so quietly we had no warning: He simply let himself in to River Cottage and had gone to wash by the time Tiger pounded into the living room. Laura was going reluctantly to bed. Turning around she suddenly found her father standing behind her. 'Get down, Tiger,' he ordered. 'Outside.' To our astonishment Tiger obeyed. No animal was ever allowed inside the cottage; they were mochadi, * Saul said. But Tiger had never before observed such rules until a well-aimed boot persuaded him. Now both man and dog seemed quieter, more confident.

Mochardi unclean, unwholesome.

In her pleasure Laura was demanding to see what was in her father's bag and to be picked up simultaneously. Laughing, Paul turned her upside down and deposited her on the sofa. His laughter could not hide his tiredness.

'Have you eaten?' Janie asked.

'Not since breakfast.'

'When was that?'

'About five this morning. I'm OK.'

Laura was clamouring to be turned over again, but Saul took her hand 'Let your Daddy rest a bit,' he said. It was the first time I had ever heard him express concern for his son's well-being. Clumsily he got up and poured a glass of beer, but Paul shook his head.

'Not on an empty stomach,' he said. Then as if realising a gesture had been made, he relented. 'Thanks, Dad. You have that one. Pour me a half.'

'Is Ian there?' Saul asked.

'He arrived this morning. His girl's going to help with the stalls.'

Janie was on her way to the kitchen but returned in concern. 'What's she like?'

'Seems OK. She's just lost her job so the money will be useful. It wouldn't surprise me if they stay with Cal and Zac. There's not much else on offer for them.'

'What happened about Phil?'

'He got sent down – three months. Zac and I drove over to see if we could do anything, but the evidence was too strong.' Saul shook his head. 'Well, he should learn to keep his temper,' Paul replied.

I felt like a prim chapel girl, drifting into a world I did not know or understand. That Paul could remain so untouched by it amazed me. Feeling out of place I followed Janie into the kitchen.

She was crying when I went in. 'I seem to have a bit of a cold,' she said, blowing her nose.

'I told you he'd come back,' I said. 'You go and talk to him. I'll get us something to eat.'

'He pushes himself too hard,' Janie complained. 'He didn't have to come back the same day as moving on.'

Through the open door we could see across the passage-way, into the living room, where Laura was sitting on her father's lap, flirting outrageously with him. For an instant Paul put his face against her hair and closed his eyes. 'There'll be trouble if those two have to part,' Janie said, voicing my thoughts.

'They'll have to do so,' I warned. 'Unless he can patch his marriage up.'

'He'll do that,' Janie assured me.

There were presents for us all, which Laura distributed like Mother Christmas. I had a shawl she announced, and some old postcards, though why Daddy should give me old postcards she could not think. He should have bought me something new. She would tell him afterwards. Sitting at the kitchen table I opened my packages. The first contained two wonderfully sentimental Victorian cards, and a foreign one made of embroidered silk. Paul had written a translation from the German and attached it to the card. Dated 1916, it said, *My dear little bride, I shall see you soon. The boys should finish the Job this year.'* The words moved me almost to tears. They were the other side of the story I had been writing.

'Open the parcel,' Laura kept insisting. Dutifully I examined the shawl. It was exquisite. 'Auntie Hilda made it,' she announced. 'Daddy asked her.'

For some minutes I sat at the table, not trusting myself to speak. Impatiently Laura put the shawl round my shoulders and took me to the mirror. I looked at my reflection and for the first time in my life I felt that I was beautiful. Then in the mirror I saw Paul in the doorway, watching me. 'Is it all right?' he asked.

'More than all right. Thank you.' Carefully I took off the shawl and folded it away.

Crossing to me, he stood uncertainly beside the range. 'I would have brought you more, but I knew you wouldn't accept it.'

'I gather you had a good time,' I said, avoiding the issue.

'Tell you what, touring with the fair doesn't half do something for your ego.'

Something in his manner reminded me of his father. 'Indeed?' I asked.

'Don't look so frosty. I've been as good as gold. Well, perhaps not gold. The Trades' Description Act might get me on that one. Brass?'

Despite my surprise I could not help smiling. 'What have you been up to?'

'Nothing. I just stood at the dodgems – and sort of brooded …'

'Hens do that,' I remarked and had the dishcloth thrown at me for my pains.

'Now you wouldn't grudge me a bit of light entertainment, would you?' The mock Irish was so overdone as to be outrageous. Then he was serious. 'Martie, I've remembered what it is to enjoy myself. The problems haven't gone away, but I've got them into proportion. Come on, I see good times for you too.' Cajoling me he pretended to read my palm. 'What have we here? Five husbands and, twenty-three children…'

242

'Get away! I replied, laughing. 'I'm off home.'

'Whatever for? You're family now. Laura wouldn't hear of you going yet, would you?' Obediently Laura shook her head and her father laughed. 'Stay and eat with us.'

So, sitting beside Laura I ate while Paul talked to his parents of relatives I did not know and of places the fair had visited. There was the woman who had complained the music was disturbing her pussies' sleep, and the Gala with the Lord Mayor wandering round and slurping mushy peas in his chain. Another day Paul had ended up piling a load of hay on the pick-up and driving a harvest festival on wheels ... We sat in amused stupefaction with the remains of our meal strewn about us. Laura should have gone to bed ages ago.

Finally Paul remembered to be firm. But she had not shown him my present she protested, resourceful as all children are at such crises. The recorder was brought out and every one of her pieces played at least twice, and suitably applauded. We were spoiling her horribly.

'You've brought her on nicely,' Paul said to me. 'Miss Felpham didn't teach her all that.'

'I can't get this one right, 'Laura pleaded, and with a cunning that made me smile, passed Paul the recorder. 'I've tried and tried.'

'That's easy enough,' Paul said and began to play. The tune was one of several folk songs in the book and he could continue beyond the few printed bars. Janie emerged from the kitchen where she had been washing pans.

'Now that always reminds me of my father,' she said.

'Play us another, Daddy,' Laura insisted, and he started to laugh.

'I wasn't born yesterday, either of you,' he said.

We looked at him in injured innocence. 'I'll play you a few tunes and then you go to bed. If you don't I'll carry you there – both of you.'

When I returned to Sweetbriar Aunt Mary was restless, struggling in and out of her chair and fidgeting around the kitchen. She had been waiting for me to tape some more of her memories. Nothing would satisfy her but that I should fetch Paul now he was back. He must listen as well.

The demand puzzled me, and I found her manner worrying. It was so unlike her customary quiet gentility. It was a warm night and through the open window I heard the recorder playing, as if Paul were sitting in the orchard, so as not to wake Laura. I did not want to trouble him. He must be very tired after so long a day.

Yet Aunt Mary became so agitated by my refusal to do as she asked that I began to feel frightened. Perhaps she was sickening for something? She was a very old lady after all. In desperation I went back to River Cottage. By then Paul had returned indoors. It was unreasonable I knew, with his parents wanting his company and him so tired, but could he come? My great aunt was becoming upset. Perhaps he need only stay a few moments and I would be able to get her to sleep. Paul was as mystified as me, regarding my great aunt's whim as a bad sign.

'I wanted to tell Martie about her mother,' Aunt Mary said as soon as we entered the chalet. 'And about Milly. Since a lot of what I have to say concerns your grandfather, I thought you should be here too.' She did not sound unreasonable; there were even some notes on a pad beside her. As Paul gave her his hand in greeting she examined a bruise across his knuckles, gained it appeared by trapping his hand between the dodgem cars. I noticed several older bruises and a cut near his thumb nail. 'You're a very foolish young man,' she said unexpectedly. 'Throwing away a talent like yours.'

In annoyance Paul glanced towards me, but I shrugged my shoulders, indicating I knew nothing of my great aunt's plans. Out of respect for her he kept his temper. 'I'm rather busy,' he said coldly.

'Not too busy to listen to me. The young must give in to the wishes of the old, if only because death may prevent them having another chance to do so.'

'That's blackmail,' I said smiling uncertainly.

'Of course it is, but can you call my bluff? I'm eighty-seven. I've already had seventeen years beyond my span. What I have to say will take an hour or so, so you might as well make yourselves comfortable. You too Paul, even if you have no wish to listen. I need a witness.'

Understanding came to Paul's eyes, and no longer hostile, he sat down.

'We have some business to do,' Aunt Mary instructed. 'Go and get the little writing desk from my bedroom.'

Almost imperceptibly Paul nodded to me, suggesting I should do as I was asked. Returning with the writing desk, I stood beside my great aunt while she found the key. As she opened the flap it dropped down to reveal a baize-covered writing mount and a row of drawers, each with a tiny mother of pearl knob. From one of these drawers she took a manila envelope containing a stiff manuscript. Gathering round the table we looked at it together. The secretary hand in which it was written was almost impossible for a lay person to decipher, but a typed transcript was attached. 'I want you to examine these,' my great aunt said, looking at Paul. 'What do you make of them?'

For some time Paul considered the papers before him. 'As far as I can tell,' he said cautiously, 'these are the deeds for an area of land to the north of Sandhill, commonly known as Lakin's Heath. They assign to the holder all rights, privileges and so on, including any mineral wealth to be found.'

Picking them up, Aunt Mary handed them to me. 'I'm giving these deeds to you Martie, as they were given to me, with Paul as witness. I have of course made the transaction more secure by naming you in my will. That has already been witnessed by Saul and Janie Booth.'

'Did your mother and father say anything to you?' I whispered to Paul.

'They haven't had time.'

'I've written out a brief statement, to the effect that you witnessed me giving these deeds to Martie to care for until my death, and that you were aware of my wish that she should inherit them at that date. I've tried to cover things both ways. If either my will or the transaction is contested, there's the other proof.' Passing him a pen she waited while he read the statement and then signed it.

Her gift appalled me. 'You're giving me an awful responsibility,' I said.

'No more than I have had myself. You'll know better what to do with the land than your father. He'll be too easily persuaded by others, and make a worry of it into the bargain. You'll enjoy yourself bullying councillors and officialdom generally.'

'You don't make me sound very pleasant,' I protested.

'Bullying's the wrong word perhaps. Persuading.' Aunt Mary looked positively mischievous. 'Having Sandhill shake its head over you won't be a new experience.'

'When has Sandhill shaken its head over me?'

'A girl who picks up with a boy like Lol Jackson and keeps the friendship going after he's married is bound to have a few heads shaken over her. Meaning no offence to present company of course, but your relationship with the Booth family has set tongues wagging, too. That's your strength, Martie. You live in your own world and don't hear the tittle tattle. Now I think you should know a little about your grandmother. She was another. It'll give you a sense of purpose to know what you're following. It will also perhaps ease my conscience.'

'You have nothing to feel regret for,' I insisted. 'Adoption was much the best course. My mother had a place in the town by being the adopted child of the Wallaces – she had her choir practices and church outings. Such things would have been closed to her as the illegitimate child of Miss Lakin.'

'But people might have understood. Milly thought so.'

'I doubt it. When I was a girl, sex was something that happened in the *News of the World*, but not in Sandhill. My mother might have been forgiven but Milly would not have been. You did your best to see both had as good a life as was possible in the circumstances, even engineering my parents' marriage. You did engineer it, didn't you?'

I saw Paul look up in amusement.

Aunt Mary smiled in satisfaction. 'I thought our Len might be a suitable husband, steady her down a bit and give her a better position. I managed to see they met at my home, accidentally, of course. It worked out easier than I could have hoped. Len was half in love with her the first time he saw her.'

'Poor Dad,' I said, laughing. 'He wouldn't have stood a chance. You gave him thirty happy years though, and that can't be bad.'

'Now get the tape recorder out,' Aunt Mary instructed. 'I want to tell you about Milly – and about how I came to love Richard. You should know what he planned for the Heath, too. I'll start by telling you a story. It'll mean more to you than a few facts. There's one day that sticks in my mind particularly.'

'But it's so late, Auntie,' I protested.

'Not too late for a story. If I don't begin now I may never do so.' Paul had stood up, ready to leave. 'No, you sit down young man. I think you should understand a few things too. You're caught between two worlds aren't you? Trying to live in both and not really succeeding. I'll be bound that wife of yours increases your unease too. It's about time you told her to accept you as you are.' A flush of anger and embarrassment came to Paul's face. 'You're a fine musician yet you ruin your hands working on the dodgems.'

I admired Paul's control. I would have replied angrily I'm sure. Sitting down again he glanced towards me in appeal.

'That's better,' Aunt Mary said firmly. 'You stay and listen. I'll tell you about your grandfather, then perhaps you'll understand more about yourself. If he were here he'd know how to advise you. •

And so began the story I have already given you, transcribed from the tapes I made that night. My great aunt spoke with remarkably little hesitation, as if her speech had been prepared beforehand. It was an increasingly strange experience with the sound of water lapping beyond the chalet, as if we were marooned on an island together. The night was close, the sort of weather that makes milk go sour. Emotion made it even more stifling. The people Aunt Mary was talking about were our ancestors, Family. If Paul and I had married as our parents predicted, Booths and Lakins and Coopers would have joined in us. As it was, a peculiar complex patterning gave everything she told us an ironic edge, as if some chess player had taken us, descendants of Isaac and Milly alike, and arranged and rearranged us on his board.

After half an hour I made my great aunt rest while I readjusted the microphone. Anxious that so much talking would tire her I tried to persuade her to continue the next day but she refused. There would not be time tomorrow. Catching her sense of urgency we resigned ourselves to a late night. So that our eyes should not be tired by the glare of the main light I fetched a bedside lamp and set it on the table beside us. Moths continually flicked at the windows, those which entered through the open transom window flying at the lamp and dying in a soft burning smell. For another hour Aunt Mary talked, pausing only when I needed to adjust the tape recorder. From the movement of his hand on the arm of the chair I saw Paul was beginning to find the situation distressing. In describing his grandfather's poverty and the town's attitude to his father my great aunt was saying things he would have preferred left unsaid. I too was becoming increasingly uneasy, my identity blurring in the darkness. All three of us were held in a magic from which it seemed only sleep – or death – could free us.

Gradually her voice began to falter. The will was still burning bright but the physical body would not bear the strain. Instead of a coherent account of events, she turned to our present selves. Paul did not value himself enough, or his family. He had been tainted by the constant insults, the sense of being on the edge of town. Just living in River Cottage, so far up a muddy track was bound to give him that feeling, but he had to live with the fact that his father had been branded as a thief. I was too harsh on myself too – I possessed charity for everyone else except myself. It sounded like the wisdom of a dying woman and Paul and I looked at each other in alarm. Perhaps I should fetch a doctor I suggested, but Aunt Mary rounded on me in such anger I did not dare pursue the matter.

We all desperately needed sleep. Making my own thirst a pretext I went out to the kitchen. There I made us a cup of cocoa. The doctor had prescribed some sleeping tablets for me when the pain in my head was at its worst, but I had not finished them. Putting one in my aunt's cup, I waited till it had dissolved and then added plenty of sugar. She complained it was too sweet, but she drank it. Then the talking began again. Natural sleep already confused her however, and the barbiturate worked quickly. Her eyes became heavy, her mouth slackened.

It was one o'clock.

Putting a cushion behind her head I went out into the kitchen, hoping Paul would follow me. 'I'll leave her in the chair,' I said when he entered. 'If I try to get her to bed it'll disturb her.'

'Did you put something in her drink?'

'Only a sleeping tablet.'

'I imagine she realised. I'm not sure how ethical it was, but it was the best thing.' His face was white with tiredness. Opening the door to the verandah he stood in the fresher air. 'Shall I fetch my mother? I don't like the idea of you being alone with your aunt tonight. I've a feeling she's about to have some sort of attack – a stroke perhaps.'

We looked towards the cottage. It was in darkness. 'Let her sleep,' I replied. 'I'll be all right. I'll sit up till first light then go for a doctor, whatever Auntie says.'

Uncertainly he watched me. 'I'll stay,' he said.

I had known him too long to suspect anything but kindness in his motive. 'You're tired,' I pointed out.

'I can sleep late tomorrow. Martie – your aunt was very good to me when I was little. So was your uncle. They helped Mum a lot when Dad was travelling and I used their piano many times before I managed to get my own. I don't like to think of her being ill – dying perhaps without someone to help. Supposing she fell? How would you lift her?'

'I'm stronger than I look,' I replied. 'Still, if you want to keep me company I'd be glad of it. We'll sit on the verandah. It'll be pleasanter there and it seems – more proper somehow.'

We made ourselves comfortable, Paul on the old garden swing and me in a deckchair. At first we were eaten alive by river gnats but I remembered the repellent in the bathroom and took us off the menu. As I passed my great aunt her face was relaxed, with the peacefulness of one who had completed her business. Gently I kissed her.

The night was still heavy; even on the verandah the air was sluggish. Talking quietly so that we would not disturb Aunt Mary, Paul and I began to watch till dawn. The light from the open door made a wedge of yellow across the boards, but we were beyond it, scarcely visible to each other. In the silence we could talk as we used to, admitting our fears and foolishness, while the darkness mercifully hid our expressions. For half an hour or so we talked of the Heath and my hopes for it, Paul making me think my ideas through. After that we turned to Paul and his life in America.

Though he was scrupulous in saying nothing against his wife I knew that he was nervous of his return. Then there was a pause filled by the sound of water lapping at the bottom of the garden.

'Your great aunt's a shrewd woman,' Paul remarked suddenly. 'She's diagnosed my sickness perfectly.'

I waited for him to explain.

'I don't know where I am nowadays, do I? Or where I belong? When I was a kid it was simple. I rejected the lot – Dad, the fair, living in a backwater like this. I wanted out, and music was my door. I almost hated my grandfather, even while I loved him.'

'Why should you hate him?'

'I felt he was to blame for all my family's problems, that he should have stayed where he belonged.'

'That's unjust.'

'Who ever said a child's just? Now, well, I wish I could call him back and ask him how it all was. He used to tell me a lot of stories – he seemed to take to me more than the others. I wish I had him to talk to now.'

'You know your trouble?' I asked gently. 'You've no purpose anymore. You used to know exactly what you wanted. I've heard you play the piano so that I could almost see the determination, and the anger. Why don't you play now? You'll never get back on the concert circuit if you don't.'

'I've sickened myself of it, rehearsing and practising all the time – and the sham of it too, the way people use you, the way you have to use others. The joy's gone from it.'

'Then write music, like you used to. You were always making up songs and things. Do as Aunt Mary say, use what you've inherited, and tell everyone else to go jump. You must have one of the richest backgrounds of any musician.' I saw him smile and shake his head. 'I don't mean in money, but culturally, however pretentious that sounds.'

In the silence that followed I listened to hear if Aunt Mary were calling, but the night was unbroken.

'You've got me interested,' Paul admitted. 'What do you mean?'

I was out of my depth and afraid of sounding silly. 'Well,' I floundered. 'You've got your mother's songs, real folk music, not the trendy modern stuff, and the fair with its music. You have your grandfather's memory too. What happened to the pieces you wrote clown for him when you were a kid? They were beautiful.'

'They're still in my books. I play *Aquarelle* occasionally.'

He paused, and I could sense that he was troubled.

'Martie, how can I be proud of the fair? Or of my family? I respect Zac, and Cal to some extent, and I've always loved Aunt Hilda, but a lot of what's said about the rest is true. Our Phil's a thoroughly nasty piece of work, and a good deal of petty thieving does go on. It's regarded as a bit of sport, not amongst the family, but the hangers on, the casuals ...' He was having difficulty expressing himself. 'In a sense I am a drifter like Aileen's people say. I can't settle in one place long; I hate the town. Yet I could never settle here either.'

'Use your heritage,' I repeated. 'It's not many men who have a Romany grandfather?'

'Don't glamorize things. What would you have me do? Play the romantic gypsy? I've no claim on that. It's all too far back. Even Grandad was a *Diddikai*. I'm a mongrel Martie, a Heinz fifty-seven variety like that daft dog of ours. I love the fair even while I'm ashamed of it. I also love being treated as something a bit special – the great new discovery – but all the while, I'm terrified of using the wrong knife.'

He was beginning to make me cross. 'OK,' I agreed, my tone sharper than I had intended. 'Make the one serve the other. Talk to the old people in the fair, like I've been talking to Aunt Mary. Your Aunt Hilda's genuine Romany, you told me so yourself. You have entry to all sorts of worlds the rest of the music world couldn't get near – it's too middle class. So your people are show people? So what? It's an honest profession. They bring a bit of life and colour into drab little towns all over the place. Is that so different from what you've been doing? I'll bet you play to the women whether you're standing on the dodgems or sitting at a piano.'

'You've sussed me,' Paul said, laughing. 'OK, I give in. It's get at Paul night, isn't it? I'm being sorry for myself and I deserve it. But don't you see my point? Belonging nowhere's quite exciting for a while, like going on holiday abroad, but you need somewhere to send your mail.'

Then we were both quiet, Paul sitting very still in his chair, presumably considering what I had said. Getting up, I went to see if Aunt Mary was all right. Thinking she looked about to wake any minute I sat with her for some time. When I returned Paul was asleep, half stretched out on the swing seat. He would wake stiff and aching. Going back indoors I found a towel and rolled it to make a pillow, then lifted his head and slid it under him. His eyes opened, acknowledged me, then closed. For a time I too dozed, awkwardly bent into my deckchair.

When I awoke the air was damp with morning. I heard the sound again and tried to place it. Suddenly leaping up I ran into the chalet.

As soon as I saw Aunt Mary's face I turned and ran back across the verandah. In the darkness I stumbled several times and wished I had stopped to bring a torch. Finally a lighted window at the Villa guided me. A night nurse answered, frightened at such an intrusion. No, they didn't have a resident doctor and she could not leave her patients to go to see to my great aunt. They were short- staffed, a chronic complaint I gathered, despite the cheery adverts. I could however use the phone and borrow a torch. And so, standing in the beautiful marble hall that had been built to my ancestors' specifications, I sought help for my grandmother's friend. As an afterthought I made a second call, to the minister at Arton. When I returned the verandah was empty.

Paul was sitting beside my great aunt. 'I've called the doctor,' I whispered.

'I guessed that was where you were going. Sorry, I didn't mean to fall asleep on you.'

Aunt Mary was talking again, her words slurred and indistinct. Isaac had promised to tell her and Milly about the war. They had rowed upriver specially to hear him. In horror I realised my aunt thought the man beside her was Isaac Booth. 'Aunt Mary, it's Isaac's grandson,' I said.

As if unable to endure the situation longer, Paul got up and crossed to the window.

But she was adamant. Gently she patted my hand. It was I who was mistaken. The children's colds would get better if they had some nice oranges to eat. I must take this basket into the cottage and ask Isaac to come out to her and Miss Lakin. They had managed to buy the children two precious oranges. Perhaps he did not like talking about the trenches. She had heard many of the men did not. Then he must tell them how he had entertained the troops, or about the time he toured the music halls before the war. Milly was tired; managing the forge was a lot for a woman and it would do her good to hear him talk.

The light of the bedside lamp scarcely reached the window and Paul's features were indistinct as he stood there. In the warmth his hair fell heavily around his face and shadows deepened his eyes, already dark with lack of sleep. The likeness to his grandfather's picture was disturbing. It only needed a flash of gold at his throat for the postcard to have taken on a physical presence. Eerily that too was supplied when he moved his hand and his ring caught the light. I felt myself becoming disorientated, sleeplessness and concern playing on my imagination.

'Come and sit with me,' Aunt Mary asked.

Quietly Paul crossed the room to her. In the better light the resemblance was less strong but Aunt Mary could no longer see beyond her youth. 'Thank you for the oranges,' he said.

I would have spoken, insisting on reality, but Paul shook his head. 'Milly is managing the forge now,' she said, and to my horror she touched my hand. 'She finds it very ...' The words were slow to form. 'Very tiring. She needs a rest from thinking about business. Tell us about when you were famous. You were famous weren't you?'

.'A little. I'll tell you about the music halls if you wish.'

Sitting down beside her Paul began to talk, as if he were indeed his grandfather and she were a young woman again. Another story began, a gentle lie to give a dying woman peace. The air was heavy with sleep. Prickles of sweat appeared above our mouths. My great aunt could no longer move her right arm so I fetched a cloth and cooled her face and hands with it. Still Paul talked, weaving images from what his grandfather had told him as a boy and the similarity of his own career. We saw the Empires and the Palaces, the noisy audiences, the gilded ceilings, smelt the cheap lodging houses afterwards. There were the juggling acts and the dancers, the singers in beautiful hats, the actors who became Hamlet for a scene, and the magicians with doves fluttering about their dressing rooms. Once again Paul was weaving stories fit to make a hearer dream.

An expression of contentment settled on my great aunt's face. Her eyelids began to lower in sleep and then open again, briefly. 'It's so good to hear you talk,' she said, though the words were almost indistinguishable. Slowly she drifted into sleep. It was four o'clock, the dead of morning.

The exact moment of death was impossible to determine. For a little longer Paul talked, then taking a spray of fern from the vase, he held it beneath her nostrils. There was no movement. Closing his eyes briefly he said something I did not catch, and feeling he should be alone with her I went to fetch a blanket. When I returned he was still beside her.

Afterwards I stepped out on to the verandah and cried a little. The air was cold on my face and I shivered, returning indoors as soon as I was presentable. I found Paul in the kitchen standing at the mirror which hung on the wall. The action had nothing to do with vanity, rather with identity, but as soon as he saw my reflection he moved away in confusion. Turning on the tap he splashed cold water on to his face and hair, then pausing suddenly watched the tap gush into the sink. Like his father he had always washed so, in running water, and usually without soap, but there seemed some significance in the habit which for the first time he understood. The towel was outside, I remembered, and went to fetch it for him. When I passed it to him his hand was shaking with exhaustion; in the last twenty-four hours he had slept little more than one hour.

'Come outside,' I said. 'It smells of death in here.'

We sat on the old swing seat together. He could not speak and his eyes had a bewildered expression. At last he turned to me: 'Touch me Martie,' he said. 'Tell me I exist.'

His hair was wet against my face as I held him and the seat rocked slightly in the early morning breeze. A bird startled into life in the darkness and then another woke, and another. I was conscious of nothing but the beauty of their song and the nearness of Paul's body to mine. In the distance a light began to flash in and out amongst the trees along the bank and I gradually accepted that there was a car coming along the track. 'You'd better go now,' I said. 'There could be talk if the doctor or the minister found you with me. Not even your parents would believe we spent the night together and simply talked. Go home – and thank you. You gave an old woman peace and helped me beyond saying.'

Getting up, Paul put his fingers to his lips and then against my mouth. 'Don't grieve,' he said. 'It was what she wanted.'

SIX: Willow

The next day blurred into unreality. I phoned home, breaking the news, and then saw to undertakers' arrangements. Janie Booth came to help me. Though I had seen death before I was too confused to do more than stand and watch as she prepared the body with gentle, expert hands. She was brisk and business-like, the sort neighbours send for at times of lying-in and laying-out, relied upon to do what was necessary without chatter or requiring thanks. In her quietness I found comfort and began to help. As we worked we talked, softly in respect for the dignity of what we were doing. I announced my intention of returning to Sandhill. She was clearly relieved. 'I've been so proud of you both,' she admitted. 'Indeed I have. Love's a mighty force and can drive people to things they regret afterwards. I wish I had another son to give you.'

'Why?' I asked in surprise.

'Like the Jewish widows in the Bible, you should still have been my daughter then, but you wouldn't want any other man, would you? The sort of love you have for Paul I had for his father.'

I had never heard Janie speak of her husband with such tenderness. 'How did you come to marry Mr Booth?' I asked.

'He came to our house for water. There was no tap in the field behind us, where the fair had pitched. I took the bucket and filled it for him, but it was too heavy for me to carry down the yard so he jumped the gate and took it from me. It was as if he took a child's seaside pail.

'I had never known a man so strong or so fine. When he turned to go I stood with my mouth open like a fool. I was finished.'

We both laughed. I wondered if we were being irreverent speaking of such things, but decided Great Aunt Mary would be interested in the conversation. 'After that you followed him?' I asked.

'He had charge of the swing boats and lifted the little ones in and out with so much strength and gentleness I could not take my eyes off him. For the rest of the week I missed work to be with him; then the fair moved on. I'm afraid I did a very foolish thing. I took what money I had and a few clothes and caught the bus to the next booking. Most men would have taken advantage of me but Saul was too kind. Since I could not go back home with my good name gone, he brought me here to stay with his parents. As soon as I was old enough he married me.'

'You must have regretted giving up your family for his sake,' I suggested.

'What woman doesn't regret marrying at times? Even more I regret what people have done to my husband. They have made him hard inside with their snobbery and prejudice. There has never been a decent job given him, not fit for a man of his intelligence, and because they call him coarse and ill-tempered he has become so. Still, I understand why and that makes it easier to go on loving him. With his goading and patience Paul is making him fight back too and I shall be eternally grateful to him. Mind you, between them both they have nearly driven me into leaving, though where I could go I have no idea.'

'Would you really leave?' I asked.

'We women lose ourselves in our men. Suddenly we look round and find we have forgotten to be people ourselves. I am beginning to learn to be myself again, not somebody's wife or some child's mother. My family must recognise that or I will be like a prisoner trying to escape. Paul is beginning to understand and I think Saul will one day. Underneath all the hurt he's still the big gentle man who carried the pail for me.'

We had finished our work and Janie could declare with pride that we had made a beautiful corpse. Two candles burnt at the foot of the bed in a thoroughly unMethodist manner. I hoped Aunt Mary wasn't offended.

After Janie had gone I began packing my great aunt's things. The writing desk was still on the dining table from the night before, and opening it I took out the deeds to Lakin's Heath, spreading them on the kitchen table. Though there were large sections of legal preamble I did not understand, the old writing gradually gave up its secrets to me. A feeling of joy filled me, however inappropriate that sounds. My great aunt had died, as she wished, still dignified and intelligent until the last moments. She had been ready for death and had called it upon herself in a sense, as Paul implied. I remembered a story Saul Booth told us when we were small, of how a very old fairground woman he knew sang herself into death, despite everyone's attempts to quieten her. My great aunt had quite literally talked herself to death. The phrase would have a new meaning for me. Now the Heath was mine and what had been delayed by war and the untimely death of others, could be fulfilled.

Locking up the chalet I went for a walk through the woods, retracing the route I had taken four weeks ago. The distance seemed nothing now, a couple of hours, no more, though admittedly not easy walking. I stood in the sawyer's pit and remembered my fear, and it was another person's emotion I was recalling.

As evening approached I returned by the top track, past Arton Villa. For some time I stood near the gate, visualising the terrace and the marble hall. I wished my cousin had not sold the house; not out of greed but because I should have loved it as the present occupants did not. A nurse stared at me as she crossed the lawn and I remembered I had not returned the torch. If Arton Villa ever came on the market again I would move mountains (or more usefully mortgages) to see if the family could buy it back.

Passing River Cottage I walked towards the top gate of Sweetbriar's land. A light had been switched on in Paul's bedroom and the sound of Laura's recorder came from the kitchen. The simple tune she was playing was haunting on the evening silence. Then in the half-light I saw a wreath lying beside the door to the chalet.

Even without opening the envelope attached to it I knew Saul or Janie had sent that wreath. Ivy and laurel had been threaded round a wire frame and into their loops were twisted spring flowers from the cottage garden, their stems bound into a backing of damp moss. It was a country wreath quickly and skillfully made. The card said, *'For Mrs Chapman, from Saul, Janie and Paul Booth'* and underneath, in Paul's writing was a message which puzzled me: *'With thanks.'* Tucked behind the card was a piece of manuscript paper. My mouth went dry as I opened it.

'My Love, how have you been? Mum says you have coped admirably. Pay my respects to your great aunt, and say thank you. She's set me writing music as if I were demented, and still the ideas keep coming. Every time I've paused my mind has been jammed with a thousand thoughts, about my family, myself, what I want for the future – and about you.

When I was at the lowest point in my life you gave me friendship without making any claim on me, though you had every right to hate me. No one else would have taken care of Laura as you did, not even my wife, not so that I could go off with the fair as I did, so irresponsibly. I would have picked myself up in the end as I always have done, but you saved me a wasted year or so.

I can offer nothing in return except the knowledge that I love you, body and soul.

There's the problem, of course. Because my soul – mind if you like – loves you I shall only have to think of you and you will be with me, but there's body in my love too and I dare not be near you any longer. When I held you last night, it brought back all the longing I had for you years ago. I'm no better than Aileen. A few weeks ago I couldn't understand how she could break her vows to me. Now I would break my own to her.

Please Martie, for pride's sake, I can't slip into an affair with you. The only way I've coped with the last few months was by feeling I was in the right, not sanctimoniously I hope, but as a matter of self-respect. I told myself Aileen would tire of her new bloke and because I recognised I had driven her to him by being away so much, that we could forgive each other. If I too am unfaithful, I shall lose that last chance of making my marriage work, and however inconsistent it sounds after what I've just written, I want to stay married to Aileen. I meant the promises I made and she is the mother of my child. Besides, divorce would cut me off from my church. It would also almost certainly mean I would lose Laura, and if I were honest with myself, that frightens me more than losing Aileen.

And so my Love, whichever way I look, I can see no alternative other than wishing you the best in the world and then keeping away from you. The only time I would consider a divorce would be if I thought I could bargain for Laura by doing so, and that's not sufficient hope to give you. We've had a good time together these past few weeks. I'm glad we met up again and there's no bitterness left between us. I love you as much as I love myself, more, for I'm an erratic sort of bloke and grow impatient with myself.

Take care. May your book be a success and your hopes for the Heath come true.

Paul.'

I read the letter through twice, then folded it back in the envelope. There was no fire, so I went into the kitchen and lit the gas, but even as I stood there with the envelope above the flame I could not bring myself to destroy it. Despite being so carefully worded, my grandmother's cards had revealed their secret to me; goodness knew who might one day read Paul's letter. All the same, it reflected only good on his character, and my own if that mattered, and no man had ever written such a letter to me before. I could not destroy it. Though the edge was charred, I took the envelope from the flame.

Harry could not take time off work at such short notice to help me and asked me to wait till the weekend. He could bring me back then, together with Aunt Mary's possessions, but I would not wait. There was a transport firm connected with the local garage. They could offer me an elderly van.

All the next morning I loaded it. At one point when there was a hitch in the undertaker's arrangements I threatened to pack a coffin in as well.

Fortunately his secretary was so horrified at the thought she promised to 'see to things'. By lunchtime I was ready. Wrapping one of Aunt Mary's necklaces in tissue paper, I slipped it inside an envelope marked 'For Laura'. No doubt I was behaving illegally with the will not yet read, but I felt sure Aunt Mary would understand me doing so. Call it a propitiatory offering if you like, a talisman. If anyone could bring Paul to me, it would be Laura.

The van proved to have been last driven by Rommel's desert army (all of them) and showed an alarming tendency to veer to the left, but by keeping the wheel permanently to the right I persuaded it to bump along the track in a fairly straight line. Reaching the main road, I set off to Sandhill at the grand speed of thirty-five miles an hour.

Even before the funeral I took Dad with me and called upon Charlie Warwick, having taken the precaution of asking Miss

McClean to be present too. They had already consulted each other, as I had suggested in my letters they should, and had begun to like my idea. Sitting surrounded by papers and cats we watched each other warily. Dad and Miss McClean never greatly enjoyed each other's company, while I slipped back into a mental gymslip as soon as I was with her. My stay at Sweetbriar had given me new confidence however. I had lain in a wood all night, tidied up after a death. My former Latin teacher, though promoted to permanent-pleated glory, could do no worse.

As efficiently as I could I explained the situation, in confidence of course. Lakin's Heath was now mine, willed to me by my great aunt and given to her by Milly Lakin. With due reverence we laid out the title deeds, having first evicted Venus and Aphrodite from the table. 'The question as I see it,' I explained, 'is how best to preserve the land for the good of the whole community.'

'You have no intention of selling to developers?' Dad asked.

'No, though I'll admit the money would be nice. The Heath was given to me – the whole family – in trust, to carry out Richard Lakin's wishes, not for any personal gain. Richard wanted the shafts to be made safe and the land allowed to return to heathland, to a sort of wild park. The idea wasn't wholly his own. It came out of his friendship with Isaac Booth. I imagine you remember him – the ferryman at Arton.' I saw Dad raise an eyebrow at the mention of the name Booth. 'I would suggest we add another project to Richard's: the creation of some sort of tourist attraction to bring money and jobs back to the town.' I had prepared my case thoroughly and could offer columns of figures on expected costs, potential income and so on, most of which Paul had helped me prepare before he left with the fair.

Miss McClean nodded. 'What sort of tourist attraction?' she asked.

'Several of the old works are still standing. They could be restored as an industrial museum. It seems to be all the rage. With folk exhibits and workshops, and an old-fashioned fair perhaps, we could make it a good place for families to come to, and for school parties. My ideas aren't original, but I think there's room for another such development round here and we have an unusually large area to work with. It might be possible to open up the Shepherd's Lead for parties to walk down – it'd be quite a thrill for a child – and there are plenty of broken bogies and rails around. I'd like to involve the school from the start and Mr Warwick could guide us on the historical side of things, I'm sure. Dad could act as a link between the school and the family.'

Charlie positively bounced. He'd files and files on the Heath, been ferreting around there for years. He could tell us which the brickworks were and where the tiles were made, and in which shaft the accident took place. There was a ballad about it by Jove, and he could find us drawings to enable us to reconstruct one of the old winding houses. All those hours he'd spent in Sandhill library reading dusty records, and being sniggered at by dolly librarians, had suddenly taken on meaning. There was work for him to do till he was a hundred.

Within minutes we were immersed in talk of Community Programmes and sponsors and participant workers which I found thoroughly bewildering. Miss McClean would handle all that, she said. She had already approached the local Community Programme manager, in the abstract of course, and she had raised the matter with the school governors. As it happened the local Manpower Services Office had not used up all its allocation and was urgently seeking projects and sponsors rather than surrender its places to the National Pool. (I had visions of a large pond with participant workers swimming round in union jack costumes.)

Splendid, splendid, Charlie agreed. He would begin further research straightaway. The Lakins had been meticulous record-keepers and there were papers galore in the library, preserved down the generations till Miss Lakin presented them to the town, though most of them had lain undisturbed for a decade. Apparently he could already feel the dust on his hands for he wiped them vigorously on Aphrodite. The most important mine had been the Shepherd's Lead of course, but there were over forty separate shafts in all – he'd found a number of them on old maps.

Then the conversation came to an abrupt halt. I suddenly realised both Charlie and Miss McClean were talking about 'starting things off next winter.' Dad and I looked at each other in horror. 'But by then I shall have less than four months left in England,' I pointed out. 'We must start before then, with volunteers if need be.'

But we would need money for materials, Miss McClean reminded me. The MSC had to have meetings. Nothing in England was ever done without at least five meetings.

'We'll raise the money ourselves then,' Dad said quietly, and I loved him for it.

'What's the hurry?' Miss McClean asked, smiling at our youthful enthusiasm.

'I owe it to my great aunt and Miss Lakin to have things sorted out before I leave the country,' I began, but my explanation sounded limp I know. Without going into the personal reasons behind my determination to reclaim the Heath, it was difficult to put up a strong case. Unexpected illegitimacy tends to sound like a Dickensian plot, and I had no desire in any case to have my grandmother's affairs talked of in the town. While the dead might be beyond hurt, there were the living, like Aunt Lizzie and Dad, even the Wallaces to consider. 'Miss McClean,' I asked, changing the subject carefully. 'I wondered if I might borrow one of the school tape recorders, a good quality one. I'd like to copy my great aunt's tapes, for safety's sake.'

The loan was arranged.

Throughout the conversation about recordings and tapes Charlie Warwick had sat in silence, as had Dad, both of them clearly thinking deeply. Finally Charlie stirred himself, so suddenly both cats shot into corners, where they crouched washing themselves to prove they had not been in the least disturbed. 'It's all very appropriate and fitting,' he declared. I would make a worthy inheritor of Miss Lakin. Strange to say I had often reminded him of her, not in looks, but in ways ... His bright little eyes watched me like the cats. There I was, full of impatience to begin, with a book to write too. Just like Milly. She burnt herself out always working. Died younger than she need because of it. It was strange how indolent one side of the Lakin family was and how vigorous the other. I must take care I did not burn myself out too; get my book written and delegate the work on the Heath to others.

It was sound advice, but too perceptive for comfort and I saw Dad watching Mr Warwick uncertainly. Getting up, I suggested we all went to the Heath together to see what was involved.

And so the most ill-assorted quartet Sandhill could have provided walked up Sandhill Rise through the lunchtime drizzle, the good weather having broken immediately on my return from Arton. From Mr Warwick's house it was only a short distance to what used to be Bircham's Coppice. Cars sped beneath us down to the valley in a brutal roar. My mind filled with anger. 'They didn't have to take it all,' I shouted. 'I'll tell you what, if there's anything I can do to change this I shall.'

'You can't change a road,' Dad replied, also shouting above the traffic.

'But you can plant trees along it. I believe there's a bit of money coming to each of us from Aunt Mary. Miss Maclean, if you can get your school to plant trees and look after them, I'll pay for them. We used to pick bluebells here.'

We stopped, each of us staring across red clay and visualising a blue river of sweetness, then we walked to a quieter place. 'I'll suggest it to the governors,' she offered. Her voice was as ever efficient but she had lingered beside the road longest of the four of us. 'I'm sure we could raise money for such a scheme ourselves, without taking what your aunt has left you. You should keep some of her bequest for yourself. She would have wanted you to do so, I'm sure.'

Making polite conversation, we walked up what remained of the copse towards the Heath.

There above the town, the drizzle was rain, driven across the old army camp by an unseasonal wind. For all its bleakness the place was beautiful, the air fresh and clean upon one's skin. Since I was last there, the flowers had changed to those of early summer though a few exposed hawthorn bushes were still white. The Heath's glory would soon be the gorse, a yellow flame flickering over rises and scrubland amongst lush new ferns that threshed in the wind. We stood so silently a rabbit ran across the path ahead, disappearing near the roots of a hawthorn bush. The grass was pocked and eroded near us, suggesting whole colonies of rabbits going about their business of feeding, breeding and bobbing, oblivious of the town in the valley beneath them. I recalled Aunt Mary's description of her ride across the Heath, and could trace the track to Twynning she had taken. The muddy hollow Richard Lakin had pointed out was a pool that day; the toad's mouth rock stood on the skyline, still remarkably like a toad. For a few moments I felt a sense of exaltation, that all this land was mine, to sell or preserve, or simply to own. The temptation to keep it to myself was strong, until practicality as well as duty returned to me. The boards over one shaft had slipped since Lol and I were there, prized off no doubt by exploring children or glue sniffers seeking shelter. The area had to be made safe and I could not afford to do the work myself.

Silently we returned to Sandhill.

Dad and I walked the last stretch down to Nightingale Road together, after we had wished the others good afternoon. 'Do you mind Aunt Mary leaving the Heath to me?' I asked. 'She originally intended to name you in her will, but decided I would know how to go about things more. I feel bad about it.'

"Course you don't,' Dad said smiling. 'You're on top of the moon to have all that land, even if you mean to give it to the town. No, I don't mind. What could I have done with it? Coping with the roof on one house is enough for me.'

'But you might have sold it,' I suggested, 'used the money to get the house done up a bit – retire early if you wanted.'

Again he shook his head. 'All that would have been nice,' he agreed, 'but it wouldn't have been what Aunt Mary or Katie would have wanted. It's harder to go against someone's wishes when they're dead than when they're alive.' Thoughtfully he watched a pigeon strut along a loft near us. 'No, it's best you have it, Martie. You have your grandmother's and your Aunt Mary's energies combined – three times what Lydia and Harry have – and you have the education, too. You'll know how to fight developers and so on. We'll do what we can to help, of course.'

'I thought Mum never told you who her parents were,' I said, flushing slightly.

'She didn't, but listening to you talking at Mr Warwick's, it was suddenly clear to me. I think I'd had an idea who her mother was for years actually. Miss Lakin used to visit Aunt Mary a lot and we always called on the Villa when we were there. I don't know who Katie's father was – do you?'

'No. Aunt Mary didn't, either.'

'Katie once told me she remembered a man hanging around the school when she was little. For some reason she thought he might have been her father. He used to watch her in the playground till one of the teachers saw him and sent him away.' Dad sighed in sympathy.

All that afternoon and evening I played with tape recorders, duplicating my great aunt's tapes. Aunt Lizzie and Dad found it a peculiar occupation, with a funeral the next day and scones to bake. In the end they put it down to grief and left me to it. I finished at nine o'clock, my brain feeling as though it too was going around on little wheels. As an afterthought I took a second copy of the four cassettes I had made on the night of Aunt Mary's death. Packing them carefully I sat for some time with the outer wrapping unsealed. Finally I found a With Compliments slip I had brought with me from work and wrote on it, '*I thought you might like to have a copy of these. They concern your ancestry as much as mine.*' Since my name was already printed I did not add my signature. Somewhere inside me a small voice was crying.

We buried Great Aunt Mary with ham and scones and sausage rolls that fell to hits on the carpet- too much fat, second cousin Hannah suggested. We did Auntie proud. The Co-op laid on two black Marias fit for a Mafia summit meeting, and the chapel on Sandhill Rise was packed. Afterwards a procession of cars wound its way through Sandhill streets to the cemetery near the Heath, the longest procession since Mr Langdon died, Aunt Lizzie whispered as we sat squashed together in a lavender-scented row. Great Aunt Mary had been respected and thirty or forty folks were willing to tramp between the cherubims and seraphims of the established dead, to the oblongs permitted the dissenters. On that windy height I felt embarrassed by my lack of grief. My continual thought was, 'She died as she wanted, thank goodness.' Everything was fit and proper and she would have been pleased with her funeral. Besides, I had such a strong sense of her presence, grief seemed inappropriate. Aunt Lizzie nudged me, instructing me to blow my nose at least, lest people think me cold and unfeeling. In deference to her wishes I sniffed and shuffled my feet.

Then we all tramped back to our cars and Aunt Lizzie's scones. There were the usual libations of spilt tea, and the equally inevitable family spats, Aunt Lizzie and second cousin Hannah still disagreeing over the recipe for sausage rolls, and my mother's adoptive sister; Maureen, seen only at funerals and other national celebrations, dropping hints about my feathering my nest by kidnapping Aunt Mary and giving her the third degree in her final

269

days. The last implication was retracted however when Harry appeared.

He had bitten her bottom at the age of seven and ever since she had had a healthy respect for his teeth. I seemed to be seeing the whole afternoon with my great aunt's cool gaze as well as my own, and the proceedings began to take on the flavour of black comedy. When I heard Aunt Mary referred to as 'such a sweet old lady' I had to go into the kitchen and talk to the cat.

To my pleasure and nervousness Lydia had accepted my invitation to attend, though she arrived after the funeral itself was over. ('Can't stand such functions, darling – too morbid.') With her characteristic sense of timing she entered during a lull in conversation, just as everyone was getting bored with eating. Her hair had changed from blonde to brown since I last saw her but her manner was just as careless, just as charming. For a while I let her greet old friends and kiss elderly relatives, winning their hearts as ever. Finally it was time for me to greet her myself. Finding it impossible to hold my cup of tea as well as my plate, I paused in annoyance near the sideboard. I would not be submerged by her personality; not this time. Jettisoning the offending cup and saucer I went towards her. 'I'm so glad you could come,' I said. 'I wish it could have been under happier circumstances. How are you? How's ...?' In horror I discovered I could not remember her husband's name.

'I'm fine, thank you. Barnaby will be here soon.' She stressed the name to remind me of my error. 'He's just popped down to the garage for some petrol.' Unfortunately instead of being reprimanded, I found the situation incredibly funny.

'Good grief, Lydia!' I said. 'Can't you call him something simpler? He sounds like a teddy bear.'

For an instant she stared at me in amazement, then she too began to laugh. 'It does rather,' she agreed. 'I call him Pootles.'

'You what?' I was giggling unmercifully. 'What's he like?'

'Terribly sweet really. He's the best one I've come up with so far.'

'You sound as though you marry one a year. What do you do with them? Lock them in your palace and chop their heads off if they don't do the washing up?'

She stepped back and considered me. 'You're thinner,' she said, 'but I like your hair short. It gives you a new image. You've changed too – got more confidence. You were getting to be a typical academic, all flat shoes and apologies. You seem happier. That's it.'

'Are *you* happy?'

The question startled her, the brightness leaving her manner for a moment. 'Who knows whether any of us are happy?' she replied. 'I've had a lot of good times and never been short of money or a man. That must be most women's definition of happiness.'

'Then why did you never answer my letters?'

'Too busy, darling. There's always something on, or somebody coming round. Besides, there didn't seem a lot to say – not that you'd understand.'

'You could have tried me,' I suggested. 'I did eventually grow up.'

We both of us looked for our cups of tea. 'I've been staying at Sweetbriar,' I volunteered. 'Aunt Mary was there with me when she died.'

'So I heard.' Again she seemed puzzled by my manner. 'Either you're pretty thick-skinned or you've more courage than I have. I've never been near the place since Mike Booth died.'

'Do you still grieve for him?' I asked.

'Why should I grieve for him? He was no more than a Tinker's son.'

'Because you loved him.'

Her face took on a hard expression of denial, then slackened. 'Sometimes,' she admitted.

With that one word a mile had been crossed.

'Have you ever heard from Paul?' Lydia asked.

'He was staying with his parents while I was there. He had his little girl with him.'

I felt my sister search beneath my calm, but for once I was stronger than her. 'How was he?' she asked. 'Has he changed much?' When my reply was slow she laughed. 'Is he still a beanpole with ears?'

'You'd hardly know him,' I replied carefully. 'He's almost as good looking as Mike or Artie nowadays, and has the additional benefit of not knowing it. I'm speaking as a mere observer, of course. I don't fool around with married men.'

'Course not, my dear,' Lydia agreed.

When you've shared a bedroom throughout your childhood and giggled into the night, a few coded words can contain paragraphs of information. My continued love for Paul and our parting were instantly conveyed and acknowledged. Barnaby had entered by now and stood looking round him in bewilderment.

'Is that Pootles?' I asked. 'He looks all right – the sort of man you can tickle without getting your hand smacked.'

'He rolls on his back and waves his paws in the air,' Lydia agreed. Poor man – if he had known he would have been hurt, but for years Lydia and I had made fun of the male of the species and we saw no reason why husbands should be exempt.

Dad came across to us. He seemed almost afraid of his eldest daughter. 'You look very well, my dear,' he said, which was his way of saying that he didn't like her hair. 'Is that your car outside? It's very fast, isn't it?'

Lydia laughed, her voice lifting above politer relatives.

'Of course not, Pops, it's hired. Don't half impress the neighbours though.'

'I thought you had a car,' Dad said hesitantly.

'No – we don't bother with one. There's nowhere to park and the underground's the best way across London. Still, there's no harm in letting Sandhill think we're doing well, is there? One in the eye for Aunt Lizzie, eh?'

'I thought you were making a lot of money.'

'London's an expensive place, Pops, and we like to enjoy oursleves.' She straightened his tic. 'I'm fine. Stop looking so worried. I'm not your little girl anymore.'

'I'd like to think you were settled ...'

'Settling's for hens. Life's too short to worry about mortgages or owning cars. Barney and I are thinking of living abroad in fact. This country's going downhill. I'd fancy a year in Montmartre.'

'Too many tourists,' I advised.

Aunt Lizzie came to claim me. The milk was running short. Could I pop down to the shop and buy some more? Funerals were such thirsty affairs. Then she sniffed, looking towards Lydia's hair. 'What colour do they call that?' she asked.

'Mahogany,' I replied, brushing her cardigan. 'You've got biscuit crumbs on your bosom.' I saw Lydia laugh quietly, and loved her all over again.

When the outsiders had gone I called a family conference. For some time I hesitated as to whether I should try to avoid Aunt Lizzie being present, but could think of no way of doing so, there being no Ladies' Bright Hour or nuclear alert that night. The delegates sat in an expectant circle, Aunt Lizzie and me, Harry and Sue, Dad, Lydia and Barnaby. I had prepared my speech but forgot it of course and ended up charging at the topic in a series of sideways assaults like a belligerent crab. First I explained about the Heath and that Great Aunt Mary had left it to me to preserve – to the whole family I hastened to add, but to me in name because she thought I would be able to fight off the developers and so on. For a good hour we discussed how Aunt Mary's wishes could be fulfilled, and to my surprise there was little protest at the land being left to me rather than to the others. Aunt Lizzie in particular had a stronger claim than me, having been the one who had had to cope with the extra work caused by Great Aunt Mary's presence. In fact it was fitting I should have the land she said.

The remark intrigued me. 'There's a second reason I called us together,' I said, 'I've a feeling you know why, Aunt Lizzie.' We watched each other, each trying to assess how much the other knew. 'Why do you find it fitting?'

The others were mystified, apart from Dad of course.

'I've often seen the likeness,' Aunt Lizzie replied.

I felt ashamed. Clearly she had known of my mother's birth for some time and had said nothing. While I had thought her no more capable of keeping a secret than of running off with the Vicar, she had kept silence. Even the Aunt Lizzies of this world are capable of surprising us.

'What the devil are you two on about?' Harry asked.

'Your mother was Milly Lakin's daughter,' Aunt Lizzie replied, embarrassed by the attention unexpectedly directed towards her, and even now caught between pity and disapproval. 'Your mother was born outside wedlock of course, but you three are Miss Lakin's grandchildren all the same. Martha is the one most like her – that was what I meant.'

'Did you know?' Harry asked, turning towards Dad.

'Not in so many words, but I'd guessed as much and Martie told me yesterday. As Lizzie said, it's fitting the Heath should come into the family though I think it will cause us a lot of trouble. You may be forced to sell, Martie.'

'Not if I can help it. If I give it to the community, the Council will have to protect it – there'll be votes in it.'

'Shrewd girl,' Barnaby said. He was an estate agent himself and the idea of having 'married into land' appealed to him. He hadn't realised he'd got such a good bargain he said, putting his hand on Lydia's knee.

When Harry and Sue had left and Lydia had taken her teddy bear to bed with her, I could at last talk to Dad. Sitting at the table together (we had found the bourbon creams) we considered Aunt

Mary. I told him of her passing and the strangeness of it, but he had ceased being surprised by his aunt long ago, having seen her stride around Sandhill in an air raid warden's hat or wade into the river after nephews determined on a watery grave. She was one on her own. Then again we went through the figures Paul and I had drawn up, and discussed the plans for the Heath. 'Don't underestimate what you're taking on,' Dad advised. 'You've got enemies already.'

'Who?' I asked in surprise.

'You're bound to have. Old school-males and neighbours who'll think you 'jumped up'', people who crossed swords with Miss Lakin years ago and will see the likeness in you... Sue thinks you should sell and split the money amongst the family – you'll need to watch her. She's slow to move, but once she gets her teeth into someone she doesn't let go. If Harry weren't so easy-going there'd be trouble there many times. Being single won't help you, either. The women will think you're after their husbands.'

Accepting his wisdom, I nodded.

'How's Paul?' Dad asked unexpectedly.

I followed the logic of his remark and smiled. 'Please Dad,' I pleaded. 'Leave Paul out of things. I'm in love with a married man and that's no good to any of us. Let me chase round the Heath and sublimate madly while he goes back to his wife. Not that there's been anything improper,' I added hurriedly.

'Of course not,' Dad agreed, but he was very quiet as he drank his coffee.

After that our privacy was ended. We became celebrities for all of ten miles around. I was bread and butter for lawyers and cub reporters, and men came to me with propositions that weren't always to do with land. There were meetings. The chief function of these seemed to be to measure the smoke-bearing properties of air in a small room, but Minutes were read and an agenda for another meeting usually agreed. At my request neither relatives nor lawyers mentioned the family's hereditary claim to the land, but as Dad had predicted, rumour got around. Like rotten meat, scandal concerning prominent citizens, even dead ones, carries a powerful smell. Lydia was for making a denial through the local paper but that might have led an old friend or resident to produce evidence we were lying. We were helpless. Old scores against Miss Lakin were being settled. Gossip has always been a powerful weapon against such women; it is less trouble than a ducking stool and just as effective. As for me – I had been too clever by half, coming top in class too often and making myself altogether too prominent ...

As families sometimes do at their best, we closed ranks and neither spotty-faced youths with pencils or neighbours could obtain the least detail from us. Even Aunt Lizzie remained silent, though it must have cost her dearly at choir practice. Having allowed such a can of worms to be opened in our living room. I felt I must start my project as quickly as possible. Since officialdom required ten meetings and six in-trays before it could consider the idea, I persuaded the school to act on its own initially, raising money for trees to be planted along the new road, and helping me to make the Heath safe for Sandhill residents to use. Even this required the inevitable jumble sales, and sponsored swims with dripping juniors presenting forms for signing. She could do with several men, Miss McClean remarked, to which I nearly replied, 'Couldn't we all?' but remembered to behave myself. 'I think Lol Jackson might be interested,' I suggested, 'so long as we'll pay expenses.'

Which is how I came to take Lol Jackson and Josie for a drink at the Green Dragon. We sat squashed in a corner while I tried to explain above the Space Invaders that I was not going to run off with Lol but merely wished to make him a business proposition. I could not afford to pay him a wage but would quietly 'see he was all right without affecting- his dole', of course. If the scheme was accepted by the MSC and the council I would do my best to see he was properly employed on it. The nice thing about inheriting land was that it enabled me to play fairy godmother to my friends.

In the end Josie was mollified; not reassured or enthusiastic, but mollified. To the end of her days she would regard me as a rival for her husband's affections, but she was confident enough of her own charms to tolerate me. She saw how much idleness degraded him and was prepared to put her own feelings to one side. I respected her for it. Lol was full of enthusiasm – that is, he nodded slowly and said, 'Well, I suppose it'll give me summat to do. Better than hanging round the house any road.' When we parted all three of us were a little merry, business being such a dry way of spending an evening.

In such comings and goings I had almost driven Paul out of my mind; that after all was part of my purpose. Yet each day when the post came I was sick with fear wondering if he had received the tapes and would acknowledge them. I didn't want a letter- just some sign that I was remembered. Finally a postcard arrived. Paul must have hunted for days for that card. It was surely the most boring postcard ever printed, a view of Styles Gasworks and Westfield Road. I laughed out loud. On the message space one word had been written: *'Thank you.'* There was not even an address or date, but that card kept me going through a whole Governors' meeting.

Hope of returning to my book had to be forgotten during those first weeks. The Heath and its needs had swallowed me just as effectively as if I had walked into one of its shafts. We made Charlie Warwick's home our base; there was room in it for another stack of files and it was nearer the Heath than Nightingale Road. Almost every day I was there for several hours, writing letters, discussing history, making plans with Lol Jackson or Miss McClean or the dozen or so teachers, chapel members, old schoolmates, who drifted onto the project, as much for something to do as out of conviction, until gradually they caught Charlie's enthusiasm. We needed legal advice but could not afford to pay fancy fees. I remembered Peter Sampson had become a solicitor in Birmingham and wrote to him, suggesting he might help his old school. At the time I wondered if he would even remember me, much less do me any favours, but back he came, looking pompous and smelling of aftershave, but under it all still Sampy. He had made a disastrous error in thinking he could enter Charlie's lair and leave after a few encouraging noises. Like the rest of us he was caught, his eyes taking on the same gleam they had had when he put dolly blue in the teachers' lavatory cistern, or tied the door handles together. We would get our legal advice. It was good to see Sampy again, and all the others in our year who drifted back to History House as we took to calling Charlie's Gothic monstrosity. Venus and Aphrodite found themselves with a crisis of laps and extra feet.

As the fruit in the garden at Nightingale Road began to mature, I thought with irritation of the crops I had sown at Sweetbriar and the strawberries going to waste. Finally I asked Harry and Sue to go down to the chalet for· me. They could have a break with the children and bring back anything the birds had not eaten. Sue would find the chalet more civilised now, I assured her. I had evicted most of the sitting tenants.

When they returned the car was laden with plastic bags full of fruit and there were spring greens and the first cauliflower heads. I had expected reports of weeds and birds stripping the plants and stood in amazement. 'Mr Booth has been keeping an eye on the place,' Harry explained. In delight I handled the crops I had sown and never expected to harvest. Those polythene carrier bags were the best symbol of hope I had seen in years.

'I didn't ask him to look after our garden,' I protested.

'He reckoned it was a crime to let good crops go to waste.'

'Can he work in the open now?'

'With a stick. He props himself on it and works with the other hand. He's started sorting his own place out, too – tying back the trees and netting the strawberries. It looks like he'll always be lame but he's learning to live with it. If you ask me he's quite proud of his fall. Every time he told me the story it got taller. Paul helps him of course, but he's deliberately making his father do more and more.'

I became very interested in sorting howls of fruit. 'Is Paul practising?' I asked. 'Seriously I mean.'

'Trying to, but with no piano at the cottage it's difficult. He spends a lot of time at his little girl's school. He's doing a bit of teaching for them – just flute and guitar – and plays their piano. He says there's no way he can appear in public again, though. His fingers are too stiff. Saul had a long talk to me about it. He told me about Paul's wife and seemed genuinely concerned – a bit late in the day if you ask me. Funny in't it? Paul's goaded the old scoundrel into picking himself up; now he's trying to goad Paul in return. He doesn't want Paul to go out with contracts broken and his reputation gone.'

'A concert,' I said suddenly.

'A what?'

'A concert,' I repeated. For the second time in six months I had had an idea, a beautiful glistening idea. 'We need money to start the Jubilee project. Paul needs something to work for. It's perfect.'

'But he's only got six weeks left in England.'

'Then we'll arrange things as fast as possible. Get it on the local radio and in the press, photocopy the tickets instead of having them printed. It can be done.' In my pleasure I had a hundred tickets sold already.

'You're asking an awful lot of Paul,' Harry said quietly.

'But it can be done if he wants,' I insisted. 'He's always worked best under pressure. Unless he makes some such effort – and soon – he's finished as a performer. Playing for us will give him a chance to make mistakes without the critics jumping on him.'

Harry helped himself to another strawberry and got his fingers rapped. 'Righto. Concert it is,' he agreed.

Why it never occurred to me Paul would refuse I don't know; pride in my own idea perhaps. Yet refuse he did, by return of post. When Charlie showed me the letter I sat in silent vexation. 'He's afraid,' I said.

'Of appearing in Sandhill?'

'Of appearing anywhere. He's pushed his own standard so high no one, not even himself can reach it. Rather than fall below he'd sooner give up altogether.'

'But that's an awful waste,' Charlie protested.

'I'll try another tack,' I offered. 'If that doesn't work we can't hound him. That would make him more definite.'

As soon as I returned to Nightingale Road I went through the cards in Aunt Mary's collection, eventually choosing one dated 16 February 1970.

'Dear Martie, can you come to Arion again? I shall have to spend this Saturday working on the boats, but I could see you Sunday. I'm going noisily round the bend practising for my grade. I've had to stop playing at home as Dad gets mad and the little ones keep interrupting, so I stay at school and do some homework there too. The walk home in the dark's a bit creepy. I'll admit I've come very near giving up, but I'm not the sort somehow. Love you, Paul.'

Putting the card in an envelope, I addressed it to Arton. He would be angry of course, say I was putting pressure on him, but I hoped he would be stung into taking up my challenge. I had not reckoned on the full force of his anger however.

There was a telephone call for me, Aunt Lizzie said. Sounded as if it was from a public house. She couldn't think who I could know in a public house. 'I can,' I replied brightly. Taking the phone I stood with my hand over the receiver till she tired of waiting and went back into the kitchen.

'Martie?' Paul's voice demanded straight away. 'What the hell are you playing at? I can't do it. Do you understand? I would if I could.'

'Sandhill's hardly the Hollywood Bowl,' I began. 'We'll be lucky if we get a hundred people in the audience. Just play as you did years ago.'

'I'm not fit to appear in public. I've had too long away from practising.'

'You'll be fine in two or three weeks. It'll give you something to work for.'

'No – and there's an end of it.' The phone slammed down at the other end, leaving me standing in surprise.

I would not let him end the discussion so abruptly, and on such a sour note. In my diary I still had the phone number of the Black Bull in Arton. Presumably he was ringing from there. My hand shaking, I dialed the number and asked the landlord to fetch him. I heard someone call Paul's name and there was a pause, as if Paul had already left the building.

'You don't give up,' Paul's voice said, and to my relief I heard the beginnings of amusement in his voice.

'I've never known you give up before,' I replied. 'You're scared.'

'I'm bloody terrified. I shall let you down, and myself. Even in Sandhill people will have heard of me, or at least remember me from last time: the wonder boy who was going to do such great things. As soon as I sit down at the piano they'll hear it's gone from me.'

'What's gone?'

'The joy – the flair, whatever you like to call it.'

'You've got to play in public some time,' I pointed out. 'Or are you going to stay in Arton forever? What about your contracts? You must have bookings lined up for your return. Or are you going to pretend you're ill? I thought there was more to you than that.'

For a long time there was silence between us, filled with talk and laughter in the background. I remembered Paul and I talking while he was with the fair, and recalled that I had been happy then. 'You owe me,' I said. 'You said so yourself. I need something to launch the project in a big way, not piffling little jumble sales.'

'I would need to stay somewhere,' Paul said at last. 'Somewhere quiet where I can shut myself away for four or five days and rehearse. It's hopeless here. The only piano I can use is at the school, and then only for a few hours.'

'Charlie Warwick will have you. He's got a baby grand – remember? You used it last time.'

'What about Laura? I can't leave her again. Besides, every day with her is precious to me.'

'Bring her. Charlie has room for half a dozen kids. I'll look after her while you practise. I'll enjoy seeing her again.'

'Martie,' His voice was strained. 'I'm not only afraid of playing...'

I understood what he could not find words to say. 'This is purely professional.' I said, 'nothing more. I'm asking you to come as a performer, not even as a friend.'

'I'll come on one condition – that you don't call it a concert. Call it *"an evening with..."* If it's informal I'll stand a better chance. You can make it as soon as you like. Staying here trying to prepare isn't going to achieve anything. It'll all have to be done at Charlie's.'

'Write me the date,' I asked, 'so we'll get it right.'

'All right, damn you. But I warn you, make me look a fool and I'll never speak to you again.'

After I had put down the phone I stood looking at the numbers on the dial. The nought was smudged by constant use and the division between the one and two was cracked. Whenever I looked at the dial afterwards I noticed that detail, and remembered the emotion I had felt when I first saw it.

We advertised *'An Evening with Paul Boothman',* though to my annoyance the local paper added the description 'celebrated pianist.' For three weeks we scurried around like guinea pigs in a run, arranging publicity, organising the school hall – none of us had anticipated the Victoria Rooms being booked for All Girls Wrestling that night. To my abject relief tickets began to sell, albeit mainly among the converted. It would have been simpler for us all to put a tenner straight into funds, but we would not have had an evening out and I would not have had a reason to challenge Paul.

From Paul I heard nothing, and had to trust he would keep his word. Until the day he turned up at Charlie's I lived with an inner nightmare that he would vanish with his Uncle Zac. Yet on the Monday evening he appeared with Laura, having carried her half-way up Sandhill Rise on his back. At least three cars could have met him at the station if we had known the time of his train but he chose to be beholden to no one. Laura was delighted by the idea of staying in a real old English house, 'almost a mansion' Daddy had told her. I was a rich lady now. Daddy had told her that, too.

'Of course I'm not,' I replied, laughing. 'I own some land, that's all, and a wild neglected place it is too. I'll take you up to see it tomorrow.'

She wanted to go that night but I explained it was dangerous to do so, and that she must in any case have some supper and go to bed. Even as I spoke I heard the piano begin downstairs.

Those days were terrible, the first almost unendurable. All through Tuesday Paul shut himself in Charlie's front room, playing arpeggios and scales till the rest of us were demented. Hour after hour he drove himself, never permitting a shred of melody, as if such sweets were only acceptable once he had reached perfection. I took Laura out on the Heath, but the weather had turned colder and clouds blew across from Twynning with an unseasonal chill. The beauty remained but it was harsh, the cry of the wind taking on an ominous note, as if all those souls who had laboured under our feet were howling in distress. To keep warm we explored two of the safer shafts, and Laura whispered in excitement, pointing out the gleam from abandoned lamps and rails amongst the darkness. When I described how the mines were worked she listened with awed excitement, her occasional questions cutting straight to the dreadfulness of it all. It occurred to us both that she was almost as old as the boys who pulled my ancestors' trucks; older than the children who worked the traps in northern pits. I introduced her to Lol and his mates afterwards, and she stared in silence at the great sandy-haired man who stood up to his knees in mud rescuing a sunken bogie. She would remember it all for years to come.

When we returned there were several members of the Jubilee Committee to see on business, and Charlie and I took them through to the study. Caller after caller went away remarking on the merciless nature of art, and was heartily sick of the sound of a piano. The tension in the house was a tangible thing, affecting us all. Paul joined us for the evening meal but he was silent and withdrawn. A cut on his hand had begun to open up and the quick round one thumbnail was bleeding. In irritation he sucked at it, but the faint line of blood kept returning. Even so, he returned to Charlie's front room after dinner and practised for another two hours while I played snap with Laura. Finally I persuaded her to go to bed. The scales had stopped, and thinking Paul might like a drink I opened the door. He was leaning forward against the piano in an attitude of absolute despair. Silently I closed the door and went away.

The second day was a little better. I bought something to paint on the cuts on Paul's hand, and as Paul's pain eased, so did ours. The scales and arpeggios gave way to practice studies, some of which I remembered hearing him play as a youth. This time however the pleasure was missing. Each piece was played immaculately by the time he allowed himself to move on to the next, for he had developed an impressive technical ability. but it was lifeless. Even Charlie could tell the difference and shook his head. 'I'm afraid you may have made a serious misjudgment, my dear,' he admitted.

'No,' I insisted furiously. 'He'll do it.'

I hoped to God I was right. I could scarcely eat. Like Laura I had become so sensitive to Paul's moods that his despair affected me physically. Laura herself had developed a haunted expression and was unnaturally quiet. If I could have cancelled Saturday's concert I would have done, but Paul would not countenance it. Having committed himself he would not admit defeat.

By Thursday he too had stopped eating, though out of politeness he sat with us trying to pretend interest in the meal before him. According to Charlie he was not sleeping either. Now I had the additional fear that exhaustion would beat determination. All his life Paul's dignity had been as much a matter of will as strength and now he was beginning to look wretchedly tired. Yet still he pushed himself, moving on to rehearsing his programme.

Then, coming out of Charlie's front room on the Friday afternoon he announced he had done all he could and was going for a walk. Uncertainly I looked at the rain.

'I'm not afraid of getting wet,' he insisted. 'I need a few hours quiet in the fresh air. May I – explore your Heath, madam?' It was the first flash of humour in a ghastly week.

'I'll show you round the estate,' I offered.

'I'd rather be on my own if you don't mind. Nothing personal.'

There was no point in arguing. 'Lol Jackson's working up there with a couple of his mates,' I replied. 'Take them a flask of coffee if you wouldn't mind. Be careful though. It's dangerous.'

And so, inexplicably, he went out into the rain. The house lightened after he had gone. 'Not easy living with the artistic temperament,' Charlie remarked, stroking Venus. 'Mind you, that young man has courage. We'll have our concert.'

As the afternoon passed I began to wonder. Paul seemed to have two parallel time schemes by which he lived; the first that of city time, and often forgotten, to the exasperation of everyone round

285

him; the second a countryman's measure, determined by light and dark and mealtimes. I hoped he would not find himself benighted on the Heath. As we ate our tea I began to see images of him trapped inside the Shepherd's Lead or lying with his leg broken beside one of the old rails. Furiously I stabbed the bread. By the time the key turned in the lock I was seething.

It was not just Paul who returned, but Lol also, both of them soaked and quietly good-humoured. They had been for a drink together after meeting on the Heath. Laura said it all for me. 'You don't deserve any tea, Daddy,' she said, 'worrying us all. And stop dripping all over Mr Warwick's floor.'

We had our concert, though to the end we avoided calling it such. During the awful few moments before the switching-off of lights and opening of curtains I was nearly the next to vanish on to the Heath. I could not bear to see if we had an audience and hid myself backstage. When Harry told me the hall was full I thought it was one of his usual jokes.

Yet full it was. People whose sole experience of the classics was Gilbert and Sullivan were there as well as press-ganged friends, school governors and teachers, the Wesleyan choir complete with Aunt Lizzie, the Lord Mayor and his Lady, and diligent – or ambitious – councillors. Even children had been brought, there being no one left to mind them. I was glad I had persuaded Paul to let Laura come in Lol and Josie's care or she would have felt very cheated. Presumably the reports from callers at History House had aroused interest, I decided with pleasure. My pleasure decreased when Harry told me a third of the congregation had come 'to see Martha Cooper's fancy man.' How that little gem got about I'm not sure. Perhaps Aunt Lizzie had made some ill considered remark, unless it was a stroke of genius on her part. Whatever the source, there was as much curiosity as love of music in the gathering that night, and I was developing quite a reputation. I would not have minded so much if it had been merited, but I had not even had the pleasure of earning my fame.

Fleeing to the back of the school I pretended to be checking refreshments. To my horror, when I returned the audience was laughing. 'Oh Lord, is it that bad?' I whispered to Harry.

'They're laughing in the right places you chump,' Harry replied. 'Paul's telling them funny stories.'

'He's what? I'm paying him to play the piano.'

'Shurrup and listen.'

Sitting cramped in the wings Harry and I listened.

'Concert' would have indeed been a misnomer. Paul had shrewdly judged that Sandhill would need a cough and a peppermint after more than a quarter of an hour of music of any sort. It was not that the town was ignorant or insensitive – no more so than any English industrial community any rate – just that lives filled with the routine of work, or unemployment, had little space in them to develop a knowledge of the arts. To have thrust a high-powered classical concert on his audience would have been snobbery, while any suggestion of talking down would have produced mutters of 'Who does he think he is?' Now I understood why Paul had wanted no printed programme. His performance was to be a one man show in the old music hall style, such as his grandfather must have given years before him.

Stories from the by-ways of musical history, illustrated by well-known pieces on the piano became in his hands a hilarious evening. We had Beethoven growling through the streets, Liszt setting out to make himself a virtuoso and running away from the first ever groupies, George Sand and Chopin adding their spice of naughtiness. All right, so the stories were old ones but few in Sandhill knew them, or had heard them told so well.

It was not what I had expected and though I laughed as loud as anyone I felt a sense of unease. Paul was saving the evening by his wit. Each piece was appropriate and immaculately played, but it was not the music I remembered, or that had won him scholarships and reputation. At the end of the first half the applause was loud and enthusiastic but I knew Paul would not be satisfied.

I found him sitting in a classroom in semi-darkness, with his eyes closed.

'It's going well,' I said.

'It isn't and you know it.'

'You're making people laugh – giving them a very pleasant evening,'

'Is that what I'm reduced to?'

'It's not a role to be despised,' I pointed out. 'An entertainer reaches far more people than a great artist, during his lifetime at least. Your grandfather didn't feel any shame in touring the music halls.'

'But I'm capable of far more.'

'So was he.' I put my face against his hair. 'Play something you want to this half. Anything so long as you love it. Never mind the audience or whether you think you're supposed to like it. Perhaps you'll play better then.'

'It's usually a mistake to alter a programme.'

'Aunt Lizzie would say "Let the spirit move you". We used to call it her holy laxative.'

Paul laughed and leant against me. 'Love you, Martie,' he said.

The audience was restless and chattery when we returned and I wondered how Paul would bring them back to him. His solution was simple. Without speaking he sat at the piano and began playing. Within minutes the hall was silent. His stage presence was as effective as Miss McClean's. Afterwards he turned to his listeners. 'It was suggested I play something of my own choice this half,' he began. 'Some of you may remember I came to this hall fourteen years ago. I was a nervous schoolboy then, scared stiff on my first big engagement. You even paid me. That five pounds lasted all of a month.' There was some sympathetic laughter. 'Part of my programme was a Sonata by my grandfather, called *Aquarelle*. Since then that piece seems to have brought me good fortune. I've played it when I've won scholarships or received important reviews. Most performers have their superstitions; some carry rabbits' feet or Uncle Alfie's ashes – I have my grandfather's Sonata. May it bring your project good fortune also.'

The notes rose and fell in my mind even before the Sonata began. I knew that at last Paul was relaxing, no longer expecting too much of himself. As he did so his playing improved, the lovely liquid sounds carrying us forward and outwards, away from a harsh little town. When they finished the applause was that bit longer, heads turned in appreciation.

How do you express the difference between the merely good and what people call art? Paul had made no mistakes in the first half; twelve hours' rehearsal a day for four clays had ensured that, but now we were listening to a different pianist. As piece followed piece the joy grew, catching us as we listened, till player and audience were held in unison. The sweet papers stopped rustling, there were fewer coughs. Charlie Warwick's expression delighted me, for he more than anyone in that audience understood music, though his hands were too gnarled for him to play more than a few hymns nowadays. The boy he had encouraged over a decade ago had fulfilled his hopes, and in pleasure he nodded towards me, indicating a photographer entering at the back of the hall. Following Charlie's gestures I realised that as well as Bert from the *Sandhill Recorder*, another reporter had arrived and was examining the audience. In gratitude I closed my eyes; if they had come during the first half and gone away they would have written a very different report.

Finally I sensed we must be nearing the last item. Paul put his notes to one side, as if once again he had decided to change his programme. 'One failing of composers,' he began, as if merely telling another story, 'is that they long to hear their own work performed. My final choice is the short, original version of what has since become a concerto, scored for full orchestra, and is called *Atchin-tan*.' For the first time that night Paul sounded nervous and in surprise I glanced at Harry, who indicated he knew nothing about the item either. 'As I've been telling you anecdotes about other composers I suppose I had better tell you something about myself. Some of you are aware my father's family runs a travelling fair. A month or so ago I joined them for a short while, and when I returned my daughter besieged me with questions.' The reporter had begun to scribble. 'I wrote *Atchin-tan* in an attempt to convey to her the atmosphere of the fair, and the vigour of the people who travel with it. The children amongst you will hear the carousel with its mechanical organ, and the music that blares from the loudspeakers all day... I hope the adults will recognise a tribute to a way of life that has scarcely changed for centuries, and which draws me, even while I must reject it. It seems I can only bridge my two worlds through music...'

Running out of words, he turned to play, then paused as if a last point had occurred to him. '"Atchin-tan" is the *Romani* word for stopping place. My father's people arc part Romany – or more strictly speaking, Mumpers – Travellers of mixed descent.' The photographer had stepped forward. 'You will recognise influences from so called gypsy music, I'm sure.'

Shrugging his shoulders in a gesture of embarrassment he turned back to the piano. I was appalled at the risk he was taking, revealing his character and his work to an audience that understood so little beyond its own closed values.

Yet that night the audience was Paul's. It would no more have derided him than miss the refreshments afterwards. Since he was writing originally for a child, his composition was in any case accessible to his hearers, and we could smile at the carousel, recognise the Victorian tunes and the modern beat, but I knew the simplicity was deceptive, even if I could not explain why. The rhythms were haunting, the time constantly changing until a sense of excitement had been created which I found almost troubling. Without being strident, *Atchin-tan* was undeniably modern and strikingly original. With a peculiar sense of awe I sensed that we were hearing the premiere of music that would be performed again and again. We were also hearing the first public work of a man who would become known in time as a composer of repute...

For some minutes afterwards the audience stayed in little groups around the hall, the more musically minded trying to speak to Paul personally. Laura escaped from Lol and Josie, but she clearly feared her father's anger if she interrupted him, and stood at a distance until Paul called her, letting her stand close against him while the reporters asked questions. Two rather battered little men, they greeted each other with suspicion when I passed them their coffee later, but they were evidently content. They had their scoop, though considering the space afforded music in the average paper it was probably more like a teaspoon. Then I found myself becoming a source of interest. Was it true I had inherited a large area of land to the north of the town? And that the concert was organised to raise funds for its reclamation? How did I know Mr Boothman? Laura came up to me as I talked. She was tired of stuffy people talking to Daddy.

'And how does it feel to have a Daddy who composes music for you, little girl?' the Birmingham reporter asked.

Laura examined him with her unnerving eyes. 'He often does,' she replied politely. It was meant as a statement of fact, not pride, but I could see the reporter marking her down as precocious, a child of the theatre, and I wanted to defend her against such injustice. Fortunately both men decided to take themselves and their pencils off home.

Nervously I went over to Paul. Only a few people remained, and most of them were friends from the committee. 'It came good,' I said.

'Good? It was bloody marvellous.' Relief had taken the tiredness from his face and he swung me round in an idiotic polka till we nearly knocked the chairs flying. There had never been any plans for a party but people kept drifting up to us to ask about profits and congratulate Paul, and a few cans of beer at Charlie's seemed a good idea, and well, a few cans led to a small keg ...

Laura should have been sent to bed of course, but she curled herself into the corner of Charlie's living room and wisely kept so quiet she was forgotten. Finally Paul called her over to him and making her comfortable against his arm told her to go to sleep. I doubt if she obeyed; there was too much of interest around her, but she lay there perfectly still while he talked and both were happy.

It was Paul's night. He could have celebrated how he wished and we would have noisily gone along, but he preferred to sit there, talking about the Heath or his own music, while his daughter dozed against him. The tension had gone from his manner, and I had never seen him so obviously content. I thought of the title *Atchin-tan* and wondered if he had indeed reached a stopping place, but he would not be drawn into discussions of intent. Such matters were too personal for sharing. It occurred to me that I had never heard him mention the fairground in public before, much less avow his father's ancestry.

The party was a good one, and all the better for being spontaneous. Bert from the *Recorder* turned up, having somehow heard rumours he was missing a free drink, and Harry told his jokes, while Sampy stood pontificating and smelling of aftershave. Finally Paul whispered something to Laura. 'It's time this young lady went to bed,' he said aloud. 'Don't break up the party. I'll come back down in a few minutes.'

'I want Martie to read me a story,' Laura announced. 'She promised me one last night.'

For the life of me I could not remember such a promise but to say so would have sounded ill-tempered. Standing on the landing I stared at them both. 'You're a rotten pair,' I said. 'What do you want?'

'To talk to you. Story first.'

'At a quarter to twelve? All right. Bed …' I had meant Laura but Paul's eyes laughed at me. 'Oh, give over,' I replied, beginning to laugh also. 'You'll ruin my reputation keeping me talking up here.'

'I'm afraid your reputation's gone already, me dear. Half that audience only came to see what I looked like.'

'Harry put it at a third,' I replied drily. 'What do you want to say to me?'

'Stay behind a bit when the party breaks up. I'll walk you down home afterwards.'

For the next hour I could scarcely focus on the chatter around me. My head felt light, as if I were tipsy, though I had drunk nothing but orange. Wherever Paul moved in the room I was aware of him: his voice cut through the babble to me, despite being quieter than most. I noticed his gestures, the way he laughed, the movement of his hands as he talked. The room was hot and my face felt flushed. At last people began to leave, congratulating each other on a thoroughly successful evening. We had raised three hundred pounds at least, Sampy announced, for Paul would not take his fee, only expenses. When we tried to persuade him otherwise he shrugged his shoulders and offered to take five pounds if it would make us happier, arguing that he was worth no more now than he had been the first time he played for us. It was all very noisy and good-humoured. Finally Harry and Sue stood beside me, wanting to take me home in their car.

'I'll stay a while and help Charlie clear up,' I said. 'Thanks all the same. I can't very well leave him with this mess. Paul will walk me home.'

'I sec,' Sue said and her voice had an ominous bitchiness to it. 'First you read the little girl stories, and then you tell us them.'

'I've no need to justify my actions to you or anyone,' I replied coldly, and immediately regretted my indiscretion. 'I shall do precisely what I said: help Charlie and then walk home with Paul- no more, no less. If you wish to think evil of me you may.'

Then I began clearing up glasses, though my hand was shaking. Harry lingered. 'I hope you know what you're doing old girl,' he said.

'Clearing glasses,' I replied. 'Don't you start.'

After they had gone I stood at the fireplace in anger. 'You didn't have to quarrel because of me,' Paul said softly.

'I'm sick of having my motives questioned all the time, and of being thought the scarlet woman. If I wanted to go to bed with you I would, but I'm not going to be the one who breaks your marriage.'

Nodding slightly in acknowledgment Paul took the glasses from me. 'You'll drop these in a minute,' he remarked. 'Come and sit outside with me a bit.'

We sat on the back step in silence. The air was heavy with the scent of overgrown bushes and damp grass, and beyond the hedge the Heath rose in a dark shadow. 'Have you heard from your wife?' I asked.

'She and Mark are living together. I had heard as much from friends, but I'm glad Aileen had the courage to tell me so herself.'

'Do you still want her?'

For a long time Paul was silent. 'For Laura's sake I have to try and persuade her to come back to me. I tried to explain how things were the other week, and told her she might have to go with her mother. I've never seen a child cry so much. It was three before I could persuade her to settle, and then she had nightmares. She doesn't like Mark any more than I do, but it's more than that. She's in tune with me and not with Aileen. She's the sort who loves too much, just as I am.' Taking my hand, he examined it as if finding the words he needed there. 'That's why I asked you to stay behind a while, though as usual I've brought you trouble by doing so. I wanted to say thank you before I left, and to tell you how I felt. All the while I was playing Grandad's Sonata I was remembering the times we had together, and the love I had for you – still have, though it's a more mature sort of love now. You put me more and

294

more in your debt, Martie. I could never have fulfilled my commitments back in the States, but for you forcing me to appear tonight.'

'We've made a good profit, and got a lot of publicity,' I said, trying to lighten the atmosphere between us, and very aware of Charlie padding about in the kitchen.

'I'm glad, though that's not why you did it. Why are you so faithful to me? Very little I've done has merited it. Ever since we were kids I've taken from you, without giving in return, though I haven't meant it to be that way.'

'I know that, 'I replied carefully, 'but I'll admit for years I thought you did and blamed you for it.'

'If it's any consolation, I did mean to marry you. I intended to ask you the weekend everything went wrong. I'd even bought you a ring but I felt a fool, and then you said it would be better if we didn't see each other anymore... It'd be nice if I could get the ring out and prove it, but I chucked it in the river after Mike's funeral, so all I can do is ask you to take my word. It doesn't much matter – just that I wanted you to know I didn't mean to use you.'

The step was cold and I shivered. 'We'd better help Charlie,' I said. 'We can talk while you walk me home.'

It was nearly two when we set off up Sandhill Rise. In the darkness we stumbled several times as we went up the path through the remains of the coppice, and neither of us wanting to break a leg or fall down a shaft, we kept to the main track across the old army camp and on to the Heath. There we stopped, looking down on the glow that was Sandhill town. Even at that time of night there was traffic moving along the new road and streetlights traced patterns beneath us. It was almost beautiful. Sitting beside the first hawthorn we watched the town below. We did not touch each other but sat apart. There was a constraint between u, an unexpressed agreement that we were being foolish, playing with fire ...

'Did you really intend to propose to me?' I asked, amused by the idea.

'On my knees. I'd have looked a right idiot. Martie – what can I say? Offer you? If Aileen will try again with me I shall go back to her. Even if she won't I'm stuck. If I loved you less I'd suggest we kept in touch but you could no more accept being my other woman than I could tolerate such a situation. We're decent, nice people – at heart, at least. Adultery isn't a word we use. Even when we made love as kids it was all wrong. We should have stayed innocent – friends and no more.'

In the darkness I touched his face. 'You do us both an injustice,' I said. 'Just as I did for years. It's easy to let the bitterness that came afterwards colour your memory of what went before.' I was not explaining myself as I had hoped. He was too near to me. 'Think back,' I asked. "It was good between us. I used to sit with my books open at school and dream of being with you. That was why I did so badly in my exams. I used to live from one weekend to another, thinking of you- what we would talk about... You told me you felt the same... how you'd walk through the woods looking for somewhere quiet we could go, or row over to the Island just to sit thinking of me.'

I saw him shiver slightly. 'We'd better go,' I said. 'Before either of us does anything we might regret.'

Getting up, I looked towards the town, though Paul sat for some time still, his face turned from me, hardly visible in the glow of the town below us. 'Take care of yourself,' he said finally. 'Don't work too hard.'

'I shan't come up to Mr Warwick's tomorrow,' I said. 'It'd only make things more difficult for us both. What time do you leave?'

'I'll go after lunch – stay in bed a bit tomorrow morning. Will you be all right? You've compromised yourself tonight, you know. There'll be talk.'

'It'll die down, once you've gone. If ever -' I could not think how to phrase my request. 'If ever you find yourself on your own, don't let pride get in the way.'

'Don't hang around waiting for me, Martie.'

'Course not,' I promised. 'I've no intention of pining, for you or anyone else. I can cope on my own, thank you. Besides, I shall be too busy to pine ...'

Taking my hands, he held them to his mouth. It was a gesture of farewell. 'No,' I pleaded, 'not here.'

'Why not?' Saying goodbye outside your house will be asking for· gossip.' Then he understood and laughed uncertainly. 'Oh give over, you're making me nervous. I'm not going away to war.'

'But you're flying from one end of an ocean to another, and driving goodness knows where afterwards.' I was tired and irrational.

'Perhaps I am going to war in a way. I've a feeling I'm going back into a hell of a lot of trouble, most it of my own making.' Letting go of my hands, he kissed my mouth briefly. 'I'd give a great deal to stay here with you, but that would be running away. Think of me sometimes my love, but go and find yourself another bloke soon – please. It'd help if I thought you were settled and happy.'

Down in the town a clock chimed three times, and we turned in its direction, reminded of the day to come.

Staying at Nightingale Road became impossible. My time was being taken up too much by family needs and my own sense of duty. I must go to chapel, help Dad, play auntie to Harry's children. There were too many phone calls, too much coming and going and too much tension. As we had recognised when I returned, I was the discordant element in the household. I squeezed the toothpaste in the middle, left my shoes where people could trip over them, and while Aunt Lizzie's bowels were naturally of interest to their owner, after a month or so of their intricacies I began to lose my temper. During the weeks leading up to the concert I'd told myself and anyone who would listen that Things would get better afterwards, but with the usual tendency Things have to do as they please, they did not. I lacked mental quiet to work on my book in the few days not gobbled by committee meetings, and I was disrupting the life of the family too much.

There was a more serious cause of tension, too. Sue had always thought I should sell the Heath and share the profits. When I declined an offer from a developer wanting to build starter hutches on my land, she was furious. I cared for no one but myself. She and Harry had scrimped and saved ever since they married, and it was they not me who had had to put up with Aunt Mary's funny ways. I had returned from overseas and within a few months had taken over Aunt Mary's affections and her estate.

Poor Sue. She had a right to feel cheated and old tensions were resurfacing. I had always been that bit too smart for our Sue. Now she had other grounds for her dislike. My morality was not all that could be desired in a strict chapel family, and not a good influence on her children Having seen Paul and me stay behind at Charlie's she drew the wrong, but understandable conclusion, and after that she stubbornly stuck to her idea, despite the fact that Paul was now an ocean apart from me. Her view was that where there's a lust, there's a way. I would have minded her innuendos less if they had been true, but I was proud of my virtue. Had a dragon suddenly appeared and eaten Aileen up I should have rung Saint George and reported the matter, then presented myself at Paul's door, but dragons being in short supply I found comfort in the knowledge I had not made him unfaithful.

As I struggled with my book after yet another discordant Sunday tea, I remembered Charlie Warwick's invitation to cry on his shoulder, and decided he might accept me a little earlier than the promised page 132.

Mr Warwick and the cats considered my problem. There were thirteen rooms in History House, not including the bathroom and a peculiar tower that was once the skivvy's quarters. With his hands getting so stiff and his time being so taken up with the thousand things still waiting to be done he couldn't keep the house as straight as he'd like. Having removed a piece of toast as I sat down, I saw his point. I was welcome to take over the attic floor he declared, so long as I straightened up a bit. Since I had a whole Heath to straighten up a bit, I decided one house, even if it was Mr Warwick's, would be a mere trifle.

And so, to my family's incredulity I took myself and my files to History House. There I had a bedsitting room furnished with a splendid three-legged bed (the fourth leg was a Pear's Cyclopaedia) a chest of drawers that stuck, a chair which despite looking like a fat lady in a crinoline was surprisingly comfortable and a wonderful view over Sandhill Rise and the town beyond. Simply looking at that view set me writing again. Sharing a bathroom proved awkward but Charlie's researcher's mind came up with a solution. We were each allotted strict times and meetings in dressing gowns were avoided.

In return for Charlie's hospitality I attacked a decade of neglect. The cats were furious. Venus took to crouching at the top of the banisters and snatching at my hair as I went past, while Aphrodite laid in wait under chairs and beds, ready to sink her teeth into my ankles. Other feline temperaments were provoked. I was the talk of Sandhill, or at least of the post office. There were references to me being Mr Warwick's housekeeper, nudge, nudge, wink, wink. Not only had I one gentleman friend, of the tall, dark and handsome variety, now I had found myself a sugar daddy with a large if eccentric house. Presumably I was hoping to inherit that, just as I had inveigled my aunt's land from her ...

Dad had warned me I would make enemies, and I should have foreseen the reaction to my moving into History House. As usual I had been floating around in cloud cuckoo land. There was humour in my being linked to Mr Warwick, whose idea of an exciting evening was a game of Scrabble, but once again I was hurt. Moving out would have meant admitting defeat however and I was comfortable with Charlie. In that wet summer it was useful to be living nearer the Heath and my book had begun to take on life again. Charlie himself was not in the least bothered by the chatter. Had someone suggested Keats was living with Fanny Brawne he would have been fascinated, but gossip regarding himself bored him.

In the way that ill winds have, the resentment against me brought me some good. It set me wondering why the Heath was considered so desirable, and what it was worth. I had the land properly valued and spent the evening with Lol and Josie recovering. Feeling I needed a second opinion I rang the teddy bear, and he and Lydia came the following weekend. Even without planning permission and pitted with shafts and derelict buildings Barnaby estimated the land could sell for over a hundred thousand.

If a developer could afford to invest in its clearance the profit to them would be two or three hundred thousand pounds. Subsidence would be a problem but an unscrupulous firm might hope there was no movement until after the builder's guarantee had expired. A scrupulous Council would of course refuse building permission, but there was an unpleasant smell about the attempt at compulsory purchase made during my grandmother's lifetime, and Barnaby suspected such a bid might be made again.

As my brother-in-law turned towards the car Lydia and I looked at each other in horror. 'Fancy Aunt Mary owning this little lot and never letting on,' Lydia remarked. For once she seemed awed.

'Ought I to sell?' I asked. 'Sue says I'm being a dreamer.'

'Of course you are darling, but there has to be room for a dreamer occasionally. Sue would have the whole world eating bread and dripping. You stick to your guns, little sister.'

I wondered at her unusual gentleness. 'We've managed without being particularly wealthy or particularly poor till now,' Lydia replied, shrugging her shoulders. 'I don't see why we need to sell Aunt Mary's land. It'd be going against the dead. I'm not superstitious but Aunt Mary would be quite capable of getting up out of her grave and pitching into us with her walking stick and so would old Isaac Booth come to that. Besides, a place like this is bound to be haunted. We might have all those poor souls who worked down the shafts chasing us.'

She was making light of matters as usual, but I heard an unaccustomed emotion in her voice. 'I feel I owe it to Mum,' I agreed, 'and to the other Lakins. To the Booths, too ...'

For some time Lydia stared across the wasteland. 'If there's anything you can do to atone to them, duckie,' she said over-brightly, 'I reckon you'd better do it. We treated those two boys very badly, didn't we? We were slumming, getting a thrill of a weekend. They deserved better of us.' Abruptly she turned, and went towards the car.

Despite their protests, when Barnaby and Lydia returned to town I stayed on my own on the Heath, sitting at the foot of the toad's mouth rock. What had begun as a dream had become a terrifying responsibility. My original intention had been to sign the land over to the council once I was assured that it would be preserved; now I decided against doing so. There was too strong a chance of someone making a profit out of it later. The Heath must remain in the family so that we could control its future. Even if I myself had no children, there were Harry's three to consider, and there was still time for Lydia to produce little pootles. I must fulfil Richard and Isaac's plans myself.

SEVEN: Enchanter's Island

Paul did me a last favour before returning to America. At my request he wrote to Christopher Lakin introducing me, and asking if I might visit him, to discuss 'matters of mutual interest.'

While there was unlikely to be any legal difficulty proving my claim to the Heath, I felt I needed to have Christopher Lakin's support – or at least to ensure he would not make trouble. It would be understandable if he felt bitter. The Heath was worth a lot of money and as Henry Lakin's son he had more right to it than me. My title was an illegitimate one, and not only more distant but from the female line. He might publicly oppose my plans, and in Sandhill the name of Lakin still had force. Hostility between him and me might cause problems for the Booths too, for River Cottage was still rented from him and my association with Paul was well known. I'll admit it however – my main reason for wanting to meet him was sheer curiosity. I was longing to know if my relative was as unsavoury as rumour suggested.

A polite reply came almost by return of post. I was invited to dinner, which gave me an excuse for a day in London before travelling down to one of those southern villages where the thatch is combed nightly and even the dogs and cats are vetted by the English Tourist Board. After Sandhill the air seemed to have been scrubbed; even Arton was seedy in comparison. Christopher Lakin himself lived in 'a delightful mews house' or so I saw a neighbour's home described in the estate agent's. It was freshly painted and groomed and smelt of quiet luxury.

He greeted me with a graciousness I found slightly unnerving; it made me suspect I had a ladder in my tights. Vanishing into a cushion I sat while he served me tea in a Japanese cup and discussed Paul's letter. I was researching a book on the old families of Sandhill he gathered, and was interested in the Lakins. As the sole surviving member of the family he would be delighted to assist me.

For an hour or so I let him talk, while I frantically took notes. Afterwards we ate dinner prepared by a woman from the village and drank wine in long fluted glasses. Still he gave me facts and figures, dates, names, all of them invaluable. Clearly he had an excellent memory and an intellect to match. As I listened I tried to place him, but could not. Though middle-aged he seemed far younger. His face had the smoothness of a boy's, and his expression reminded me of a slightly spoilt but pleasant child. I felt I should have brought him popcorn instead of wine. The same youthfulness affected his room; there were bright scatter cushions and wall hangings that looked as if they had genuinely been brought back from Peruvian travels. Yet his manner was weary, and his voice suggested knowledge of disappointment despite the immaculate Oxbridge accent. I found myself recalling Oscar Wilde's Dorian Grey – a man granted perpetual youth but decaying inside. Yet almost as soon as I thought the idea I felt I was unjust, that this man meant well.

We talked for a while of Arton Villa and River Cottage. 'It was good of you to let the Booth family stay on,' I remarked.

'Paul Booth asked me to,' Mr Lakin replied, as if that were sufficient reason. Then almost as if to deny my conclusion that he had been generous in friendship added, 'The rent is useful. It's a steady bit of income and I shall sell the cottage and orchard for a good price in a few years.'

'Do you regret moving south?' I asked.

'Would you?' His glance took in the rose garden beyond the french windows and the manicured lawn. 'Why live in a place like Arton when you can afford better? I'm no idealist my dear.'

'I believe you write short stories?' I asked in the pause that followed.

'Occasionally. I work for a publisher's editing hard-back novels down for a popular series. There's a lot of money in Romance nowadays my dear, far more than in your academic books.'

Finally I forced myself to explain why I was there. In my embarrassment I made several false starts and got the relationship between Mr Lakin and myself confused.

'I hope you don't mind,' I ended lamely. 'With my mother being illegitimate…'

'Why ever should I mind?' he replied. 'What would I want with the Heath? I knew of course that my aunt had left her estate to a friend. It was necessary for me to know in case I made enquiries. It was no more than I would have expected of her.'

His reply was so enigmatic I could not judge whether he approved or not. 'Did you know of my mother's existence?' I asked.

'No. She kept her secret well. None of the family can have known.' Then suddenly there was a flash of humour under all that sophisticated poise. 'Well, well. I did my aunt an injustice. I thought her incapable of such things.' Getting up, he fetched a decanter off the sideboard. 'I think this deserves a brandy. I'd offer you a cigar if I thought you'd like one.'

Uneasily I smiled. 'You're not angry then?' I said. 'I shan't make any profit out of the Heath myself.'

'Then more fool you.'

'Would you sell it?'

'Of course.'

I lay awake in my hotel room many hours that night, feeling a peculiar sadness. Somewhere in that gracious, luxurious man there was another man, crying. He had sold his talent and his heritage.

Many do the same, but he was different. He knew what he had done.

Still, he had given me his blessing – of a sort. He had taken me by the hand and wished my 'strange little scheme' success.

And after my return? One campaign is very like another and there seems little point in boring you with details of how I got my way. The school Jubilee Celebrations were fixed for the beginning of November, just after half-term, and the reclamation of the Heath was well under way. Soon I wanted more than rubbish cleared and shafts filled. I wanted the old tile works restored as a local history centre. Other towns had their Victorian streets and Tudor banquets; I wanted to go Edwardian, to the youth of Richard and Milly. I wanted more than a museum, though. My original vision had been of light filling the tile works and forges and I was determined we should not have turnstiles closing at five. Paul had suggested the packing room would make an excellent small theatre, perhaps refurbished in the style of Sandhill music hall, a seedy building demolished in the sixties but more than Twynning ever had. We found old playbills and pictures of the exterior and could reconstruct the interior from reports in the library.

The Committee suggested the tile works could become a centre to which local people could come all week, for amateur actors, for craftsmen like Ben Tithe our only remaining chain maker, and for Mr Taylor's photographs. What I had begun was developing its own momentum, leaving the Jubilee Celebrations as a minor gesture.

Then, as I walked in what remained of Bircham's Coppice I realised the school could create a much richer symbol than a few trees planted along a road. I wanted my Bluebell Woods again. We must plant whole thickets of trees, and scatter bluebell seed. In a frenzy of activity I talked people into giving money, even persuaded Josie to undertake a sponsored slim and cost her a whole new wardrobe. My dream had become an obsession. When people laughed at the idea of moving a whole wood I replied that Macduff had done it, and I didn't see why we shouldn't as well. Since most people thought Macduff was a Scottish football player, my explanation hardly helped them.

Sue had decided that rather than greedy or immoral I was positively mad, which was a relief even if it led her to use the tone one adopts to sick children. The others probably shared her opinion but were too kind to say so.

It was impossible for me to keep up so much effort without over-tiredness, and after Charlie, Lol and Dad had each lectured me I agreed to take a holiday. Hiring a car, I set off to the West Country, aimlessly, booking in at bed and breakfast signs along the way. Even then I could not relax, but visited any tourist centre I passed, stealing ideas. Finally, almost unintentionally, I found myself on the road to Harlech. I was mentally as well as physically exhausted, needing to give way to emotion for just a little while. A desire to see where my grandmother had stayed afflicted me, coming over me like a cold in the. head. There was a 'Vacancies' notice in the window, and on an impulse I went inside and booked a room.

Afterwards I sat in the lounge looking out over the dunes beneath the town and listening to the chatter around me. At dinner I watched the woman who served us, and wondered if she were related to Paul, but there was no likeness between them, and perhaps after all she was a hired help. Later I explored the castle, thinking of my grandmother doing so before me, waiting for her child to be born. I almost envied her.

The visit was a foolish one, dwelling on the past and bound to leave me feeling alone. The town seemed to be full of young families and people walking hand in hand. I was in danger of feeling sorry for myself.

Then I met Hannah. She too was alone, and sitting at our separate tables we began to talk. Within hours we were walking the sand dunes together, sharing our lives. At present she was resting between appearances with a repertory company up north, and in delight I shamelessly scribbled her ideas for the Sandhill theatre in my diary. Like myself she was recovering from a love affair of sorts, having discovered her feller had been two-timing her. She'd presented him with a plate of fish and chips in his lap on hearing the news. We giggled at the image she created, and laughed at men in general, wandering around the town awarding points to those we passed on a scale from nought to ten. I never did manage to introduce myself to Paul's relatives, nor to ask after my grandmother, but I seemed to sense her presence and was happy. On the night before we parted Hannah and I sat for a long time considering Milly's story, and wondering if we would have done the same. We would never see each other again, but we had helped each other through a bad week in our lives.

When I returned to Sandhill I was calmer than I had felt since Paul left. In my absence Sampy had solved the legal problems involved in the preservation of the Heath. Leased at a peppercorn rent to a cooperative of enthusiasts, the land would remain mine in name. When I returned to Australia the cooperative would oversee a Manpower Services project continuing its reclamation, and employing one full-time warden and a team of part timers, with voluntary help manning the museum after it opened. Sampy was confident of approval, though there was a whole in-tray of paperwork to be copied in triplicate before the scheme could be approved. Still, it was an idea to be looking out for eligible employees he suggested, passing me a bewildering list of regulations.

'Lol Jackson,' I said, returning the papers. 'We'll have him as full-time warden.'

'But it would involve being management if you see what I mean,' Sampy pointed out dubiously. 'Lol's a good worker, but could he take charge of others?'

'People have always followed Lol, one way or another,' I reminded him. 'I doubt if he'd enjoy thinking of himself as Them instead of Us but he loves the Heath and he's used to working there. He knows every shaft and tree, and he doesn't mind the weather.'

'He has a – he's been in trouble, Martie.'

'What do shafts and trees care about that? It's my land and I want him looking after it.' Trying to persuade him, I smiled. 'Come on – we've all been in bother some time. I distinctly remember a certain prefect being hauled before the Head, for putting dolly blue in the teacher's loos.'

In all such activity I had nearly driven Paul from my mind, but Charlie was worried about him. He had expected a letter from him after the concert. For several years after the first concert, Paul had kept in touch with him, out of gratitude to an older man who had encouraged him, I suppose. This time Charlie expected at least an acknowledgment of his hospitality. He found it strange and rude to have no thank you letter. I too found it worrying. Once again Paul's image began to trouble my sleep. Several nights I was woken by a sense of foreboding. One time I was wandering a building site trying to find an examination room long after I should have begun the paper; another I was running from some unidentified terror while a whole street laughed at me. Part of my unease was the result of being in so prominent a position in the town, but there was a continued sense of concern for Paul that I could not explain. Several times I saw him in my sleep as I had seen him as a boy, thin and ill, watching our game.

Then in the third week of September Charlie at last received a small packet. It included reviews of *Atchin-tan*, which had just received its American premiere, performed by full orchestra with Paul as soloist. The critics' opinions ranged from 'Brilliantly original' to 'Incoherent' but the good outweighed the bad. There was a scribbled letter with the photocopies, written on notepaper headed with a motel address. Paul thought the Committee might like to see the enclosed as there were references to the Sandhill concert. He apologised for not writing sooner but was very busy touring. As I returned the letter I felt a sense of unease. Something did not ring true.

All evening the unease stayed with me.

In the middle of the night I woke crying with fear, my mouth clamped shut. I heard Charlie knock at my door. 'Are you all right, Martie?" his voice asked.

'Just a bad dream,' I called back. 'Thank you.'

As his footsteps went back down the landing, I realised how loudly I must have been shouting for him to hear me a floor below. I felt a fool.

The nightmare stayed with me however, and as I lay in the darkness I tried to recall it. The fair had come to Arton again but this time Paul was managing the carousel. Just as before I was standing watching him. The carousel started and the children riding it laughed as the horses went up and down. I noticed that Laura was seated on a magnificent gilded horse on the second row and she waved to me. As she did so the carousel began to go faster, the horses rising and falling more quickly and beginning to float outwards. To my surprise I saw Paul was still standing at the centre, holding firm despite the continual motion. Suddenly the horses began to speed up again, too fast for the little ones, several of whom began to cry. In horror I saw the horses had begun to take on life, their heads turning as they moved, their painted teeth becoming real. At once the children screamed and parents ran to snatch them away. One by one Paul lifted the children down and passed them to safety though the horses reared and bit at his hands as he did so. The organ played louder and louder till I put my hands over my ears to protect them from the pain. Laura was furthest from her father, and as he tried to reach her a huge gelding struck him with its hooves. I called to the crowd to help but they were running away. Dropping to his knees Paul tried to protect himself and in the distance I heard Zac Booth shouting instructions. When the roundabout stopped Paul lay motionless across its centre...

My dream was absurd, childish, but the fear it had given me would not go away. Further sleep was impossible, and putting on my tracksuit I went for an early morning run, towards the Heath.

'You make me feel old,' Charlie complained when I returned. It was the first time I had heard such an admission from him.

'Nonsense,' I said, passing him the butter. 'It's only us unquiet spirits who need early morning runs. Sensible people stay in bed.' He watched me curiously but made no comment. 'Would you mind if I looked at those reviews again?' I asked, trying to sound casual. 'I was too tired to read them properly last night. I'd like to show them to Lol, too. He'd be interested I'm sure.'

With a clearer mind I tried to identify what had caused my anxiety and the dream which had expressed it. The mere act of sending the reviews was an inconsistency for though Paul had tolerated his mother's pride, it was out of character for him to boast about a performance of *Atchin-tan* to others. Nor did the quality of the letter paper or the address at its head suggest the sort of hotel a well-known musician would stay in while on tour. Such details had obviously been noticed by my subconscious last night, but they did not themselves explain the terror I had felt in my sleep.

Making up a flask of tea I walked to the Heath afterwards.

Lol was there already, hauling out one of the old bogies that had lain submerged in soil for at least a century. Such debris was dangerous but if restored could provide us with museum exhibits. Two of his mates were working on the other side of the track and I nodded to them. Lol always preferred to work alone. His stomach and chest had tightened over the last months, and the days spent in the open air had reddened his skin, till he reminded me of a Scots chieftain. We sat against a pile of rails, drinking tea, sharing the cup because I had forgotten to bring a second. 'Well?'

Lol said at length. 'What is it you wanted to talk about? You always want a chat when you bring me tea.'

I laughed. 'And here I am ferrying your tea out of the goodness of my heart,' I protested. 'Shame on you for a suspicious mind. As it happens however...'

'What is it?'

'Do you believe in dreams?'

Lol considered my question. 'Course I do. I have 'ern regular. If you mean do I think they can tell you things, well, I reckon you can probably work out things in your sleep. What've you been dreaming about?'

'I'll tell you later. Read this.' I passed him the packet of reviews and Paul's note. 'I've a feeling I'm missing something obvious.'

Lol read it all through and then reread it while I finished my tea. 'There's nothing about the little 'un,' he said.

'How stupid can I be?' I replied, seeing the truth at once. 'I'd say he and his wife have split up, and she's got the kiddy. He'd have at least mentioned her starting a new school, or sent her love to Mr Warwick. They got quite fond of each other while she was staying here.

'If Paul's lost Laura he's going to be so low...'

'Perhaps that's why he sent the reviews in the first place. I mean, it in't like him to boast about what he does. Why should he be staying in a motel in any case?'

'Or so near home?' I continued. 'He's driven all over the Eastern seaboard. He wouldn't stop short of driving home if he was in the same State.' I considered the address again. 'I've not been thinking straight, have I? He's on his own, and his wife has everything, apartment, child...' A hawk was wheeling in the sky ·above me, caught on the wind. 'Those reviews were a cry for help, though he's too proud to say what's happening. He's ill. I know he is.'

'What was your dream about?'

'If you laugh I'll never forgive you,' I promised. 'It wasn't just one dream. It was a sense of fear night after night.' Foolishly I explained.

'Send him some stuff about this place,' Lol suggested.

I understood him at once.

That night I made up a bundle of newspaper reports about the project, adding as an afterthought one of my With Compliments slips. We were doing well. There was more hope in the town than there had been for years. Perhaps some of that hope would pass to him.

Paul did not acknowledge my package, nor the letter Charlie wrote thanking him for the reviews. I had no way of knowing whether he was still at the same address, and was reluctant to contact his parents, for fear of worrying them or making myself appear foolish. As mid-October approached I recalled that the Boothmans' fair had an annual booking during that week, in connection with a regular autumn fete held in Talchester, a few miles north of Twynning. Persuading Harry to take me there, I asked him to drop me outside the town while he continued to some clients in the area. Then I walked the last half mile to the fairground.

Zac remembered me at once and made me welcome, apparently not in the least surprised that I should appear unannounced. People were always dropping in on them he said, taking me to meet Paul's Aunt Hilda. It was kind of me to call while I was local. Sitting at the table in their van I drank tea and chatted. For days afterwards the smell of polish and flowers lingered in my mind. I was wondering if they had heard from Paul I asked, during a pause.

Shaking his head, Zac looked concerned. 'He usually sends me the paperwork back regular,' he said. 'He does the accounting for me you know – has done for years. It's cheaper even with the postage to send him a bundle of receipts than employ an outsider, and I trust Family more. He checks through all my additions and spots anything I've overlooked. This month's stuff's late, and last month it came back to me with just a scribbled note. He's always written a proper letter before.' Sitting down beside me the old man rubbed his chin. 'Things ain't going well for him – you don't have to be a genius to see that. I've told him he can come back to us and help me out. He could have a share of the business, like Artie. Now there's only our Joel and Phil's such a hothead we could do with one more.'

'Did he say what was wrong?' I asked.

'Just that he'd got the whole mafia of money and respectability against him – those were his words. His wife's living with her fancy man, I know that, and Paul's on his own. If it was me, I'd tell her to get lost and find meself another woman, but that ain't the way our Paul docs things, and I can't help but admire him for it. He's me Dad all over again.'

'Have his parents heard any more from him?'

'They got a couple of short notes letting them know his new address. I got our Joel to drive me over I was so worried, but they've had nothing lately.'

Thanking them for their hospitality I got up. 'What's a woman like you doing, caring for a fellow like him?' Paul's aunt asked unexpectedly. 'Oh I know he's been educated and all, and he's not really one of us, but he's not your sort neither.'

'Who's to say who's anybody's sort?' I replied. 'I don't imagine you expected to be running a fair when you were a girl.'

Laughing good-humouredly she settled back in her seat. 'No,' she agreed. 'I married beneath me, but you wouldn't understand that.' Laughing again, she took out some lace she was making. 'I didn't do too badly. I'd have had to look a long way to find a better man than my Zac.'

It was a long walk back to the bus, and it was raining.

The plans for the School Jubilee were well in hand, though there were the usual last-minute problems, and at times I found Miss

McClean's manner patronising. Though we both tried devotedly, she could not stop picturing me in a gymslip, and I could not stop remembering my Latin lessons.

Then, the week before the Jubilee, my father brought me a letter which changed all my plans. As soon as I had deciphered the postmark my hand became unsteady, though I did not recognise the writing. '*Deer Miss Martie,*' it began. '*I thought as you should no Paul and Laura is here, only for a week. For the babby's sake more than his you ort to come and see them. You always understood our Paul, and mite no what to say, we dont. Ive told him hes daft not to rite but he's too proud. Hes divorsing his wife and the babbys been sick over it. It grieves Janie and me to see them.*'

Jubilee Celebrations, Heath, everything was insignificant compared to that appeal, probably the only letter Saul Booth had written in a decade. 'When did this arrive?' I asked my father.

'This morning. I thought you'd want to see it straight away, seeing as it was postmarked Arton.'

I kissed him for his understanding. 'What would you do?' I asked, passing him the letter.

Silently Dad considered Saul's appeal. 'Go, of course!' he said.

'If Paul had written to me himself I wouldn't have hesitated, but you can see what his father says – he's too proud. If he thinks I've come out of pity he'll turn against me, and I shan't have another chance.'

Reading the letter again Dad nodded slowly. 'I know Paul almost as well as you,' he agreed. 'But you'll have to risk it. Not to go will leave you feeling mean, and if Paul finds out his father wrote and you didn't come he'll have every right to think you cold and unfeeling. I don't know how to advise you, my dear. Do as you feel right.'

All the way to the city my mind turned with the wheels. I was as nervous as I had been before Paul's concert. Saul had said his son was too proud to write to me. Perhaps he simply did not want me.

Having returned from one battlefield, why should he risk marching into another? And why risk me?

It was midday by the time I approached Arton. Ahead of me a man was leaning on a walking stick, resting while his dog panted near him. Not till I recognised Tiger did I realise the man was Saul.

'Thought you'd come,' he greeted me laconically, beginning to stomp homewards.

'Thank you for sending for me,' I replied. 'What's wrong with Laura?'

'She'll mend – when her heart heals. Pack of clever people tearing a babby in two. They've even got the trick cyclists on to her. She doesn't need no psychologising. What she needs is a bit of loving.'

We walked towards River Cottage together. 'Tell me what's been going on,' I persisted.

'What I wrote you.'

I would not let him give me so inadequate an answer.

'I dunno it all,' he replied grudgingly. 'From what I can gather the kiddy was supposed to stay with her mother when the family split up. It was all done legal - a separation don't they call it? It happened right after Paul returned I think. Not a divorce, our Paul wouldn't agree to that. His wife kept the apartment and the kiddy. There's equality for you. Her people were against Paul of course, reckoned he was a drifter, not fit to have their grandchild. Why they should have thought their Aileen and her fancy man could do any better, Lord knows. They put her straight in school. It was a very good school.' Saul's mockery was bitter.

'Laura wouldn't settle in another boarding school,' I commented.

'You know that, and I know that, but they didn't. Within six weeks the headmistress had asked for the child to be taken away. She was disruptive she said. So they put her in another school. She ran away from that one. Paul don't talk about what happened after that, but it all seems to have gone very wrong. Well, I can't help but feel there's justice in it. I had enough strife with that son of mine; now he knows what it feels like.'

'Laura had set her heart against going with her mother from the start,' I agreed.

'A y, and she's fair worn herself and everyone else out till she got what she wanted. You'd best go in alone. Don't be surprised at the change in them. They've both aged a hundred years.'

Stopping to throw a stick to his dog, Saul let me walk on ahead. When I approached the cottage I could hear the sound of sawing and of Laura's laughter, just as I had heard it months before. The privet hedge was high and thick and I could not see them, nor they see me. 'Time we got this mop cut,' Paul's voice said. Laura laughed and I could visualise him tousling her hair. 'Do you reckon Sam Stables knows how to cut little girls' hair? I'd feel saft taking you to the Ladies' salon.'

'Grandma shall cut it,' Laura announced.

'That's an idea. She used to do mine. Which do you prefer? Pudding basin or meat tin?'

They sounded so at ease together I could not understand why Saul should have sent for me. Going to the gate I bent to open the catch. My shoes made no noise on the grass and neither man nor child saw me till after I had seen them. The shock made me catch my breath. Laura looked like an illustration from a Victorian novel, her eyes huge and dark in an old face. My heart went out to her in pity even before she ran to me. For a moment I could see nothing for her arms around my neck. Finally I disentangled myself, sufficiently to open the gate. As I did so I saw Paul standing uncertainly, as if he too wished to come to me and dared not. He had lost weight. Ironically it made him look younger, more like the boy I remembered.

'How did you know we were here?' he asked.

'Your father wrote to me.'

Saul was level with us now. 'I thought Martie should know,' he said defensively. 'The kiddy needs her even if you don't.' I recalled the bad-tempered man of Paul's youth, the burnt music and the occasional blows and could not fathom them. Neither Saul's present kindness nor his past anger were the whole man; they were both aspects of a composite called Saul, just as his son's pride was as much part of his character as his gentleness.

We went into the cottage together. Janie had seen us but she did not come to greet me, remaining at the sink like a resentful bird. 'He's traded his church for his child,' she said when I joined her.

'He wouldn't do it lightly,' I replied. 'You know that.'

Paul began making us coffee. When I visited the cottage last time it was Saul's presence one sensed. If he was irritable we placated him; as soon as he wanted logs sawing, Paul did so. Now it was Paul's personality I felt, a quieter but equally strong presence. 'Go and see if there's any eggs,' he asked Laura, passing her a bowl. 'Please.'

'I want to talk to Martie,' she protested.

'So do I. You know the story already. Let me explain it to her.' After she had gone he turned to me. 'Has Dad told you about the divorce?'

I nodded. 'How will you cope?' I asked.

'I'm renting a house over there, and there'll be Auntie Janet. She seems a capable sort and her references are impeccable.' His hand moved restlessly on the table. 'My in-laws have come good, or I wouldn't be able to afford a place of my own till the apartment's sold.' I was conscious that Saul and Janie were listening. 'I have the upper hand of course – I have their only grandchild and right now no one else can do anything with her. They paid for us to fly here. I shall pay them back, of course.' Laura had come back, carrying five eggs in a bowl.

'There's only five,' she complained, near to tears. 'And I've looked and looked.'

Grudgingly Janie bent towards the bowl. 'Hens don't lay so well as autumn comes on,' she agreed. As if against her will gentleness entered her manner. 'Five's enough. That's one each.'

Calling the child to me I sat her on my lap and listened to her talk about airplanes and how Daddy had taken her fishing yesterday. 'We flew overnight,' Paul said quietly. 'It was the only flight I could get at short notice.'

We talked together for about half an hour though it seemed longer. Laura's conversation was erratic, some times aggressive, at others over-emotional and the change in her disturbed me. Outside it was one of those unseasonal Indian summers with which England can surprise its sodden inhabitants, warmer on an October day than in most of July. The light shone through the open door. Laura's needs were great, but her father needed rest, too.

'It's a lovely day,' I suggested. 'Janie, would you look after Laura an hour or so, so that Paul and I can spend some time together?'

'I want to come,' Laura insisted, jumping up.

Saul took her hand. 'Your Daddy's given a great deal for you,' he said firmly. 'Now you give a little in return. You and me'll feed the goat.' He was cajoling her. 'We'll do a few jobs together nice and easy, while Daddy has a bit of a holiday. Everyone needs a holiday now and then.'

Taking a bundle of lettuce leaves, he led her outside.

We gathered some of Janie's cakes and a flask of coffee, then took the skiff from the jetty. By unspoken consent Paul rowed upstream, towards Enchanter's Island, completing the journey which had been begun on the day of Mike's death. I was afraid of the water. In all the years since, I had never been past Enchanter's Island by boat.

'Most of the time we sat in silence. 'You underestimate your father,' I said at last.

'Not anymore.'

'Why didn't you write to me?'

'What could I say? "Please, Martie, my wife doesn't want me"? You would never have known if I loved you or simply wanted comfort.'

The water slapped the oars; Paul rowed strongly and evenly under the overhanging willows. Low in the sky, the sun coloured the river a rich gold and made our eyes dazzle. Though the shadow struck cold, beyond the leaves it was warm, a beautiful unexpected gift. We paused at the channel where Arton Brook entered the river and sat watching each other. 'You and your With Compliments slips,' Paul said. 'At the lowest point in my life I get a With Compliments slip and a packet of stuff about a museum. That must be the most original love letter yet.'

'What makes you think it was a love letter?' I asked, teasing.

'Because you understood my thoughts an ocean away. I sat in my motel room and read your stupid packet and didn't know whether I was laughing or crying. How did you know things were going so badly with me?'

'Because you wrote to Mr Warwick and didn't mention Laura.'

'Zac could use you. We've not had a fortune-teller since Annie left.'

'All I did was put two and two together from what I saw before me.'

'Precisely.'

'It was Lol Jackson too – he helped me work it out. He'd look good in a headscarf and earrings.'

Taking the oars again Paul rowed up-river. In the distance Enchanter's Island came into sight, a dark fist within gleaming waters. As I looked towards it I was afraid. 'I dreamt of you,' I admitted. 'It sounds pretty silly now. I was afraid you were in trouble.'

In answer Paul inclined his head slightly, accepting my statement. The Island was near us now, a pair of crows cawing as if they had been charmed into waiting for our return. The waters parted into fast moving currents at the furthest tip, but the Island

319

itself was beautiful in the sun, a dangerous paradise. Despite the dryness of the autumn the river came down with a stronger flow the nearer we reached the division in the waters, and Paul had to row hard merely to hold firm as we crossed to the safety of the nearside bank. Even on so calm a day twigs swirled in the eddies set up by the current, and shreds of reed tangled in the branches overhanging the water, as if a nymph had laid a paperchase round it to doom unwary lovers. Looking at the height of that pale line I could not help but remember floods swirling downstream and a branch the size of a small tree borne on them. My hands felt sticky and cold, though in that peculiar October warmth the effort of rowing brought pricks of sweat to Paul's mouth and brow.

My fear was irrational, out of proportion to the mere sight of a dangerous place. Breath seemed to swell in me until I could not expel it or gain fresh air. The sensation of water filling my lungs was vivid as if it were actually happening again. I was struggling to free myself, caught under an upturned boat and tangled in twigs trailing from the sodden bough. I could see nothing but mud churned up by the flood. Sitting hard on my hands so as to hide my fear, I turned back, trying to remember which overhanging tree I had caught hold of, and at which point I had seen Mike go under for the last time.

'You've gone very pale,' Paul said. He seemed uneasy himself. 'We'll stop a while and let you rest.'

'Not here.'

'Yes. We both of us need to stare it out of our minds.'

Pulling the skiff into the bank, Paul sat looking down the river. Whatever personal tragedy it had brought, the place was beautiful, golden, a couple of ducks waddling tranquilly along the muddy edge of the Island, and the reeds bending and straightening as the river lapped their roots. Beyond them the elms stood, untouched by disease though so many of their species downstream had died. In their shadow I lay down as a seventeen-year-old schoolgirl, for whom anxiety was a matter of homework dates and what the other

320

girls said; when I got up it was as a woman, with a woman's fears, of pregnancy and loneliness. It was the same time of the year, a similar golden day when the leaves were beginning to fall as golden edged feathers. With the sophistication of adulthood I saw the symbolism and smiled to myself, grimly. I wondered what Paul was thinking. He gave no indication what role I should play: the old friend come to comfort, the former lover... I doubted if he knew himself what he wanted of me. He was still too involved in a dying relationship to recognise the fragile tenderness we were creating.

'This past few months have felt like a judgment against me,' he said unexpectedly. 'For years I held my anger against you like a stone, turning it over and over till it was shiny and hard. Now I know how it feels to be blamed for things that were not my fault. My every mistake has been used against me. Even travelling with the fair was cited by Aileen's lawyers, as proof that I was unfit to have Laura.'

'You shouldn't have mentioned it,' I replied, shaking my head. 'It was bound to be misinterpreted.'

'I let it slip when we were talking about money, about how I'd managed over here. It would still stand against me if I hadn't been able to argue I was gathering material for *Atchin-tan*. That's the only sort of motive the Russells could understand.'

'How have they come to take your side?' I asked. 'There's so much you haven't told me.'

'My mouth goes stiff when I try to speak of it. Sometime Martie. Some time. I kept telling myself things couldn't get any worse, and the next day they did. I got that packet of yours out many times.'

Setting off again, he rowed us up-stream till the ferry came into sight, making its beetle way across the river, obsolete of course but cheaper to run than a powered boat, and so long as it held together, allowed to remain. Paul's aunt Sal still operated it, she too seeming scarcely changed. She made a fuss of us, calling us into her cottage for 'A little drop of summat,' whereupon a black-haired grub of a boy she called Johnnylad appeared with home-made wine, and a girl of sixteen or so followed him carrying glasses.

Johnny lad was Sal's grandson Paul explained softly. The girl was called Ann Matilda and was Cal's granddaughter. She was not strong and as winter came on stayed with Sal at the ferry, not being able to cope with the mud and travelling all weathers.

'How's the little one?' Sal enquired. 'I heard she's been poorly.'

'She'll mend,' Paul replied. Clearly he did not want to talk about Laura.

The ferry was busy, with some of the customers from the Fisherman's Rest on the opposite bank deciding to explore the river. It was a glorious day for the time of year they agreed, better than the whole summer put together.

One fat man in a suede jacket assured us he always drove out for a pub lunch when he had the time; couldn't get better value than at the Fisherman's Rest. A group of bikies crowded around the forecourt across the river, revving their engines and shouting. Their voices carried over the water. One of the girls shrieked as her boyfriend lifted her up and pretended to drop her over the car park wall into the river. Johnnylad wanted to see their motorbikes and persuaded his grandmother to let him cross when the ferry made the next trip.

Rather than be in his aunt's way Paul and I took our glasses and sat on the bank near the jetty. For a while Ann Matilda sat with us, obviously pleased to see Paul. They talked of the fair and her grandfather and the work she had found helping at a neighbouring farm two days a week. Then she went indoors to finish preparing her aunt's meal. Paul and I sat watching the ferry. Inevitably I thought of my Aunt Mary and Richard and Milly sitting there also. The effort of visualising Sal as a dark-haired morsel of a child defeated me. It amazed me to realise she was seventy-four. She wound the cable as firmly as any man.

Till then neither of us had expressed any desire to eat. Now a sense of peace and relief made me remember I had travelled a long way and eaten very little. Our meal consisted of wine and cakes, and in the quietness of early afternoon we began to talk. It seemed I was to be the old friend, the sympathetic listener who turns up when needed and then goes away. I felt a sense of disappointment even while I was glad Paul had not been offended by my coming. Across the water I heard the girl shriek again, and glancing up saw she was running away from her boy in a game of lovers' chase. I envied them their freedom.

'I began to feel sorry for Aileen in the end,' Paul admitted. 'She'd started something that was meant to be smart and clever – everyone round us was doing it – and ended up as a nightmare.'

'You sound as though you love her still,' I pointed out.

'Part of me will always stay married to her, and part says it ended as soon as she went to Mark. My mother would say the first is true; my father believes the second. I understand both extremes. What I don't understand is why people make laws and then pay a lot of money to have themselves declared exceptions.'

The girl was laughing, and distracted by the sound we both looked up.

With her boy she had boarded the ferry and was fooling around. Paul watched them, a waterman's sense of danger giving an added keenness to his interest.

'That couple of idiots' going to get into trouble,' he said at last, and getting up, went towards the landing stage. 'They're daft, messing about ... I think Aunt Sal may need some help.'

His uneasiness infected me, and I followed. The two teenagers were messing about so much Sal spoke sharply to them, her voice carrying to us above the whirl of the wheel. As she did so the youth mouthed some obscenity to her, and made a rude gesture. 'I've seen their sort before,' Paul commented. They often end up at the bottom of the river.'

By this time the boat was pulling close to the landing stage, the young couple already waiting to leave, the boy boasting he would be first. I knew exactly what would follow. The lad would leap from the side of the ferry to the bank to prove to his girl he did not need to wait, and would not allow for the drift-away. As Sal wound the last yard of cable he would fall between boat and bank, into twenty feet of water.

'He'll go in,' Paul said to me. 'I've seen it before.' He was already taking off his shoes.

It happened precisely as I had known. With the lad poised to jump, the ferry neared the bank, then drifted back outwards on the current, opening the gap again. With an expression of horrified amazement the boy went feet downwards into the water. It would have been funny had it not been so deadly.

At once the girl began to scream, in earnest this time. She was useless, a black-jacketed, hysterical idiot. 'Help him!' she wailed. 'He can't swim.' Grimly Sal held the ferry steady on its cable but I scarcely saw her. Kicking off my shoes I ran down the bank towards the point where the boy had entered. At the same time Paul was running onto the jetty. Diving cleanly into the water he began swimming hard around the ferry so that he could outpace the current. By now the boy had surfaced and was threshing at the water and gulping great mouthfuls of it. The noise of the two voices screaming was terrible. I swam the last few yards to bring me to the side of the ferry, then holding onto the rail to prevent myself being carried downstream, I worked my way towards the drowning boy. The weight of his leathers was dragging him downwards even as the current carried him along the ferry's side. Reaching out to him as he drifted past I grabbed his jacket. He was heavy in my hand.

Still the girl screamed. Rounding the bow of the ferry Paul swam towards me. The weight of his own clothes was slowing him and a less determined swimmer might well have drowned himself. My shoulders ached with the boy's weight. Then I heard someone run down the path and from the jetty leap onto the ferry. It was Ann Matilda. Leaning over the rail she too clutched the boy's jacket. At the same moment Paul reached me.

Voices were calling from the bank and there was screaming from the direction of the pub. I heard fresh steps running along the path towards us. Together Paul and I bundled the boy along the ferry's side while Ann Matilda took his weight. Finally between the three of us we pushed and hauled him onto the deck. For the first time I noticed my legs were aching with cold.

The whole incident had taken no more than a minute or so. Lying on the boards where we had dropped him the boy began retching, his girl still useless, crying now. The tourists who had run along the river path stopped in an excited group, and someone called, 'Well done, the three of you!' 'What happened?' a woman's voice asked and there were half a dozen volunteers ready to explain. 'Who's the couple?' a man asked his companion. 'Dunno who the woman is, but the bloke's Paul Booth, Saul's boy – you know. Those tinker lads always could swim like fishes.' It was not an ill-intentioned remark but I hoped Paul had not heard. Fortunately he was kneeling over the boy and seemed unaware of the voices.

'He'll survive,' he said to his aunt. Then he turned the boy over. 'Don't ever let me see either of you round here again,' he warned. 'Your sort risks other people's lives as well as their own. If your girl had gone in after you you'd have lost her.' He looked towards me. Standing in dripping jeans and sweater I felt a fool. 'You could have cost me mine,' he added quietly.

'You should have left him,' Sal said. 'You heard what he called me? In my day young people respected their elders.' Rolling onto his front the boy was violently sick. 'Look at the mess he's making of my ferry!' she almost screamed. Grabbing a bucket from the stern she dunked it in the river and threw the contents over boy and deck. She was merciless in her anger.

'Let him be,' Paul said. He turned to the girl who was still crying. 'He'll be all right,' he assured her. 'If I were you I'd make sure he stays off the booze when he's out with you. How was he going to drive you back? You'd have been smashed to pieces. It's always the pillion that dies.' His warning was chilling and the girl watched him with horror. 'You'd better take him back to his mates,' he added to his aunt. 'Martie and I will go and clean up.'

The tourists parted to let us through and somebody thumped Paul on the back. I had no sense of having been in any way brave and could not understand the awed chatter. It had been common sense. In fact I felt acutely embarrassed. The little fat man in the suede coat winked at me and I glared in return.

Afterwards we stood in the scullery of Sal's cottage, trying to squeeze the worst of the water from stubborn sweaters. The main room was covered by a square of old carpet and we would not go in for fear of dripping all over it. My shoes were somewhere on the riverbank, near Paul's jacket presumably. I wondered where my bag was. Impulsively Ann Matilda reached up and kissed Paul, and then not knowing what to do about me, kissed me too. Paul put his finger under her chin, making her look up at him. 'You did well,' he said. 'I couldn't have lifted him on to the deck on my own. Not from that angle.'

We stayed long enough to dry our faces and hair and for Ann Matilda to go in search of our belongings. Sal was slow returning, no doubt seeing to the couple being taken into the Fisherman's Rest and telling the story a dozen times. While Ann Matilda was away we held each other in relief that we were safe, wet as we were. Her return startled us and I saw an expression of surprise enter her eyes, but she made no comment. 'We'd best go,' Paul said. 'Apologise to Aunt Sal for us.'

'You could stay here,' Ann Matilda offered. 'Your lady could have my coat and I'll find you something.'

Smiling, Paul shook his head. 'I'm not sitting around starkers in a blanket,' he objected. 'Please Ann, let us go before your great aunt comes back. She'll make a fuss and I can't face it at the moment.'

So, soaked and shivering we got back into the skiff and Paul rowed us home. 'Are you all right?' he asked.

'Cold and miserable, but all right,' I replied. 'I feel a fool.'

'Why? You did just what you should have done.'

Afterwards we were silent, half-drifting, half rowing towards the Island.

Some time we must brave that current again; it was a matter of self-respect. When you fall off a bike you get back on before fear grows in your mind. We had let fear grow and it needed putting back into its place. Sense made me decide not to suggest then, however. We were cold and wet; we would catch our death as Aunt Mary would have put it. 'You row now,' Paul said, surprising me. 'I'm tired and I don't see why I should do all the work.' I knew what he was doing, forcing me to take over when I was most afraid, and forcing himself to trust me perhaps. Holding the skiff stable at the bank, we changed places. 'You can just about let us drift, so long as you keep to the bank,' he advised. 'Don't get into the current.'

The flow of the river carried us safely down-stream, though my stroke would have been the despair of Saul. There was warmth in the late sun and I felt my clothes beginning to dry, and the colour coming back to my face. With a sense of bewilderment I knew Paul was watching me through half-opened eyes, and considered him in return. He was a stranger to me; he had married another woman, discussed the milk bill with her, arranged school for their child. A world of experience separated us, yet once we had made love together. At the time it had seemed a sin. Now we were more sophisticated, afraid of commitment, but we were still drawn to each other.

Some flame of physical attraction had always burned between us, and chance had woven our families into an intricate pattern. Even so, I could not know what he was thinking; those dark eyes had never revealed much to me. As a boy he was self-contained, inward looking; the past months had made him more so.

After the brightness of sun on water the chalet was dark, smelling of damp. It had been shut up since Harry and his family stayed there. A child's model car reminded me of their presence. 'There's an old gardening shirt of mine might fit you,' I suggested.

'It's you who's supposed to come out of the bedroom wearing my shirt.'

'I'm all for reversing the roles.'

He smiled, watching me. 'I remember a lot of things about you,' he remarked. 'But beauty isn't one of them. You look beautiful to me now. Almost as beautiful as when you wore that shawl.'

'Like this?' I asked, laughing. 'You must be in love.'

'I think I am.' I did not know what to say or how to behave, wanting to hold him but kept back by some instinct that it was not yet time. 'When I swam round that ferry and saw you'd already got the boy to safety I wanted to shout out for joy. All my doubts about you went. You acted instinctively – without stopping to think. You'd have done the same for Mike if you'd had chance. You weren't to blame for his death. If anyone was, it was him.'

My throat had gone tight. 'Why do you say that?' I replied.

'I've no wish to speak ill of the dead, especially my own brother, but for all his skill Mike could never work out how that current flowed. Several times he got into difficulties and Dad had to yell at him to row different. When we sat near the Island today I saw what had happened. As that branch came down Mike rowed against the current instead of using it to carry him to safety. All he managed was to turn the boat round.' Crossing to me Paul stood looking at me. 'I do love you, Martie.'

We stood awkwardly, afraid of each other. 'Go and get changed before you catch cold,' Paul said at last. 'I'll dry myself in here.'

'Put the gas on,' I suggested. 'It'll warm the place up.' Nervously I tried to make conversation. 'Make us a cup of tea while you're at it. There's tea bags in the caddy and dried milk in the cupboard, so long as the earwigs haven't got it.'

'Oh yes, the tea. We English always make tea...' Hesitantly he held out his hand to me. 'Thank you for coming, Martie. I wanted so much to write to you, but I couldn't think what to say.'

Going into the bedroom, I stood for a few seconds looking at the damp patch on the wall and at the edge of the bed. A feeling of sickness came over me, very similar to the fear I had felt as we passed Enchanter's Island. Shivering, I looked for some dry clothes. After I had changed I sat on the edge of the bed. Perhaps I was suffering slightly from shock. For the first time I realised both Paul and I might have drowned that afternoon. We had been given another chance. Not many people are granted that. And neither of us had proved a coward.

Paul came along the hall. 'Your drink, madam,' he said, placing a mug on the dressing table. He had taken off his wet sweater and shirt.

'You'll catch cold,' I said. 'I've found a shirt of Harry's. Put it on.' Fetching the shirt from the wardrobe, I took it to him. There was a hollow along his collarbone which had not been there in the spring and in concern I traced the line of his throat and shoulder with my fingers. His skin was cold under my touch. In embarrassment he glanced towards the unmade bed.

'Can you stay tonight?' he asked.

I could scarcely reply. 'If you want. I brought a few things with me, and Charlie s not expecting me back unless I turn up.'

Without answering Paul went out, back to the kitchen. When he returned he brought matches. Silently he lit the paraffin heater, turning it low afterwards. As he bent, the line of his back fascinated me, making me want to reach out and touch him, but I could not do such a thing outright. I wanted to tell him he was pleasing to me, but all the descriptions I thought of were owned by men. Then standing up, he moved away from me, towards the window. 'Martie, I'm sorry...'

'What for?'

'I want to turn to you and I can't. I'm too hurt inside. It throbs like a pain distracting me all the time. Be patient with me. If there was time I'd court you again, buy you things, try to talk to you... Come back to the cottage with me, where it's warm.'

'I'll stay on one condition,' I said. 'That you're not just using me to get back at Aileen. I have pride too.'

'I don't know Martie. You'll have to judge that yourself.'

We went back to River Cottage, Paul going upstairs to change while I tried to distract attention by talking too fast about visiting Arton Ferry. Saul and Janie were suspicious, wanting to know why I had changed, Saul evidently coming to the wrong conclusion. 'We got a bit wet rowing,' Paul replied casually enough afterwards.

'You should know better than that,' Saul said scornfully. 'You're no better than a city man nowadays.'

'I'm out of practice,' Paul answered, but I saw his mouth tighten. For the next half hour the atmosphere was strained, though Laura talked enough for us all, wanting Daddy to take her out on the river at once. Neither of us had meant to lie about what happened at the ferry but we did not know how to begin the story. Then there was a bang on the door, startling us. Janie went to answer. I heard a boy's voice and caught snatches of a breathless message. Grandma wanted to know how Paul and his lady were. They shouldn't have gone without telling her. She was cross and we would catch our deaths. Getting up, Paul apologised. 'I'm sorry we offended her, but we wanted to come home and change.'

'What's all this about?' Janie asked Johnnylad severely.

'There was this fella Aunt Janie, what fell off the ferry. Paul and his lady got him out. Everyone's saying they should get a medal. Grandma made me run all the way to see if they were safe here.'

Laura had run to the door and I heard her father say, 'It's OK, pet, it's nothing to worry about,' but when they came back he was holding her to him.

330

After that the afternoon burst open. The story was incoherently told between Johnnylad and Paul and me. When she realised her father had been in the river Laura's edginess turned to fear. 'Don't be silly,' Paul said. 'There was no danger. We knew what we were doing.'

But she would not be consoled. 'You might have been drowned,' she argued. 'Then you'll die and I shan't see you again.' By the time Johnnylad left she was working herself into a hysterical state, though over what we could not determine. Paul would not take her on the river. He preferred Martie to her. He would get drowned and she would never see him again. Not knowing what to do, I held back, worried by that first suggestion of jealousy, while Paul tried first to tease her out of her emotion, and then to comfort her. In fury she pushed him away, only to cry for his return. Her eyes began to go red and sore, the skin under them puffing so that her whole face looked swollen. Little blotches appeared around her nose and mouth while great gulps of sobbing shook her. In despair Paul looked towards his mother.

Janie could not hold out against such an appeal. Taking the child to her, she rocked her in the chair before the range. 'There, there, poppet,' she said. 'Don't you cry so. Don't you take on so.' The rhythm of her words fitted the rhythm of the chair rocking back and forth. 'Don't you take on so.' The child's body still shook. 'Don't you take on. Your Daddy's safe. He's not going to go away from you. Not anymore. You have us too. Don't you take on so.'

Saul was watching them. Awkwardly he got up and put his hand on Laura's shoulder. 'You mustn't cry,' he said. 'You're upsetting your Daddy.' I looked across at Paul. He was sitting with his eyes closed, almost in tears himself. 'You mustn't cry,' Saul repeated. 'Come on, *dordi*.' He too did not know how to treat her.

'Get her a drink,' Janie suggested. I would have gone but Saul was at the sink immediately. A cup of water was brought and I put it to the child's mouth. Slowly she drank. 'That's better isn't it?' Janie asked, rocking her again. 'Indeed it is.' Though deep shudders of grief still passed through her, Laura became gradually quieter. Paul extended his hand to her and getting up suddenly, she ran to him and hid her face in his jacket. For a long time he held her.

'My watch has got water in it,' he said. 'Look. It's supposed to be waterproof.' Unable to resist, Laura turned her head.

After the noise of her crying the room seemed silent. Janie got up and made the fire higher. She wasn't having us catch pneumonia; it wasn't the time of the year. Quite what was the time of the year for pneumonia she didn't explain. I discovered the colour of my jeans had rubbed onto my ankles. I hadn't realised they ran I admitted, and was assailed by an image of my jeans chasing me round the laundry. For an absurd reason I was filled with happiness, though there was nothing good in the situation of a crying child, nor the suffering which had led to that grief. Quietly I took her to wash her face after so much grieving and she did not push me away. Then we returned to the kitchen and the inevitable cup of tea.

'I don't know what all that was about.' Paul said to us. 'Strain I suppose,' but I knew he was lying. There were facts which he had not told me, and without which I could not know how to behave.

We sat talking over our tea, Paul joining in hesitantly, with long spaces for thought. He hoped that when Aileen and Mark were married, his wife would hanker less for Laura and he might be able to return with her permanently to England. Till then he would spend fewer months performing and more composing and teaching, so that she should not be without him too long. There was a cottage coming on the market soon, near the edge of Arton Forest – old Molly Marshall's place. A mate of his had tipped him off yesterday. He was thinking of making a bid for it. Zac had always promised him a share in the business, in payment for his advice and doing the figures. In the past he had refused it, but the fair was doing well now and could support another member of the family. The money would help him pay off the cottage. There would be years of work to do on it, but it would be years before his reputation was sufficiently established for him to risk living in such an out-of-the-way spot, even for part of the year. In the meantime it would provide him with a base in England. He would need to come back regularly so that he could build up contacts.

Finally, the conversation turned to me. When was I leaving for Australia? My sabbatical must be ending in four or five months' time.

Staring at my cup I considered my answer. I would have to return in March I agreed, but would begin looking for something in England before I left. What had begun as a nice idea for a school project had become a sense of mission, however pious that sounded. If possible I would find other employment to keep me going during the first few years, but the Heath was mine and ought to be able to support me. I would have to fulfil my notice at work, and I wouldn't want to leave colleagues in the lurch, but as soon as I could, I would come back to Sandhill.

'You won't get back into the academic world here,' Paul warned me. 'Not from what I've heard.'

'I'm not claiming any great revelations about ivory towers,' I replied, shrugging my shoulders in confusion, 'but these past few months have changed my whole view of myself. I doubt very much if I could settle back into nine-thirty lectures and Faculty Club dinners. I would keep hearing miners' ghosts on the wind.'

Janie and Saul were listening very carefully. They were observers, waiting while Paul and I negotiated our futures. No promises were being made; life was too unpredictable, but if we wanted we might be able to sort something out…

'I doubt if you'll make much money out of the Heath,' Paul advised.

'You won't make much out of composing. Have you sold anything yet?'

'As it happens, I have. I have a book of children's piano pieces accepted, and a commission to write a film score.' Janie and Saul

333

glanced towards each other. 'It's about the circus. Type-casting, I'll admit, but it's a start.' Laura was getting restless. 'Come and give the hens their mash,' Saul invited and she leapt up in pleasure. Gramp was OK – he had so many interesting things to do. Making an excuse that she had to see to the goat, Janie also went outside.

Determinedly I turned to Paul. 'What has been going on?' I demanded. 'What was all that crying about?'

'Leave it alone, Martie. Let it be.'

My temper snapped. There had been too many conflicting emotions during the day and I was tired. 'How the hell are you and I ever going to get on?' I shouted. 'You won't talk to me, explain anything. No wonder your wife left you.' It was cheap and mean, and I was sorry afterwards. Trying to unsay what I had said I drew him to me, but he was hard and unresponsive to my touch. 'You must talk to me,' I pleaded. 'How can I help Laura if I don't know what's happened? The kid's in a state of shock.'

It was a guess, no more, but it turned him to me. 'She disappeared. The police thought she had been abducted.' He was furious at my persistence.

'Your father told me she had run away from school.'

'We didn't know that at the time. It was while Aileen and I were both on tour. Laura just vanished, on a school outing. A shopkeeper thought he'd seen a man with her. The Head contacted the police and Aileen's parents. She'd left the address for when she and Mark were touring. The Russells were sure it was me that had taken Laura. They knew I was grieving at losing her, and thought I'd decided to take her back to England; that perhaps I'd used connections in the fairs to hide her.'

'That's absurd,' I said.

'It's happened before. You read about such things in the papers.'

'You mean the police accused you?'

'They picked me up and questioned me, hour after hour. My agent had to plead with them to let me perform that night, and then they took me back to the station straight away.'

334

'My Love…' I did not know how to express my concern.

'I was charged with abducting my own daughter. It was a small town, a bit narrow – they didn't like musicians, theatre people of any sort. There was a lot of evidence against me. I'd been seen round a fair nearby, getting material and I'd visited Laura the week before without Aileen's knowledge.' His eyes seemed sore. 'I kept thinking of Dad, all his life being tried for a theft he didn't commit. Then, well, the next morning the station officer withdrew the charges, but he ordered me to report wherever I was on tour. I had a whole series of short bookings. I didn't dare give them up. It had taken me long enough to re-establish myself after my return, and it would have been the end of me professionally. But I couldn't sit around a hotel room waiting for the phone to ring, so as soon as the performance was over I drove back down to New York. That day was almost as awful as the first. Aileen and I were blaming each other, and the police were blaming us both. Then it sort of settled into a pattern. You can get used to anything after a while. Each night I drove down after my performance, and in the afternoon I drove back.'

'What about sleep?'

'Could you have slept? I pulled into a layby and dozed a few times.'

'How long did you keep that up?'

'Four or five days. I forget. Then I terrified myself by falling asleep at the wheel. After that I had to settle for going alternate nights…'

There was such weariness in his expression I felt ashamed of my earlier irritation. 'It got better in a way,' he went on. 'There was no point in fighting when we were all out of our heads with worry, and Aileen's parents felt bad about getting me into so much trouble. Sometimes I had a meal with them before driving back.'

I did not know what to say, and reaching across the table stilled his hand as he fidgeted with the sugar bowl. 'How long did it all last?' I asked.

335

'Eleven days. The police warned us Laura was almost certainly dead – and if she wasn't we'd probably lost her in other ways. She's a pretty kid – a bit striking. Someone would have picked her up. After that I tried looking for her myself. I drove round and round the streets, went into places she might be – I saw things…' He could not speak and sat staring at my hand. 'Kiddy porn's quite a problem in New York. Then the police asked me to identify a murdered child. She had been… It wasn't Laura.'

There was a long silence between us. Standing up I went around to his chair and stood hesitantly beside him. How could I comfort? The things he spoke of were beyond my experience. 'And you managed to play through all that?' I asked.

'I had to. Besides, it was a relief. When I was on stage I could drive it all away from me. Poor Aileen spent the last few clays under sedation.' Again there was a pause. 'People were very kind. It got around that my daughter was missing. I don't know how much longer I could have gone on without sleep, but ironically I got very good **reviews.'**

Throughout, he had spoken carefully, his face turned away as if he were trying to give an honest account of someone else's story, but now his voice slid and he had to wait till he could control it. 'You should have told me this before,' I said. 'Do your parents know?'

'I tried to tell them…'

We heard Laura's's voice outside. 'How did she turn up?' I asked.

'I got a phone call, from somewhere I'd performed the week before.' In remembered relief he closed his eyes. 'She'd seen my name on a handbill and decided to find me, but it had taken her longer than she had expected. It was about a hundred miles from her school.'

'That's one determined little girl.' I remarked.

'I drove straight over, but when I got there I blacked out.' The image in my dreams suddenly returned to me and I felt a cold chill on my skin. 'It was exhaustion, that's all. There was no way I could drive us home and I wasn't having Mark fetch her, so I rang my father-in-law. He came and fetched us. We struck a bargain. I offered to let Aileen have her divorce if she would let me have Laura. My father-in-law agreed, for Laura's sake, and the rest of them fought it out while Laura and I slept.'

Recalling my own night alone in the woods I shook my head in bewilderment. 'It amazes me that she survived,' I said. 'Where had she been?'

'She's told us almost nothing. She was filthy and exhausted, but she hadn't starved. I imagine she was thieving. She said something about a greengrocer having a lot of apples. Frankly I don't want to know. I'd thieve if I was on my own and trying to survive. I've told the police she'd learnt how to live rough from me. It's partly true. If I'd known she'd taken to the country I'd have been much less worried.' He shook his head.

'Funny, isn't it? I ran away several times when I was a kid. It seems to be hereditary.' There was another long silence. 'It's a case of trying to get her back to normal living now. She's lost her trust in everyone.'

'You speak of her all the time,' I said. 'You look ill yourself.'

'I'm a bit dazed still, that's all. It was fortunate I could take this week off. I have to be back to rehearse on Monday, but these few days'll do me good. I've been down into hell and come back. Now I'm seeing everything with new eyes somehow, and it's all incredibly beautiful. I've got Laura, and you've turned up without my asking. That's getting jam on both sides.'

The others returned, wanting something to eat. At Janie's suggestion we gave Laura her tea first. She was tired after her crying fit and it seemed best for her to go to bed early. While she ate Paul spoke quietly to his mother in the kitchen, asking some favour of her with his arm round her shoulders. Few mothers could have resisted a son so persuasive. As soon as he had gone upstairs with Laura, Janie started bringing in our supper, while I helped her lay the table.

It was a meal fit for a celebration. There was cold ham, and bread and pickles, specialities Janie must have prepared for Christmas, nasturtium seeds and pickled walnuts and a bottle of homemade wine which Paul put on the dresser after he came downstairs. Saul's expression as he did so was amusing. Evidently it was his best wine and hoarded for a special occasion. Getting up, he protested softly to Paul who replied equally quietly. Finally we sat down together.

All through the meal I was aware that Saul was watching his son. There was a sense of expectancy in the room, as if I were the only one who did not know what was being awaited. On the table were several small loaves of Janie's bread, plaited cobs, a third having already been eaten. 'Would you like more bread?' Janie asked me, and out of politeness rather than hunger I accepted. Silently Paul took the loaf and instead of cutting it, broke it and passed me a piece. The timelessness of his gesture startled me, and looking at him I tried to assess whether it had any significance. Saul was also watching. A small flicker of emotion began to burn in my mind. Staring at my food, I realised I was no longer hungry.

The meal was half-over, but the wine had not been opened. For several minutes Paul stared out of the window at the darkness. The curtain was open and the shape of the apple tree was outlined by moonlight. There would be the first frost of the season despite the warmth of the· day. Taking up some crumbs from the cloth he rubbed them aimlessly between two fingers. Finally he seemed to come to a decision. As if idly, he took the saltcellar and stirred the salt in it with the spoon. I had never noticed that spoon before. It was silver, and made from a shaped coin. Like the cut-glass cellar in which it stood and many of the other objects around us, it would have worth to a collector, yet it was merely part of Saul and Janie's life. Taking some of the salt on the spoon, Paul let it fall back into the cellar. It seemed an inconsequential gesture yet I felt the atmosphere tighten at once. Again Paul took up the salt. This time he poured some of it into his hand.

'Do you realise what you're doing?' Saul asked. He sounded almost angry.

'Yes.'

'I shall hold you to it. So will Cal and Zac.'

'Of course.'

In bewilderment I glanced at Janie. There was sadness and resentment in her expression.

Silently Paul held the salt out to me, as he had held the bread. 'If you take the salt from me Martie, you agree to stay with me,' he said. 'Call it a betrothal if you like. I can't offer you legal marriage yet, but I give you my word. As you heard Dad say, the family will keep me to it.' Looking down at the salt in his hand he flushed with embarrassment.

The small flame of emotion flared in my mind. I could scarcely see for its light. Silently I took the salt from his hand.

'Throw it over your shoulder – for good luck,' Saul advised.

I did as he asked. The emotion of the whole day welled into my mind and I began to cry, wordlessly. Immediately Paul got up and ignoring his parents, held me.

Saul looked at the clock. 'Those hens need shutting up,' he said. 'They'll have put themselves to bed, if they've any sense.'

'Is the chalet unlocked?' Paul asked me. 'Dad had best check that heater.' Mumbling my thanks, I found the key and passed it to Saul. Some unexpressed understanding passed between father and son, then Saul and Janie went out.

They remained outside a long time, leaving us to each other. Even after I heard them return they went upstairs and seemed to go out again. We sat motionless on the old sofa, not daring to speak lest we destroyed the preciousness of the moment. There was no time, no place, only that silent moment. Then crashing in on our peace, Saul and Janie returned.

'I suppose you'll be wanting that bottle opened,' Saul suggested.

'That was the idea,' Paul replied.

'You were very sure I'd accept,' I commented. 'What would you have done if I'd refused?'

'Put it back in the cellar. Thrift, me dear.'

We drank Saul's wine, a clear champagne he assured us was dandelion. Disturbed by our laughter Laura appeared at the head of the stairs and calling her down, Paul sat her in the armchair beside him. 'Martie's going to stay with us a few clays,' he said.

'Do you mind?' I asked. 'We could go on the river together, walk in the Tourney Field, things like that.'

Silently she nodded. She was very tired. Saul poured a small amount of wine into a glass and added water. 'Drink your Daddy's health,' he invited. 'And Martie's. They're promised to each other. Do you know what that means?'

Again she nodded but I could not judge what she thought. Perhaps she was too sleepy to care. Carrying her back upstairs, Paul left me with his parents for a few moments. 'Is Paul serious?' I asked Janie.

'He never jokes about such things. He offered you the salt for his father's sake, and because it was a way of saying something he couldn't put into words.'

I loved her for that reply. 'You don't approve,' I remarked. 'Yet you laid out that meal for us.'

'No, I don't approve,' Janie agreed. 'As far as I'm concerned he'll never be married to you, though to Zac and Cal what you did was a form of marriage. Paul agreed to a divorce so long as he had custody of Laura – he'll stay a Catholic at heart. It isn't something you can just trade. Still I want him to be happy, any mother would, and you understand him and make him laugh. Ever since you arrived he's begun to look better. The kiddy likes you, too. I can't stand against you.' She glanced towards her husband. 'And nor will he. He thinks Paul's marriage ended as soon as Aileen went to another man. It's the way they do it in the fair – the older people, anyway. I'm the odd one out. I can't fight you all.'

It was almost ten o'clock. Paul glanced at the clock.

'I'm going round to the chalet with Martie,' he said. 'I don't know what time I'll be back. Laura shouldn't wake but you can fetch me if there's any problem.'

'We'll see to her,' Saul said, too loudly. He poked the fire to cover our confusion.

Outside, the moon was hung on a blackened bowl and the air was breathtakingly cold. Yet as soon as I put on the light in the kitchen I looked round in astonishment. The heater had been turned up, making the atmosphere almost warm. My clothes were drying over a rack near it. A vase of late chrysanthemums splashed gold and red on the table; eggs and rashers of bacon under a cover had been set out for the morning.

'Who did all this?' I asked.

'Dad. Mum's helped I think. The flowers have her touch.'

'Even though she doesn't approve?'

'He can be very persuasive.'

A nightjar screeched as it flew towards the woods, and I wondered foolishly if it was the same one I had heard months before. Crossing the room, I closed the curtain. Voices shouted in the distance, drinkers leaving the Black Bull perhaps. Their noisy goodnights made the silence of the chalet deeper. I did not know what I was doing there, nor how I had come to be in such a situation. 'Your father's not the only one who's persuasive,' I remarked. 'You could talk the boots off your grandmother.'

'Now what would I be wanting with my grandmother's boots?' The Irish lilt was perfect and I laughed despite my confusion.

'Were you serious just now?' I asked.

'I'm always serious – except when I'm joking.'

'Stop clowning for a minute, Paul. Be serious.'

'I can't. I'm too happy. I'd begun to think I'd never laugh again.' Taking my hand, he considered it. 'I won't break the promises I made. As far as I'm concerned they're absolute and binding. I didn't just offer you that salt to please my Dad, but also to please myself.'

'You don't believe such things,' I pointed out, a little sharply. 'You don't belong in the fair. You like your home comforts too much – your audiences, your books ...'

'True, but my father's ways begin to make more and more sense to me. Martie, I've tried playing my life the conventional way, the legal way if you like. The law didn't hold Aileen and me together. If anything it drove us apart. We were sorting things fairly sensibly till the solicitors came in. It was after that everything started getting so bitter. I don't expect you to regard your promise as binding unless you want to, but I shan't marry anyone else. I've loved you as long as I can remember, since before I loved Aileen, and after I think. I'm the sort that gets stuck, lumbered. I'm not explaining myself very well. I just wanted you to know I loved you – for good. I dunno how we'll sort things, but we can if we want.'

In exasperation he turned from me and stared at the sink. The tap was dripping. 'Let's go and sit in the other room,' I suggested.

There were flowers there too and the curtains were already drawn, making the room more private. We were beginning to be at ease together, sitting while the heater spluttered. 'We used to talk a load of tripe, didn't we?' I asked. 'Sitting together like this. All that stuff about being famous.'

'It did the trick, though. I had determination, sheer bloody-mindedness if you like, but I had no one but you to cheer me on.' We watched the heater flare, and I was conscious that at last I was at peace. Unexpectedly Paul laughed. 'You were a revelation to me,' he admitted. 'You believed in me. You weren't what girls were supposed to be either. Most of the time you were either upside down or climbing a tree. If you did wear a skirt, it was tucked in your knickers. I got more views of your knickers than was good for me. They were usually navy. School regulation navy.'

'If we're going to get personal,' I warned him, 'I'll tell the one about you and the goat. First musician in orbit.' Teasing me, Paul

342

grabbed my wrist and we fought as we used to, like a couple of idiots, till I called 'pax,' getting the worst of it. 'It's so good to be with you,' Paul said.

'Do you remember the time you pushed me in the mud?' I asked. 'Aunt Lizzie still hasn't forgotten it. We were fooling about like now and I slipped. You rotten devil – all you did was laugh!'

'You must admit you looked funny. I think that was when I first realised I loved you. No, it was before then. When you brought me those biscuits.'

'I knew it was then,' I boasted. 'I ran all the way back to the chalet to tell Harry and Lydia, and all Harry said was "Yuck, mush" and Lydia was out. What were you doing hiding from your Dad? You never told me.'

'Can't remember. Mending a guitar when I should have been helping him I imagine. I dunno how my ears managed to stick out when I was a kid. They got flattened often enough.'

The heater flared, its wick damp and dirty. Getting up, I went to adjust it. I was aware that in the foolishness of our teasing we were clearing ground, making a new relationship possible.

'You did something earlier I rather fancied,' Paul said and took off his shirt.

I burst out laughing. 'Now that's what I call dropping hints,' I agreed.

Going to him, I traced the line of his shoulder and collarbone with my fingers as I had done before. He held me to him and it was as if we had never parted; as if we were once again on Enchanter's Island while the river flowed beyond the trees. 'Are you willing to treat it as a marriage?' Paul asked. 'Not just tonight, but always?'

'Yes.' I closed my eyes. 'Yes.'

'We should have married years ago.'

'Neither of us could have given up our ambitions when we were kids and we wouldn't have known how to fulfil them together. Even if you didn't expect me to be the little woman at home, our families would have done. I'd have had your children and loved them, but I'd have hated you for tying me down.' I paused, listening to the water beyond the garden gate. 'I have several friends like that.'

'Will you still have my children?'

Wordlessly I nodded, the colour flaring in my face.

In the silence of that first frost of Autumn we were at peace, both of us exhausted by emotion and the events of the day. It was nearly midnight when we went to bed, our feet echoing on the wooden hallway. Remembering the unmade blankets and the damp on the wall, I felt a sudden disappointment, and the sickness which had overcome me in the afternoon returned. Then, opening the bedroom door, I caught my breath. The bed had been made, a bright patchwork quilt spread over it. A nosegay of everlasting flowers lay on the dressing table, a bridal bouquet.

'Those are from me,' Paul said. 'They'll last longer than fresh ones this time of year.'

Putting them back into place I stood beside him, shivering. 'I'm afraid,' I admitted. 'Afraid we'll quarrel again – or that I'll never see you again after you return to America.'

'If I told you I was frightened stiff you'd laugh at me, but I am. I've had two chances of happiness and made a mess of them both. Getting a third is more than anyone has a right to expect.'

Mechanically I sat on the edge of the bed, not really knowing what I was doing. An earwig scuttled from beneath my hand. Involuntarily 1 screamed. 'Your Dad put that there deliberately,' I swore.

'Oh come now,' Paul pleaded. 'Not even Dad's that thoughtful.'

'Bloody earwigs,' I said, looking round for more. 'They get all over the place. You can see them in the morning pushing each other on to the window-ledge. The first one lowers a rope for the others. I'm not making love with earwigs selling tickets.'

Lying down, Paul began to laugh. 'In't it marvellous?' he asked. 'I get a lady into bed with me, and she finds an earwig. They can sit in rows eating crisps for all I care. They couldn't be worse than some of the audiences I've had.'

The schoolyard was packed. Near the gates, the first-year children waited in an excited clamour, clutching their packets of seeds in mittened hands; behind them the second years queued with their shrubs, spiky bundles wrapped in polythene. Third in line were the older children, each with a sapling also wrapped for protection. The staff attempted to keep some sort of order but were not achieving a great deal. Dad had given up 4G ten minutes ago and found a pressing need to visit the staffroom. Fortunately the babble was well-drowned by a resurrected Sandhill Band, which played with gusto and a considerable amount of gasp. Like Thursday's child they had far to go and intended to get there noisily. A few mangled notes hardly mattered in such general confusion, though Mr Warwick winced. Class Two majorettes were on form, Mrs Pendleton-Smythe making a formidable major, her bosoms jiggling to the music and her glasses catching the November sun. The spectators admired her efforts (and her bosoms) and congratulated each other on such a lovely day.

Our Sue was resplendent in a new red coat and hat to match, looking like a Victorian pillar-box; one of those double-sided ones with Town on one slit and Country on the other. Her conviction that I was stark, staring mad had not altered, but she had come to support the school, and her children. Harry and his trousers were parting company as usual and Aunt Lizzie was certain he would catch cold in his kidneys. Going over to him, I dusted him down and tucked his shirt in. 'That's from Aunt Lizzie,' I said.

Rumour had it (Rumour in Sandhill being like children, prone to having things), that a fair had come to town, but when I pestered Harry as to whether it was true, he began cracking silly jokes and avoiding the issue, so I went over to Lol Jackson. 'Glad you could get back,' he said. 'You'd have been cut up to miss all this. Most of it's your doing. Mind you, these past few days have been a bit fraught. People get edgy when summat's about to happen, in case it goes wrong I suppose. Miss McClean's had to keep us in order. That woman do arf scare me,' he admitted, grinning. 'She called Councillor Oakey "a fat little man" on Wednesday.' Lol's emphasis made the phrase positively libellous and I laughed outright.

I could not lie to him. 'I haven't been away on business,' I confided. 'I've been with Paul.'

'I wondered if you might have been. You looked so - well — happy last night. You're mad you know, with him married.'

'He's divorcing his wife,' I replied. 'He'll come back some time.'

'I've heard that one before,' Lol warned.

'Please,' I pleaded. 'Don't spoil my day. I'm happy, whether I have any right to be or not. I've had five days that would make up for a lifetime, and now we're moving the Bluebell Woods. What more could I ask?'

Nodding Lol accepted my reply. 'Harry's got the fair,' he said. 'Did you know?'

'Which fair?'

'The Boothman's. He managed to trace them through the trade, and booked them for the weekend as a surprise for you. They're pitched on the open land in front of the tile works. We'll be christening the museum project too if you see what I mean. Families will go up to the fair so we've decided to open the front part of the works for them to have a look round. It's safe enough there. Old Charlie's putting up some photos and things. It was a bit of a last-minute idea. You're not cross with us for doing things while you were away?'

'Of course not. You've done marvels.'

Going back to Harry I stood hesitantly beside him. 'You're a lovely man,' I said. 'Even if your jokes are awful.'

Harry took my judgment as a compliment, of course. 'Did I tell you the one about reincarnation?' he asked.

'No.'

'They say it's making a come-back.'

I shook my head. 'No, you didn't tell me. I'm glad you didn't.' Kissing him on the nose I straightened his collar. 'Thanks for getting the fair.'

The Band began leading the procession, experiencing some difficulty in keeping in step without losing sheets of music to the wind, but they led us effectively enough, Major Perkins (retd) being a difficult object to lose. Harry Parkes could scarcely see over his drum and there was some danger of him taking the wrong turning at the Victoria Road junction, but Bobby Harthill poked him with a cornet and the crisis was averted. Next came the majorettes, valiantly keeping in step to two different tempos, there being a disagreement between the bell-lyre and the trumpets. Finally the schoolchildren followed, trying to walk in time with a sapling acting as a third leg. Miss McClean clapped her hands helpfully whenever the crocodile's tail overtook its head, and the new gym mistress demonstrated potential as a marathon runner, taking messages up and down the line in bewildering whispers. At one point I was told Mr Parkes' teeth were coming in a jar, but decided he was going to the Heath in a car, which seemed more likely. The helpers and cooperative shuffled along at the rear, being a thoroughly ungovernable lot. Charlie Warwick darted off persistently, greeting bystanders, shaking hands, and Sampy would not march on principle – 'None of your paramilitary stuff for me.' Lol Jackson had only two paces, walking and even slower walking. As for Harry, he had no pace at all, his permanent gait being a well-meaning shamble, punctuated by trouser hitching.

Finally we reached the top of Sandhill Rise and straggled towards the muddy ground near the new road. Miss McClean raised her finger and temporarily silenced a force eight gale.

Much of her speech was carried away on the wind, but the shreds which caught on hats and buildings seemed effective. She explained about the school's Jubilee, and what it meant to her and the school staff and then described he origins of the project in which we were now engaged. Many had mourned the loss of the Bluebell Woods. It had been one of the worst examples of official vandalism in the area. Here he glared at Councillor Oakey. Well, times were changing now and attitudes with them. People were beginning to value the country-side again and the flowers and animals who were after all our brothers and sisters on this island earth. I wasn't sure how a bluebell came to be my brother and wondered if it too had problems with trousers.

Unperturbed by Sandhill winds and mixed metaphors Miss McClean spoke on. What had begun as a small project, the planting of a few trees to screen the new road, had become the beginning of new life for the town. With Dr Cooper's vision the screen of trees had become a patch of woodland, another Bircham Coppice, for Bluebell Woods, moved to the west and blooming again, just as Lakin's Heath would bloom again someday. That evening everyone was invited to take a stroll up the hill and see what had been achieved so far, and in the meantime the families might like to enjoy the fun of the fair. Since part of the Lakin's Heath project was to establish a folk museum, and the fair was a traditional one, with a beautiful hand-painted carousel she believed, it would provide a fitting start... Mr Charles Warwick, chairman of the Sandhill History Society had mounted an exhibition of old photographs in the tile works, so there would be that to see, too ... Now she would call on the instigator of both the school scheme and the wider project to plant the first tree.

As arranged, I went forward, and began planting my tree. Since the saplings were each tagged with a child's name, I hoped the school children themselves would look after the new Bluebell Woods I said afterwards, my voice fading on the wind. While it had taken less than a week for the bulldozers to erase the Coppice, it would take Nature thirty years to replace it, but many of us standing there would see that happen. Perhaps the children would come some day in the future and picnic together under the trees with their own children ...

Then Miss McClean planted her tree, managing to look immaculate as she did so, whereas I had two inches of mud on my boots. Following her came the school staff, the gym mistress finishing before her seniors. Democracy not being Sandhill Grammar's strongest point, her enthusiasm was felt to be uncalled for. Probably a CND supporter, Miss Henry suggested. Finally the schoolchildren began their digging, with staff and helpers paddling about in wellington boots, trying to prevent elms being planted upside down and oaks developing a list to starboard. When every tree and shrub was planted, we dug holes for the bluebells, a few token bulbs for each member of the project Committee, and a determined sprinkling of seed by the first years. How many of those seeds fell on stony ground I would not like to say; most were probably blown down the hillside or trodden into inhospitable clay, but the gesture was being made. When the time and earth were more propitious, I would come secretly and make another sowing. It would be my last action before returning to Australia.

My throat ached at the thought. Inevitably my mind turned to Paul and Laura. Watching the First Years, I realised they were already older than that little girl who had wandered a hundred miles to reach her father. I wondered how many of them could survive eleven days on their own, even if their father had taught them a good deal beforehand. Lol's warning began to jar on me. Lol was so rarely wrong, but then, the only time I had known Aunt Mary wrong, it was about Paul.

It was only then that I saw Laura. Amongst so many excited schoolchildren she had been unnoticed; not even Charlie Warwick had recognised her. Dropping my spade I ran through the crowd towards the road, leaving Harry and Charlie staring after me. By the time I reached the edge of the crowd I could not see her and wondered if love had turned likeness into identity. Suddenly I felt Paul watching me. He was leaning against a car, his collar turned up against the wind, and I had walked straight past him, not recognising in the well-dressed spectator the man I had known in Arton.

'What the hell are you doing here?' I demanded. 'You're supposed to be catching a plane.'

'Had a puncture on the motorway.'

I touched the nearest tyre with my boot. 'Looks all right to me,' I said.

'Naw, flat as a pancake. That's the trouble with hired cars – can't trust 'em. Didn't give us no spare either.'

'How long have you been here?' I persisted.

'You dig holes very well – for a woman.'

'Watch it isn't a hole to push you into,' I warned. 'Why didn't you tell me you were here? You've been spying on me.'

'Not spying. I wanted to see your big day and was afraid I'd make you nervous. I also have something to give you – from Dad.' Opening the car he passed me an old envelope. Dubiously I turned it in my hand, feeling something hard inside. 'Don't drop it if you can help it,' Paul advised.

'Is it breakable?'

'No. I'm being superstitious.'

Puzzled, I unwrapped the tissue inside the envelope. Three gold sovereigns lay in my hand. 'Why has your Dad sent these to me?' I asked.

'He put away a handful of sovereigns when he was married – as a sort of family heirloom. I've heard him use the word *sumadji* for it. As each of us married, he gave us our share, to give to our partner as a sign of love, and good fortune.'·

'Why didn't he give them to Aileen?' I asked. 'Or did you ask for them back?' For an instant I felt the bitterness of jealousy.

'Aileen never had my share. I wrote to tell my parents I was married but Dad wouldn't trust the post. When I finally brought her over he didn't like her and conveniently forgot. All last night he was going on about bringing me bad luck by keeping them. He insisted I give them to you as soon as possible.' Bewildered by the

350

change from tree-planting to emotion I stared at the coins in my hand. 'Please, my love. Humour him and take them. I could do with a bit of luck. It hasn't exactly been with me first time round.'

Taking my hand he closed it over the coins. I wished crowds and noise and Sandhill a thousand miles away. 'How long can you stay?' I asked. 'The fair's on the Heath. Harry booked them as a surprise for me.'

'You mean Cal and Zac arc here?'

'Have you time to go up and see them?'

With obvious regret Paul shook his head. Laura had found us and stood hesitantly near me. 'I wish I could, Martie, but if I go up there it'll be hours before I get away. I must catch the next flight. I managed to change the booking, but I daren't do it again. Mark and Aileen are coming to see Laura tomorrow and I promised to have her home in time. If I don't it'll prove I'm irresponsible - and all the rest of it. You go up to Zac and say hello. Tell him I've written to him but my letter won't have reached him yet. I sent it on to a booking I knew he'd have in a few weeks' time.'

'I wouldn't know what to say,' I protested.

'I'll give you a note to take.' Finding his diary, Paul wrote a quick message on one of the memoranda pages, then tore it out, and folding it, passed it to me. 'Give this to Zac. You can read it after I've gone, but not till then.'

'Come with me now,' I said. 'I have to see to the refreshments.'

Paul shook his head. 'This is your big day. I don't want to steal it from you. Laura can go with you a little if she wants.'

'The children are having a drink and a commemorative badge,' I said. 'We'll find her one.' Taking Laura's hand I went back to the frame tent we grandly called the marquee. The committee were serving hot tea in those plastic cups designed to spill boiling liquid over your hand, but there was squash for the children. As I found Laura a cup she thanked me. Though she spoke quietly her accent made one or two heads turn. 'Where's Paul?' Charlie asked in surprise. 'Where's there's Laura, there's Paul.'

'By the road. Cover for me Charlie, please. Just a few moments.'

The crowd had begun to drift away, the wind proving too cold for chatter. It was a nice idea, people said. So long as the vandals left the trees alone, they'd make the place a bit brighter, wouldn't they? It'd be interesting to see what they were doing on the Heath. Might even look in on the fair too. Taking Laura by the hand I ran across to the road. Paul was sitting in the car, though he got out as soon as he saw us. 'We must go,' he said.

Laura was near to tears. 'I want to stay with Martie,' she said.

'So do I,' her father said.

'I'll come at Christmas,' I offered. 'I can come over at Christmas, can't I?'

Immediately Laura was happy. In five days her face had filled out, but she still had an alarming way of swinging from one emotion to another. 'You can see our new house,' she invited, clapping her hands.

'Of course you can,' Paul said. 'I'll send the money for the ticket.'

He too had improved, handsome enough now to make two fourth form girls hang around on the wall near his car.

'No you won't,' I insisted. 'Aunt Mary'll pay for that. She would have wanted to. You pay for everything your end.'

'We'll have the biggest tree in the street, and we'll put it in the front with neon lights on it flashing *'Happy Christmas Martie'*. And I'll dress up as Santa and come down your chimney in the dead of night...' He closed his eyes for a second. 'Give me a year or two, my love, to build up connections back here and fulfil my obligations. Then Laura and I'll join you.' Once again Laura's eyes were very bright. 'Come on pet,' he said. 'We have a long drive to the airport. We'll stop at the first service station for something to eat.' Still he could not bring himself to turn away. 'Love you,' he said, holding out his hand to me.

The band had begun to play, ready to lead the majorettes and the school children back down the hill. 'Lord, don't let me get trapped behind that lot!' Paul said. Getting himself and Laura into the car at once, he turned it rapidly in the narrow space. For an instant he paused beside me, winding down the window so he could speak. 'Go up to Zac,' he insisted. 'For your own sake, if not mine. You might need their help some day.'

After that the car was gone. The band marched onto the road and the school followed, with the majorettes coming last this time, to mop up any stragglers who preferred Lakin's Heath to ham salad in the hall. A couple of hundred parents and well-wishers walked alongside, calling across to children and joking with the Committee. The tune of *Colonel Bogey* was actually recognisable and there was talk of a bit of a party that evening up at the tile works. Charlie would need help to take down his exhibition, and well, while we were doing it... Lol fancied a ride on the carousel, too.

Dropping back so that I could speak to Dad, I waited. The procession was already half-way down Sandhill Rise, a couple of dogs lending their support. There was even a police escort, with Constable Hope cruising along trying to look as though he knew what he was doing. The wind had begun to nip the trees, sending leaves spinning like golden-edged feathers. Below me in the valley I saw Paul's car turn left along Low Town.

'All right, old girl?' Dad asked, stepping to one side. His eyes watched the car, like mine.

'Of course.'

'You did well. We'll have the town looking almost nice by the time we've finished.'

'What do you mean, "almost"?' I asked. 'We'll have it looking like bloody Kew Gardens.'

'Aren't you coming down with us?'

'I thought I'd go and see the fair – check everything's all right at the tile works. See you later.'

Dad nodded. 'Don't get giddy on the carousel,' he advised.

After the last people had passed I opened the note Paul had given me. It was addressed to his uncle Zac.

'I'm sorry I couldn't see you today, but I have to catch a plane back to the States this afternoon. There's a letter on its way to the Red Lion explaining things. I'll send the usual paperwork back as soon as I can. Sorry about the delay. Life has been a bit chaotic lately.

You will remember Martie. For my sake, see she has addresses where she can contact you. Should anything go ill with her, take care of her and treat her as Family. She's very precious to me. She also owns the Heath on which you're camped, but don't hold that against her.'

Folding the paper, I stood watching the procession snake down Nightingale Hill, then I walked towards the Heath.

Epilogue

Do you recognise yourself in that solemn-eyed child? Do you even recognise the events I have described? That is how I remember them, but each of us has our own truth. Already, with the distance of nearly a year and ten thousand miles I may have distorted reality, put words I wish had been said in place of what was actually spoken. I have tried to tell you the truth. If it is not your truth, consider a little whether it might be so. Writing to you has at least kept me occupied. I did not recollect loneliness until I recollected love. By the time I had thought of explaining to you I had caught up on all those journals I had meant to read, and had put to one side, finding life much more interesting. I had even rechecked the proofs of my book, catching two commas and an ibid.

There's more to the story than I have told you of course – the phone calls from one country to another, the bewilderment of friends, the marriage between bookings. I was grateful to have the fair to retreat to during those last weeks in England when Sue and Aunt Lizzie found even Family can become too outrageous for support. Travelling isn't a life I could lead permanently and I chose the coldest February in years, when puddles cracked underfoot and metal burnt stiff hands, but those weeks gave me a sense of its appeal, and an idea for hook number four. They also gave me time to plan my future. In fairness, I have promised to complete another year of my lectureship here in Australia, but after that I will return to Lakin's Heath. I trust your father will join me but am universally declared to be a Romantic on that issue.

Forgive me if with the selfishness of adults we caused you pain. I hope we will make up for it, but I imagine Snow White's stepmother had good intentions, too. By the time you read this you will probably think me awfully dull, mortgages and gas bills having a way of catching up on us all. You will wonder how I could have known such things.

May your life have as much sweetness as mine has now. I have travelled to Enchanter's Island, and beyond, to countries I did not dream of eighteen months ago. Like an explorer entering exotic lands, I must close my eyes at times, and snap them open to be sure of what I see.

Take care, my love.
Martie

Other novels, novellas and short story collections available from
Stairwell Books

For further information please contact rose@stairwellbooks.com
www.stairwellbooks.co.uk
@stairwellbooks